---

# TANGLED IN VENGEANCE

---

## THE SINFULLY CORRUPT SERIES
### BOOK 1

## LEILA MATTHEWS

Tangled In Vengeance: The Sinfully Corrupt Series

Copyright © 2024 by Leila Matthews



This book is a work of fiction, and any resemblance to any person, living or dead, any place, events, or occurrences are purely coincidental and not intended by the author.

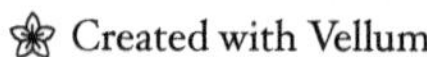 Created with Vellum

# BLURB

My name is Isabella Blackhart, but this gilded cage is not my choosing.

I'm a pawn in a game I didn't know I was playing, forced into a dark union with a monster.

A prisoner in a world of opulence and terror. A world where one death marked the continuation of my nightmare.

Now, caught in a web of deceit and danger, my life hangs by a thread. My captor is out for vengeance, gunning for his brother's murderer. And I'm his number one suspect.

In a life filled with danger, betrayal, and forbidden desires, I navigate through a treacherous path where love is both my weakness and my strength.

As secrets unravel and the line between enemy and savior blurs, I must make a harrowing choice. A choice that could cost the life of the one person I've unexpectedly come to love.

# TRIGGER WARNINGS

The book contains themes of abuse, torture, abduction, bloodshed, death, graphic violence, profanity, emotional and psychological abuse, themes of power and control, forced marriage, and other mature content. If this offends you, please do not read this book. If you're fine with this content, please enjoy!

Leila Matthews

"You have to leave that place," Seraphina's voice crackles through the phone coated with worry.

She's my best friend, and we grew up together. She was in a mansion with more rooms than days of the month, and I was a little less wealthy but still wealthy, nonetheless. Despite the gap in our family's wealth, she never flaunted her silver-spoon upbringing. Instead, she'd scuff her designer shoes, playing tag in the mud with me.

She's down to earth and takes no shit from anybody. She relaxes at home, watching TV or reading a book, and loves shopping as much as the next person, but she's not doing it to show off her wealth. Seraphina has a keen fashion sense, and she loves clothes.

She's always been this way. Unfazed by the façades and the facelifts. Nor the expectations to primp and parade around like a show pony. She's always been there for me. My rock when life got hard.

"I know," I sigh, feeling the familiar knot of disappointment and frustration in my stomach. "It's just... it's getting harder each time. Dad's slipping further away, and I'm always caught in the middle."

"You can't keep bailing his ass out of trouble, Isabella," she insists. "It's not your burden to carry."

"Isabella!" Dad shouts from downstairs. I hear the door slam shut and his brisk footsteps as he heads toward his office.

I sigh in agitation. Usually, when he storms into the house like this, it's because he's gotten himself into trouble. I come from a wealthy family, and our lives used to be great. Then, my mother died from cancer, and I realized it was my mom who kept everything together.

A knot of disappointment forms in my stomach. It's a familiar sensation that's been nestled there ever since Mom passed away. My father would rather be out making terrible decisions than be a father to his only child. He's not the man I thought he was, and each day, that realization stings more than the last.

"Is that your dad?" Seraphina asks. "He sounds angry, and I don't like it."

I wonder what trouble he's gotten himself into this time. My mind drifts back to a time when I was thrust into a pit of chaos. A vivid image of my father, his hands bandaged and immobilized, flashes before me. I can still hear the roar of his voice when he barged into my room, panic-stricken, admitting he'd squandered away the fortune my mother left us and he owes people money.

His reckless obsession with gambling had finally caught up to him. I shudder, recalling the cold, merciless eyes of the thugs who had broken his fingers as a warning. Their threatening words echoed in my ears, promising a snapped neck if the money wasn't produced within twenty-four hours.

It was the first time I'd been forced to pick up the pieces of his mess. I remember the desperation in my voice as I pleaded with these faceless criminals for more time. The account I had wisely hidden from my father was my secret lifeline.

It wasn't easy to access, but the imminent threat to my father's life had propelled me forward. When I finally managed to unlock the funds, it was a painful relief to find just enough to pay off his debts. The memory of handing over my money to those criminals still leaves a bitter taste in my mouth.

Pulling myself back from the haunting memories, I focus on the present commotion. I can hear his pacing figure, which brings me back to the pressing crisis at hand. It's a pattern, a cycle of chaos and desperation, and now it's spiraling into something far more terrifying.

"He sounds panicked," I tell Seraphina. "I refuse to bail him out of trouble this time."

"You can always stay here if you need to. I'll come by right now and pick you up. I don't want to see you get hurt," she says, and I can hear her gathering her things.

I glance towards the door as Dad's voice booms from below once again, his tone laced with panic and agitation.

"Now, Isabella!" he shouts.

"No, don't. I have to go," I say quickly and hang up the phone before I make my way downstairs, each step heavy with a mix of dread and anxiety.

I never thought I'd still live at home at twenty-four. I wanted to go to college, have my own apartment, and have a nice job. Unfortunately, my dad's life choices derailed my future. Despite all the shitty things he's done, I can't leave him. He's all the family I have left.

"Yes, Dad?" I ask as I walk into his office.

"I've really done it this time," he says as I watch him pace back and forth. "I've done something terrible."

I sigh heavily before stepping closer. "What have you done this time?"

"I stole money from the Blackharts," he replies as he stops pacing to look at me.

"You stole money from the Blackharts, Dad!" I shriek. "They're not known for being forgiving."

They're a family that truly lives up to their name. Their hearts are as black as can be, stained with the blood of their crimes. It may never have been proven, but no one messes with them for a reason.

Anger crosses his face, and he takes a step closer. "Watch your tone with me, little girl. I don't need you to tell me who they are."

"Clearly you do," I say with a snort. "I don't have any money, Dad. I can't pay whatever debt you owe, assuming all they want is for you to pay them back."

I stare at him, my chest tightening as I recall the countless times I've bailed him out of situations like this. The world we live in is a cruel and unforgiving place. Once you owe, you're owned. It's an unspoken rule among the elite and the wealthy. You borrow, you return, and if you can't, they have ways to make sure you do. Ways that often involve pain and fear.

It's a dangerous game of power, wealth and control, and my father, he's played it one too many times. Those who can't pay their debts end up as examples. Their fates are whispered in hushed tones at elite gatherings. Family empires crumble, reputations are ruined, and lives are lost. It's a gamble, and this time, he's taken a bet against the Blackharts, a family notorious for their ruthlessness.

"I've handled it," he says.

I suck in a sharp breath, not liking the tone in his voice. There are unspoken laws that govern our world. A world where the elite's power plays and hidden agendas shape our lives more than any public laws ever could. In our circle, reputation is more than a social currency. It's a lifeline.

The façades of affluence and propriety mask a world rife with silent battles for dominance. Here, debts aren't just financial. They're personal bonds of power and control. To owe someone is to be ensnared in their grasp, subject to their whims and mercy. It's a high-stakes game among the privileged.

"How did you handle it?" I question. "Please tell me you did do something reckless."

"I gave you to Jackson Blackhart and he accepted as payment for the debt," Dad tells me as if it's no big deal.

"You did what?" I shout. "You can't be serious? I am not a piece of meat you can sell to settle your debts."

The hand comes so fast that I don't have time to block it. My head whips back from the force of his slap. My cheek stings, and I rub it before turning back to look at him with anger in my eyes.

"Mind your tongue, little girl," he snaps. "I had no choice. Jackson would have killed me. Marriage was the only way."

I reel from the sharp sting of his slap, with a bitter taste creeping up my throat. A rush of anger swells within me, hot and wild and fierce, yet there's also a chilling realization that spreads through my veins. This is not the father I once knew. This is not the man who held me when I cried, who taught me to ride a bike, who showed me the stars and made me believe in magic.

That man is a ghost, replaced by this monster of desperation and greed. Sorrow for my once happy family is replaced with a burning resolve. I will not be a pawn in his game of debts. I will not let my life be dictated by his mistakes. I am not his to barter.

"So, I have to marry that monster because you got greedy?" I scream, not caring if he hits me again.

My dad has done a lot of fucked up things, and I've forgiven him for it. However, this takes the cake. I've not once used my body to get him out of trouble, and he offers me up on a silver platter to save his own ass like it's nothing.

"It's a good deal," he says. "Jackson's reputation is all rumors. The Blackharts are upstanding people."

"Yet, he's willing to accept an unwilling woman as his bride?" I snort. "Yes, really fucking upstanding."

Jackson Blackhart is a name whispered with a mixture of fear and respect in our circles. Rumors of his ruthlessness are as dark as they are numerous, but there are also whispers of a different kind. Some say he's not just the cold-hearted villain he's made out to be. I don't know what to believe, but I do know one thing. Being bound to Jackson Blackhart might be more complicated and dangerous than I could ever imagine.

"Look at me, Dad," I implore, trying to hold back the tears that threaten to spill from my eyes.

I see him glance at me, and it's a look I've seen far too often. It's not one of guilt or remorse but of desperation, a wild fear that he's been cornered without an escape.

"I know you're scared," I say as calmly as I can manage. "But this...this isn't the way. You can't just trade my life away to save your own."

"I can and I will," he replies without remorse.

"I refuse to do this!" I snap, angry that he can be so careless with my life.

Dad's arm whips out quickly, and his clammy hand wraps around my throat. He tugs me closer until we're nose to nose.

"The wedding is in three days. You will walk down the aisle, marry Jackson, and you will do it with a fucking smile on your face. Understood?" he growls.

I grab his hand, trying to pull away from him. "I will never sell my body to pay your debts. You'll have to find some other way. I won't do it."

"You will, or I will sell all of your mother's possessions and sell this house," he growls.

He knows how much I miss my mom and how I love my childhood home. However, I don't think I love it enough to trade my life away to a monster. I don't think Mom would want me to, either.

"I won't do it," I say, defiance clear in my tone and eyes.

He releases my throat, and I sigh in relief. Until his meaty hand wraps around my hair and tugs.

"You don't have a choice," he replies as he pulls me from his office by my hair. "You will do this. I'll keep you locked up and monitored until you're officially Mrs. Jackson Blackhart. After that, you'll never have to see me again. Do your year and leave him."

I kick and scream all the way to the cellar, where he tosses me on the ground. He turns around and storms out before shutting the door behind him. I scramble up as quickly as I can and bang on the door.

"Let me out of here!" I yell. "If you make me do this, you better hope I never see your sorry ass again!"

In the dim light of the cellar, I think back on everything my father has done. I refuse to be passive, to let my spirit be crushed by the weight of my father's sins. No matter how hard I try or how much I scream, Dad ignores my pleas.

He keeps me in the cellar, bringing by food and water. He escorts me to the bathroom to relieve myself and then back to the cellar. I put up a fight the entire way. I don't care about the hits, but he doesn't listen. As the three days draw to an end, I'm taken out of the cellar, told to shower, walked out to a car, and driven to a church. The city blurs past as I inch closer to the church. I never thought that living in Henderson City, home of the world's elite, would make me feel trapped.

Upon arrival, I'm ushered into a room where a woman

greets me and tells me to put on a wedding dress. It isn't just her in here. There room is filled with guards to make sure I don't bolt out the door.

"I'm not putting it on," I tell the woman defiantly.

The woman gives one look at the guards, and they stomp forward with determination in their eyes. One grabs me by the arms while the other starts ripping off my clothes.

"Let go of me, asshole!" I scream. "Get your filthy hands off me."

It's no use. They don't listen, but I fight them every step of the way. Unfortunately for me, I lost the battle. Soon, my father has a death grip on me as we walk down the aisle. I spot Jackson standing in the front, and his gaze makes my skin crawl. The way he's leering at me makes me want to puke.

He's tall with golden locks and piercing blue eyes. I'm short with long, curly brown hair and eyes like emeralds. To anyone looking, we'd make a beautiful couple. However, there is no love between us. This is no fairytale. There's no one here but me, my father, Jackson and his thugs, and the priest.

I'm walking toward the precipice of my worst nightmare as the organ plays the haunting melody of the wedding march. The fabric of the gown feels heavy. An unwanted burden, and the eyes watching me feel even heavier. I have no choice but to do this because as much as I hate my father at this moment, he's all the family I have left. The pit of my stomach is churning with a whirlpool of dread and fear, yet my mind is strangely clear.

As I inch towards Jackson, my mind is not on the man waiting for me at the altar or on the vows that they expect me to make. Instead, it's on the promise that I make to myself, a solemn vow echoing within the confines of my soul.

"I will not let this break me," I tell myself, steeling my heart against the horrible fate that awaits.

I will not be a damsel in distress, and this is not my end. I refuse to let it be my end. I will fight. I will resist, and one day, I will break free from this prison, from the shackles of this forced marriage. Jackson Blackhart may think he owns me, but I swear he will never own my spirit.

# CHAPTER 1

## Isabella

I delicately dab the concealer under my left eye, wincing as I brush over the tender skin. Trying to camouflage the telltale marks of abuse has become an art form. One that I've sadly perfected over time.

Every stroke of the brush feels like a betrayal, an acceptance of the reality I'm living in. Jackson's rage, once an occasional occurrence, has now become my daily storm. Each day holds the promise of a new bruise, a fresh reminder of the torturous existence that is marriage to him.

As I look in the mirror, I see the reflection of a woman trapped in a daily saga of fear and despair. I've been married to Jackson for what feels like a lifetime, with each passing day feeling harder than the last. The memory of when I first arrived suddenly swirls in my mind.

*The silence in the car is deafening. My emotions swirl all over the place. From sadness and betrayal to anger and bitterness. I can't believe I'm married to Jackson Blackhart. My heart pounds in my chest like a sledgehammer, every beat echoing the truth I can hardly bear to face. I glance at Jackson, on his harsh profile silhouetted against the car's dim light.*

*His eyes are focused on the road, but the rigid set of his jaw tells me he's just as aware of the tension coiled between us. As the city lights give way to the looming shadows of our destination, my stomach churns with a gnawing uncertainty. The house that awaits us, my new home, feels like a prison already. Each mile that rolls by under the car's tires enhances the growing sense of dread.*

*"Isabella," Jackson's voice cuts through the silence like a knife, cold and harsh. "You will play the part of a dutiful wife. I will expect you to fulfill your wifely duties." His words hang in the air as a chilling decree.*

*"Go to hell, Jackson," I hiss and my words are laced with venom. "You and my father may have forced me into this marriage, but I will never share my body with you."*

*The impact comes a split second later. His backhand strikes my cheek with a force that jerks my head sideways. I can taste coppery blood where I've bitten my lip.*

*"You would do well to remember who you're talking to, Isabella," his voice is dangerously low. "I won't tolerate your disrespect."*

*As the car pulls up in front of Jackson's home, I can't help but let out a gasp. It's not a home, it's a fortress. Tall, imposing walls of stone and glass stretch out before me, their stark elegance softened only by the moon's glow. Lavish gardens sprawl around us, their greenery soaked in silver. Fountains glisten in the moonlight, and their opulence is intimidating. The mansion's grandeur takes my breath away because it's so beautiful.*

*I step out of the car, and the crunch of gravel under my shoes echoes ominously in the silent night. I take a moment to take it all in. The grand staircase led up to a set of massive oak doors, the walls lined with ivy, and the windows aglow with the warm light from inside. Everything is meticulously maintained, reflecting a richness that feels alien. This isn't a home, it's a cold testament to Jackson's wealth and power.*

*Jackson walks away, leaving me standing there, gaping at the enormity of his mansion. My eyes follow him as he strides confidently* toward the entrance, his broad shoulders set with an air of authority. I quicken my pace to catch up with him as my shorter strides struggle to match his long, powerful gait.

The front doors swing open, revealing an interior that leaves me momentarily breathless. The lavishness is almost overwhelming, with tall marble columns supporting a high, ornate ceiling. Crystal chandeliers hang down, their light refracting in a thousand directions to paint the grand foyer with a warm, inviting glow.

I had grown up in a wealthy family, yes. But this? This is Blackhart wealth. It's a level of affluence that's almost obscene in its extravagance. The walls are adorned with exquisite paintings, the floors are covered in plush carpets, and the furniture is made of the finest leather and wood. I can hardly believe this place is now my home. This isn't just wealth. It's another world entirely. Jackson turns to the housekeeper, who has been waiting silently off to the side.

"Mrs. Collins," his voice echoes in the vast entrance hall. "Show Isabella to our bedroom."

I stiffen at his words, and my heart pounds in my chest. "I'm not sharing a room with you, Jackson," I declare, my voice shaky but determined.

He pauses in his steps, turning slowly to look at me. A chilling smile curls up from his lips as he chuckles.

"Fine," he drawls. "I'll give you this one night. You can have a separate bedroom tonight to get used to the idea that you're Mrs. Blackhart now."

"But..." I start to protest, only for him to hold up his hand, cutting me off.

"No time for arguments, Isabella," he warns, glancing at the large grandfather clock that stands imposingly in the corner of the hall. "We have dinner at my brother's place in an hour, and you need to change."

As Jackson strides away, the echoing click of the shutting door grates against my every nerve. I take a deep breath to keep my rising fear at bay. Mrs. Collins, a delicate, older woman with a kind face, gestures for me to follow her.

*Upon reaching a spare bedroom, Mrs. Collins ushers me inside. The room is tastefully decorated, but its magnificence does nothing to comfort me. She guides me to the walk-in closet, where racks upon racks of women's clothing hang neatly.*

*"Madam, perhaps you'd like to pick something to wear for this evening," Mrs. Collins suggests in her soft, pleasant voice.*

*"Mrs. Collins, you don't have to call me Madam," I reply, trying to keep the tremor out of my voice.*

*"Very well, Mrs. Blackhart," she nods, her voice respectful.*

*A shiver runs down my spine at the sound of my married name. "Please, don't ever call me that," I plead, meeting her kind eyes with a desperate gaze.*

*"I... I understand, Miss Isabella," she replies with a hint of sympathy in her voice.*

*I hesitantly reach out to touch the clothes hanging in the closet. "Whose clothes are these?" I ask as my fingers brush against the silky fabric of a dress.*

*"Mr. Blackhart always keeps a selection of women's clothing here," she explains somewhat hesitantly.*

*Realization washes over me, and I pull my hand back in disgust. He keeps clothes here for the many women who rotate through here, no doubt. Without another word, Mrs. Collins exits the room, leaving me alone with the unwelcome remnants of Jackson's past.*

*Before I know it, I'm dressed in one of the countless gowns Jackson keeps in the mansion. We're in the car, headed to his brother's house. As we pull up, my eyes widen in disbelief. His brother's house is even grander than his if that's even possible.*

*"Jackson," I begin, trying to keep my voice steady. "What's your brother's name? Is there anyone I should know?" I've heard of him. I've never met him, but I know he runs the family.*

*He doesn't even look at me as he replies. "You don't need to know, Isabella. All you have to do is stand there and look pretty. You're not required to speak unless spoken to. You're to be seen, not heard."*

*His words sting, but I don't let him see my hurt. "You're a jackass,*

*Jackson. I'm not some shiny object that you pull off the shelf to show off whenever you want," I snap.*

*He parks the car suddenly and grabs my chin, turning me to face him. His eyes are cold, and his grip is firm. "That's exactly what you are, Isabella," he says, his voice deadly calm, "And you better get used to it."*

*We leave the car and walk inside. No sooner do Jackson and I step into the sitting room than everyone turns toward us. An older woman, tall and thin, rolls her eyes.*

*"Jackson," she chastises, her voice dripping with disdain. "How many times have I told you that family dinners are not for the floozies you hook up with?"*

*Jackson just laughs and strides over to her. He bends down to give her a hug, leaving me standing there, wallowing in my awkwardness.*

*"She's not just a floozy, Mom," he counters with a smirk as he walks back over to me. "She's technically my wife."*

*The room explodes in a flurry of gasps and hushed whispers. Jackson's mother looks like she's been slapped, her face now flushed red as she reels from his announcement. She steps back as her eyes widen in shock.*

*"Your what?" she splutters, her voice rising in pitch.*

*At her side, a younger woman, most likely his sister, judging by the uncanny resemblance, stares at me with her lip curled in a sneer.*

*"You've got to be kidding," she scoffs, her gaze raking over me with visible disdain. "This...woman?"*

*The room is thick with tension, and the air is heavy with unspoken accusations. Their eyes are all on me. Each stare is a blow that makes me wince as if I'm not good enough to be in this family. I stand my ground with my heart pounding in my chest as I stare right back at them. I am not the one who should be ashamed. I am not their plaything to be insulted and mocked.*

*Suddenly, another voice cuts through the tension. "Jackson, what the fuck have you done?"*

*The voice belongs to a man of imposing stature standing at the entrance of the room. His gaze is as cold as ice, his features hard and unyielding. This must be his brother. The head of the family. I catch his gaze from across the room. There's something unsettlingly captivating about him. It's a magnetic pull I can't quite explain.*

*Despite myself, I feel a flicker of something dangerous, an unwanted intrigue that I quickly pushed aside. His eyes are a deep blue, unreadable, yet I feel a shiver run down my spine. Why did his gaze linger? I quickly look away with my heart strangely fluttering.*

*Jackson turns to face him with a neutral expression. "Damien," he greets, deceptively calm.*

*"I demand an answer, Jackson," Damien's voice booms through the room, the fury clear in his icy gaze.*

*His authority is tangible, radiating off him in waves that seem to shake the very foundations of the grand mansion. There's a power about him that's compelling, intimidating, and strangely mesmerizing all at once. His tone is accusing. His piercing blue eyes fix on Jackson with an intensity that makes my breath catch.*

*Jackson, on the other hand, remains eerily calm. His shining eyes meet Damien's head-on. His voice is smooth, almost nonchalant, but I can sense a tremor of fear beneath the cool façade. It's subtle, almost undetectable, but it's there, like the faintest whisper of a secret trying to break free.*

*"I didn't think it was necessary to inform you, Damien," he says, his tone light, almost dismissive.*

*I can see it, though. The tightness around his eyes and the way his hands clench into fists at his sides.*

*"That's where you're wrong," Damien snaps in a cold, sharp tone. "As the head of this family, every move you make is to be communicated to me. You've crossed the line, brother. What happened that you came home hours after I saw you married?"*

*Jackson raises his head in defiance. "None of your business, Damien. You may run things, but I have a say in the things I do."*

*Damien tilts his head to the side, his eyes narrowing on Jackson. "You're wrong again."*

"Well, it's done now," Jackson says with a shrug, trying to mask the apprehension in his voice.

I can see him, the real Jackson, hidden beneath the bravado. He's scared of his older brother. The tension is thick, and the air is heavy with the weight of unspoken words and simmering anger. This is a battle of wills, a clash of titans, and I can't help but wonder where I fit into this strange, new world.

"That's not the point, and you know it!" Damien roars, his fists clenched at his sides. "You've disrespected the family. You've disrespected me."

Damien's anger seems more than just about family respect. His eyes occasionally flicker to me, a stormy mix of disapproval and something else, something unreadable, that makes my heart unexpectedly skip. Damien motions his head, a signal that Jackson seems to understand instantly. Without a word, both walk towards a pair of large doors at the end of the room.

Their heated voices can be heard echoing through the hallways until a door slams shut, silencing them abruptly. I'm left standing in the grand room. The tension is replaced by an awkward silence. His mother, a woman of regal stature, steps forward first.

With a forced smile, she introduces herself, "I'm Donna, dear."

The younger woman, who is the spitting image of Jackson, follows. "I'm Aurora," she states in a flat tone.

Before I can even open my mouth to respond, they start bombarding me with questions, each laced with an underlying insult, probing every aspect of my life that they deem unsatisfactory or unfit for their family. Their questions come so fast that I don't have a chance to answer any of them. Not that I wanted to, anyway. I don't know how long this goes on, but suddenly, Damien and Jackson stalk back into the room. My attention instantly goes to Damien.

"So, you whored yourself out to the highest bidder? It's no surprise that you'd want the status and extravagance that come with being a Blackhart," he says, his words slicing through the tense silence like a knife.

*His icy blue eyes are boring into mine, searching for a reaction. I feel a rush of anger surging through me, the heat of it stinging my cheeks.*

*"Go to hell, asshole," I snap, unable to keep the edge out of my voice. "I didn't do anything. I don't want anything to do with your damn brother. All of you can fuck off!"*

*As soon as the words leave my mouth, I feel Jackson's hand squeeze my arm in a silent warning, but it's too late. The words are out there, hanging in the air like a challenge. I can see the surprise flash in Damien's eyes, but it's quickly replaced by a cold, calculating look. This is not over, not by a long shot.*

As those memories fade, I'm brought back to the cold reality of the present. Since that fateful day, I've learned to play my part all too well. At the dinner table, I laugh gracefully at jokes I don't find funny, my eyes meeting Jackson's with a well-rehearsed glint of admiration. Nobody at the table would guess that behind my smile lies a storm of disdain. In public, I'm the picture-perfect wife, always smiling, always charming, a dutiful spouse by Jackson's side.

I speak only when necessary, creating an illusion of a perfect marriage. Which is a far cry from our reality. At home, it's a different story entirely. I give it Jackson as good as I get, never backing down, never yielding. He may have forced me to share his bed, but he has never possessed my body. No matter how hard he tries to persuade me, I remain steadfast. To satiate his desires, he brings home an endless stream of women, each one more forgettable than the last. I couldn't care less about his indiscretions, and the fact that I remain unaffected seems to irk him to no end.

"Isabella!" Jackson shouts from downstairs. "Move your ass. I don't want to be late."

"It wouldn't take me so long to get ready if you'd stop leaving bruises in places people can see," I mumble to myself.

Not that anyone would care, nor would they say anything

if they did. These are the Blackharts we're talking about. Their word is law around here. I roll my eyes at Jackson's voice echoing through the mansion as I add the final touch to my makeup with a deep red lipstick that perfectly matches my fitted dress. With one last glance in the mirror, I slip my feet into the killer heels waiting by the door, grab my purse, and prepare myself for what's to come. It's another dinner at Damien's house. Another part of the never-ending cycle of family traditions.

I've lost count of how many of these dinners I've attended, every single one mandatory, all at Damien's insistence. The awkwardness that hangs in the air, the undercurrent of resentment, the obvious tension, it never changes. Stepping out of the room and into the sprawling hallway, I steel myself for another long night.

Mingling with the Blackharts is like walking on a tightrope. One misstep, one wrong word, and it's a long drop down. As I make my way towards the front door, I can't help but wonder how much longer I can endure this. How much more of this charade can I put up with before the façade shatters?

# CHAPTER 2

## Damien

"You fucking did what?" I yell at Jackson, and he flinches at the anger in my voice.

I'm standing in the shadowed expanse of my office at Blackhart Enterprises, the lines of my face set hard as Jackson shifts uneasily before me. I only knew something was up when Victor, my right-hand man, called with a tone of irritation whispering through his usual calm. He told me murmurs were circling. Talk of a problem, a serious one, with Jackson's name at its center.

I don't like bringing in the dirty side of the family business here. Blackhart Enterprises is a legitimate business. A business that handles investments in various sectors, including stocks, bonds, and perhaps venture capital funding. In this field, we can't afford to look like we're doing shady shit, or the SEC and police will cause all kinds of Hell for us. Yet, the tone in Victor's voice caused me to call Jackson here right away.

So, here we are. I called Jackson in and demanded straight answers because, in this game, a whisper can mean a mountain of trouble. Now, as he spills the story, I feel the weight of a colossal fuck up settling on my shoulders. A mess I never foresaw. Jackson's words are a flame licking at the edges of my hard-earned empire.

"I oversaw the shipment like I was supposed to," Jackson says with a defiant lift to his chin. "Chico disrespected me in front of everyone. So, I chopped off his head."

My teeth grind in anger at his brazen disregard for the delicacy our operations require.

"That was uncalled for, and you know it," I growl, feeling the weight of responsibility choking me.

Jackson narrows his eyes, and his voice is laced with a challenge. "You would have done the same, and no one would have batted a fucking eye," he snaps back. "Why is it wrong when I do it?"

The fury pounds in my temples, and I slam my fist down on the desk. "I am the head of the fucking family! I run this company and our family business. Not you." My voice is a whip, each word striking with intent. "You cause nothing but fucking problems, Jackson."

The air between us is thick with the unspoken threat that he's veered too far from the line. He knows it, too. I can see it in the way his bravado starts to crack, just a fraction.

As I stand rigidly, the fury within me simmers, a seething cauldron threatening to spill over. Reflecting on Jackson's reckless string of stunts, I am infuriated by the chaos he effortlessly brings into my carefully structured world. For years, I've played the firefighter, extinguishing the fires he lights with a carelessness that borders on arrogance. His audacity to disrupt the balance of our operations with his impulsive whims has quickly become a grim and tiresome cycle. One I'm forced to navigate meticulously.

Every time he strays, it is I who must steady the ship, righting wrongs and smoothing ruffled feathers. Now, as we stand in the aftermath of his latest fiasco, it's clear I'm condemned to repair the bridge he gleefully burns, all while containing the anger lashing against my calm exterior. I can feel it burning through my veins, a reminder of the inconvenient burden his impulses continue to cast upon my shoulders.

"First, you're spending more money than usual," I tell him, my voice cold and even. A shadow flits across his eyes, a hint of something deeper, but it vanishes before I can understand it. "Yes, I keep up with your spending habits," I continue, locking eyes with him.

"You think you know everything," he snaps with a veneer of defiance plastered across his face.

"It seems like I'm the only one in the fucking family that works," I tell him as I sit back down in my chair. "Then you go off and get married to a money-hungry socialite, and now you do this?"

A sneer curls his lip as if the accusations I hurl can erase his own failings.

His control snaps as his anger bubbles forward. "Stop treating me like a child!" he dares to tell me, his voice rising just a notch too high.

I'm on my feet in an instant, and the roar of my frustration echoes off the walls. "Stop acting like one, and I will!" My words slice through the tension between us, leaving no room for rebuttal.

The room falls deathly quiet. The only sound is our heavy breathing. The office becomes a battlefield of wills as we stand, locked in a silent standoff, each unwilling to bend. My voice comes low and steely as I fix Jackson with a withering gaze.

"Now, because of your damn stunt, I've gotta smooth things over with the Valdez family and fast. They aren't known for letting insults slide, and the last thing we need is a war on our hands. This isn't a game, Jackson. Your impulses could sink everything I've built."

Jackson, with that infuriating air of defiance still clinging to him, sneers right back. "What's wrong with you, Damien? You've gone soft."

The sharpness in my eyes sends a strong message. One that silences him more effectively than words ever could.

"Get the fuck out of my sight," I hiss, feeling the barely constrained rage coiling in my chest like a serpent. "Before I do something. Something I won't regret but will surely make Mother unhappy. Don't fool yourself into thinking I've gone soft, brother. Test me again, and you'll find out just how wrong you are."

His eyes meet mine one last time. There's a flicker of something, a challenge perhaps, or the beginning of understanding. It's hard to tell. Then, without another word, he turns on his heel and storms out, the door slamming shut behind him with a resounding echo. The silence that he leaves in his wake is deep, broken only by the steady pulse of my own heart beating a fierce rhythm of control and simmering fury.

I sigh heavily, sinking back into the chair that feels too much like a throne. I close my eyes for a moment, chasing the tendrils of tension from my forehead. Jackson's probably headed straight home, back to that new wife of his. My mind conjures her image without permission. The curve of her smile, the arch of her brow, features etched with a beauty that's as undeniable as it is infuriating.

Even now, just the thought of her, the memory of that instant magnetic pull I felt upon first laying eyes on her, sends a ripple of forbidden warmth through my veins. The idea of Jackson with her, his hands where mine ache to be, ignites an unfamiliar possessiveness that claws at my insides, fierce and unyielding.

She's a vision, but visions can be deceptive. She's painted in whispers and rumors, hues of greediness and entitlement. Jackson's description, not mine. A money-hungry socialite, he called her. I can't help but wonder if there's more to her than the spoiled brat he's painted. These thoughts are a danger, a line I've drawn firmly in the sand.

Isabella is off-limits, untouchable, the wife of my brother, a complication in an already tangled web I cannot afford. So, I force my thoughts away from the softness of her lips, the laughter in her eyes, and the silk of her skin. Stay away, I remind myself. Some prices are too high, even for me.

I press the intercom button with more force than necessary. The frustration of my encounter with Jackson is still simmering beneath the surface.

"Tina, in here, please," I demand, my voice taut with the effort of maintaining my composure.

The door opens almost immediately, and she steps in. "Yes, sir. What can I help you with?" she asks with a glimmer of something more than just professional attention in her eyes.

I manage to suppress a sigh. Her unspoken advances are the last thing I need right now. Tina's competence is the only shield saving her from being fired. Her ability to run the office through my intermittent absences is, admittedly, invaluable.

I meet her gaze, all business. "Cancel my meetings for the afternoon. I need to clear my schedule. I'll be occupied for the rest of the day." The words are clipped. "Also, take over the gala preparations. I trust you know what to do."

She nods, and the slightest flicker of disappointment passes over her features before she locks it down and responds. "Yes, sir."

With no further comment, she exits as quietly as she arrived, closing the door gently behind her. I stand in a fluid motion, driven by a need to move, to act. Shrugging into my suit jacket with a practiced ease, I walk to the door. My stride carries a tension, a marked purpose as I reach the elevator. The doors slide open, and I step inside, descending from my high-rise domain into the city below.

The moment I step outside, the brisk air strikes my face, drawing a sharp contrast to the stifling atmosphere I left behind. I weave through the crowd with my mind running calculations and strategies. Within minutes, I'm seated in the leather confines of my car with the engine purring to life beneath my hands. I waste no time dialing Victor's number, the call connecting as I navigate through the dense traffic with practiced ease.

"Meet me at Casa Valdez," I command the moment he answers, my tone leaving no room for argument.

Casa Valdez, the inconspicuous family restaurant, brimming with the aroma of spices and secrets. To any outsider, it's a place to savor authentic cuisine. To us, it's a lucrative façade. The Valdez's have been allies of the Blackharts for decades, and their restaurant serves as both a meeting point and a front for our more discreet operations. Namely, the transport and sale of weapons. Our services carry a weighty price tag, but one that's justified by the risks and always, always paid.

I pull up to the restaurant just as Victor's car slides into view. He steps out, his presence radiating the kind of strength and reliability that only years on the frontline can forge.

"What are we doing here?" he asks, eyes searching mine for the turmoil that's roiling beneath my calm exterior.

"Fucking damage control," I growl. I can see his mind already turning, piecing together the fragments of information that point to a singular, disastrous event.

"What the fuck did Jackson do now?" Victor probes, his voice steady despite the gravity of the situation.

"Those whispers you heard?" I say, allowing a fraction of my frustration to seep through, "Well, apparently, Jackson cut off Chico's head."

Victor curses a sharp, hard sound that slices through the quiet morning air. His hands move with a practiced motion as he checks his gun, an action that's second nature to him. Preparedness is his creed. He's lived by it ever since he took a bullet meant for me years ago.

The memory comes on swiftly. Victor grew up impoverished, every day a battle, every night shadowed by uncertainty in the cold walls of too many orphanages. His past is a patchwork of hunger and survival, and yet, there's an unmistakable strength that adversity has etched onto his character.

I remember that fateful, gritty evening in the bad part of town. The smell of gasoline was strong, mixed with the threat of impending violence. I had stopped at a gas station, a wrong turn on an otherwise ordinary night. I was a teenager that got lost on the way home. Suddenly, a group of thugs approached me. Their intentions were as cold as the steel they pointed in my direction. The fear I might feel in such a scenario now is dulled by the life I've built, shielded by affluence and security. Back then, invincibility clung to me like a second skin.

Before my mind could race to the next move, he was there. Victor, a boy with nothing to his name but the fire in his eyes, stepped between me and the looming threat. His voice cut through the tension as he demanded the thugs to back off. However, words aren't armor, and a scuffle broke out, revealing the courage within Victor as he dispatched their violence with a swift, practiced might.

It could have ended there, but as the thugs relented, the bite of a gunshot shattered the momentary calm. Time slowed. Inches and seconds collided as Victor shoved me out of the bullet's deadly path. A shove that sealed an unspoken bond.

Since that night, our lives have been interwoven with loyalty and an unwavering sense of brotherhood. That moment cemented his status as my right-hand man. There's nobody I trust more within the treacherous balance of our world than Victor, a man who's seen the darkness in me and stands by my side regardless.

The click of the firearm snaps shut, drawing me back to the present. The stakes are clear. We have to smooth this over with the Valdez family or risk igniting a conflict that could consume everything I've worked to build. I can feel Victor's resolve, as tangible as my own, radiating off him as he follows me into the restaurant, ready to face whatever comes.

The scent of simmering spices and the low hum of conversations are abruptly cut off as the doors close behind us. Inside, the men at the tables rise as one, the scrape of chairs against the floor almost drowned by the sudden chorus of weapons being drawn. A silent tension swells in the room, like the calm before a storm. Our hands instinctively go up, open and empty. We both know it's a universal language of peace or at least non-aggression.

"We want to speak to Jose," I state, my voice steady despite the adrenaline that begins to surge. "I want to smooth things over and to apologize. My brother is an idiot."

An older gentleman breaks from the shadows, his steps measured as he motions for his men to lower their guns. "Damien," he acknowledges, his voice carrying a weight that sees beyond years.

"Jose," I return the greeting with equal gravity, my eyes holding his in understanding that stretches back to stories my father used to tell.

Without another word, Jose turns on his heel, inviting us to follow him. Victor and I exchange a glance, words unnecessary between us, and step in line with Jose. The eyes of every man in the room watches us pass, their silence speaking volumes of the precarious peace we're here to negotiate.

The room's air is thick, and even the occasional clink of glass from the bar area does little to cut the tension. We sit across from Jose and a duo of his most trusted men, our chairs drawn up to a solid, unadorned table that has undoubtedly heard more secrets than I can imagine.

I break the silence first, my voice steady but inflected with regret. "Jose, I'm here to express my sincere apologies for what my brother has done. His actions were rash, and he was not thinking clearly."

Jose's face is set in stone, every line on it speaking of hard-earned respect and years in command. "Your apologies are fine words, Damien," he begins, his tone controlled and his eyes fire. "But your brother is a reckless idiot. He's gone too far this time."

I feel a surge within me. Anger mixed with familial loyalty. Keeping my voice level commands all the control I have. "Watch how you speak about him, Jose. He's still my brother."

The moment my words hang in the air, the room's temperature seems to drop, and Jose's expression contorts with fury. "Your brother," he hisses, the veneer of respect cracking. "Killed my only son. He's a murderer!"

Victor's hand rests on his weapon, an unconscious motion, and I nod minutely, telling him to stay calm. "I understand your pain, Jose, and I swear to you, we'll make this right. Jackson's actions will not go unpunished by our own code. But let's talk. There has to be a path to keep the peace between our families."

There's a cavernous pause before Jose speaks again, his voice now a low rumble. "Peace? Your family's actions have ripped a hole in the heart of mine, and you expect talk of peace?"

"Without peace, this escalates. More blood. More loss. Neither of us wants that," I keep my eyes locked with his. "Tell me, what does justice look like to you?"

"Justice?" Jose spits the word as if it leaves a bitter taste. "You offer me your brother's life for my son's?"

"I offer compensation and restraint. Jackson will face the consequences, and we will provide reparation in gold and influence. Is there nothing that can balance the scales, at least enough to avoid war?" There's a cold fire in my words. A leader's gambit laid bare.

Jose's eyes narrow, and for a moment, the only sound is the distant clinking from the bar. Then, slowly, he nods. "I'll give you one chance, Damien. For the sake of the peace that's lasted decades between our families. Make this right. But remember, if you fail, it will be war."

I nod, my head a mere tilt of acknowledgment of the gravity that Jose's conditional reprieve carries. Victor and I stand in unison, our chairs scraping sharply against the faded tiles, and we walk out. The heavy air of Casa Valdez releases its grip as the door swings shut behind us, and I curse under my breath. Jackson's impulsive act, murder, there's no other word for it, threatens to dismantle everything our family has built with blood and time.

"He's a damn fool," I mutter, feeling the knot of anger and responsibility tightening in my chest. My brother's actions demand justice. Our code demands it. Though it will tear me apart, I must be the one to mete out that justice.

I turn on my heel to face Victor. "Get Jackson. Take him to the warehouse. Secure him there. I'll meet you shortly."

Victor nods. Not a word passes between us, but his eyes acknowledge the task's severity. He heads to execute the order, leaving me to prepare for what must be done. As I slide into the driver's seat, the leather creaks under my weight.

My hands are steady as they clutch the steering wheel, but

my mind races with the weight of what's to come. As I drive, I play the upcoming scene over and over in my head. Beating Jackson won't just be a reprimand. It's a necessity, a statement that I will not tolerate insubordination or actions that endanger our precarious peace.

I need to make it clear. To Jose, to my family, to every last soul that whispers my name, that my authority is not to be questioned. The approaching violence is distasteful yet unavoidable. A grim act that must be cloaked in the guise of discipline, though every strike will also be an apology to the Valdez family.

I confess to myself, in the dimming light of the car, that a part of me is desperate for it to be enough. Glancing at the fading sun, I sigh. It's a sound muffled by the confines of the car. I'm ready for this day to be over, for the actions that must unfold, and for the semblance of peace they may bring.

# CHAPTER 3

## Damien

I pull up to the warehouse on Center Street, and there's tension gripping my muscles as I turn off the engine. I take a deep breath to steady the anger coursing through me. I know what I'm about to do, and the weight of it sits heavy in my chest. We operate under a code, and Jackson broke it in the worst way.

It's not about wanting to hurt him. It's about the message it sends. He crossed the Valdez family. They could've demanded his head on a silver platter, and he should count himself lucky they didn't. Now, I have to make an example out of him.

I step out of the car, and the cool night air bites at my skin as I close the door with a resounding thud. Every step towards the warehouse door is heavy with the weight of what must be done. The door creaks open as an eerie prelude to the scene inside.

Jackson is there, suspended in the air with his hands bound securely above him. He hangs in a cruel limbo, a marionette awaiting the pull of strings. His eyes flash with a mix of fear and defiance as they lock onto mine. The dim light casts shadows across his face, painting a picture of a man who knows the gravity of his situation. There's a bitter taste in my mouth as I take in the sight.

"Finally, you're here," Jackson spits out, with a strain in his voice that gives away his attempt at bravado. "You've put on your show. Now let me go."

I close the distance between us, my footsteps hollow against the concrete. "I can't do that, Jackson," I say, my irritation simmering below the surface. "You put me in a tight spot. Now, I'm forced to do something about it."

His eyes widen, and the façade of toughness wavers for an instant. "You can't be serious?" he questions with a tremor of panic in his tone.

"I'm dead serious," I reply, my voice low and resolute. "You killed the only son of one of my clients because of your fragile fucking ego. Your behavior alone is enough to warrant an ass-kicking, but I've been letting it slide. I can't let your latest stunt go unpunished."

"I'm your fucking brother, Damien!" he yells as fear flashes in his eyes for just a moment. "You're going to let someone dictate how you run your family? Your business?"

A laugh, humorless and sharp, cuts through the tension in the air. "No one is dictating shit," I snarl. "I'm showing everyone that I govern my own. That when they step out of line, there will be consequences. That I'm the one they must deal with. You have no one to blame but yourself for what's about to happen."

"I won't let anyone disrespect me," Jackson snarls. "You wouldn't either, so what's the difference?"

"The difference is," I say, steadying the rage swirling in my chest. "I've earned my place. I make decisions that keep us strong, keep us alive. You? You let your ego and your dick lead you, and that's reckless. The family, our people, they look to me to guide them, to protect them. That's a job I don't take lightly, and I do it with their respect."

Jackson's face hardens with defiance in his eyes. "That's what I'm doing! Getting respect."

I lean in close, making sure my words leave no room for misinterpretation. "You don't get it, do you? You put yourself first. Not the family. That's why you're in this predicament. Not because you're not respected but because you didn't respect the order that keeps us all alive and thriving. The difference between you and me is that I command respect with my mere presence alone. You demand respect by flapping your fucking mouth."

I reach up and unbind Jackson's hands. He lands the short distance to the ground almost gracefully, but he stumbles, displaying a flash of weakness before righting himself. I step back, creating distance as I strip off my suit jacket and carelessly toss it aside. I unbutton the cuffs of my dress shirt methodically before rolling up the sleeves in preparation for what's to come.

"You want respect?" I ask Jackson, my voice a blend of challenge and disdain. "I'll give you a chance to earn a little of it. Right here. Right now. Fight for your respect."

He's standing now, unsure but defiant. A small, tenacious flame in the eye of a storm. The air between us crackles with the promise of violence. An old and primal ritual of power.

"If you win," I continue, the corners of my mouth hinting at a mocking smile. "Everyone will know you got the best of Damien Blackhart. It will do wonders for your reputation."

I square my shoulders, letting the cold, hard reality of our situation sink in. "Just know, I'll take great joy in kicking your ass while you try." My fists are closed tight and ready. "When I beat you into submission, and I will," I assert, every word a nail in his coffin. "I'll send proof to the Valdez's to keep them at bay, and you'd better not step a fucking toe out of line again."

Jackson lunges towards me like a wounded animal, desperate and ferocious. I sidestep his first few punches with ease, the memory of a thousand past fights guiding my movements. His heavy breaths are already demonstrating fatigue, but there's a fire in his eyes that refuses to be extinguished. Cocky, foolish determination. I can't help but admire it just a little, even in this moment.

I let him land a few jabs, his knuckles connecting with the hard planes of my body with no effect. The dull thuds are almost amusing. I chuckle under my breath, feeling nothing but the rush of adrenaline warming my veins.

Then, with a swift pivot, I'm behind him, watching as he stumbles from his own momentum. He's been with me long enough to know better, yet here we are. It's clear Jackson is no match for me. His movements are too predictable and heavy with emotion rather than strategy.

So, I dance around him, a predator playing with his prey, throwing punches, which I pull at the very last moment. It's a show more for the shadows lurking in the corners of the warehouse than for the man spinning in the center of my controlled storm.

"You'll have to do better than that, little brother," I taunt, dodging another one of his punches. He growls, frustrated and wild, and I can see it in his eyes, that moment of realization. He's outclassed, and whether his pride lets him admit it or not, he knows it. Yet, despite it all, he doesn't give up.

That's when I decided enough is enough. Playtime is over. I narrow the distance between us with my fists clenched and ready. I unleash a tight combination, a left and a right, straight into his guard, breaking through with sheer force.

Jackson's attempts to counter are clumsy, with desperation making him sloppy, and I exploit every opening.

I hammer another punch that catches him square in the jaw, feeling the shock of the impact jolt up my arm. I'm relentless, a barrage of jabs and hooks that snap his head to the side again and again. He's feeling it now, and each blow I deliver carries a lesson. It's not just about respect. It's about consequences.

With a swift uppercut, I lift him off his feet for a split second. I step back, and watch him struggle to keep on his feet. This is the hierarchy of power. This is how respect is earned and maintained. I deliver another punch, and he falls to the ground.

I look down at Jackson. His face is bloodied and beaten, and the fight is gone from his eyes. He's barely conscious, trying to stay upright in his defeat. I grab him by the front of his torn shirt, yanking him up to level his gaze with mine. My fist connects violently with his face, again and again, each punch a clear message in this brutal conversation. When he begins to mumble incoherently, probably pleading for an end, I finally stop. I release my grip, and he collapses to the ground in a pitiful heap of desperation.

I step away, breathing heavily, my chest rising and falling with the adrenaline still coursing through my veins. Jackson's eyes are swollen shut, and with a pitiful act of defiance, he spits out blood onto the dirty warehouse floor before finally falling back, unconscious. I walk over to where I tossed my suit jacket and slide into it, straightening the fabric with a sense of cold satisfaction setting in.

Meanwhile, Victor snaps pictures, capturing Jackson in his debilitated state. These will be the images sent to the Valdez family, a demonstration of the consequences of stepping out of line with me.

"Go home, Vic," I say as the weight of the night hangs heavy on my shoulders.

He nods, packing up his things, and leaves without a word. I take a moment to look over Jackson's limp form. He's a mess, but he's still family. I stoop down, lifting his unconscious body with surprising ease, and make my way out of the warehouse. Fitting him into the front seat of my car, I slam the door and slide behind the wheel. As I start the engine, I glance at his battered face once more. This is the cost of power. Of respect.

The drive to Jackson's house is a quick one, as the streets are almost empty at this hour. Every now and then, Jackson groans, a low sound of pain that escapes his lips despite his unconscious efforts to hold it back. Pulling into the driveway, I kill the engine and sit for a moment, staring at the house. So normal and peaceful. I get out, open the passenger side door, and carefully hoist Jackson's limp form into my arms. His head lolls around, but I've got him.

Inside the house, the heavy sound of silence greets us. I walk over and lay him down on the couch, not giving a second thought to the blood that might stain the fabric. Suddenly, Mrs. Collins enters the room. Her startled gasp fills the space like a sudden crack of thunder.

"What happened?" she asks, her voice shaky and afraid.

"He'll be okay," I say flatly, cutting off any further questions. "Just get him some painkillers and something to drink."

My voice leaves no room for argument. I'm still the man in charge, even here in this domestic scene that feels worlds away from the warehouse's grim shadows.

Mrs. Collins scurries away, leaving me alone with my thoughts as the heaviness settles in my chest. It's not guilt that creeps at the edges of my mind, nor is it sadness. I didn't want to do this to Jackson, but the harsh truth is that our world doesn't care for what we want. Money and power govern us all. In the circles we run in, in our world, I'm the highest power and authority there is. Jackson's screw-up was a slight against me, as much as it was against the Valdez family.

I should feel justified, but there's a hollow ring to it all. It's the cost of maintaining order, of ensuring that the gears of our operation turn without resistance. My thoughts are like the dark waters of a deep lake. Still on the surface but with undercurrents running wild below. I'm aware, bitterly so, that respect within our ranks is often measured in bruises and broken bones.

A soft gasp snaps me out of my thoughts, sharper than the snap of a bone. I turn, slow and deliberate, to find Isabella standing at the entrance of the living room. Her eyes are wide, reflecting the gruesome scene before her.

"Damien," Isabella says. "Are you alright?"

Silence hangs heavy in the air for a heartbeat or two as my gaze locks with hers. Lost, that's what I am, caught in the moment, admiring the vision standing before me. She's in silk pajama pants paired with a spaghetti strap top that clings to her form, failing to obscure the fullness of her breasts. My eyes are drawn to her, compelled by the vibrant green that seems to spark a wild forest within them, and I can't help but notice how her hair, a tumultuous cascade of curls, sits atop her head like a wild, untamed crown.

Desire, unwanted yet undeniable, flows through me, a current driven by the sheer force of her presence. It's an ache, a longing to reach out, to forget the blood and violence, if just for a second. Her clearing of the throat is the anchor that pulls me back, the simple sound somehow slicing through the thick tension.

"Yes, I'm fine," I manage to reply, my voice coming out steadier than I feel inside.

"Okay, good," she murmurs, her gaze avoiding the crumpled form on the couch as she starts to turn away.

"You're not going to ask about Jackson?" I find myself calling out, my voice oddly gruff, stopping her in her tracks. My tone has a cutting edge to it, revealing more of my own turbulent emotions than I intend.

"I wasn't," she says. "Clearly, he'd gotten himself into trouble, and you were there to save him. He's home, and that's what matters."

"You're right. He did get himself into trouble," I admit, my voice low and unwavering. "But I didn't save him. I'm the one who beat the shit out of him." My confession hangs heavy between us, and the tension in the air grows thicker.

Stepping closer to Isabella, I can feel the electric charge of our proximity. It's like standing too close to a sparking wire, the danger clear yet impossible to resist. The undeniable pull between us seems to vibrate through the cramped space, a silent dance of desire that neither of us had planned for, yet both are acutely aware of.

Isabella's breath hitches as she processes my words, her gaze never leaving mine. In that prolonged look, in the shallow rise and fall of her chest, I feel the wild beat of my heart mesh with hers. Despite the violence and the bloodshed, there's an undercurrent of want, an unspoken acknowledgment of tension that neither of us can deny.

"What kind of man does that to his brother?" Isabella questions in disgust and her words snap me out of the lustful daze.

Rage bursts inside me like a lit fuse. "The kind of man you don't fuck with," I respond angrily as I step away from the intensity of the moment. "It doesn't matter that he's my brother. He overstepped, and he had to be taught a lesson. You'd do well to remember that, Isabella. Women like you never learn their lesson."

Isabella steps back, her expression turning to a frown, her

pride clearly wounded. "Women like me?" she echoes, disbelief edging her tone.

"Money-hungry, status-driven whores," I spit out. "You move on from one man to the next, taking all you can."

Her face contorts as if I've struck her, and she rears back. "You don't know me, asshole. You can take your insults and shove them up your ass," she snaps with a venom that matches my own.

She turns on her heel and stomps away, her every step radiating indignation and scorn. I watch her retreat, the tension not dissipating but morphing into something harsh and jagged.

"It's not an insult if it's true," I mutter under my breath, voicing a bitter truth only to her retreating back.

Mrs. Collins shuffles back into the room, her hands unsteady as she tries to rouse Jackson just enough to swallow the painkiller. She maneuvers with a persistent, matronly efficiency that surprises me, given the state of things. Despite the protest in his groans, Jackson's better off now, taking what's meant to dull the worst of it. I don't linger.

I pivot around, already forgetting the scene behind me. I can feel the press of other matters, the weight of the world that doesn't pause, not even for blood spilled or pride shattered. I step out of the house with my mind already flipping through a catalog of troubles that waits.

The door of my car slams with finality. The engine purrs to life like an eager beast that's all torque and raw power. As I'm about to pull away, something catches my eye. Isabella's figure is stamped against the window. Her silhouette is defiant, and right then, her arm lifts. Slowly but surely, her middle finger rises like a flag of her own fierce battle standard. It's bold, it's brash, and I can't help but let out a rumbling laugh. She's fire, and under different stars, I might have admired that spark in her even more.

Peeling off down the driveway, I shake my head, reveling in the dark humor of it all. Jackson, the fool, might have hurt himself in all manner of ways, but he managed to marry a woman with the kind of fire and attitude that could have set the world on fire. Too bad she'll burn for the wrong sinner.

# CHAPTER 4

## Isabella

Today is a day I can relax and be myself. I can let my guard down and enjoy my time away from Jackson's mansion. Taking a deep breath, I relish the freedom that accompanies stepping outside the mansion's suffocating confines. It's always a relief to spend time with Seraphina. She's the one person who doesn't judge me or question my motives.

Of course, Jackson couldn't care less where I go or who I see. It's not like he's concerned about me. However, he always makes sure I'm watched everywhere I go and ensures I have a driver. He doesn't trust me, believing I might seize the opportunity to escape his clutches. He's not wrong.

His treatment confuses me. On one hand, he seems indifferent; on the other, he exerts control as if fearful of losing his grip on me. He came home last week, beat to hell, but I couldn't care less. Whoever he pissed off, he obviously deserved it. I was surprised to learn it was Damien who hurt him, though Damien seems like the kind of man you don't want to piss off.

"God, Isabella. This would look amazing on you,"

Seraphina says, holding up a flowing, off-the-shoulder number that's far more daring than anything I'd usually wear.

We're at the mall because she wanted to go shopping. I readily agreed, eager to get out of the house because I had nothing to do. However, I'm finding it hard to match her enthusiasm today. As I sift through the clothes, a thought of Damien intrudes unexpectedly. I don't understand why his cold, stern eyes and commanding presence invade my thoughts at the most random moments. It's infuriating.

She notices my solemn demeanor. "How are you? Is that marriage of yours still as shitty as when it started?" she asks.

I let out a bitter laugh, running my fingers over the delicate fabric of the dress. "Terrible. I can't wait to get away from Jackson," I confess, my voice barely above a whisper.

Seraphina's smile fades as she turns to look at me, her voice full of concern. "You know, Isabella, you can't hide everything. I've seen the bruises."

My cheeks burn at her words, and my grip on the dress tightens.

"I can handle it," I say quickly with a defensive edge in my voice. I force a smile to deflect the worry in her eyes. "I just need to find a way out. Trust me, I'm working on it."

Shaking her head, she turns away, and we continue browsing the racks in silence. A few minutes later, she holds up a dress that catches my eye. It's a striking crimson number with delicate lace detailing and a plunging neckline.

"I think this one would look great on you," she suggests with a grin.

I pause as the dress captures my attention. "It's cute," I admit with a small smile, "But I'd never buy it."

As Seraphina plunges deeper into the throng of shoppers, I find myself trailing behind, merely a spectator in this shopping excursion she insisted we go on. Despite Jackson's countless admonishments to 'look the part' and his incessant demands that I spend his money, I've never relented. I refuse to spend a single dime of his money, much to his irritation. Sure, I'll put on the clothes he buys, the extravagant dresses and the exquisite jewelry, because I have to.

I'm trapped in this role he's cast me in, but that's where I draw the line. Beyond that, I stick to what's mine. The clothes I had transported over from my childhood home that now lie abandoned. I can feel their familiar fabric against my skin, a constant reminder of the freedom I once had. The memories, though painful, provide a sort of comfort. A reminder that I'm still me underneath all the charades and the façade.

Seraphina's voice pulls me from the abyss of my thoughts. "You're stronger than you realize, Isabella. Remember, I'm always here for you. I may not be Blackhart wealthy, but I am wealthy. I'll help you get out."

Her words remind me of the strength I've been forced to cultivate, a bitter armor forged in the fires of my marriage. I give her a grateful nod and smile. This conversation has turned sad.

"So, enough about my disaster of a love life," I say, shifting the focus away from my own problems. "What about you? Any exciting romantic developments on the horizon?"

A blush creeps onto her cheeks, her eyes twinkling as she grins at me. "Well, since you've asked, there might be someone...," she says, her voice tinged with excitement.

I can't help but laugh at her enthusiasm. "Really? Tell me!"

"His name is Ethan," she begins, her face lighting up at the mention of his name. "He's kind, funny, and... he treats me with respect. It's a refreshing change from my previous relationships. You know how men in our world can be."

The happiness in her voice makes me smile despite my own troubles. "He sounds wonderful. I'm genuinely happy for you."

She grins back, and her spirit is infectious. "Thank you. It's the early days, but... it feels different. It feels right."

A pang of longing echoes in my chest as I used to wish for such simple happiness. However, I push it aside, focusing on my friend's joy. "That's good. Keep me posted, okay? And hey, maybe one day I'll get to meet this, Ethan."

"You'll be the first one to know. It's about time we had some good news around here," she promises with a nod.

Feeling her happiness wash over me, I can't help but feel a sense of relief for Seraphina. It's not often that women in our social circle find someone who treats them with kindness and respect. The sad reality of our world is that we women are mere objects in the grand scheme of things.

We're paraded around, shown off when the men want us to be seen, and then shelved once they're done with us. They dictate to us. They tell us what to say, where to sit, how to act, and when to speak. It's not just unfair. It's downright demeaning.

The constricting societal norms, the expectations, the control, it's all too much sometimes. Though for now, I push those thoughts aside, focusing on the spark of hope that Seraphina's news has ignited. Maybe, just maybe, I'll find someone who treats me that way. That's if I ever get away from Jackson.

We shop for a few more hours, the store's fluorescent lighting illuminating Seraphina's excited face as she chatters away about Ethan. As the afternoon lingers into the evening, I finally decide to call it a day.

"Harrison," I instruct my driver when we exit the department store. "Take me to my house, please."

"Yes, Mrs. Blackhart," he acknowledges, his gaze steady on the road, and I cringe at my name.

The house, my real home, has sat vacant since the day I tied the knot with Jackson. Each time I visit, it's like stepping into a time capsule. Every room reminds me of simpler, happier times. I don't live here anymore, but I can't bear the thought of this place gathering dust or my family's possessions being neglected.

As we pull up to the modest residence, my heart aches with nostalgia. The front lawn, once a vibrant green, is now dull and overgrown, but the structure of the house stands firm, just as I remember. Inside, I start dusting the furniture, adjust old family photos, and check that everything is secure. The familiar routine brings a strange comfort, a whisper of normalcy in the chaos of my life.

I move from room to room, the rhythmic routine of cleaning soothing my frayed nerves. Then, a noise from my father's old office stops me in my tracks. My heart thuds in my chest. No one should be here. I haven't seen anyone in this house since the day of the wedding. I creep towards the door, my hand instinctively reaching for a letter opener lying on the hallway table. It's sharp and pointy, perfect to instill some fear.

If it's him, if it's my father who sold me off to that beast without a second thought, he's going to get a piece of my mind. His betrayal stings more than Jackson's physical blows. I grip the letter opener so tight that my knuckles turn white. He'd better hope I don't decide to let him feel a fraction of the pain I've been bearing silently.

As my hand pushes the heavy wooden door open, a feeling of shock washes over me. The office, once in picture-perfect order, has been turned into a disaster. The air is thick with the scent of disturbed dust. My father's desk, a once imposing figure of polished mahogany, is overturned, its drawers opened for all to see.

The sight sends a shiver down my spine. It's as if a whirlwind had swept through, leaving no regard for the sanctity of this space. The disorder is jarring, a stark contrast to the meticulousness my father maintained. Whoever did this was searching for something. This is a clear violation of the last piece of my past life.

Another noise echoes in the silence, and instinctively, my gaze whips towards the window. A wave of fear rolls over me as I take in the scene. It's open. My heart hammers in my chest as my grip tightens around the letter opener so more. There's no room for fear, not now. I stride over to the window, swallowing the lump of dread in my throat.

Peering out, I catch sight of a figure dressed in all black, scaling down the exterior wall to the ground. The figure is not moving very fast, and their movements are hesitant like the intruder is not used to doing this.

"Hey! Who the hell are you!" I yell, pushing down the chill of fear.

The intruder looks up, but a mask conceals their face, leaving me clueless as to their identity. With a swift movement, the intruder hits the ground and almost falls before taking off running, albeit slowly.

Anger flares in my chest. "Stay the hell away from my house!" I shout after them, my voice echoing off the empty walls of the house. "If you're looking for my father, he isn't here! If you find him, tell him to kiss my ass!"

The intruder pauses and turns to look at me before turning around to run again. Pulling away from the window, I turn back to the chaotic mess the intruder left. An ache forms in my chest as I look at the destroyed office. The intruder didn't just violate my privacy, they tarnished the memories embedded in this room. Memories of my mother, whose laughter used to echo in these halls. Although my father is a bastard, I won't let his mistakes ruin my mother's home.

I begin to pick up the scattered papers, each crumpled sheet feeling like a stab to the heart. Among the wreckage, I notice a pile of shredded documents dumped carelessly on the floor. They must have been in a hurry, looking for whatever it was they needed.

As I continue to clean, something catches my eye. The paper shredder, overturned in the chaos, has a thick stack of papers jammed in the feeder. I reach for it, and my fingers are barely able to grasp the compressed mass. The papers are stubborn, resisting my attempts to dislodge them. I pull harder, but my hand slips. With a final, determined yank, the papers come free.

I carefully smooth out the crumpled, shredded papers, revealing fragments of text and half-visible letterheads. The words 'legal documentation' and 'trust' jump out at me from the top of the page, followed by my own name. It's a document from a law firm, one that faintly rings a bell, but I cannot immediately place it. My mind is a jumbled mess of confusion as I try to piece together the torn sentences, but I can't make heads or tails of it.

The document speaks of a trust, but it's frustratingly incomplete, with sentences breaking off just as they seem to be revealing something important.

*"...under the condition set forth by the trust established... the sum will be released to Isabella...,"* my eyes squint, trying to decipher the disjointed phrases. *"...on the event of..."*

The rest is lost, shredded into confetti. With a sigh, I sit back, the paper limp in my hand. It must be related to the money my father squandered away. I turn the paper over in my hands, hoping for more clues, but find none. Frustrated, I place the papers on a shelf and force myself to continue cleaning.

Exhausted and mentally drained, I finish cleaning the last of the chaos. The room, though far from its previous state of perfection, looks considerably less like a hurricane hit it. I step out of the room and pull the door closed behind me with a soft click.

As I step outside, the cool evening air hits me. The sky, now a blanket of twinkling stars, brings a hint of peace to the turmoil inside me. Harrison sees me, and he steps out and opens the car door. I take a deep breath, gather my strength, and walk towards the car. As I slide into the backseat, he shuts the door behind me, enclosing me in a cocoon of silence.

"Take me back," I request quietly when he slides back into the driver's seat, with my gaze lingering on the house one last time.

"To Mr. Blackhart's residence," I clarify, never referring to Jackson's house as my own. The mansion was never a home to me, only a gilded cage. Harrison gives a curt nod before pulling away, leaving behind my comfort and solitude and my true home fading into the distance. The noise of the engine is a dull hum in the background, barely registering as I lean back into the seat and close my eyes. I let the rhythm of the journey lull me into a state of dull tranquility.

The ride comes to an abrupt end, and before I know it, I'm back at the mansion. I walk through the ornate front door with my shoes echoing off the marble floor. My heart beats in rhythm with each step I take towards the bedroom. The bedroom I'm forced to share with Jackson. With a deep breath, I push open the door and stand there in complete shock. There's a woman on top of Jackson, and it's clear they're having sex. While Jackson has been bedding women since the day we married, he's never brought them back to the same bed he forces me to sleep in.

Jackson sees me standing in the doorway. "You're home earlier than expected," he says as he grabs the woman's hips and brings her down hard on top of them. The moans of plea-sure they both let out make my skin crawl.

The woman turns around, still riding Jackson like a hoarse, and looks at me. "Do you mind? We're in the middle of something, bitch," she says before moaning again and bending down to kiss Jackson.

"I guess she wants to relax in bed," Jackson tells the woman when they finish kissing. He smacks ass her before pulling out of her. "Come on, get up. Let's get this over with so my *wife* can relax," he says.

He says wife in a mocking way, making me even angrier. I watch, stunned that, one; the woman doesn't seem to care that his wife is standing in the room, and two; he's so damn obscene about it. Jackson turns her onto her hands and knees, positions himself behind her, and starts hammering her from behind. I turn around and slam the door behind me, effectively muting the disgusting sounds they're making.

I stumble blindly through the maze of hallways with the echoes of their vulgar pleasure haunting me. Each step in this prison reminds me of the stark contrast to the life I'd envisioned. A life I wanted where I was free, now tainted by the cold, gilded cage I find myself in. A spare bedroom emerges up ahead, and I decide to seek refuge from the sickening reality. I step inside, desperate for solitude, and shut the door behind me, hoping to drown out those disturbing sounds. The room is cold and impersonal, but it offers the peace I desperately need.

In the sanctuary of the spare room, my composure crumbles. Anger, hurt, disgust. It's a maelstrom that threatens to consume me. I wrap my arms around myself, seeking solace in solitude, away from the ugly reality that lies beyond these walls. Slowly, I approach the bed. I slip under the covers and curl my body into a tight ball. The chill of the sheets against my skin is a welcome sensation, grounding me, pulling me away from the nauseating images playing on repeat in my mind.

With a deep, steadying breath, I shut my eyes, forcing the world to fade away. I focus on the silence, the darkness, and the neutral scent of the unfamiliar bedding. Anything that isn't the memory of Jackson, the woman, and their disgusting display. As I try to settle my racing thoughts, I yearn for escape. Not just from this room, this mansion, this life, but from the all-consuming bitterness that's become my constant companion.

## CHAPTER 5

### Isabella

A knock on the door pulls me from the depths of slumber. My eyes flutter open, heavy with the remnants of sleep and the weight of last night's events. I sit up, smoothing the tangled mess of hair from my face, just as Mrs. Collins enters the room. In her hands, she carries a tray filled with breakfast. The scent of toast, eggs, and freshly brewed coffee wafts through the room, though my stomach curdles at the thought of food.

"Good morning, Mrs. Collins," I manage with a hoarse voice.

"Good morning, Miss Isabella," she replies kindly, setting the tray on the bedside table. I notice the slight tremor in her hands and the thin lines of worry etched across her face.

"Mr. Blackhart has already left for the day," she informs me, her eyes not meeting mine.

"Has he?" I ask, a wave of relief washing over me. A day free from Jackson's presence is a rare and welcomed gift.

"Yes, indeed, and that harlot from last night, she has also left," Mrs. Collins adds, her words careful, her tone gentle as if to buffer me from the harsh reality they depict.

"Thank you, Mrs. Collins," I manage to murmur, staring at my hands, my fingers worrying a wrinkle in the sheets.

"I could have come down to eat," I tell her. "You didn't have to bring this all the way up here."

She waves a hand to dismiss my statement. "Nonsense. It's my job. Now, let me look at you," she says as she inspects my face.

The bruising is slowly fading away but is still noticeable.

She smacks her lips as she steps away. "I'm sorry you have to deal with that monster."

"It's not your fault," I tell her. "Never apologize for that asshole's actions. As soon as I can get away, I'm gone."

As Mrs. Collins leaves the room, I sink back into the pillows, appreciating the solitude. I reach for the remote and flip through the numerous channels before settling on a mindless comedy show. The light-hearted banter fills the echoing silence of the room. In the quiet of the room, my mind inexplicably drifts to Damien.

His fierce gaze and harsh words at the dinner linger in my memory. There's a strength in him that's both intimidating and... oddly compelling. There's an undeniable attraction. Its unwanted but there, nonetheless. I wonder if things would be different if Damien had been the one I married. I shake my head, frustrated at myself for even thinking about him.

My fingers dance over the screen of my cellphone, initiating a conversation with my only confidante. The bright light of the screen illuminates my face as I send a quick message.

Me: Are you busy? I really need to vent.
Jackson, the jackass, is gone for the day.

I smile as her response chimes through almost immediately.

Sera: I'm helping my mom with catering right now. Call me later. Stay strong. We'll get you out of there soon.

Boredom sets in as the hours pass. This room, my sanctuary, now feels like a gilded cage of its own. The television drones on, the comedy show long replaced by a documentary about some exotic wildlife. I glance around the room, and a flash of defiance sparks within me. If Jackson wants to be an ass to piss me off, he's in for a surprise.

I stride out of the spare bedroom with determined steps and a focused mind. The hushed silence of the mansion echoes around me. I reach Jackson's bedroom with the door looming ominously before me as a symbol of our twisted relationship. Swallowing my apprehension, I push it open and step into the room that was once my prison.

I move to the walk in closet filled with a sea of designer dresses and high-end attire, all bought by Jackson to mold me into the perfect socialite wife. Ignoring them, I reach for my own clothes. Simple and comfortable, a reflection of the life I once lived before Jackson. My hands tremble as I pull them free from their hangers, each item a silent reminder of the woman I used to be. The woman I am still fighting to reclaim. I grab the suitcases stuffed in the back with more of my belongings that I never took out.

One by one, I carry my things into the spare bedroom. Each trip back and forth feels like a journey, a small victory in the battle against this gilded cage. The bedroom gradually fills with my possessions, pieces of my life seeping into the cold, impersonal space, making it a little more familiar, a little less daunting.

As the day stretches on, the room slowly transforms. My clothes hang neatly in the wardrobe, my favorite books line the bedside table, and family photographs are displayed with careful reverence. The room now radiates a sense of home, of comfort, of me. I stand in the middle of the room with a sense of accomplishment washing over me. This is not just a room anymore. It's a sanctuary, a safe haven through the storm that is my life.

The finishing touches are just in place as Mrs. Collins returns, bearing a tray filled with dinner. Despite the dread that has shadowed me all day, I'm grateful Jackson isn't home yet. Mrs. Collins hesitates at the threshold, her eyes sweeping over the transformation of the room.

"Miss Isabella," she starts, her voice wavering slightly. "Mr. Blackhart... he won't be pleased about this. About you moving rooms."

I lift my chin, meeting her gaze with a hard stare. "Well, Jackson can go fuck himself."

She flinches at my words but doesn't disagree. Instead, she sets the tray on the table and turns to face me, her hands wringing nervously.

"Miss Isabella," she says again, her voice a soft plea. "Wouldn't it be easier if you... if you just did what he wants?"

I freeze as my heart pounds in my chest. My defiance falters, and the reality of my situation crashes down around me.

I swallow hard before forcing the words out. "I can't, Mrs. Collins. I can't stop fighting. If I give in... that means they win. Jackson wins. My life... my life will never be my own. All I've ever wanted is to be on my own, to make my own choices, to be respected, to be loved..."

My voice trails off as the weight of my hopes and dreams settles heavily in the room. Mrs. Collins purses her lips before nodding her head slowly. Without another word, she turns and leaves the room, closing the door softly behind her. I'm left alone with the bitter taste of defiance on my tongue.

I pick up the phone and dial Seraphina's number. The ringing echoes in my ear before it's replaced by her voice.

"Hey, Isabella. How are you doing?" she asks, her tone gentle but laced with worry.

"I'm okay. I'm hanging in there," I respond, trying to keep my voice steady. I take a deep breath before I dive into the truth of last night. "The asshole brought a woman home last night. I caught them in the same bed we sleep in."

Silence hangs in the air, heavy and palpable. "Seriously?" she whispers, the shock evident in her voice. "I'm so sorry. Did you... did you have to see them?"

I wince at the memory as the image of them together burns in my mind. "Yes," I say quietly, my voice barely a whisper. "I saw them, Sera. It's like he's trying to torment me, to degrade me even more."

Seraphina's sigh of empathy travels through the line. "I wish I could take away your pain, Isa," she says, her voice choked with emotion. "But remember, you're going to get out of there. You can come over tomorrow, and we can create an escape plan." Her words are comforting, even if what she's saying sounds like an impossibility.

I force a smile even though she can't see it. "Thank you, Sera. I don't know what I'd do without you."

We talk a little more about our day before she has to leave to attend an event with her mother. I disconnect the call and cradle the phone close to my heart. Seraphina's words echo in my mind, reminding me that there's a way out of this nightmare. Slowly, I get up, and my body is heavy with exhaustion. I cross the room to the bed, pull back the covers, and sink into the soft sheets.

I settle in, pull the covers up to my chin, and close my eyes. Despite the anxiety bubbling just beneath the surface, I feel a strange sense of peace. As I drift off to sleep, Seraphina's words replay in my mind like a mantra. If only it were that easy to leave.

A sharp pain slices through the fog of sleep, catapulting me into wakefulness. I shriek in pain. My voice echoes around the room as my hair is yanked viciously by something pulling me off the bed. My heart hammers in my chest as terror grips me. My eyes snap open, instinctively searching for the source of my pain. The reality of my situation crashes over me like a horrifying wave.

"You think you can move rooms, bitch?" Jackson snarls as he continues to pull me out of the room.

"Let go of me, you despicable bastard!" I scream as I fight against his grip.

Pain explodes through my scalp with each vicious tug. His fingers are like iron bands in my hair. I can barely breathe, let alone think, as I claw futilely at his hand with my screams ricocheting off the walls. I can feel my heart pounding like a wild drum against my ribs. Each beat is a sharp testament to my terror.

"Stop, stop," I gasp in a voice barely a whisper, but my pleas fall on deaf ears.

"My *wife* sleeps in the same bed as me," he says as if I hadn't spoken.

We reach the bedroom, his grip unyielding as his booted foot kicks the door shut with a deafening slam. In an instant, I'm airborne as he hurls me onto the bed. The back of my head hits the plush comforter, the impact jarring but at least cushioned. Before I can so much as draw a breath, he's climbing on top of me using his weight to pin me down. Panic floods me and my heart is stuck in my throat. I look up at him, trying to mask my fear, but his eyes bore into mine, cold and unfeeling.

"You think you can disrespect me in my own house?" he

asks. "I think its time I show you what it's like to fully be my wife."

"You're delusional," I spit at him as he unbuckles his pants. "I will never sleep with you!"

"You don't have to be willing, Isabella," he says as he starts ripping my clothes.

"I wish you'd die and rot in the deepest, darkest pits of hell," I scream as I fight him.

I kick, scream, and fight against him. He punches me in the face, and I'm momentarily dazed. The pain has my face throbbing, and it's hard to focus until I realize his hands have moved to my pants. My focus comes back, and I resume fighting harder. Just as he raises his fist again, someone bangs on the door. Jackson leaps off the bed, fixes his clothes, and opens the bedroom door.

"What the fuck do you want?" he snarls at the butler.

"Sir, your brother called. He says there's an important matter that you forgot to take care of and to meet him at the warehouse," he says. "He sounded very upset."

"Shit!" Jackson hisses before turning back to me. "Your ass better be in this fucking bed when I return."

As the door slams shut behind him, I let out a shaky breath I didn't realize I'd been holding. My heart is still hammering in my chest. The silence in the room is deafening, amplifying the lingering echoes of my screams. My body trembles as the adrenaline slowly ebbs away, replaced by a bone-deep weariness. I squeeze my eyes shut, willing away the tears pricking at the corners.

The fear I felt... it was like a living thing, a monstrous beast clawing its way up my throat, threatening to swallow me whole. It wrapped around my heart, squeezing until I thought it would burst. It was the kind of fear that left you gasping for breath, your body cold and rigid, your mind trapped in a whirlwind of terror and hopelessness. I can still feel its icy tendrils, a chilling reminder of the nightmare I'm living in.

With trembling hands, I push myself up off the bed. My body is already aching from the struggle. The room spins for a moment as I stand, and I brace myself against the dresser until the dizzy spell passes. Glancing at my reflection in the mirror, I barely recognize the woman staring back at me.

"I am not a victim," I whisper to myself as a look of determination replaces the fear in my eyes.

I gingerly remove my torn clothes, dropping them onto the floor with a grimace. The shower is quick, impersonal, merely a means to wash away the taint of his touch. Once done, I dress in new clothes, choosing the most comfortable ones in anticipation of what's to come.

As I put on my clothes, every movement is measured, every sound calculated. If he dares to come back, to try and take what isn't his, he'll be met with resistance he never expected. I make my way quietly downstairs, each step more calculated than the last. The house is covered in an eerie silence. The only sound is the pounding of my heart against my chest. As I reach the kitchen, I feel around the drawers until my fingers close around the cold steel of a kitchen knife.

The weight of it in my hand lends me a bit of courage. Back in the room, I slide the knife beneath my pillow as a silent promise to myself. If he comes back, if he dares to force himself on me again... I'll be ready. I'll kill him if I have to. This nightmare will end, one way or another.

**6**

## CHAPTER 6

**Damien**

The warehouse is dimly lit. The faint smell of rusted metal and old wood lingers in the air. The silence outside belies the flurry of activity within. I stand in the middle of it all, my gaze sweeping across the room as I oversee the latest shipment. Men scurry around, their faces hardened and their movements quick and precise. My fingers drum against the cold metal of the table in front of me as my mind churns with thoughts, plans, and strategies.

Echoes of terse conversations fill the air, punctuated by the occasional thud of heavy crates being moved. I can feel the weight of their gazes on me, their silent respect and fear equally present. The room is grimy, and the air is thick with the scent of sweat, blood, and determination.

Here in this warehouse, I'm not just Damien Blackhart. I'm the man who keeps the family's darker secrets, the man who handles the business everyone else is too afraid to touch. Victor strides towards me, his worn leather boots echoing ominously in the cavernous space. His face is a mask of calm, but the twinkle in his steely gray eyes betrays his amusement.

"Damien," he begins, his baritone voice resonating

through the room. "The shipment's ready. Weapons are packed and ready to roll out."

I nod, not taking my eyes off the flurry of activity around us. Victor's laid-back demeanor belies his lethal competence, making him just as deadly as me. He's the quiet storm to my thunder, the chill to my fury.

"And the Hawthorns?" I ask, my jaw tightening at the mention of our rivals.

Victor says as his fingers drum rhythmically against the table, too. "They're poking their noses where they don't belong," he says with irritation seeping into his voice. "They're fucking with our operations."

A growl of frustration rumbles in my chest. "They're starting to piss me off," I say, turning to face him. "We need to deal with them and fast."

My tone is firm and authoritative. There's no room for discussion here. Victor simply nods, understanding the gravity of my words. Our territory, our operations, and our family. We will protect it all, no matter what.

"We'll get the information we're looking for," Victor tells me. "I'm going to enjoy beating the shit out of their henchmen. Where the hell is your brother? He was supposed to be the one overseeing this shipment."

I lean against the table as my eyes scan the room, but Jackson is still nowhere to be seen. My hands clench in irritation. Jackson's absence feels like a glaring spot in my otherwise structured world. Lately, he's been more reckless, his actions bordering on self-destruction. His duties and responsibilities, he's shoving them aside, leaving me to clean up his messes. Apparently, beating the shit out of him didn't help to change his behavior.

I'm glad it was enough to keep the Valdez's off our backs. That and reduced costs for their shipments for an extended period of time. The anger bubbles inside me, a steady drumbeat matching the pounding in my head. I clench and unclench my fists as my nails dig into the palms of my hands. If Jackson only knew half of what I was dealing with, he wouldn't be wasting his time playing house.

Thoughts of Isabella sneak into my mind uninvited. Jackson's words echo in my head, painting an unflattering picture of a spoiled vixen hell-bent on climbing the social ladder by any means necessary. She's reportedly obsessed with money, social status, and the finer things in life. This perception of her is repugnant, sickening even. It's like she's the embodiment of everything I despise in my world.

Greed, vanity, and deceit. I grit my teeth and swear to myself that I'd do everything in my power to protect my family fortune from her. The creaking of the warehouse doors shatters my thoughts, and in strides Jackson, late as usual and uncaring about the inconvenience his tardiness causes.

"You're late, Jackson," I say with a controlled calm that contradicts the anger simmering beneath the surface.

Jackson shrugs, and his nonchalance stokes my fury. "Relax, Damien. I'm here now," he replies with a cocky grin playing on his lips.

"That's not the point. You were supposed to oversee this shipment. Instead, I get pulled in to cover for you again," I snap, my temper flaring.

Jackson rolls his eyes, and the disrespectful gesture ignites my fury. "Take the stick out of your ass, Damien," he drawls in a dismissive tone. "I said I'm here now, so I'll handle it."

My fists clench at my sides, and my anger is a solid force between us. "While you were off gallivanting around, some of Hawthorn's men destroyed our last shipment," I growl through gritted teeth. The surprise on Jackson's face is satisfying, but it does little to quell my rage. "We've captured some of them, and we need to interrogate them. Now."

Jackson raises an eyebrow. "Fine, you handle the men. I'll get the shipment out."

I snarl at him as my patience has worn thin. "This is not a fucking game, Jackson," I snap before turning on my heel and storming away. My thoughts are a whirlwind of anger and frustration.

Victor and I stride through the warehouse, and our boots echo ominously against the concrete. We enter a room separate from the rest, a harsh, unforgiving space filled with four men, two strapped to chairs and two to metal tables. I recognize them. I've seen them sniffing around Blackhart Enterprises.

The room is chillingly silent. There's fear in the air as Victor and I stand tall, our imposing presence filling the space. The rancid stench of urine fills my nostrils as the two men strapped to the chairs piss themselves, their bodies trembling with raw, primal fear. I curl my lip in disgust as I shake my head at the pitiful display.

"Now, gentlemen," I begin, my voice echoing off the cold, bare walls of the room. "Let's get to the point. Why did Hawthorns destroy our last shipment?" Silence hangs heavy in the room. The men shift uncomfortably under my gaze. "And what," I continue, my gaze turning icy. "Do the Hawthorns plan to do next?"

The men remain silent, but their eyes are wide with fear. Victor and I exchange a look, a shared understanding passing between us. It's going to be a long night, one filled with pain and blood, but we will get our answers one way or another.

I unbuckle my suit jacket and hand it to one of my men standing off to the side. I begin rolling up the sleeves of my shirt, and Victor and I waste no time, our cold, calculated methods of persuasion taking center stage. I grab a steel rod, its surface shimmering threateningly under the harsh fluorescent light. As I run my fingers along its cool length, a shiver of dread ripples through the men, their eyes wide with terror. The screams begin when Victor picks up a pair of pliers, the metal gleaming menacingly before their eyes.

At first, they scream for mercy, and their pleas echo off the cold, blank walls, but it falls on deaf ears. Nothing but the truth will end their suffering. Victor is relentless, his methods unkind but effective. Every now and then, the metallic *clink* of the pliers meeting teeth reverberates through the room, followed by a blood-curdling scream. It's gruesome, but this is our world. It's harsh and unforgiving. We are monsters in the eyes of many, but we do what we must to protect our own.

I put down the blood-covered metal rod before picking up the brass knuckles. "Still won't tell me what I want to know?" I say just before my fist connects with his jaw.

The man groans in pain, but it's not enough. I punch him again, this time in the stomach. He's covered in blood, his eyes are swollen shut, and he's missing a few teeth, but he can still talk. I go on and on, hitting him, and he lasts longer than I thought he would, giving nothing up. If he were one of my men, I'd be proud of how strong he is, but he's not. The Hawthorns will be collecting his body, and they have no one to blame but themselves for his death. I have no sympathy because he chose the wrong side, the wrong people to fuck with, and his death is his reward.

My patience is all but gone as I move to the next man. I return to the steel rod, its cool weight a grim promise of what's to come. The first blow lands with a sickening *thud* and bones crunching under the force. Agony-filled screams rico-chet off the walls like a chilling symphony of pain and desperation.

"Are you going to go out like your friend, or tell me what I want to know?" I ask him.

"Fuck you, man," he spits at me. "The Hawthorns will kill me."

I swing again and smile at the scream he lets loose. "I'm going to kill you. The Hawthorns are the least of your troubles."

The interrogation continues. Our patience yields little but the blood-curdling screams of Hawthorn's men. My fists clench around the steel rod, and each blow lands with the force of a truck. Minutes turn into hours, the passage of time marked by the growing desperation in their pleas. Every bone crushed, every tooth pulled, only hardens my resolve.

Their resistance infuriates me. It's a slow-burning rage that fuels my determination. Questions hang in the air, the silence between their screams tormenting me with its emptiness. Despite the sound of their wails, there's a deafening silence that fills the room when we're done. The silence of unanswered questions. The only thing we know is that the Hawthorns want more money.

Finally, Victor and I emerge from the room with our clothes splattered with blood. Our faces are twisted, and our anger is simmering beneath the surface, fueled by the stubborn resolve of Hawthorn's men. The scent of fear and blood clings to us, a bitter reminder of the fruitless hours spent in the interrogation room. Victor and I step outside, and the cool night air cools the tension inside me.

"So, the Hawthorns want more money," I mutter as I wipe my bloody hands clean. "They're disrupting our trade. What the fuck do they need more money for? They're almost as wealthy as us."

"Yeah," Victor replies, running a hand through his hair. "But that's not all. The last guy... he said something strange."

My attention snaps to him. "What did he say?"

Victor hesitates before speaking. "He mentioned a player... a silent one. That we have no idea what's happening."

I scowl. "What did he say exactly?"

Victor shifts uncomfortably. "He said, 'You think you've

got all the players on the board, but what about the silent one? There's an informant. The one closest to you, yet farthest from your world."

The words hit me like a punch to the gut as a wave of confusion washes over me. A mole? Among us?

"Start snooping around, Vic," I command, my voice steady despite the turmoil churning within me. Just as I say that, out walks Jackson, his casual demeanor contrasting the heavy tension hanging in the air.

"You guys look like shit," he remarks, eyeing our bloodied clothes and the dark.

I shoot him a cold look before responding. "One of them said something...strange," I start, my voice low and serious. "He talked about an informant. Someone close to us."

Jackson's casual demeanor vanishes, his eyes narrowing at the serious tone of my words. "Who do you think it is?" he asks, his voice just above a whisper.

"I don't know," I admit, with my hands balling into fists at my sides. "That's why I need you to keep your eyes and ears open, Jackson. We need to figure out who this person is...and fast."

Jackson nods, understanding the urgency of the situation. "I spoke to Aurora before coming out here. Of course, she was whining about her birthday being during the week and that if she had a party on her actual birthday, nobody would come. Since it's the weekend, I told her we'd have a party at my house tomorrow for her. Now, we have to deal with a supposed informant, but you know we can't cancel the party. Aurora will have a fit, and it will make us look bad.

I sigh once again in agitation. "Fine, what time is the party?"

"It starts at seven, so be on time," Jackson says before walking away.

The stench of blood and fear still lingers on my skin. I

can't help but think about the success we've had with the weapons and the power it's given us. Now, the stubborn silence of Hawthorn's men, has left us in the dark. We have an informant, a mole within our ranks. The thought leaves a sour taste in my mouth.

As I run through a list of names in my head, one name stands out, Isabella. Everything was fine before she showed up. Our operations were running smoothly, and our territories were secure. I'll have Victor keep an eye on her from this point on, just to be sure. This isn't a coincidence.

"Clean up this mess," I instruct the men. "And clear out, we're done here for the night."

Victor and I leave the warehouse with the sounds of cleaning echoing behind us. The tension still lingers, but we'll get through this. We always do.

# CHAPTER 7

## Isabella

I wake up, relieved to find Jackson's side of the bed empty. My heart had pounded like a drum last night when he stumbled into the room with the heavy scent of dirt and sweat coating him. I was prepared, my fingers clutching the cool blade hidden under my pillow, ready to strike at the slightest provocation.

Fortunately, he simply collapsed onto the bed with his snores filling the room moments later. Whatever task his brother had set for him must have been exhausting. I let out a sigh as the tension in my muscles ease. For now, it seems I'm safe.

I reach for my phone to check the time, and I see a text from Jackson, which is an unexpected sight. He's not one to call or text, which makes the sudden message that much more unusual. His words are curt and straight to the point.

Jackass: We're having a party tonight. Fix your fucking face and be presentable.

I sit the phone back down and let out a soft sigh as his words echo in my mind. "Asshole," I mumble under my breath, the bitterness lacing my words proof of the resentment simmering beneath the surface.

The morning light peeks through the narrow slit in the curtains, and the soft rays illuminate the room. I push myself up and swing my legs over the edge of the bed, wincing as my feet touch the cold floor. Each step toward the bathroom feels like a Herculean effort, but I continue, driven by the necessity of maintaining appearances.

In front of the mirror, I take in my reflection. My skin is pale, and the dark circles under my eyes are glaringly obvious. My fingers trace the contours of a bruise on my cheek, a bitter reminder of Jackson's temper. I reach for the concealer and skillfully dab it over the discolored skin. A bit of foundation and some blush, and the damage is masked, hidden beneath layers of makeup.

Next comes the outfit. I rummage through the closet and pull out a simple dress. The fabric is soft against my skin, and the fit is perfect. A matching pair of shoes and a touch of perfume complete the ensemble. Glancing in the mirror, I hardly recognize the woman staring back at me. She looks put together and confident, the complete opposite of the storm inside me.

Stepping out of the room, I slowly make my way downstairs to see the house buzzing with activity. Decorators rush from room to room, their arms loaded with streamers and decorations. Their faces are flushed with the bustle of their preparations. The staff is busy cleaning, their movements precise and efficient as they scrub and polish, ensuring every inch of the house is spotless.

The scent of cleaning supplies mixes with the faint smell of baking, a sign that the kitchen staff is hard at work. As I navigate through this whirl of activity, I can't help but feel a pang of envy at their obliviousness. At their ability to focus on the task at hand, undisturbed by the undercurrent of danger that seems to follow me.

As I venture closer to the kitchen, the rhythmic chopping of knives, the sizzling of pans, and the murmurs of the cooks fill the air. The heat from the oven hits me, the warm scent of roasting meat and caramelizing onions enveloping me. Peering inside, I'm taken aback by the sight. There are more people in the kitchen than I've ever seen in a sea of white hats and aprons, all bent over their tasks.

Countertops overflow with an assortment of ingredients. Stacks of fresh vegetables, slabs of meat, and bottles of spices are all around. Pots and pans simmering on the stove, each one harboring a different, tantalizing aroma. Judging by the amount of food being prepared, they're cooking enough to feed an army or, in this case, a house filled with guests.

I can't help but marvel at the precision and coordination on display. They navigate around each other, and their movements are so well-choreographed that it's almost like a dance. Despite the chaos, they're an impressive sight, their focus unwavering and their dedication evident. Spotting Mrs. Collins from the corner of my eye, I managed to slip away from the chaos to approach her. The older woman is standing by the counter, her tiny frame dwarfed by the massive cake taking shape in front of her.

"Mrs. Collins," I begin, forcing a smile onto my face. "What's the occasion?"

She beams at me as her eyes twinkle with excitement. "Oh, Miss Isabella! It's for Aurora's birthday."

I frown as my displeasure seeps into my expression. The last thing I want is to suffer the presence of Jackson's crude family and socialize with strangers who know nothing of the reality of my life. The anticipation of the oncoming night fills me with a sense of dread.

Mrs. Collins gives me a sympathetic look, patting my arm

gently. "Why don't you go back to your room, dear? I'll bring you up some breakfast in a moment."

I nod, relieved to escape the bustling energy of the kitchen and retreat to the bedroom. True to her word, Mrs. Collins appears a few minutes later with a tray in her hands. The breakfast is simple. A soft-boiled egg, a couple of toast fingers, and a small bowl of mixed berries. A steaming cup of tea, the aroma of Earl Grey wafting from it, completes the meal. Despite my sour mood, I can't help but appreciate the comfort this simple meal provides.

As I pick at my food, Mrs. Collins moves towards the closet with her eyes scanning the myriad of clothing. "You'll need to look your best tonight, Miss Isabella," she says, her tone laced with a resignation that mirrors my own. She pulls out a few dresses, each more extravagant than the last.

I shake my head with my fingers absently tracing the edge of the eggshell. "I don't feel like dressing up tonight, Mrs. Collins."

She sighs, and her gaze softens. "I understand, dear. But you know it's necessary."

I push the tray away with the remains of my breakfast untouched. "I'll pick something out later, Mrs. Collins. I need some time alone."

She nods and steps away from the closet. "Of course, dear. Take all the time you need."

Standing in front of the mirror, I let my gaze travel over my reflection. I'm draped in a rich velvet dress, and the emerald color enhances my pale complexion. Its off-shoulder design exposes my collarbones, the material hugging my body before flaring out at the waist into a full skirt. Matching emerald heels complete the ensemble, adding extra elegance. As I trace the delicate embroidery along the bodice, I can't help but appreciate the craftsmanship, yet the heavy fabric feels like a shackle, a beautiful façade for the farce that is my life.

The thought of spending the evening with Jackson's family fills me with apprehension. Behind closed doors, their disdain for me is evident. The snide comments, the rude dismissals, and the cold indifference. Yet, in public, they masterfully masquerade as the ideal family. Their pretentious smiles never reach their eyes, and their words drip with insincere kindness.

It's a perverse game we play, each of us concealing our true feelings behind a mask of pleasantness. Their false pretenses fuel my resentment, a bitter pill I must swallow for the sake of appearances. It's a cruel irony that the glitz and glamour of my attire tonight serve as a reminder of the ugliness of the reality I endure. Tonight, like every other night, I will put on a brave face and play my part in this grand charade.

Descending the grand staircase, the party unfolds beneath me like a display of wealth and affluence. A sea of elegantly dressed men and women mill about in the grand hall, their laughter and conversation blending seamlessly with the gentle strains of the orchestra's symphony. The room is bathed in a soft, golden light emanating from the elaborate chandeliers that hang from the high ceiling.

The long, heavy drapes are drawn back to reveal tall windows that overlook the sprawling estate, the moonlight casting an ethereal glow over the manicured gardens. Silver trays filled with champagne flutes and hors d'oeuvres are circulated by uniformed waitstaff, their movements well-choreographed in a dance of servitude. Large, ornate mirrors along the walls reflect the magnificence of the room, amplifying the grandeur of the party.

However, beneath this veneer of elegance and class, under each carefully chosen word and a polite smile, lies a thick tension. A subtle currency of power and influence exchanging hands, discernible only to the most astute observer like me. I take a deep breath, steeling myself for the night ahead. This is the world of the wealthiest elite. A world of ostentatious displays and meticulously crafted personas. As I step off the last stair and into the throng, I am once again reminded that this is a world where I must tread lightly.

Out of the corner of my eye, I spot Jackson, secluded in the kitchen area with a beautiful blonde playfully toying with his suit lapel. The sight of them is a bitter reminder of the discomfort I feel in this world of extravagance and deceit. Yet, as soon I step into his line of sight, his demeanor changes abruptly. His eyes widen slightly, and a flicker of anger fills his eyes. With a sudden jerk, he pushes the blonde away, straightening his suit and clearing his throat.

A mask of nonchalance replaces his earlier smirk, but it does little to conceal his surprise at my presence. The sudden break in their intimate tête-à-tête leaves the blonde bewildered and her painted lips parting in a silent protest. The spectacle leaves a sour taste in my mouth, but I swallow my disdain before forcing a smile onto my face. Tonight, after all, is simply another act in this grand scheme.

"Hey!" the blonde says to his retreating back.

Jackson strides toward me with confident steps. As he gets closer, he scans my body, checking out what I'm wearing as he walks a circle around me. When he stops in front of me, he grabs my chin and turns my face from side to side, inspecting my makeup. Whenever Jackson comes too close, I feel myself tensing up. Somehow, I find myself searching for Damien. His presence, for reasons I can't fathom, feels like a safe harbor in the storm.

"This will do," he says. "You're presentable enough. Remember to keep your fucking mouth shut and just smile."

He grabs my arm, and we head toward the ballroom. I

paste the biggest, fakest smile I can and start counting down the hours until this is over.

Jackson's grip on my arm is firm, almost mechanical, as he guides me through the crowd. We're not walking together. More like he's parading me around, proud of the trophy he's showing off. No one speaks to me. Their eyes glaze over me, a mere accessory to Jackson's grand presence. They laugh at his jokes and clink their glasses with his. Their fake laughter echoes in my ears. Whenever someone does address me, their words are empty, mere obligatory remarks about my dress or the weather. I respond with a curt nod and a pleasant smile, keeping my words as minimal as possible.

I excuse myself and head toward the bathroom to give myself a break. As I hurry through the hallway, I bump into Damien. Our eyes meet, and I feel a sudden warmth rush through me. He's talking on the phone, and he looks angry.

"Have him waiting for me," he says, looking directly at me. "I want him hanging. Only give him water. I'll stop by in a few days. That should get him talking. If not, I'll beat it out of him."

My heart races as I stare into his eyes. My breath catches at seeing the darker side of Damien Blackhart. A side I'd never believed really existed. I look away, not wanting to confront him or delve deeper into the secrets he keeps hidden.

"Sorry," I murmur before quickly moving away.

I have no idea why his presence affects me like this. In the bathroom, I heave a sigh of relief before checking my makeup to ensure no bruises are showing before heading back out to the party. I've become adept at this game of concealment, of revealing just enough to satisfy their curiosity but with-holding enough to keep them at a distance. I carry on this charade, one nod, one smile at a time, counting the seconds until I can retreat from this pretentious spectacle.

 

Soon, we're nestled in the midst of his family, all eyes turned towards the guests. Damien begins to command the room as he saunters towards the center with a glass of champagne glinting in his hand. The room falls silent as a hush of expectancy infuses the air. His voice slices through the silence as smooth as velvet.

"Ladies and gentlemen," he begins, his voice resonating with an authoritative yet warm tone. "Tonight is an extraordinary night, a night that we gather not just in celebration of wealth and prosperity, but more importantly, in celebration of family."

His gaze travels around the room, and for a fleeting moment, our eyes meet. His gaze is piercing, quietly assessing, and it sends an unexpected tremor down my spine. I swiftly look away, unwilling to acknowledge the unnerving effect his gaze has on me.

"We are honored to celebrate our dear Aurora," he continues, his eyes now focused on his beaming sister. "Beautiful, charismatic, and undeniably intelligent, she has made an unforgettable mark on our hearts. Here's to a future filled with joy, love, and endless possibilities."

As he raises his glass, the room erupts in applause. Yet throughout his toast, his eyes keep finding mine, quietly assessing, sending tremor after tremor down my spine. The kind of tremor I don't want to acknowledge because I don't want to find him attractive. However, during the laughter and applause, I find myself drawn to him, my heart pounding with a rhythm I dare not decipher.

The applause rings through the room as Damien finishes his speech, and we're all escorted to our tables for dinner. I find myself seated with Jackson's family, tucked between Jackson on my left and an unfamiliar face on my right. The chatter around me becomes a white noise, a mere backdrop to the whirlwind of thoughts storming in my mind.

Through out the dinner, I can't help but feel the weight of Damien's gaze on me, which causes goosebumps along my skin. His unreadable eyes seem to hide an ocean of secrets, drawing me in despite my best attempts to remain detached. For now, I focus on the clinking cutlery and murmur of voices around me, waiting for the evening to end, one second at a time.

"Hi, I'm Victor," the guy to my right says to me with a smile.

I stare for a moment because he's so handsome. His eyes are a smoky grey color, warm and inviting, a contrast to the cold scrutiny I've received so far. His hair is a tousled mop of chestnut brown, giving him an air of approachable casualness despite his immaculate suit. However, I can sense the danger that lurks beneath his smile.

He leans closer and smiles again. "This is where you introduce yourself. You're Isabella Blackhart, right?"

Hearing that name snaps me out of my thoughts of his handsomeness. "Just Isabella," I say before staring straight ahead.

Victor leans over again. "Are you enjoying the party," he asks.

I continue staring ahead, and when the waiter brings out the next course of food, I start eating, effectively ignoring him. He leaves me alone and starts talking to Damien. Meanwhile, Jackson's been ignoring me since we sat down. A few minutes later, Victor leans over again.

"How's the food?" he says casually. "I think my meat is overcooked."

"Please leave me alone," I hiss at him.

Jackson grabs my hand, and my head whips toward him, thinking I've pissed him off by talking to someone. His eyes are wide, and he's staring at me with his body stiff as a board. A weird sound comes out of his mouth, and I frown.

"Jackson, let go of me," I say, quiet enough that only he can hear.

I try tugging my hand away, but he's got a tight grip on me. It's starting to hurt, and I feel my hand going numb. He's shaking, and another weird sound comes out of his throat.

"I said let go," I tell him a little louder this time before pushing him away.

He falls out of his chair and starts convulsing on the ground, making gasping noises. I sit there, shocked at the scene before me. Everything seems to happen in slow motion, but it happens fast as Victor pushes me out of the way and starts administering aid.

The room erupts into chaos around me. Shrieks of panic echo against the gilded walls, piercing the once harmonious atmosphere. A sea of party-goers scramble in every direction, their faces masks of fear and confusion. The finely dressed servers are lost in the chaos, leaving trays of untouched food abandoned on their tables. Jackson's mother and sister are at his side almost instantly, their faces draining of color.

I hear his mother's high-pitched cries slicing through the air as her hands flutter helplessly over his convulsing body. Her tears leave streaks of mascara down her face, and despite the terror of the situation, I find myself momentarily hypnotized by the black streams that distort her carefully applied makeup.

Jackson's sister clings onto their mother as her own sobs blend into the chaos. Damien, who until now had been the epitome of charismatic charm, morphs into a commanding presence at the head of the room. His face is etched with determination and anger. He bellows out orders, his words a clear beacon through the chaos.

"There! Clear a path!" he roars, pointing to a group of men in black suits who I hadn't noticed before. Their presence is intimidating. They spring into action, forming a wall against the onlookers and creating a clear path towards Jackson.

Despite the terror that grips the room, I find myself rooted to the spot, unable to comprehend the nightmarish scene unfolding before me. I clench and unclench my hands, the sensation grounding me during the pandemonium. The room spins around me, yet in the chaos, I feel a strange calmness seep into my bones. One second at a time, I tell myself, one second at a time.

I watch in stunned silence as an older man walks in with a bag, kneels, and begins to appraise Jackson's condition. His hands move with a mechanical precision that suggests he's done this multiple times before. My heart skips a beat as he pulls out a white sheet from his bag, a body bag.

"Move back!" commands another man, his voice barely cutting through the chaos. The crowd parts like the Red Sea, creating a path for the men carrying Jackson's lifeless body. The sight of his still body in the body bag is a horrifying sight that sears itself into my mind.

Victor steps back from the scene with his face twisted in anger. He walks over to Damien, placing a firm hand on his shoulder.

"He's gone, Damien," he says, his voice barely a whisper. "Jackson is dead."

**8**

# CHAPTER 8

## Isabella

I stand among his family dressed in a black dress and veil. It's been a week since Jackson died, and I've felt nothing but relief since. While I do feel sorrow for his family, I'm glad to be free of him. He made my life a living hell and got what he deserved. As I stand here, the past week rolls over me in waves of memories. From the moment of Jackson's death, everything became a blur comprised of a series of funereal rituals and preparations.

Every day was filled with decisions and choices. The selection of a suitable casket, the most poetic epitaph for his tombstone, and the extravagant floral arrangements that would blanket his final resting place. Each decision was overwhelming, a surreal reminder of the permanence of Jackson's absence. I remember visiting the funeral home and choosing the charcoal grey and mahogany casket, the one that seemed to match the Blackhart's wealthy persona.

The funeral director, an older gentleman with sympathetic eyes, led us through the process with a somber grace. He showed us an array of burial clothing, and we chose a suit, black as midnight, the one that resembles the one Jackson wore all the time. His mother clung to it with her tears soaking the fabric.

There were endless discussions about the order of service. Deciding who would deliver the eulogy was a battle in and of itself. Victor offered for me to do it, saying it would be the final gift to Jackson as his widow. Before I could refuse, Donna suggested that each of us say something, and that was the end of the conversation. The discussions, the choices, the planning, it was all a haze of grief and disbelief.

I recall the visit to the cemetery where we chose a spot under an ancient oak tree, a place befitting the Blackhart legacy. Every detail was scrutinized, and every decision weighed heavy on their hearts as we prepared to say our final goodbyes to Jackson. It was a week of suspended reality, a week where I navigated through putting on the façade of a grieving widow as if I cared that he died.

The priest's voice brings me back to the present. His voice echoes solemnly in the silence of the church, his words a soft balm against the harsh reality of the loss.

"We are gathered here today to celebrate the life of Jackson Blackhart," he begins, his voice steady and comforting. As he talks about Jackson's life, his accomplishments, and his dreams, tears begin to flow freely from everyone's eyes. Everyone except for me, but I make sure to look as sad as I possibly can. The cries of Donna and Aurora fill the air, their grief piercing the solemn silence like a knife.

Meanwhile, Damien stands there like a statue in his expensive black suit, looking as stoic as always. His face is unreadable, a mask hiding whatever turmoil he might be feeling. His eyes, however, hold a visible anger. The priest finishes his speech, and Damien steps forward. He steps up to the podium and clears his throat. His gaze sweeps over the crowd, a sea of somber faces, before landing on me.

"My brother was a man of strong convictions," he starts,

his voice firm. "He lived by his own rules, and his fierce determination often got him into trouble. Trouble I'd usually have to bail him out of."

He pauses, gripping the sides of the podium tightly. His knuckles turn white under the strain. "Many of you knew Jackson as the charming, charismatic individual he was. He had a way of gaining attention when he walked into a room."

I try not to snort at the shit Damien is saying. Jackson was an asshole who treated people like shit. Everyone here knows it, so there's no use in feeding them shit and convincing them it's good for them. Damien pauses as he gets lost in thought, and I can see his features soften a little. But as quickly as it comes, it's gone, replaced by a cold, hard edge.

"Jackson wasn't just my brother," Damien continues, his gaze hardening. "He was a Blackhart, a force to be reckoned with. While we mourn his loss today, we must also remember who we are. We do not forgive, and we do not forget."

His words hang heavy in the silent church, vibrating with a promise of retribution. The stoicism he had showed cracks, revealing a flicker of the fury burning beneath. It's a side of Damien I don't want to see, a side that sends a chill down my spine. Just as quickly as it appears, it's gone, replaced by the composed, stoic demeanor everyone knows.

"My brother may be gone," he concludes. "But his spirit, his fight, lives on through us. We owe it to him to ensure his legacy is not forgotten. To ensure the world knows who he truly was. To ensure that those responsible for his untimely death face the consequences of their actions."

As he steps down from the podium, the church bursts into applause, a thunderous sound that drowns the eerie silence. I watch him as his tall figure retreats to his seat with a strange mixture of admiration and fear bubbling within me. His eulogy wasn't just a farewell to his brother. It was a declaration of war.

Donna and Aurora take their turns at the podium, their tearful eulogies for Jackson a glaring reminder of the love and bond they shared with him. Donna, her voice shaky yet filled with strength, recounts tales of a mischievous Jackson in his boyhood days. Aurora, her eyes filled with unshed tears, shares memories of the protective older brother who was always there for her. Their raw pain is apparent, etching deeper lines of grief onto their already sorrow-stricken faces.

As their words fade into the heavy silence of the church, I know it's my turn to speak. My heels click against the church's stone floor in a rhythm that matches the pounding of my heart. As I step up to the podium, I glance at Jackson's family.

"I am sorry you lost Jackson," I say in a voice barely above a whisper.

That's all I can muster to say. I'm not an actress. I can't make tears fall anytime I want. There's no love lost here, and I can tell by the narrowing of their eyes that they expect me to say more, but I don't. As my words hang in the air, I turn to the priest, silently motioning for him to close out the funeral. My part in this ceremony is done. I have said my words and offered my condolences, and now it is time to move on.

The ceremony comes to an end, and I'm ushered into the receiving line. I sigh with relief as I perform my final duty. I stand with a downcast gaze with my lips pressed into a thin line as a steady stream of people approach, each face a blur of sympathy and sorrow.

"I'm so sorry for your loss, Mrs. Blackhart," a woman says in a voice choked with emotion. She looks familiar, but I can't quite place her.

"Thank you," I murmur in response.

Another figure approaches, an older man with a weathered face. "Jackson was a good man. A loss to us all," he mumbles, his eyes moist with unshed tears.

"Thank you," I repeat, my tone as cold and unyielding as the winter frost.

One by one, they come. Each bearing their condolences as if they were offering me a lifeline, unaware of the fact that I never wanted to be saved. I despised Jackson. Their words of comfort fall on deaf ears, and their pity is misplaced, but they don't know. They don't know that with each passing moment, with each 'sorry for your loss,' I feel a sense of relief washing over me. They can't see it. They don't see that I didn't shed a single tear for Jackson. I won't. Not now, not ever.

As soon as everything is over, I head toward the car as fast as my feet will allow me. I want to get as far away from the Blackharts as I can. I don't make it a couple of feet before a hand grabs me and turns me around.

"How could you just stand there?" Aurora yells at me. "I saw you at the party. You did nothing. You let him die!"

I stand there silently, not giving her the satisfaction of replying.

"Answer me, bitch!" she says before slapping me in the face.

My head whips to the side, and I turn toward her with anger in my eyes. I shove her hard, and she stumbles.

"Touch me again, and I will kill you," I tell her before walking away.

I can hear her screaming behind me, saying that this isn't over. As far as I'm concerned, this is over. I'm free, and I can't wait to move on with my life.

I climb into the car and tell Harrison to take me home. My childhood home. I made sure to have my things moved back there during the funeral preparations. I knew that when the funeral ended, I'd never return to Jackson's home. It can rot and decay for all I care. Not that his family would ever let that happen.

As the car pulls up to the quaint house I once called home, a sense of familiarity washes over me. I step out, and my heels click against the cobblestone path as I make my way to the front door. The key slides into the lock with ease, and I push the door open, stepping into the comforting embrace of the past.

Slipping out of my heels, I let out a sigh of relief as the tension in my body slowly fades away. I discard my black dress, trading it for a pair of comfortable jeans and a loose-fitting shirt. The fabric is soft against my skin, a stark contrast to the stiff and confining clothes I've been forced to wear.

The room is bathed in the warm glow of the setting sun, painting everything in hues of gold. The bed, my old bed, calls to me, and I can't resist its allure. I slip under the covers and let the cool sheets soothe my skin. Laying my head on the pillow, I let out a long breath, allowing myself to relax completely for the first time in what feels like forever.

My phone rings, piercing the comfortable silence of the house. A smile crosses my face when I see Seraphina's name flashing on the screen.

"Hey, Sera," I greet her, my voice light and cheerful.

"Isabella," she sounds relieved as she speaks. "You sound...happy."

"Yes, I do," I admit openly. There's no use in hiding it. She's one of the few people who truly knows what I've gone through.

"I would give you my condolences," she says, and I can almost see her smirk over the phone. "But we both know how much you despised Jackson, so I won't waste my breath."

I chuckle at her statement. "No condolences needed,

Sera. Actually, you won't believe what happened after the funeral."

"Oh?" She questions, her tone intrigued.

"Aurora. She had the audacity to confront me, blamed me for Jackson's death, and slapped me across the face," I recount the encounter with a steady voice.

"You're kidding!" Seraphina shrieks, laughter bubbling up in her tone. "Please tell me you punched the bitch in the face."

"No, but I did threaten to kill her if she ever touches me again," I confess, joining in her laughter.

"Well, that's a start, I suppose. Next time, though, don't forget the punch," she advises with amusement.

Our laughter fills the silence, and in that moment, I'm flooded with a sense of fulfillment. The chapter of my life involving Jackson and the Blackharts is closed, and I have people like Seraphina in my life. I can finally live in peace.

"Sera, I need to think about my next steps," I say, shifting my position on the bed to prop myself up. "I need... a job, maybe even school. Who knows? Maybe I'll even start dating," I suggest, and we both burst into laughter again at that.

"You, dating? Now that's a sight I'd like to see," she teases in a light tone.

Despite our laughter, I know she understands the weight of my words. I'm talking about building a life, my life, without Jackson. Without the weight of elite social expectations. We chat about possible jobs, debating the merits of different careers. Sera even brings up her cousin's school, knowing my love for learning before my life turned to shit.

"Make sure to go out," she adds. "Meet new people. Take a chance."

"I will, Sera. In due time," I assure her, the anticipation of a fresh beginning stirring within me.

After we say our goodbyes and hang up, I rise from the bed, and stretch. I make my way to the bathroom to run a hot bath to soothe my stiff muscles. As I wait for it to fill, I look at my reflection in the mirror. I'm going to wash away the remnants of today's sadness.

As the water laps against my skin, I soak in the tub, the comforting heat slowly seeping into my bones. The scent of lavender from the bath salts fills the air, giving a calming presence in the quiet bathroom. Time seems to lose its meaning as I simply exist in this moment of tranquility, letting the warmth soothe the lingering tension from today's events. It's only when I notice my fingers turning pruny that I realize how long I've been in the tub.

With a sigh, I slowly rise out of the bath, the cool air making my skin tingle as droplets of water trickle down my body. I wrap a fluffy towel around myself and pad back towards the bedroom, relishing the soft carpet under my bare feet. Slipping under the cool sheets, I can't help but smile. For the first time in a long time, I can anticipate a peaceful night's sleep. The promise of a fresh start when the sun rises is a comforting thought, and as I close my eyes, I let it lull me into a deep, restful slumber.

# CHAPTER 9

## Damien

My grip tightens on the railing of the balcony as I stare out into the night. Crickets chirp loudly while the light breeze softly touches my cheeks as my mind wanders to my brother again. Yeah, the guy was an asshole, but he was my brother. I sigh heavily as tiredness seeps in, but soon, fury boils my blood, demanding that I get my pound of flesh for the crime committed against my family.

Once news from the family doctor reached my ears, I knew my brother's death wasn't an accident. Someone had poisoned him, and they did it right under my fucking nose. The audacity of this person to come into my brother's home and disrespect my family has me shaking with a vengeance. I've been working for the past week to figure out who my brother's killer is. There were a lot of people who had access to Jackson, and I'm slowly making my way through each and every one of them. I walk back into my home office and sit at my desk. Victor walks in and takes his usual seat on the couch.

"What have you got?" I ask, leaning back in my chair and

interlacing my fingers behind my neck. My intense gaze rests on him.

Victor shifts back further into the couch with a sigh of frustration. "Nothing. I've got nothing. I haven't found anything that links anyone to your brother's murder," he says with a growl.

The room suddenly feels tenser. I rub my temples as more anger seeps into my bones. I had hoped Victor would have found something, anything, by now.

"Are we sure it's not the fucking Hawthorns?" I question, my mind trying to piece together the puzzle.

They were my first and most obvious guess, given our history, because they never shied away from taking credit for their actions. However, they're silent on this. I'm sure my brother had his share of enemies, but I can't think of a single one.

Victor shakes his head. "No, they haven't claimed ownership of this crime," he responds.

I let out a sigh, running a hand through my hair. This complicates things. If it's not the Hawthorns, then the list of suspects just got a whole lot fucking longer. I glance at Victor, my determination simmering beneath the surface.

"Then we have to widen our search, look at every possible angle," I declare.

He nods in agreement. "What about the supposed informant? That must be how they got close enough to Jackson. They knew him."

The moment I first heard about a potential informant, I dispatched my most trusted men to probe the shadows, to listen for whispers that could lead us closer to the truth. I had them tail several of the Hawthorns, keeping a keen eye on their every move. I even went as far as to assign a few of them, specifically to Isabella, feeling a strange mix of suspicion over her sudden marriage to my brother. There was a moment today, a mere second, when our eyes met, and I felt... something.

Isabella Blackhart is nothing but trouble. My men keep eyes on her. However, it's all in vain. They all report back with the same answer. Nothing. Not a single lead. Not a hint of betrayal. It's as if this informant is nothing but a fucking myth, but I know better. Someone is out there messing with our operations and my family. The frustration gnaws at me. We're back at square one, and Jackson's killer is still out there.

"I'm working on that. That's why I've been interviewing every person from the party," I tell him. "Go finish your search and send in the next person waiting."

I've got more interviews to conduct. It might be the day of Jackson's funeral, but I won't rest until I exact my revenge. Victor opens the door, and James walks into the room, his face pale and his hands shaking slightly. I motion for him to sit in the chair opposite me. My tone is cold as I start the questioning.

"James, you were Jackson's driver on the night of the party, correct?" I ask, my gaze penetrating his, forcing him to meet my eyes.

"Yes, sir," he responds, his voice barely above a whisper.

"Did you notice anything unusual that night? Anyone lingering around his drink, perhaps?" My words are razor-sharp, intended to convey the severity of his situation.

"No, sir... Everyone was... I mean, it was just a normal party," he stammers, his eyes darting around the room nervously. "It was at his home, so when he came back from conducting business, I never saw him again."

"James," I lean forward, my voice dropping to a dangerous whisper. "Do you understand the position you're in? Should I find out you're lying or withholding information, the consequences will be severe."

James swallows hard, his Adam's apple bobbing. "I-I understand, sir. I... I don't know anything, sir."

I lean back, and my gaze never leaves his face. "You better hope for your sake that's the truth, James. Dismissed."

As James practically sprints out of my office, I don't even need to signal for the next person. She walks in a mere second later. Mrs. Collins has been around for a long time. She's known my brother and me since we were kids. My demeanor softens slightly out of respect for the history we share, but my tone retains a stern edge.

"Mrs. Collins," I begin, gesturing for her to sit. Her back is straight, an indication of her years of impeccable posture, and her eyes meet mine unflinchingly. "You've been with our family for years. I need you to think back to the night of the party. Did you see anything unusual?"

She hesitates just a bit before answering. "Mr. Blackhart, it was a regular party. Nothing was out of the ordinary that night."

I lean forward with my eyes drilling into hers. "I need you to be absolutely certain, Mrs. Collins. Did you notice anything? Anyone new or out of place?"

She ponders on this for a moment, then shakes her head. "No, sir. I didn't see anything or anyone unusual."

Maintaining my gaze, I let my tone drop a notch. "You understand the gravity of this situation, Mrs. Collins? If you're withholding anything..."

She interrupts me, a touch of steel in her voice. "Mr. Blackhart, I've been loyal to this family for a long time. If I knew anything about your brother's death, I would tell you."

Her conviction rings true, and I find myself nodding. However, until I find my brother's killer, no stone can be left unturned. "Very well. That will be all, Mrs. Collins."

The room empties, leaving me alone with my thoughts, each one darker than the last. Anger bubbles beneath my skin, a hot, raw force that threatens to consume me from the inside. I clench and unclench my hands, trying to tame this beast within me. It's not just anger. It's guilt, sorrow, and a deep, relentless need for vengeance. My brother was taken from me, and every cell in my body screams for retribution.

I rise from my chair and pace the length of the room, each step echoing in the silence. I stop to stare out the window into the descending darkness. Somewhere out there is the person who poisoned my brother. I swear an oath to myself, and the words echo in the empty room. I will find out who did this, and when I do, they will pay. They will understand the consequences of crossing a Blackhart. Victor walks back into my office.

"Don't you ever knock?" I ask him as I walk back to my desk. "Also, aren't you supposed to be out finding me answers?"

"I brought back another person. Besides, I've got men working on it," he tells me. "You delegate to me, and I delegate to them. There are some things I'm doing myself."

Just as I'm about to respond, the next person walks in. It's Harrison, Isabella's driver.

"Harrison," I begin, my tone sharp as a knife. "You drove Isabella frequently, correct?"

"Yes, sir," he replies, his voice steady under my scrutinizing gaze.

"Tell me about her activities. Where did she go? Who did she meet?" My words are clipped, a clear warning of the consequences if he's found lying.

"Well, Miss Isabella, she wasn't one for going out much, sir. She mostly stayed at the house," he starts with a soft respect coloring his words. "Sometimes, she'd meet her friend, Miss Seraphina. She used to stop by her family home. Cleaned and dusted it. Kept it nice since it sat empty. That's all she did. She's a really nice woman."

I stay quiet for a moment as I weigh his words. There's no apparent deception, no hints of untruths. I nod at him, keeping my tone as imposing as ever. "That's all, Harrison. You may leave."

Harrison nods, and with a final "sir," he's gone.

"Was he describing the same Isabella that Jackson told us about," Victor says to me, surprise clear in his voice.

"She's the only Isabella, so yes, dumbass," I reply. "Clearly, the woman knows how to manipulate men."

"She did seem standoffish at the party. I tried to talk to her, and she snapped at me to leave her alone," Victor says.

"Maybe she was too busy slipping the poison to my brother," I growl. "Send in the next person."

Victor gets up and walks out to get the next person. There's a commotion outside before the door bangs open.

"Get your filthy hands off me, you son of a bitch!" the woman says as she's pushed inside. She stumbles before righting herself.

She turns toward me with a glare. "You didn't have to have your goons drag me to your house like that, asshole. Clearly, the Blackharts never say please."

"Please isn't in my vocabulary. How do you know Isabella?" I ask, my voice deadly low.

She snorts before taking the seat in front of my desk. "I thought you would know that since your men kidnapped me. The Hawthorns have been friends with the Storms for ages. That's how I know her."

My eyes narrow on her. "Hawthorn? What are you doing hanging out with Isabella?"

"First of all, I have nothing to do with this whole Blackhart vs. Hawthorn rivalry going on. I honestly couldn't care less what the hell you guys do and neither does Isabella. She knows nothing about that side of our families. Secondly, I've known Isabella since we were kids. Say what the fuck you want, so I can go home."

I find myself sitting back in my chair. My body is rigid in shock as her words hang in the air. The insolence of this woman causes me to clench my jaw. Most people wouldn't dare to address me this way, but she's a Hawthorn. Their bloodline is almost as wealthy and powerful as the Blackharts. The audacity of her to show this level of disregard and bravado, is somewhat impressive. Still, she's a crucial part of this deadly puzzle, and I can't afford to let her boldness distract me from my purpose.

"Tell me about Isabella. Why did she marry Jackson? Was it money she wanted?" I snap.

Seraphina leans back and laughs. "You really didn't know your brother at all. It's clear you don't know much about Isabella, either. If you dragged me in here to question me about Isabella because of your brother's death, you're an asshole."

She gets up, heads toward the door, and I stand abruptly. "All of this started when she came into our lives," I snarl, and I can see a tremor go through her at my tone. "Someone will pay."

She looks at me with wide eyes and fear before storming out of my office.

"Man, she's got balls," Victor says. "I should have known she was a Hawthorn."

I glare at Victor, and he puts his hands up before going to get the next person.

Victor returns, guiding Jackson's butler, Jensen, into the room. I watch as the old man sits across from me, his eyes reflecting a lifetime of servitude. I begin the interrogation, but my mind is elsewhere, simmering with the words of Seraphina Hawthorn.

"Jensen, you were close to Jackson, correct?" I ask, my tone startling him.

The butler nods. He looks older, worn down by the events of the past few days. He clears his throat, his voice a soft echo in the room.

"Yes, sir. I served Mr. Jackson faithfully for years," he replies, his gaze never leaving mine.

"Tell me about Isabella. Tell me about their marriage." I demand, my tone filled with an impatience I can't hide.

Jensen hesitates, his eyes growing distant as he recalls the past. "Their marriage...it was difficult, sir. Miss Isabella often expressed her unhappiness. She...she used to say she wished Mr. Jackson would die and rot in hell." The words hang heavy in the air, a damning indictment of his brother's wife.

"Do you think she did it, Jensen?" I ask, barely a whisper.

"I believe she could have, sir. She said once...that as soon as she found a way out of the marriage, she would take it." His words drop like stones in still water, sending ripples of fury coursing through me.

A cold, bitter rage begins to swirl within me, replacing the shock with a hard, unyielding resolve. Isabella killed him.

A raw, guttural anger pulses through me, a dangerous current of red-hot fury and betrayal. The room around me seems to blur, and my vision taints with a deadly shade of red. My breathing becomes harsh, and each exhale sounds like a growl in the silent room.

I grab the glass on my desk and fling it across the room. "Where is she?"

"I know she never returned to Jackson's house after the funeral," Victor says.

"Search her childhood home," I growl, barely able to contain my anger. "I bet that's where she is. Find her and bring her to me."

Pushing myself off the desk, I stride towards the glass

doors leading to the balcony of my office. The chill of the night air hits me as I step onto the cold, stone surface. My hands rest on the cool metal of the railing, fingers gripping it tightly as I gaze out into the inky darkness. The silent night is a stark contrast to the turmoil churning within me. Isabella. That name seems to reverberate in my mind like a bitter echo that stokes the fire of my anger.

I can feel the promise of retribution. Every beat, every pulse echoing a single, resounding thought. She will pay. I imagine her fear when she realizes she's been found, the shock in her eyes, the tremors of her hands. It fuels me, this image of her suffering, of her realizing the consequences of her actions. As I stand in the solitude of the night, I make a solemn vow under the silent, watchful stars. Isabella will suffer for what she's done. I will ensure it.

# CHAPTER 10

## Isabella

In my dreams, I'm far away from the confines of my life. I'm in a field of wildflowers, the wind lightly tugging at my hair and the sun warming my skin. The scent of fresh flowers fills the air, and I can hear the sound of birds chirping in the distance. A sense of freedom and peace fills me and makes me feel light as a feather. I twirl in pure bliss, with my heart swelling with joy. This is the life I've always yearned for, away from the bitterness of the Blackharts and my father. A life where I'm just Isabella, not a pawn in their deadly game.

Suddenly, my peaceful reverie is shattered by a loud banging. My heart jumps into my throat, and my eyes snap open, the floral paradise of my dream dissipating into nothingness. I'm jolted back into reality, sitting upright in my bed with the sheets twisted around me and my breathing ragged. The room is dark, the only light coming from the moon trickling in through the window. I glance around in confusion as the remnants of my dream still cling to me.

The banging sounds again, echoing through the emptiness of the house, and I realize it's coming from the front door. My heart pounds in my chest as I throw the sheets off and scramble out of bed. Fear laces my veins as I make my way downstairs. The banging continues, growing louder, more insistent.

"Isabella! Open the damn door!" Seraphina's voice flows through the door.

My fear dwindles as I realize it's just Seraphina. However, I wonder what she's doing at my house so late.

"What's going on?" I ask as soon as I open the door.

She rushes in, grabs my shoulders, and looks me dead in the eyes. "You have to leave. Now!"

I take in Seraphina's frantic state, her usually composed features twisted in urgency. Her hands, cold and trembling, grip my shoulders with a desperation I've never seen before. Her eyes are filled with panic and fear. The sight of her, the strongest woman I know in such a state, sends a shiver of trepidation coursing down my spine.

The atmosphere is thick with a tension that tugs at my nerves, setting them on a razor's edge. Questions buzz around my mind like a swarm of bees, but all I can do is stand there, rooted to the spot by a gnawing, unnamed fear.

"What... what the hell are you talking about?" I stutter as fear takes hold.

"Damien has been interviewing people from the party, and he's been asking questions about you. I think he thinks you killed his brother," she says. "His men grabbed me from my house and dragged me to his office. He questioned me about you. His eyes, his tone, his look. I'm telling you, Isa, he thinks you did it."

I stand rooted to the spot as Seraphina's words sink in. Damien thinks I'm a murderer. The Blackharts think I killed Jackson. A bitter laugh escapes me, a sound of pure disbelief yet laced with a creeping sense of dread. This must be the worst thing that could happen. I just got my freedom from the shackles of my marriage, only to be ensnared in a much more terrifying accusation.

While I'm processing Seraphina's words, her actions form a blur in my peripheral vision. She's moving around frantically, snatching up my shoes and coat from the hallway closet. The sight of her frenzied activity brings me crashing back to the reality of the situation. The urgency in her movements mirrors the fear that is now steadily taking hold of me. I jump into action, moving as fast as my legs would allow.

"What the hell are you doing?" she asks.

Ignoring Seraphina's question, I bolt towards the other closet and yank out a suitcase. I can hear my heart pounding in my ears and the adrenaline rushing through me, lending a surreal quality to the moment. I zip from one room to another, my hands shaking as I stuff family photos, books, and my mother's belongings into the suitcase.

Each item is a painful reminder of what I'm leaving behind, of the life that's being ripped away from me. Though, there's no time for tears, no time for goodbyes. When the suitcase is full, I take a moment to collect myself, setting it down and turning towards the stairs.

Suddenly, Seraphina is there, grabbing my arm and trying to hustle me towards the front door. I jerk out of her hold as a spark of defiance flares within me.

"I need my phone and clothes," I tell her, my voice steady despite the fear gnawing at me.

"I've got everything for you already," she says as she steers me toward the door. "Remember, I was preparing for your eventual escape from Jackson the jackass. I've got a car, burner phone, some clothes, and an envelope of cash waiting for you."

I stop and stare at Sera. "You really were going to help me?"

"Of course I was," she replies. "You're my best friend.

There were only so many times I'd let you call me about Jackson's abuse. Honestly, I was really close to kidnapping you to get you away from him."

A lump forms in my throat, and I swallow hard, fighting back the tears that threaten to spill. I feel a surge of gratitude towards Seraphina that leaves me overwhelmed. The reality of her dedication, her willingness to put herself in danger for my sake, hits me hard. I've taken her friendship for granted, but at this moment, I understand the depth of her love and care. I press a hand to my heart in a futile attempt to contain the wellspring of emotion.

"Thank you, Sera," I whisper in a voice choked with gratitude as I hug her. The words feel inadequate for the magnitude of my feelings, but they're all I have.

She pats my back before pulling away. "Hug time is over," she says. "Get in the car and drive far away from here. Only call me when you're safe."

Before I can respond, we hear a car speeding down the long driveway.

"Get out of here," Seraphina says before dragging me out of the house, pushing me into the car, and slamming the door.

I give her one last look and hightail it down the other end of the driveway. My heart hammers against my ribs as I push the gas pedal to the floor. The car rumbles beneath me, speeding down the other end of the winding driveway and away from the nightmare that my life has become. Fear rises in my chest at the sight of the car in the rearview mirror, its headlights blazing in the darkness as it gives chase. It is them. The Blackharts, pursuing me like prey. A shudder runs through me, but I force myself to focus on the road ahead.

Turning my gaze back to the mirror, I see Seraphina still standing there, a lone figure among the chaos. Relief washes over me as the car speeds right past her to chase me. I gulp in a long breath, the first I've managed to take since the truth came crashing down. My best friend is safe for now.

The roar of engines fills the night air as I swerve the car around a turn. Tall, foreboding trees loom on either side of the winding road, their shadows dancing ominously under the moonlight. My knuckles are white on the steering wheel, each jolt and bump from the car behind sending a fresh wave of adrenaline coursing through my veins.

"Keep it together, Isabella," I mutter to myself. The approaching headlights in my rearview mirror grow brighter, casting long, monstrous shadows in front of me.

Tightening my grip on the wheel, I force my eyes to stay on the road. My heartbeat pounds in my ears in a chaotic symphony of terror. The car behind me edges closer, so close now I can see distorted faces, their eyes full of menace in the rearview mirror. My breath hitches as the monstrous grille of their car rams into my bumper. A screeching metal sound tears through the night, followed by a shudder that goes through the whole car.

"No, no, no," I stammer, fighting the wheel as it jerks violently from the impact.

The road ahead twists and turns like a serpent, its surface slick with rain that had fallen earlier. Fear claws at my insides, and I feel like a wild animal desperate to escape. I swerve to avoid a pothole, and my car skids dangerously. Determination replaces fear. I won't let them catch me. I can't.

"Over my dead body, Blackharts," I whisper fiercely, my voice barely audible over the roar of engines.

The trees give way to an open stretch of road, with the moon casting an eerie glow across the deserted landscape. I push the accelerator harder, and the car lurches forward with a burst of speed.

Suddenly, their car pulls up beside me. The suspense is agonizing, and the car inches closer to mine like a predator closing in on its prey. Then it comes, a thunderous crash as they slam into the side of my car. My heart leaps into my throat as my car skids dangerously to the edge of the road.

"No!" I scream, and my hands tremble as I wrestle with the steering wheel. "They're trying to fucking kill me!"

The realization hits me like a punch in the gut, stealing my breath away. I'm not just being hunted. I'm being driven to my death. I can't let this be the end. I won't. Summoning every ounce of courage, I jerk the wheel hard to the right, and my car careens into theirs with a shattering impact. The sudden move catches them off guard. Their car veers off the road and smashes into a ditch.

I watch in my rearview mirror as the monstrous car skids to a halt with a cloud of mud billowing around it. A wave of relief washes over me as I finally pull away from them, and the adrenaline continues to surge through my veins.

"Take that, assholes!" I mutter under my breath, with a grim sense of satisfaction spreading through me as I speed away, leaving their wrecked car behind.

I let out a shaky sigh of relief, feeling as though I'd been holding my breath for an eternity. But I can't, won't, allow myself to relax, not yet. There's still a long road ahead, and it's crucial to put as much distance as possible between myself and the Blackharts. Their relentless pursuit has shown me how far they're willing to go, and I refuse to become their victim. I press my foot down on the accelerator, pushing the needle further on the speedometer, and continue driving. The roar of the engine and the rush of the wind are the only sounds accompanying me in this night-bound escape.

Dawn is breaking as I drive into a small town. The low hum of the car's engine has become a comforting lullaby. The night's adrenaline has worn off and is replaced by a heavy fatigue that's dragging my eyelids down. Every muscle in my body aches with the tension and stress of the past few hours. I glance at the rearview mirror frequently, half-expecting to see the Blackharts' car surging towards me, but the streets behind me remain empty.

Up ahead, the neon sign of a motel flickers into view. Its warm glow feels like a beacon of safety in the otherwise silent town. With what feels like the last ounces of my energy, I steer the car into the motel's parking lot. The squeak of my brakes shatters the quiet morning air as I bring the car to a halt. The thought of a soft bed and a few hours of undisturbed sleep makes my heart flutter with anticipation. I climb out of the car with shaky legs and make my way toward the motel reception, hoping to find a sanctuary from the relentless Blackharts.

The chill of the early morning air grazes my skin, causing me to shudder. The dead silence of the small town wraps around me like a blanket as I walk towards the reception. The motel lobby is dimly lit, with the faint glow from a solitary bulb casting long, ghostly shadows.

"Good morning, ma'am. How can I help you?" A rough voice breaks the silence, pulling me from my thoughts. I glance up to see the motel clerk, a grizzled older man with a friendly smile, looking at me expectantly.

"Hello, I need a room for the day," I respond, trying to keep my voice steady despite the fatigue weighing heavily on me.

"Sure thing, ma'am." He hands me a form. "Just need your name and ID."

I freeze when he says this. I hadn't thought this far ahead. Using my real identification would be a one-way ticket back into the Blackharts' clutches. I reach into my bag, my hand brushing past a wad of cash and landing on a plastic card. It's an ID. The name reads Destiny Jones. A small sob of gratitude escapes my lips. Seraphina. Gathering my courage, I hand over the counterfeit ID to the clerk along with the cash for the room.

"Thank you, Ms. Jones," the clerk smiles while handing me a key. "You're in room 6. Enjoy your stay."

I nod, offering a weary smile in return. I turn to leave and clutch the key in my hand like a lifeline. I can't help but send a silent prayer up for Seraphina's foresight.

The key turns in the lock, and I step into the dimly lit motel room. The scent of musty linen greets me as I close the door behind me, shutting out the world. I shed the grimy, sweat-soaked clothes, leaving them in a heap on the cold tiled floor of the bathroom. The soothing heat of the shower does wonders for my aching muscles, washing away the grime and the fear, if only temporarily. I pull on a pair of clean jeans and a soft t-shirt, the fabric feeling like heaven against my weary skin.

Setting the alarm on my phone for a few hours from now, I sink onto the bed with my eyes fluttering shut almost instantly. My dreams are not a refuge but a battlefield. Damien's dark eyes bore into mine, filled with a hatred so profound it chills my very soul. I plead with him, my voice barely a whimper in the face of his fury.

*"Please, Damien," I beg, my heart pounding in my chest. "Don't do this." But he doesn't listen. His hand lifts, preparing to deal the final blow. I brace myself for the impact.*

The shrill blare of my alarm jolts me awake, saving me from the nightmare. Heart pounding, I sit up in bed, and my skin is slick with sweat. For a moment, I just sit there, taking slow, deep breaths, trying to calm my racing heart. The nightmare may have been a product of my fear, but it doesn't make it any less terrifying.

I step back into the shower, washing away the remnants

of the dream along with the sweat and fear. Once dressed, I leave the safety of the motel room behind, venturing into the quiet town in search of food with the echoes of my nightmare lingering in the back of my mind.

I stroll down the empty main street, taking in the whimsical charm of the small town. Its quaint buildings and the silence that envelops it feel almost therapeutic after the chaos of the past few hours. Rounding a corner, I come across a diner. A nice little restaurant in this sleepy town. I push open the door, and the soft tinkle of a bell announces my arrival.

"Good morning, ma'am! Table for one?" The waitress greets me with a warm smile, her name tag reading 'Maggie'.

"Yes, please," I reply, returning her smile.

After being led to a cozy booth by the window, I order a steaming cup of coffee and a plate of pancakes. As I wait for my food, a 'We're Hiring' sign in the window catches my eye. I think about this quiet town. It's far from the Blackharts, in the middle of nowhere, and it seems small. This could be my fresh start. My lips curve into a thoughtful smile just as Maggie returns with my food.

The comforting aroma of the pancakes, topped with a generous dollop of butter and drizzled with syrup, fills my senses as I take my first bite. The delicious taste, coupled with the idea of a new beginning, brings a sense of optimism. Once I finish, I flag down Maggie.

"Could I speak to the owner, please?"

Maggie nods, leading me to a back office where a man in his late fifties sits behind a desk, engrossed in paperwork. He looks up as we enter, and a friendly smile crinkles his eyes.

"Hello, how can I help you?" His voice holds a fatherly warmth that is instantly comforting.

"Hello, I'm Destiny," I lie smoothly. "I saw your 'We're Hiring' sign and was wondering if I could apply?"

"Hello, Destiny, I'm George," he says with a friendly smile. "We are hiring. Do you have a resume?"

His question causes me to hesitate. "I'm sorry, I didn't bring one. I just got into town this morning. I happened to see your sign while I was eating."

He leans back in his chair, assessing me with curiosity. "Tell me about yourself and your qualifications."

"Well, I'm uh, twenty-four. I don't have a college degree, but I'm a quick learner, and I'm always on time." My voice trails off because that's all I have to say. I don't even know what qualifications are needed to work in a restaurant.

George studies me for a moment before responding. "Destiny, huh?" he says. "I'll be straight with you. This town is small, in the middle of nowhere, and there isn't much to do. People don't just move to this town because it's nice."

"I, um..." I start, but he cuts me off.

"Whatever your story is, you don't have to tell me. We're a close-knit community here, and you'll be safe. Just make sure your trouble doesn't affect anyone else, and we'll be fine. Welcome aboard."

A sense of relief washes over me at his words. Perhaps this could indeed be a new beginning.

# CHAPTER 11

## Isabella

I sigh and wipe the sweat from my face as I squeeze the mop out before dipping it into the dirty water again and repeating the process. The mop slaps against the floor as I mop up the mess one of the customers made when they threw up on the floor. My stomach heaves as I try not to throw up from the smell and sight alone. I'm one of those people who, if I see someone regurgitating, I'm going to start regurgitating, too.

"I'm so, so sorry, Destiny," the customer stammers, standing uneasily beside me. His face is as white as the diner's starchy tablecloths, a stark contrast to his earlier robust complexion.

I offer him a reassuring smile as I shift the mop in my hand. "It's okay, really. It's part of the job," I tell him, trying to ease his embarrassment. The smell is making my eyes water, but I push on, focused on cleaning up the mess.

The customer hesitates, his gaze flitting between me and the mess on the floor. "I could help clean it up..."

I shake my head vehemently, already guiding him back towards his seat. "No, no. You just sit down and rest. Drink that," I say, pointing to the glass of lemon-lime soda that I'd brought him. "It'll help settle your stomach."

With a shy nod, he accepts the glass, his hands trembling slightly as he takes a careful sip. I watch him for a moment, ensuring he's okay before I return to my task. It's been a couple of months since I fled, and life here has been nice. There are no ridiculous expectations and no elite image to maintain. To them, I'm Destiny Jones, a woman who ran away from an abusive relationship. Not Isabella Storm, a woman running away from a ruthless family because they believe she's a murderer.

Things here are nice and quiet. Well, except for today. Apparently, the meat has gone bad because everyone who's eaten a burger has an upset stomach and is throwing up left and right. Irene, bless her old soul, has no idea how to cook anything, and I went to the kitchen, took one look at the burger meat, and knew instantly that it was bad. I never understood why George hired her in the first place until I realized she's his mother and she's struggling with dementia. Having her here is the best way to keep an eye on her, but she keeps getting into shit and creating a problem.

Maggie's voice echoes from the other side of the diner. "Destiny! George needs you in the kitchen!"

I glance over at her, eyebrows raised in question. "What's up?"

"Irene's cut her hand again," she sighs, a worried frown tugging at her lips. "George has to take her to the hospital. He wants you to help out in the kitchen."

With a nod, I hand the mop to Maggie with a playful grin on my face. "Enjoy," I say, leaving her with the mess. I make my way to the kitchen and wash my hands thoroughly before starting.

Moments later, George joins me in the kitchen and his face is drawn with worry. "Sorry about this, Destiny," he says, the corners of his mouth pulling down in a frown. "I know this isn't in your job description."

I wave off his apology while keeping my gaze on the stove. "It's okay, George. We're all family here, right?" I give him a reassuring smile. "Besides, it'll be nice to have a break from mop duty."

George chuckles, his eyes crinkling at the edges. "That's the spirit, Destiny," he says before his expression turns serious. "I just...I worry about her."

"I know," I reply, turning to face him. "But you're doing the best you can for her. And we're here to help, too."

He nods, a grateful smile on his face. "Thank you, Destiny. That means a lot."

With a final nod, he leaves me to the task, and I turn my attention to the cooking, finding solace in the familiar rhythm of the kitchen. The spoiled meat gets dumped in the trash, and I spend the next few minutes thoroughly cleaning the kitchen area. Once satisfied, I start cooking fresh batches of burgers and fries. It's strangely soothing, the rhythm of the kitchen, sizzling burgers on the grill, the bubbling oil in the fryer, and the clatter of pots and pans. I lose myself in the work, forgetting about the chaos of my past life.

The door chimes as more patrons come into the diner throughout the day. The sound of laughter and chatter fills the air, reminding me of the sense of community in this small town. Maggie and another waiter, a young man named Tommy, join me in the kitchen occasionally, grabbing dishes to serve or help chop some vegetables. We share laughter and jokes, the atmosphere easing the stress of taking over the kitchen.

Tommy walks into the kitchen, holding up a tray of freshly washed dishes with a flourish. "Your chariot of clean plates awaits, dear Destiny," he declares with a cheeky grin on his face.

I chuckle while taking the tray from him. "Oh, my knight in shining armor, whatever would I do without you?" I play along, shooting him a teasing smile.

From the corner of the kitchen, Maggie shakes her head in mock disapproval. "You two are like a pair of teenagers," she scolds, but she can't stop her smile.

Tommy feigns a look of hurt. "Maggie, you wound me. I am nothing but the embodiment of maturity and professionalism."

I snort, nearly dropping a plate in my laughter. "Tommy, the day you become the embodiment of maturity is the day George trades his diner for a spaceship."

Maggie bursts into laughter, her eyes sparkling with amusement. "Now that's an image," she says, wiping a tear from her eye. "Imagine George floating around in zero gravity, flipping burgers."

We all share a hearty laugh, the tension of the day melting away in the kitchen's warm atmosphere. As I trade banter with Maggie and Tommy, I can't help but feel grateful for the unexpected family I've found in this small town. I've kept in touch with Seraphina, but it's not the same. I truly do miss her.

As the evening falls, the last customer leaves, and it's time to wrap up. I clean up the kitchen with a sense of satisfaction washing over me. I've successfully run the kitchen for a day, an achievement I never thought I'd experience. As I hang up my apron, my heart is full of gratitude for this strange, chaotic, but beautiful new life.

I flip the sign to 'Closed,' turn off the lights, and lock the front door of the diner. With the jingle of keys in my hand, I breathe in the crisp night air. I live a simple walk away in a small apartment within a stone's throw of the diner. This life is humble and modest in comparison to the lavish lifestyle I once had, but it's peaceful, it's safe, and it is mine.

It usually takes me about ten minutes to get home. The rhythmic sound of my shoes against the pavement is comforting, a predictable pattern in this new life. But tonight, an uncomfortable sensation prickles at the back of my neck, a feeling of dread washing over me. The hairs on my body stand on end as an unsettling realization hits me. I feel like I'm being watched.

I whip my head around to view the desolate street stretching out behind me. The quietness unnerves me, and instinctively, I pick up my pace. The faint echo of footsteps behind me sends a jolt of fear down my spine, and without a second thought, I break into a run. The footsteps follow suit, quickening in tandem with my own footsteps. Panic surges within me, and without any other plan, I take a sharp left, darting down an unfamiliar street.

I spot a parked car a few feet away, and without slowing down, I crouch low behind it with my breaths coming in short, ragged gasps. The footsteps thunder past, and the intimidating sound of the pursuit gradually fades. I wait, and every second feels like an eternity as my heart pounds in my ears. Finally, after what seems like forever, I stand up on shaky legs. With one last glance down the street, I break into a sprint, my apartment building a beacon of safety in the distance. I barely make it half a block before a guy in a black suit steps out of the shadows and grabs me.

He takes out his phone. "Got her, Boss," he says, and with a nod, he hangs up the phone and starts dragging me down the street.

The man is a giant compared to me, and he's bulky as hell. His expression is harsh, stone-like, with a permanent scowl on his face. His hair is short and dark brown, and his eyes are cold and merciless, sending shivers down my spine every time he looks at me.

"Help!" I scream as loud as I can.

The man places a meaty hand over my mouth, effectively cutting off my cry for help. Soon, I'm stuffed into the trunk of a vehicle, and darkness closes around me.

"Let me out of here!" I scream as I hit and kick around. "Please, let me out. I didn't do anything."

Panic engulfs me as the car roars to life, each vibration a chilling reminder of my grim situation. I'm trapped in the trunk, and my pleas for freedom are absorbed by the steel confines. The journey is a disorienting blur of turns and accelerations, a terrifying ride to an unknown destination.

The car finally screeches to a halt, and the sudden silence is deafening. With a jolt, the trunk opens with the harsh glare of a single overhead light stabbing at my eyes. I'm hauled out as a rough hand grips my arm, forcing me to stumble along. The surroundings blur into a haze, but I register the sheer size of a looming warehouse.

Without a shred of decency, I'm tossed into a room. I hit the cold, concrete floor hard, and a strangled grunt escapes me as a searing pain shoots up my wrist. I curl into a ball with the bitter taste of fear in my mouth.

Before I can recover, the thug pulls me up and shoves me onto a stiff chair. My protests fall on deaf ears as he binds me to the chair, the ropes cutting into my skin. I try to keep a brave face. To swallow down the terror that threatens to consume me, but the reality is daunting. I'm alone, helpless, and at the mercy of strangers. With a final glance, the man turns on his heel, leaving me to the chilling silence of the room. I tug at the binds that confine me, and they don't budge. I don't know how long I struggle but I refuse to give up. A scream of frustration rips from my throat.

Some time later a different thug walks into the room. I move as far back as the chair will allow me as he gets closer.

"The boss wants you stripped and hanged," he tells me before unbinding me.

The thug grapples with my body, heaving me over his shoulder with a brute strength that silences my protests. I thrash wildly, my fists pounding against the hard expanse of his back, but it's like hitting a brick wall. There's no effect. When he finally sets me down, my legs are unsteady. Swiftly, he grabs my wrists, and the cold metal of cuffs clamps around them with an ominous click, sealing my fate.

With a press of a button, my world shifts, the ground receding beneath me as I'm hoisted off the floor. Suspended, only by my arms, five feet above the ground, I can't suppress a wince of agony. As the thug's knife cuts through my clothes, each shred falling away, I fight the surge of humiliation. Displayed in nothing but my bra and underwear, I'm left hanging. The room falls silent once more as the thug leaves, the creak of the door a harsh reminder of my chilling predicament.

The adrenaline that had been pumping through my veins starts to fade, replaced by a shivering cold that creeps into my bones. I look around and take in my surroundings for the first time. The room is bare, save for a few ominous tools scattered across a table in the corner. The sight sends a fresh wave of terror through me. This isn't just a room. It's a torture chamber. My shaking intensifies, and my teeth chatter with the bone-deep chill of both fear and cold.

Images of what horrors Damien might have planned for me swarm my mind, each one more terrifying than the last. With a thud that reverberates through the hollow room, two men in suits enter. They position themselves at the door, one on each side, like grim, impassive statues. The room brims with an unspoken tension as they stand there, silent and unyielding.

"I didn't do anything," I plead, my voice hoarse and strained. The echo of my words hangs heavily in the air, each syllable a desperate cry for mercy. I look at them, straining against the binds with my heart pounding in my chest. "Please, let me go. I haven't done anything."

Their silence is answer enough. They don't move, don't so much as glance in my direction. It's as if I didn't speak. Desperation surges within me and with newfound vigor. "I don't even know why I'm here. I'm innocent!"

Again, only the echoing silence responds. The suits remain undeterred, with their gazes firmly fixed ahead, ignoring my existence. The cold reality sinks in. Pleading is futile. My words, no matter how sincere or desperate, fall on deaf ears. I don't know how long I've been pleading, but my words bounce off the walls, their heavy silence mocking my desperation.

Then, as if on cue, the monotony breaks. One of them, the one on the right, answers his phone. He listens attentively, his face impassive. I hold my breath, my heart pounding in my chest. When he hangs up, he looks at me, his cold gaze sending shivers down my spine.

"The Boss is on his way," he announces, his voice devoid of emotion. I freeze, my blood turning cold. This is it. Damien is coming. He's coming to kill me.

## CHAPTER 12

### Damien

The ringing of my phone echoes through my office, mixing with the sounds of the night. I tear my eyes away from the surveillance video from the night of the party. So far, nothing stands out. I snag my phone out of my pocket and answer on the fourth ring.

"Speak," I bark into the phone.

"Got her, Boss," one of my men says.

"Take her to the warehouse," I growl before hanging up the phone.

I stand and walk around my desk to the liquor bar and pour myself a glass of whiskey. A hollow chuckle falls from my lips as I take a sip. Alcohol, as I've discovered in the last few months, has the ability to take away the rage, if only for a little while. I've finally got Isabella in my clutches, and I will get the answers I seek. I will finally make her suffer before letting the police have her.

A wave of relief washes over me, one I hadn't realized I'd been waiting for until this very moment. The glass of whiskey in my hand suddenly feels lighter, as if a weight has been removed from my shoulders. The weight of my brother's unsolved murder. Sitting alone in my office, the sweet taste of vengeance dances on my tongue, more intoxicating than the finest whiskey. Isabella is finally in my grasp.

I imagine the look on my mother's face when I tell her the news, the glimmer of relief in her eyes. The promise I made to her that Jackson's killer would pay is finally on the brink of fulfillment. It's not just her. My sister, too, has been living under this dark cloud. Her eyes, usually so full of life, have been dulled by sadness since the day we lost Jackson. I can't help but hope that my actions might be able to bring back a fraction of the happiness that used to light up her face.

The pain in our hearts will never fully subside, but perhaps now, we can start to heal. We might start to find a semblance of peace, a glimmer of hope in the wake of Jackson's death.

I sink back into my swivel chair, pressing play on the surveillance footage. My focus sharpens on Isabella. I'm not scrutinizing her actions this time. Instead, I'm drawn to her allure. Her slender form and her curves beckon like a siren's song. Her smile, though not quite reaching her eyes, is undeniably hypnotic. Her beauty is undeniable, a fact I'd noted the first time our paths crossed, but one I had forced myself to disregard.

The soft glow of the monitor hits her face, casting a delicate light on her features. Her high cheekbones, her full lips that I imagined more times than I'd dare admit. Her hair falls in cascades, making me yearn to run my fingers through it. I swear under my breath, damning myself for these unexpected, unwelcome desires. Against my better judgment, I find myself consumed by a bitter realization. Had I met her before my brother, I would have had her in my bed by now.

However, this woman, as captivating as she may be, is nothing more than poison. A gold digger, a viper hiding in the shadow of a beauty. She's the one who silently crept into my brother's life, enchanting him only to sting lethally when he least expected it. The video continues to play, and her image dances before my eyes as a constant reminder of what I shouldn't long for.

The bitter taste of self-admonishment roils in my mouth as I reach for the power button, extinguishing the haunting image of Isabella from the screen. I wrench my gaze away, feeling a surge of self-loathing for the unbidden desires. I snatch my suit jacket off the back of my chair, shrugging it on as I stride towards the door of my office. I'm caught between anger and lust. It's an intoxicating, dangerous mix.

Fishing my phone out of my pocket, I dial one of the numbers saved in my contacts. The line barely rings before one of my men answers.

"I want her stripped and hanging," I command, my voice edged with a ruthless determination.

Without waiting for a response, I end the call, the finality of the disconnected line mirroring the grim resolution in my heart. I step out into the chilly night, the cold wind biting through my suit as I make my way to my car. The sleek vehicle roars to life as I slide into the leather seat, the low rumble somehow grounding, bringing me back to the harsh reality of the situation. Before I pull out of the parking lot, I dial another number.

"I'm on my way," I announce, my voice as cold as the steel of my resolve.

Then, the call ends, leaving me alone with the purring engine and my swirling thoughts. With a determined grip on the steering wheel, I guide the car onto the deserted street. The city lights blur into a streak of colors as I drive away with Isabella's fate hanging in the balance.

As I navigate through the maze of city streets, my mind churns with a barrage of conflicting emotions. The thought of Isabella, vulnerable and at my mercy, fills me with a dark satisfaction. Yet, her image, the soft glow of the monitor highlighting her stunning features, continues to haunt me. The intoxicating blend of her beauty and the danger she represents sends a thrill coursing through my veins.

I try to rein in these unwelcome desires, steering my thoughts towards the cold, hard truth. That she is my brother's killer. The journey to the warehouse stretches ahead, shrouded in the unknown, much like the path my life is now taking.

I arrive at the warehouse ready to make Isabella suffer for her crime. Upon walking inside, I make my way to the back room to see her hanging in her bra and underwear, shivering from both the cold and fear. Her eyes widen when she sees me, and she starts to struggle against the binds she's hanging on.

"Your attempt is futile, so you may as well stop," I tell her as I approach.

The murderous intent that had been simmering within me begins to waver as my gaze rolls over her body. She's a sight to behold, with her perfect curves barely covered by the scraps that pass for her undergarments. A spark of desire, unwelcome but undeniable, flickers to life in the pit of my stomach. My eyes trace the contour of her slender waist, the gentle swell of her hips, and the tantalizing promise of her breasts. The sight of her, vulnerable and exposed, awakens a primal hunger within me.

A sudden wave of possessiveness washes over me, a violent tide threatening to capsize my rigid self-control. The thought of my brother being intimate with her, touching her, ignites a fire in my veins. The notion of his hands on her skin, where mine long to be, is a torment that gnaws at my insides. A growl rumbles in my throat, echoing the primal claim that roars within me. Her eyes, wide with fear, meet mine, and in them, I see a reflection of the savage desire that I'm barely holding in check. This woman, this bewitching siren, belonged to my brother. At this moment, with her bound and at my mercy, I can't escape the raw, possessive need that she ignites in me.

The room reeks of cold dread and apprehension, but beneath it all, I detect a hint of something intoxicating. A hint of her. The scent wraps around me like a siren's call that tugs at the buried desires I've fought so hard to suppress. Murderous thoughts slip away, replaced by a carnal longing that tightens its grip with each passing moment. My resolve wavers dangerously. Isabella, the woman I should detest, stands before me, igniting a flame of desire that threatens to consume my better judgment.

"Release me, you lunatic!" she yells, breaking me out of my improper thoughts.

"Such brave words for someone who's going to pay for their sins," I tell her as I unbutton my suit jacket and hand it to one of my men.

"Let me out of here!" she screams again.

I begin taking my cuffs off and rolling up the sleeves of my dress shirt as anger takes over. "No. You will tell me what I want to know. I will take great pleasure in torturing the answers from you."

"I don't know anything," she screams.

"You murdered my brother!" I yell.

I walk over to a table and grab a knife, lifting it up to inspect its sharpness. My brother was in pain as the poison made its way through his body. He couldn't breathe, couldn't move, and she just stood there while it happened. I turn toward her and walk back with the knife.

"Why did you kill my brother?" I ask.

"I didn't kill him," she answers with fear coating her words.

I grab her by the hair, pull it harshly, and marvel at her yelp of pain. "You murdered him, and you dare lie to me."

The knife digs into her abdomen, slicing, and blood drips down. I bring the knife up and slice across her cheek, piercing her skin, and she winces in pain. My mind shifts as I take in her beautiful features. I don't want to hurt her. Despite my need for vengeance, to make her pay, I can't help but feel the attraction to her. I'm battling with my need for retribution and my desire, a battle on equal footing. However, I need answers, and there's no way I'll let a pretty face sway me.

"Please, stop," she cries as tears flow down her cheeks. "I had nothing to do with your brother's death."

I don't hear her words because desire consumes me. Unable to resist the allure of her lips, I lean down and kiss her. Her lips are soft but in a tight line, refusing to move as I kiss her. My grip tightens in her hair, and a small gasp breaks free, opening her mouth and allowing me to dive in. I delve deep, kissing her long and hard. A throat clearing brings me back to the present, and I stiffen.

"Please, let me go," she whispers through the haze of desire showing in her eyes. "I didn't do anything."

I back away and sit the knife down on the table, cursing myself for getting a taste of her delectable lips. "Still telling the same lie? No worries. When this is over, I will have the truth."

I move to sit at my desk in the corner. Two of my men move toward her, ready to extract information, and I have a front-row seat to the show. I give the signal, and they begin. I watch as my men approach her, their faces void of any emotion.

"Why did you kill Jackson?" One asks, his voice is as cold as the icy wind outside.

Isabella grits her teeth against the pain as they start their work. "I... didn't..." she manages to gasp out. Her voice is laced with pain, but there's a hint of defiance that makes me grind my teeth.

"Who are you working for?" The other one growls, his face inches from hers.

She screams in agony, the sound echoing around the room and making me clench my fists. When she answers, her voice is steady. "No one. I didn't kill your brother."

It's infuriating.

"Who paid you to poison him?" I find myself barking out the question before standing from my chair and striding over to her.

She flinches as I get closer, but her eyes meet mine with a stubbornness that takes me aback. "No one... no one... I didn't do it."

I stare at her for a moment, her words hanging in the air between us. I can't, won't believe her. She's lying. She has to be. My men continue their work, and her screams fill the room once more.

The men continue their relentless assault on Isabella, not asking any more questions but plainly inflicting pain. I watch as her body absorbs each blow, her skin marred with cuts and bruises, blood seeping from various places. There's a sick satisfaction in the pit of my stomach, a desperate hope that this treatment will make her sing the truth next time.

Her screams are a song of pain and terror, and each note she belts out sharpens my thirst for vengeance. I know my men aren't using their full force, but they make sure to inflict enough pain, nonetheless. With a terse nod, I signal my men to resume their questioning. She must crack sooner or later, and when she does, her confessions will be the sweetest melody to my ears.

One question catches me off guard. "Are you the informant?" one of my men asks, and Isabella looks at him with genuine confusion.

"Informant?" she mumbles through the pain. "Don't know what you're talking about. I don't know anything, and I didn't do anything."

Her denial rings hollow in my ears, another lie to add to her collection. One of my men grabs her by the chin, squeezing hard as he gets in her face. "The butler said you wanted Jackson dead. Why?"

To my surprise, she laughs before spitting blood on his face. "Jackson was an asshole who treated people like shit. I didn't kill him, but I send my thanks to whoever did."

She laughs again before groaning in pain as he hits her. The amusement in her eyes vanishes, replaced by a gleam of defiance that fuels my anger.

My men ramp up their efforts, their hands relentless and forceful as they continue their assault. Every strike, every harsh word, seems to magnify her screams until her agony fills the room like a haunting song. The air thickens with her cries, and it's a chilling reminder of the monstrous path I've chosen. I feel a twinge of something, regret, perhaps, but it's quickly smothered by the flames of my vengeance. Her pain is a necessary evil, a means to an end. The truth has to surface eventually, no matter the cost.

"Are you working with the Hawthorns?" he asks, and her eyes snap to him with even more confusion.

"Hawthorns? What do they have to do with anything?" she asks.

Her response leaves me questioning my men's tactics. Then, her eyes widen before she puts up a weak struggle.

"If you've hurt Seraphina, I will kill you!" she threatens.

Her words echo in the room, a chilling promise that roots me to the spot. I sit up straight, my body rigid as her words send a shockwave through my system. The confusion in her eyes and the tone of her voice all paint a picture of genuine surprise.

She has no idea about the informant or the Hawthorns. Her concern is elsewhere. She speaks of her friend with such worry, such fear. A chilling realization creeps up my spine, causing my heart to stutter in my chest. Is it possible that Isabella had no hand in my brother's murder?

Then, why would she run? A treacherous thought nags at the back of my mind, casting a shadow over my newfound doubt. Could this all be a ruse? Is she merely a talented actress playing her part to perfection? The thought is both tantalizing and terrifying. The room around me blurs as my mind races, trapped in a whirlwind of confusion and skepticism.

"Enough," I say, silencing the screams and the sounds of struggle. My men halt mid-action, turning their eyes to me. "Clean the tools. We're done for the day." I keep my face impassive and my tone unyielding. I can't afford to reveal the storm of thoughts brewing in my mind.

I can see their surprise, but they don't question my orders. They know better. I watch them clean up in silence, and my gaze never leaves Isabellas. She's panting, collapsing back and hanging as they release her. Her face is a mask of pain, but there is a stubborn light in her eyes that refuses to fade.

"Leave two men to guard the place," I order, standing from my chair and walking towards the door. I pause at the doorway, turning back to look at the gruesome scene one last time. "We resume tomorrow."

As I leave the room, I can feel their eyes on my back, but I keep my stride steady and my posture straight. It's crucial now more than ever to maintain control, to project an image of uncompromising command. No matter the doubts gnawing at the back of my mind, I can't afford to let them see I'm anything less but control.

As I step into the chill of the night, the door slams shut behind me. I pull my phone from my pocket and dial Victor's number. The ringing echoes in my ear, a sharp contrast to the quiet around me.

"Victor," I say into the phone. "Pick up Daniel Hawthorn and meet me at our other warehouse."

There's a moment of silence before he answers. "Are you sure, boss?"

I feel a growl rise in my throat. "Yes, I'm sure." I snap. I end the call before he can respond.

In the stillness of the night, my car roars to life, cutting through the quiet as I speed away. My thoughts whirl in my head in a chaotic storm that refuses to be tamed. The image of Isabella, bloodied and broken, flashes in my mind over and over, each time followed by a pang of remorse that cuts through me.

If she's innocent... The thought hangs in the air like a haunting reminder of the mistake I could be making. I've lived by one rule. I don't hurt innocents. The thought of breaking it, of causing pain to someone who doesn't deserve it, claws at me. If Isabella is indeed innocent, if she had nothing to do with this... I wouldn't be able to forgive myself.

The city lights blur past in a colorful haze that mirrors the confusion in my mind. As the distance between Isabella and me grows, so does the weight of my actions. The night stretches out ahead of me, filled with uncertainty and regret, a mirror to the turmoil within me.

# CHAPTER 13

## Damien

I skid to a halt in front of the warehouse, with dust billowing in my wake as a gritty announcement of the hastiness of my arrival. Not wasting any time, I step out of the car and slam the door shut behind me. The familiar scent of oil, metal, and damp earth wafts toward me as I head inside.

The warehouse greets me like a long-lost friend, with its darkness wrapping around me like a blanket. The silence is deafening, broken only by the occasional drip of water onto the cold concrete. The place holds an essence of death, a chilling aura that clings to its very core. It's a menacing presence that's noticeable, lurking in the corners, hiding in the cold steel of the abandoned machinery, whispering in the echo of my solitary footsteps. Victor's figure emerges from the shadows with a sense of urgency marking his features.

"Daniel's waiting," he says, his voice echoing in the hollow space. "Wasn't easy to get him, so make it quick, boss."

I nod in acknowledgment. This might be the key to unraveling all the mysteries, the final piece of the puzzle. I walk towards Daniel, each footstep echoing through the silence, and a sinister smile etches onto my face when I see him.

"I've got some questions for you, and if you know what's good for you, you'll tell me the truth," I challenge Daniel, my tone icy.

He scowls at me as defiance crosses his face. "I'm not scared of you, Blackhart. Do you know who I am? My father will kill you."

I can't help but laugh at his desperate attempt at intimidation. "I know exactly who you are," I respond, my voice thick with contempt. "And your father can go fuck himself."

Without another word, I land a punch on his face, feeling the satisfying crunch of his nose breaking under my fist.

"Why did you destroy my shipment of weapons?" I demand with my gaze piercing into his.

He spits out a mouthful of blood before responding. "Fuck you, man," he snarls. "Your brother fucked with us, so we fucked with you."

"What the hell is he talking about?" Victor asks.

My fist buries itself into Daniel's stomach, knocking the wind out of him. "Explain," I snarl, my gaze boring into his.

Daniel doubles over, wincing as he tries to catch his breath. After a moment, he straightens, his eyes weary but defiant. "Your brother," he grunts, glaring at me. "He...he wanted you gone. Wanted your power."

I flinch at his words as my heart clenches at the mention of Jackson. I remain silent, my gaze unyielding.

Daniel continues with his voice full of venom. "Jackson hated you, Damien. He hated you so much that he was willing to partner with us, The Hawthorns. He wanted to take your place."

I feel my blood run cold at his revelation. However, I don't let my emotions show. I keep my face impassive and my gaze steady.

"What did the Hawthorns have to gain from this?" Victor interrupts in a sharp tone.

Daniel smirks and it's a chilling sight. "It was a win-win situation, you see. We gave Jackson money, a lot of money, to hire mercenaries to take you out, Damien."

He pauses for a moment, letting the words sink in. "And the best part? It would look like one of your enemies did it. No one would suspect Jackson...or us. Then we'd be running everything."

His grin widens, and the sight sends a chill down my spine. I feel a growl rise in my throat, and my hands ball into fists. The walls close in on me, the air growing thin as the betrayal stings me.

A whirlwind of emotions engulfs me, leaving me standing in the shadows, staring at Daniel's smug smile. My mind is a battlefield of thoughts, struggling to process the betrayal that's being laid in front of me. My brother. The one I've always protected and always looked out for. Could he really have done this? As I look at Daniel, his satisfaction at my shock mirrors the truth in his words.

It's a bitter pill to swallow. My mind recoils at the idea. Yet, the possibility that there's truth in his words gnaws at me. There's a burning rage simmering within me that's fueled by the betrayal. It's also tempered by a sadness so profound that it threatens to consume me. It's a tormenting mix of disbelief, anger, and shattered trust, spinning around in my mind, leaving me torn and battered.

Daniel's voice cuts through my spiraling thoughts. "The plan would have gone off without a hitch, Blackhart," he says, his tone filled with a mocking kind of regret. "But your brother, that fool... he trusted the wrong people with our money."

He laughs bitterly. "He gave it to some two-bit hustler, claimed he was reputable and could facilitate the entire operation smoothly. But the bastard ran off with the cash. Disappeared without a trace."

His voice drops lower with a hint of anger creeping in. "That's why we attacked your shipment. We needed to recoup our losses. Jackson... he cost us. Big time."

"My brother wouldn't do that," I growl. "You're lying to save your own ass."

My fist collides with Daniel's face once again, and the impact vibrates through my knuckles. His head snaps to the side, but he starts laughing. A manic, deranged chuckle that echoes around the empty warehouse.

"Stop," he gasps out, coughing to clear his throat. He straightens up, and the glimmer of amusement in his eyes is replaced by a harsh, cold stare. "Let me finish."

Blood drips from his mouth, and his gaze never leaves mine. "Jackson came to us," he says, his voice quiet yet firm. "He said he had a way to get a large sum of money."

A sickening feeling washes over me, but I remain silent with my eyes locked on Daniel's.

"He told us he'd pay us back *and* pay for the hit on you," he continues. "We believed him."

A bitter smile twists his features. "Then he got married and went months without talking to us. No word, no nothing. We had no idea where our money was or what the hell was happening."

His gaze hardens, and his eyes seem to bore into my soul. "Your brother... he betrayed us all."

My mind recoils at the thought, a thin veil of denial desperately attempting to shield me from the harsh reality. Suddenly, a thought strikes me like a bolt from the sky. Isabella. Could she be the one feeding information to the Hawthorns? My heart clenches at the thought. The woman I've found myself undeniably drawn to potentially embroiled in this web of deceit.

"Who gave you the information?" I demand. Daniel looks at me, a hint of surprise in his eyes. "It's Isabella, isn't it?"

A burst of laughter escapes him. "Isabella? Oh, you've got to be fucking kidding me, Blackhart," he smirks, his gaze gleaming with amusement. "That clueless bitch doesn't know a damn thing."

"Why did you kill Jackson?" I ask, and my voice struggles to remain steady. Daniel looks at me, his bloody smile sending a shiver down my spine.

"We didn't," he says, his eyes gleaming with a cruel amusement. "Jackson, it seems, had other enemies."

A cold dread washes over me at his words. I can see the truth in his eyes, his sinister smile confirming my worst fears.

"The informant only passed on the information about how Jackson was going to get the money *after* he died." He chuckles. "If we had known *before*, we would have killed him ourselves."

Daniel's laughter rings in my ears. It's a chilling reminder of the betrayal that stings harder than any physical wound. He stares at me with a menacing glare. "We're still going to get our money."

I don't like the way he phrases that. The smugness in his voice, the arrogance in his eyes. It's all too unsettling. I flick my gaze towards Victor, trying to gauge his reaction. His face is an impenetrable mask, revealing nothing. Are we missing something here? Is there another piece to this treacherous puzzle that Daniel isn't telling us?

"What the fuck do you mean?" I snarl.

Before he can answer, the doors to the warehouse burst open with a deafening crash. A group of men storm in, their faces hidden beneath the shadows of their masks. Victor and I instinctively draw our guns. I barely have time to register the situation before we're in the thick of it, bullets flying and the deafening sound of gunfire echoing off the warehouse walls. We take aim, and two of the men crumple onto the concrete floor, the shock of our quick response evident in the eyes of their comrades.

"Cover me," I shout to Victor, but the words are barely audible over the chaos. Victor nods, his face set in grim determination as he provides me with the necessary cover. His bullets created a deadly no man's land between us and the attackers.

I feel the familiar recoil of the gun in my hands and the scent of gunpowder tainting the air. Time seems to slow down, each moment stretching on longer than the last. I'm acutely aware of every movement, every second that ticks by.

I spare one last glance at Daniel, and his smug face is now covered with a shocked expression. He's huddled in a corner with his hands over his head, and for one fleeting second, I almost feel bad for him. Then I hear the chilling sound of an empty chamber. My gun, it's out of bullets. I drop the useless weapon with my eyes scanning the room for the nearest threat.

A man lunges at me, but I react faster with my fist connecting solidly with his face. He stumbles back, and surprise flashes in his eyes before he slumps to the ground, unconscious. I move, darting between attackers, landing precise, powerful punches. My adrenaline surges as I knock one man to the ground before snapping his neck in one swift, ruthless move.

I snatch the gun lying next to the man I've just taken down. The cold metal feels reassuring in my sweaty palms as I urgently scan for any more attackers. My eyes find Victor, and he continues shooting, his bullets finding their targets with unerring precision.

"Victor!" I shout, my voice barely carrying over the roar of gunfire. He turns swiftly, still firing his gun. "We need to get out of here!"

"Agreed!" he yells back. "Cover me while I find us a way out!"

I nod and then turn my attention back to the intruders. I squeeze the trigger, my aim steady despite the chaos around us. Each bullet finds its mark, buying us valuable seconds as Victor searches for our escape route. The sounds of warfare fill the warehouse, but all I can focus on is survival. Escape. Victor calls out, pointing to a narrow exit at the back of the warehouse.

"There!" he shouts.

I nod, squeezing off a final round before we make our move. We dart towards the exit, and the pounding of our shoes on the concrete echoes the rapid beat of my heart. Bullets fly past us, ricocheting off the walls. We burst through the exit into the cool night air with our breath coming out in ragged gasps.

My car is parked a few yards away. We leap in, and the roar of the engine fills the quiet night as I slam my foot on the accelerator. The car fishtails, tires screeching against the asphalt, as I steer us out of the gunfire. Bullets ping off the car's exterior, and the sound is a grim reminder of the danger we've just escaped.

The city streets blur past us as I weave through traffic, driving like a man possessed. I know the roads of this city like the back of my hand, every twist and turn, every speed trap and police stakeout. I veer onto less-traveled routes, taking a roundabout way to my house to avoid any law enforcement lying in wait. My foot never leaves the accelerator, and the needle on the speedometer pushes dangerously into the red.

We finally skid into the driveway of my house with the car's engine growling in protest. I kill the engine, and the sudden silence rings in my ears. We made it, but the night is far from over, and the puzzle is far from solved. As I open the car door, I can't help but think of Daniel and the cryptic words he left us with. Whatever the hell is happening, one thing is clear. This has gotten a lot more complicated.

Victor and I step out of the car, and the cool night air washes over us. Its freshness does nothing to clear the chaos that swirls in my mind. I stride ahead, and Victor follows closely as our footsteps crunch on the gravel pathway leading to the house. Upon entering, we immediately head toward my office.

"Fucking Hawthorns," I snarl as I slam the office door shut.

Victor falls onto the couch with a heavy breath. "What the fuck did you expect by kidnaping the son of your biggest rival? I told you to hurry up."

"I expected to get answers," I snap. "But I didn't expect those answers."

Victor leans forward as his demeanor turns more serious. "Do you think the bullshit Daniel said about Jackson was true?"

"I don't know what to believe," I say with a sigh.

"What are you going to do about Isabella?" he asks hesitantly.

"Release her, feed her, clean her up, and let her go. I'll apologize and hope she forgives me. I found out that she never signed a prenup, so everything of his goes to her. It won't fix what I've done to her, but it's the least I can do."

As I stand there, the weight of the night's events pressing heavily on me, my mind begins to wander. Thoughts of my brother's betrayal swirl around, each revelation more stunning than the last. I can't help but wonder what exactly he was up to. What sinister plot he had been weaving behind my back.

Then I think of Isabella, sweet, innocent Isabella. The thought of her hating me twists my stomach into knots. I can't blame her, not after everything that's happened. I've done a terrible thing, a move I can't erase with a simple apology or a generous settlement. I can see her now, those wide innocent eyes filled with resentment, maybe even disgust.

As these thoughts consume me, I can't help but feel a sudden sense of isolation. The office, once a haven of control and order, feels cold and foreign. I'm left alone with my guilt and regret, a silent testament to the chaos of the night.

# CHAPTER 14

## Isabella

Sunlight pours through the cracked windows of the warehouse, bathing the cold concrete floor in a warm, golden glow. It rouses me from a disturbing sleep as all I could dream about was yesterday's events. My body aches with a stiffness that's foreign, and the numbness creeps in from hours of hanging in the same position. I flex my fingers in an attempt to dispel the numbing sensation. The movement sends sharp, prickling sensations up my arms.

My shoulders throb from the strain, a dull pain that's grown familiar over the course of the night. I wince, trying to shift my weight to alleviate the discomfort, but it's a futile effort. Every inch of me screams in protest.

The crunch of approaching footsteps sends a wave of terror flooding through me. Each footfall is a rhythmic reminder of my grim reality, echoing ominously through the silent warehouse. Panic bubbles in my throat as the door creaks open. The sudden influx of daylight momentarily blinds me. As my eyes adjust, I see them. Two large silhouettes standing ominously in the doorway. They stride toward me with a purposeful gait that leaves no room for misinterpretation. My heart hammers in my chest, each beat a frantic plea for escape.

"Stay away from me," I croak out despite the dryness of my mouth, but they continue their approach, their cold, emotionless gazes telling me that my words carry little weight in this twisted game of survival.

The men pay no heed to my pleas. With a chilling indifference, they unlock the bindings that bite into my flesh. Their rough hands grab me unceremoniously. I can't hold back a groan as they jostle me around, and the abrupt movements send spikes of pain coursing through my body. They manhandle me into a car, my battered body sinking into the cold leather seats. As the car lurches forward, I am filled with a dreadful assumption. They're taking me somewhere to kill me.

I brace myself, each passing minute a countdown to my impending doom. The car slows down, and I am taken aback as I recognize the familiar structure of Damien's house. My heart flutters with an unplaceable emotion. Relief? Fear? I don't know. I just know that whatever comes next, I won't go down without a fight.

The car door opens, and I'm ushered inside with the grand entryway of Damien's house sprawling in front of me. A butler in a crisp uniform and a maid in a traditional black and white outfit greet me at the door.

"Good morning, Miss Isabella," the butler greets me, his voice filled with an uncanny warmth that doesn't quite reach his eyes.

"Morning," I reply hesitantly, barely above a whisper.

The butler looks at me contemplatively before he finally speaks again. "May I inquire what type of food you would prefer for your meal?"

His question catches me off guard, and I just stare at him in confusion for a moment. "I... uh... just a sandwich will be fine," I answer.

"Very well. I will get that prepared for you," he responds, nodding once before disappearing into the depths of the house.

The maid, who had been standing silently by my side, speaks up. "Miss Isabella, please follow me."

With a deep breath, I follow her through several grand corridors before finally ending up in front of a beautiful room. The room is surprisingly cheerful with its bright, airy atmosphere. Light streams in through the large windows, illuminating the cream-colored walls and casting long shadows on the polished wooden floor. A large, comfortable-looking bed sits in the middle of the room, its crisp white sheets contrasting with the rich burgundy throw blanket. Despite the circumstances, I can't help but marvel at the elegant simplicity of the room.

The maid motions towards an adjoining door, her voice polite but detached. "Miss Isabella, a bath has been drawn up for you," she says, pointing to what I can only presume to be a door leading to a bathroom. "There are clothes in there as well. Your food will be waiting for you when you finish," she adds in a tone devoid of any emotion.

The words hang in the air as she turns on her heel and leaves the room with the door clicking shut behind her. I'm left standing in the middle of the room with a chill running down my spine. A bath? New clothes? Food? The normalcy of it all hits me like a bucket of cold water. It's too calm, too...mundane. It doesn't make sense. It can't. Not after everything that's happened. Not after the heart-stopping fear and the gut-wrenching dread.

With a shaky sigh, I move towards the bathroom, half expecting to find another surprise awaiting me. All that greets me is a large bathtub filled with warm water, a fluffy towel laid out on a stool, and a set of clean clothes folded neatly on the counter. It's all so incredibly ordinary, so incredibly surreal.

I stand before the mirror, still in my bra and underwear, taking stock of the damage etched across my body. Multicolored bruises coat my skin, while the cuts, though painful, aren't as deep as I'd initially thought. My fingers move tentatively over them, the sensation more unnerving than agonizing. I flinch, not from the pain but from the realization that my tormentors hadn't used their full force.

Could it be that Damien only intended to inflict enough pain to extract the information he wanted? My mind whirls with questions I can't answer, but I never gave him what he wanted. Was that why he abandoned me in that godforsaken warehouse?

Shaking my head, I turn away from the mirror, forcing myself to push away the unnerving thoughts. I can't afford to lose myself in conjecture. Not now. Stepping into the tub, I'm greeted by the perfect temperature. As I sink in, my muscles relax, and the tension I hadn't realized I was holding onto gradually fades away. I close my eyes, basking in the feeling of calm that seems so alien in my current predicament. I don't know what's going on, and part of me is afraid to find out. One thing is certain. Once I've cleaned up and eaten, I'm out of here.

I make sure not to linger in the bath because the comfort it offers is a bittersweet illusion I can't afford to dwell in. As soon as the tension is eased from my body, I step out, and the air in the room chills my heated skin. The cuts on my skin are barely visible since the blood is washed away. Toweling off quickly, I slip into the clean clothes that had been laid out for me. It feels strange, almost wrong, to be treated with such common courtesy in a place where I'd encountered nothing but terror.

Exiting the bathroom, I find a sandwich waiting for me on

the small table. My stomach growls a sudden reminder that it's been hours since I've had anything to eat. As I bite into the sandwich, I find my thoughts drifting back to the small town I'd made my home. It hasn't been long since I'd left. Maybe George would let me keep my job if I returned. I'm not certain, but it's a chance I'm willing to take. No sooner have I finished eating than there's a knock on the door.

"Come in," I call out hesitantly.

I jump from the bed as the door swings open to reveal Damien in all his terrifying glory. His entrance is as commanding as ever, and I can't help but feel a wave of fear wash over me.

"Damien," I begin, swallowing the lump in my throat, "What do you want?" My voice is steady, much to my surprise.

He hesitates for a moment, and his eyes narrow slightly before he answers. "I want to apologize, Isabella. I was wrong."

His words hit me like a punch to the gut. Apologize? He wants to apologize? A bitter laugh escapes my lips before I can stop it.

"You're sorry? Really?" I snort, crossing my arms over my chest. "You can take your apology and shove it up your ass, Damien. I don't accept it."

His expression doesn't waver, but I see a flicker of surprise in his eyes at my words. Good. Let him be surprised. I'm done playing the victim.

I watch him intently, his jaw clenching tightly as he struggles to control his temper. He steps forward with determination flashing in his eyes.

"Too damn bad. I'm apologizing anyway," he snaps, and the force of his words makes my eyes widen. "I apologize for being vicious towards you...for not listening to you."

His admission hangs in the air between us. I can see the

regret in his eyes, the remorse, but I refuse to make this easy for him.

"I never deserved your wrath, Damien," I whisper, my voice trembling with suppressed anger. "I never deserved any of this." My tone softens, just a fraction, as I meet his gaze. "I may have hated your brother, but I am truly sorry for your loss."

"If you hated Jackson so much, why did you marry him," he asks, and I can hear the judgment in his tone.

"My father forced me to. It's not something I wanted," I snap at him.

"So, you hated my brother for your father's actions," he states like it's a fact, and it pisses me off even more.

"Your brother was a narcissistic woman-beating asshole, and I'm glad he's dead," I spit out, and my eyes blaze with righteous anger.

Damien recoils as though I've struck him, his eyes widening in shock before quickly morphing into a steely glare.

"He hit you?" he demands, his voice laced with disbelief and something akin to horror.

"Like you didn't know," I scoff, crossing my arms over my chest. "You're all the same."

The accusation hangs in the air between us like a venomous bite lingering long after the words have left my lips.

"I have never hit a woman, and I never will," Damien growls, and his temper barely restrained. "Why didn't you say something?"

My laugh is bitter, a harsh sound that echoes in the silence following his question. "Are you serious?" I yell, throwing my hands up in exasperation. "You sure as hell had no problem cutting me or having your men hit me. You thought I was some lying, money-hungry whore who killed your brother and only glared at me in hatred every time you saw me."

I plant my hands on my hips, meeting his gaze head-on. "Tell me, would you have gone to talk to someone like that when they make it clear they despise you every time they see you?"

"I only wanted the truth, and then I was going to hand you over to the police. My men only did enough to cause pain, not to seriously injure you. And I never despised you," he murmurs, the softness of his voice at odds with the turmoil in his eyes.

"You sure as hell acted like it," I reply with my heart pounding in my chest. "Like I said. You and Jackson are the same."

Before I can move away, he grabs my arms, and the sudden contact sends a jolt of electricity through me. He pulls me closer until we're face to face, his breath fanning across my cheeks as he stares me down.

"You don't know me. I'm starting to think I didn't know Jackson either," he admits in a voice barely above a whisper. "You're his widow. That means what was his is now yours."

"I don't want anything of his," I snarl at him. "Not his money. Not his house. Not his possessions."

This angers Damien, and the arguing continues. We continue to shout and argue, and there's a tension weaving its way through us. It's not just anger or resentment but something else. Something that sends the adrenaline coursing through my veins. It's a tension of a more primal kind, a tension that has nothing to do with our hatred for each other and everything to do with the undeniable attraction that lurks beneath our heated exchanges. It's a sexual tension, thick and palpable, threatening to consume us even as we're at each other's throats.

"Let me go," I say, noticing how his breathing has

changed. With him this close, I can really see how blue his eyes are and how full his lips look. "Get away from me."

"Just talk to me," he says. "Why are you trying to escape? I want to make things right."

I blink in surprise before a look of disbelief crosses my face. "Are you serious right now? You and your family made my life hell. Why wouldn't I want to get away from you? I hate you, Damien."

My voice cracks towards the end. He's still so close that I can feel the heat coming off him. An unwanted wave of desire courses through me, a conflicting feeling in the midst of our clash. It's disconcerting, as though my body is betraying my mind's firm resolve. I can't ignore the pull, the strange magnetism that seems to draw me closer to him. The heat of his closeness, the intensity of his gaze, it's all so overwhelming. An unmistakable tension hangs between us, a heady mix of resentment, regret, and an attraction I wish I didn't feel.

"Yes, I know you hate me," he replies. "I also know something else. You feel this attraction between us. You can't deny it, so why are you fighting it?"

"Get off me, Damien, or I'm going to scream," I tell him, pushing him away from me, but he doesn't move.

"Go ahead and scream. No one will hear you," he says as he leans closer. "Why are you fighting this?"

"I have to!" I scream. "I can't give in to you. I can't allow myself to act upon the attraction to the very man who had me tortured. Who tortured me himself. Who thought I was a murderer."

My words have no effect on him because he simply smiles and pulls me closer. Our chests press against each other, and he threads his fingers in my hair, arching my head back. His lips graze my lips, and I gasp at the electricity that flows through me from the touch.

"Just give in," he says against my lips before slamming his mouth on mine, connecting us in a kiss.

The kiss is everything and shifts the balance of this hate-filled relationship we have. The moment his mouth touches mine, I freeze, too stunned to do anything but kiss him back. Goosebumps break out over my skin, and tingles zip down my spine.

As his lips move over mine, a moan escapes, unbidden and uncontrolled. It's a raw, primal sound that seems to vibrate through the air between us. The kiss is rough yet ironically gentle, stirring a torrent of forgotten sensations. Heat flushes through me, causing my breath to hitch and my heart to pound in a rhythm that matches his. The intimate contact sparks a moistness, an arousal that I haven't experienced in a long time. It's as though my body has awakened from a deep slumber, responding fervently to his touch.

Every inch of me is hyper-aware of him. The taste of his mouth, the press of his body against mine, and the subtle masculine scent that clings to him. The intensity of the sensations coursing through me is unnerving, but the unfamiliarity only adds to the raw, all-consuming desire that threatens to consume me from within. He angles my head and deepens the kiss like he's trying to reach my soul. Our tongues duel each other, and when he moans, it snaps me back to reality.

I push him away hard. My hand whips out faster than I can think, and I slap him on the cheek. The sound echoes around the room. My hand bounces back from the force of the hit, leaving an angry red handprint on his cheek. His head whips to the side, and he looks at me in shock. My chest rises and falls, and our heavy breathing fills the air as we both stare at each other. His eyes narrow as they travel along my body, burning with lust despite the slap.

His expression isn't what scares me. It's the burning desire I still feel coursing through my veins, buzzing with anticipation as his touch reminds me of what it feels like to be caressed by a man. And he's all man. His allure calls to a primary, basic need, and apparently, my body doesn't care who fulfills that need. I want to run away from the lust forming between us.

The weird, indescribable pull I feel toward him tugs me in his direction, whispering promises of pleasure my body has been deprived of for so long. I feel as though I've lost my mind. I don't understand how I can react to this man or even think about doing naughty things with him.

All the self-loathing in my mind can't stop me, though, when he steps toward me. In a second, I'm in his arms again, with his hands gripping my hips painfully. He twists around and lays me down on the bed before laying between my legs, fusing our mouths together again, and a sigh of relief escapes me.

15

## CHAPTER 15

### Isabella

There's no going back. From the moment we kiss, I can only focus on the sensations flowing through me. Hatred and desire battle against each other, screaming at me to choose one or the other. I hate Damien Blackhart with everything in me, and I will never stop, but if he's the one who gives me a break from all the turmoil in my life and gives me a moment of feeling precious and cared for, then I'll welcome it and won't judge myself about it later. I want this moment. I just want to forget about everything and experience something other than pain. I miss the touch of strong hands on me, reminding me that I am a woman.

I can't shame myself for succumbing to an act of indiscretion if it promises to soothe the ache within me, regardless of how fleeting its effects may be. So, instead of resisting Damien, I open myself to him, choosing to mute the voice in my head that warns me to desist, to flee from this insanity that is likely to consume me eventually.

In this shared moment, there's nothing but his body and the sensual sensations it induces within me. The second our tongues intertwine, our shared moan reverberates through the air, and my skin prickles into a landscape of goose-bumps. He escalates the intensity of the kiss, tilting me back until I adjust my head to reciprocate every stroke of his tongue.

The fiery passion of our kiss overshadows any lingering guilt and replaces it with an overpowering need that compels my thighs to tighten around him. My nails rake the back of his head as I part my lips further to amplify the depth of our kiss, if that's even possible.

His palms slide up and down my sides, gripping me harshly beneath my shirt, and I gasp into his mouth as his hands move lower to unbutton my jeans. He tugs them down, and when I feel the cool sheets against my bare thighs, I snatch my mouth away, gulping for air. Our eyes meet in a silent, electrifying duel, and a breathy murmur of objection escapes my lips as he retreats a step. He roughly unbuttons his crisp dress shirt and flings it aside.

He closes the distance once more, his body heat radiating into me like an inferno, setting my senses ablaze. My gaze dips, drinking in the sight of his flawlessly sculpted abs and pristine skin. Leaning in, I run my tongue over his collarbone, nipping lightly at the skin, relishing the heady taste of him that's amplified by his uniquely masculine aroma. It's intoxicating to be in proximity to such a raw, masculine man. His hand finds itself in my hair, halting my actions as he tugs me back.

"Isabella," he whispers with so much heat in his tone.

I place a finger on his lips, silencing him before any more words can shatter the all-encompassing bubble I've built around us. His eyes turn stormy, a passionate blend of lust and fury, yet he remains silent, seemingly unwilling to relinquish this precarious chance at desire that teeters on the edge. One moment, I'm like a captive held in his iron grip. The next, a surprised gasp is torn from my throat as he pushes me further up the bed. His lips descend upon mine once more, but the nature of the kiss has shifted.

Gone is the earlier gentleness. It's replaced now with a fervor so raw it is overwhelming. The kiss engulfs me whole while his hardened arousal presses into me, sliding with a teasing friction that offers me a provocative preview of what it might bring to my body. As our mouths melt together, I silently plea for him to alleviate our shared agony and satiate this mutual, insatiable craving we both have.

He nips my lower lip, causing me to jerk from the sensory overload as his teeth tug on the sensitive flesh before kissing me again in a soothing gesture. The dual sensation is a heady mix of pain and pleasure, and I can't help the whimper that escapes me. He leaves my lips, moving down to my chin, and the subtle scrape of his stubble against my skin sends shivers down my spine. His mouth travels further, over the curve of my throat, his teeth nipping at the sensitive flesh of my neck. I know he's leaving marks that will be hard to conceal.

His stubble grazes my skin, surely leaving red, irritated imprints as evidence of our wild passion, but I find myself not caring. The biting and the scraping. The pain and the pleasure. It all blends together into a storm of sensations that makes me crave for more. As long as there's the promise of pleasure at the end of this journey, I don't care. I don't care about anything but the feel of him against me, inside me. The world outside our bubble ceases to exist, and all that matters is the here and now.

"Your lips feel as good as I imagined," he says against my neck, and I moan from the sex exuding from his tone.

"This body was made for my hands," he says, biting my skin and causing a gasp to erupt from my throat.

I wiggle, trying to get him to kiss me again so I don't have to hear the sound of his voice. He may sound like sex and sin, but his voice is only a reminder that what I'm doing is wrong.

Unable to move in his firm grasp, I feel him move down, and his breath gently caresses the curves of my breasts. A soft kiss is followed by the sensation of my nipple being pulled between his lips, ghosting through the delicate fabric of my shirt.

He nudges it down to reveal my breast before greedily drawing it into the warmth of his mouth, his tongue lavishing it with wet strokes. My back instinctively arches, and an involuntary moan causes me to swiftly clamp my mouth shut for fear of his staff hearing me. I already feel ashamed enough to give in to my desires. I don't need his staff giving me disgusted looks when they see me. That would make me feel even worse.

"I want to hear you, Isabella. Be as loud as you want. No one is going to hear you," he says and moves to my other breast, sucking and driving me wild.

The soft fabric of my shirt is an infernal barrier, searing my skin with every moment it denies me the full contact of his flesh against mine. I want to tear it away, to allow the raw, unfiltered touch of him to consume me whole. Each flick of his tongue is a spark of madness, igniting a blaze that incinerates all semblance of my sanity, leaving me gasping and pleading for silent surrender. The sweet oblivion of this moment is a refuge, a haven from the harsh realities that await beyond the boundaries of this room.

As another wave of pleasure surges through me, a moan, louder and more desperate than the last, escapes my lips. It's an indication of the potency of the electric current coursing relentlessly through my veins. It has me trembling and helpless within his unyielding grasp. My core is a storm of desire, a torrent threatening to drown me, growing wetter, hungrier, screaming for any form of relief as the inferno within me blazes unchecked, ravaging everything in its path.

Driven by a primal need, I roll my hips forward, seeking

solace in the hardness pressing against me. He doesn't yield to my silent plea and doesn't grant me the release I desperately seek. His refusal is a frustrating torture.

"We'll get there, Isabella," he says, his voice a soft murmur among the storm of my own vehement protests. "Let me enjoy this."

I stubbornly shake my head, rejecting the sensations he's trying to enforce upon me. His hands, strong and adamant, enclose around my hips again, clenching with a pressure that I know will later blossom into an area full of bruises. In this heated moment, such considerations dissolve into irrelevance. His every caress, his every tender assault, deepens the increased yearning that's simmering at my very center.

He gives one last bite on my nipple before he positions me in the center of the bed. I watch as his mouth trails lower, leaving kisses on my exposed skin as he goes lower. His lips kiss my stomach, then my navel, periodically nipping my skin and leaving wet imprints in his wake. When he's low enough, he moves my legs over his wide shoulders, making sure my shirt is pushed up so it's not in the way. His piercing blue eyes meet mine, and I suck in a breath at the intensity of his gaze. Such raw, sexual hunger stares back at me.

I feel hot, and the shirt feels rough on my skin. I sit up slightly and tug the offending piece of clothing off while his hot breath fans over my core right before he rubs his face along the inside of my thigh. A whimper slips free as he sucks on my skin, eliciting a moan from deep within me.

I lean back and enjoy the teasing sensations, but a part of me wants to tug his hair and bring his mouth to the center of my need. Yet, I hesitate, stopped by the allure of his next move. The moment he shifts his attention to my other thigh, nibbling at the skin, I can't help but hiss out from the sting and pleasure of it. My heels rub against the firm ridges of his back. This time, impulse overrides restraint. My fingers weave into the silken threads of his hair, guiding him with silent urgency to the very core of my aching, inflamed desire.

"Tell me what you want, baby," he says as he kisses my center through my panties, making me moan in pleasure and frustration. My need only intensifies, and he does nothing to soothe the ache.

"Stop talking, Damien," I tell him with a groan. "You know what I want, so stop teasing."

I grind against his face, but he chuckles against my center, slightly biting me through my underwear before kissing it.

"Say you want me," he demands.

I remain silent as his breath tickles me and causes more waves of sensations to flow through my body.

He rubs his nose against my wet center. "You won't get my tongue until you say it, Isabella. You want my tongue, don't you?"

I nod, knowing he can't see it. If he won't relieve this all-consuming ache I have, then I'll do it myself. I slide my hand to my core and slip my panties to the side before slipping my finger through my sensitive folds, moaning so loud I'm sure his staff can hear me, but I don't care. I've lost all decency in my quest to relieve this ache. I slide my finger over my wet center again, enjoying the slight relief it gives me, and move to pinch my clit before rubbing it, moaning at the pleasure flowing through me.

If he wants to play games, then I can get myself off. I don't need him. Especially if he continues to be stubborn. I hear him growl as a hand wraps around my wrist. He brings my fingers to his mouth and sucks my juices from them. I lift my head to find his gaze on me, and my breath hitches at the raw desire in it. My core clenches, wanting him inside me, awakening parts of me that have been neglected. My desire flares, and I know my fingers won't be enough to relieve me of the throbbing need I have.

"No one is getting you off but me," he says as he slides his hands under me and lifts my center to his mouth. "I'm going to show this pussy that it wants me, even if you won't say it."

He attacks my core, dipping his tongue inside me, causing me to arch my back and cry out as tiny pricks of electricity flow through me. My body is on fire as his tongue laps at my lips, making my body hunger for more of his touch. He pulls his tongue out only to slide back in again, swirling side to side and up through my folds.

I moan and whimper as I dig my heels into his back. I grab my breast, tweaking my nipples and grinding against his face in a silent demand for release. However, he only applies enough pressure to drive me crazier. He continues to flick his tongue up and down my pussy before sucking on my clit. I cry out again and thread my fingers through his hair, pushing him closer to my core. He continues licking, bringing pleasure that takes me higher and higher. I'm on the brink of orgasm. It's almost within my grasp, but he slows his onslaught. I tighten my hold on him, shifting to get more friction, causing him to growl, sending vibrations through my flesh.

I groan in frustration. "Please, Damien."

"Please what, Isabella," he asks, giving me a slow lick.

I jerk in response and try to rub against him, but he grabs my ass to keep me in place.

"Make me come," I reply and groan in relief when he returns to licking my pussy, swirling his tongue deeper and deeper. I roll my hips and grind against his tongue. I'm almost there when he pulls back again.

"Say you want me, Isabella," he snarls, and I can tell that he's reaching his breaking point.

"Please!" The word bursts from me, a concoction of frustration and a burning anger directed at my own vulnerability.

I despise the vulnerability he instills in me, this need to

beg, yet find my body betraying my pride as my legs encircle him more tightly. The grip of my thighs against his face is both a plea and a chastisement, but it does little to sway the deliberate course of his actions. My trembles with a maelstrom of conflicting emotions.

"Say it," he commands, and the timbre of his voice slices through the fog of my desire as his hand trails deliberately to my core.

The pad of his thumb begins an insidious dance, eliciting a slick rhythm up and down, up and down, propelling me to the precipice of sanity with every glide. Then suddenly, he plunges two fingers inside, stretching me to a chorus of my own gasps, even as his mouth finds my clit, enveloping it with a fervent suction.

"Tell me what you want," he insists, and the dual assault verges on cataclysmic. A sheen of sweat covers my skin. My breaths are shallow, my senses singed at the edges, and all of them converge on the elemental force of his ministrations.

"I want you," I say finally, giving in because I need to come.

"What's my name?" he growls, and for a moment, everything in me stills.

The air in my lungs and the blood in my veins are stilled by the commanding rumble of his voice. I'm teetering on the edge of coherence, and he knows it, but defiance flickers within me, spurring me to hold my tongue. Yet when he draws his tongue along my trembling flesh and delves inside with a force that causes my heart to stutter, the resolve begins to crumble.

I'm caught between the need to speak and the need not to. Both paths are a form of surrender. Then, with a deliberate cruelty that wrenches a groan from the depths of my soul, he withdraws his mouth, leaving me gasping and bereft in the aching silence that follows.

"Say it!" he finally snaps.

"Damien!" I say as shame washes over me at acknowledging him.

He steps back with a smile on his face as he strips out of the rest of his clothes. My eyes widen as I take him in. Tattoos line his body. His abs are cut, and his thick muscled thighs are sexy, but it's his dick that draws my attention. It's long, thick, and angry looking from being denied pleasure for so long. Precum leaks from the tip as he strokes himself. He's back on me within seconds, grabbing my hips and pulling me closer.

I wrap my legs around him, and his erection touches my core. He rubs it against me, getting it wet with my juices as he leans forward and kisses me. He swallows the groan that escapes as he thrusts into me, stretching me in ways I've never been stretched before.

We groan in unison, and the sound mingles with the heated air between us. My fingers tangle in his soft, dark locks before pulling him closer as I arch my neck, inviting a deeper kiss. Our tongues intertwine, chasing away the shadows that lurk in my mind with each impassioned stroke. He retreats for just a moment, only to surge forward once more with his hips rolling in a rhythm that drives him deeper into my core. I'm nearly overwhelmed by the force of him. It's a potent mix of pain and pleasure.

Clasping my legs around him more firmly, I yield to his fervent kisses. Each thrust of his body wraps me in a scalding embrace of lust and delight that seeps into every part of my being, intoxicating my bloodstream. He snatches his mouth away and trails kisses down my neck. I move my hips and meet him thrust for thrust, moaning and clawing at his back. He speeds up his pace, sucking on my neck, no doubt leaving hickeys while he pounds deeper inside me.

Each stroke takes me higher, and he moves faster, deeper.

I rake my nails down his back, wanting to mix pain with pleasure, the same sensations he's giving me. My pussy quivers as it gets tighter and tighter around him, welcoming every drive of his hips.

Then it happens. Arching back, a scream tears from my throat as my orgasm hits me. Heat spreads all over my body as wave after wave of pleasure flows through me. It's nothing like I've ever experienced before.

"Fuck, you feel so good, baby," Damien says as he moves faster.

It's even slicker now from my orgasm, and Damien grips my ass and grinds deeper. He thrusts a few more times before moaning against my neck. He spills inside me, gripping my ass so hard I know I'll have bruises when he lets go. As the last spasms leave his body, he raises his head and kisses me. When he lifts his head, he gazes into my eyes as he rubs a hand on my cheek.

"Are you okay?" he asks, and the world comes crashing back into focus like a ton of bricks.

His dick is still inside me, and his voice brings the shame of what I'd just done. With this realization comes the hate and self-loathing for allowing myself to give in to this.

"Get off me," I say as I push his shoulders.

He doesn't move. Instead, he gazes at me with concern.

"Get off me now," I say more forcefully.

He pulls back, and I wince as his dick slides out of me. I hop off the bed and dress hastily, making sure to keep my gaze away from him. After I'm dressed and adjusted my clothes, I look at him with hatred in my eyes.

"I'd like to leave now," I say. "Unless you plan to hold me hostage."

"You're not a hostage, Isabella," he says as he jerks on his clothes. "Where will you go?"

"That is none of your concern," I snap. "Once I'm gone, you'll never see me again."

"We need to talk about this," he says, walking toward me with confident strides.

I back up a few steps. "There's nothing to talk about. We got it out of our systems, and now it's over. I never want to see you or your family again."

With that, I turn and walk out of the bedroom. I leave his house to the waiting car and tell the driver to take me home. The driver looks out the window, and I turn to see Damien standing outside. He gives a quick nod, and the driver leaves. As we roll down the long driveway, I never look back.

# CHAPTER 16

## Damien

I drop a couple of ice cubes into a glass, and they clink against the sides with an overture that sets the stage for the night. Tilting the bottle, I pour myself another shot of whiskey, and the amber liquid catches the dying light filtering through the blinds. A little celebration, or perhaps a somber solace for the day's grueling endeavors.

I walk over to the heavy wooden desk that commands the room. As I sit back in the chair that's molded to my form from endless hours, I take a sip of the whiskey, appreciating the trail of fire it leaves as it makes its descent. It's a warm day. The sun relenting its fury just enough to let the chirping of the birds permeate through my open window.

Shuffling through the stack of papers, a list of transactions made, and favors owed, I glance over the names, one by one, each a reminder of deals brokered in the dark. The weight of the compiled evidence, the cold, hard reminders of debts pending in weapons and drugs, feels reassuring in my grip. The paperwork is meticulous. A necessity in this line of work.

Then, there's the Hawthorns. William, with his arrogance,

Daniel the liability; Julian shrouded in his own machinations; and Seraphina, the untouchable. I don't trust easily, and certainly not the likes of this storied family, so I've kept my own dossier on them. Details about their lives, enough leverage for if and when the time comes, I need it.

In this game, it's not just about having power. It's about holding the strings that could unravel empires, even ones as deeply rooted as the Hawthorns'. Taking another slow sip of whiskey, I let the complexity of the flavors distract me momentarily from the storm of my thoughts.

I flip through the papers with mounting irritation as the words and figures blur into insignificance. Nothing jumps out, no figures are misaligned, and no names are unwittingly exposed. Each page is a meticulous account of transactions, all clean, too clean for the gut feeling gnawing at me. This isn't just about keeping our operations running. It's about safeguarding the legitimacy of our company, a legitimacy that Jackson threatened with every step he took into the shadows.

With each thought of his wayward antics, my focus on the legitimate business at hand blurs a bit more, and I desperately attempt to steer my concentration back to the empire that depends on my vigilance.

Victor's sigh, weary and drawn, drifts across the room from his slouch on the leather couch. I look up from the maze of paperwork sprawled before me to see a frown on his face, shadowing his usually unreadable features.

"What's eating you?" I ask, flicking between his troubled expression and the disorderly stack of papers in his hands.

He rubs a hand across his face, and the sound of his exhalation is a low rumble of frustration in the quiet.

"I can't find anything, Damien. Not a damn thing out of place," he admits, his voice a mix of anger and disbelief. "Everyone's sticking to their roles. Moving through their predictable, day-to-day motions. It's like they're taunting us with their normality."

I can't help but snort at that, leaning back in my chair with fingers drumming a restless beat against the leather armrest.

"Maybe that's exactly what they're doing, Vic," I say, the possibility already taking shape in my mind. "Maybe they already know what went down with Jackson and the Hawthorns. It's possible they're deliberately keeping to the shadows, sticking to the routine to throw us off their scent. Someone out there helped them, and the last thing they'd want is to end up on our radar."

Victor's eyes meet mine, a silent acknowledgment of the truth in my words. "They're clever, I'll give them that. *Too* clever," he mutters, tossing the stack of papers onto the table with a huff of disgust. "But they can't hide forever. No one slips by us indefinitcly."

"No," I say, my voice low and certain, "They don't."

The memory of Isabella's lips on mine sends a pulse of heat through my veins. It's been two months since our bodies were entwined in a dance of passion, but the images are as vivid as if it all happened mere moments ago. Her moans resonate in the back of my mind, stirring up a craving that tightens my muscles as a raw reminder of the intensity we shared.

I shift uncomfortably, the growing hardness a testament to the indelible mark she's left on me. She thought she could just walk out of my life, but no one leaves Damien Black without consequences. I've had my men on her tail since she decided to disappear. Every couple of days, they report back, and every time they do, it's like I can feel her presence all over again.

I'd be lying if I said I haven't been tempted to call off the surveillance, to let her slip away into oblivion. But that's not who I am. The empire I built wasn't founded on the whims of desire, no matter how phenomenal the sex was. Beautiful faces are a dime a dozen, but loyalty and trust are rare. So I keep watching because it's not just my empire that's at stake; it's my everything. She might seem innocent. She might even believe she's got nothing to do with the chaos unfurling in my world, but I can't afford to take chances.

I shake my head roughly as if the motion could scatter the vivid memories like leaves in the wind and push myself up from the chair. The familiar weight of my suit jacket settles on my shoulders as I slide into it, buttoning it up to resume the mantle of authority. It's like armor, each button a forging of resolve and power.

"Keep looking, Vic," I command. "Dig deeper. There's something we're missing, and we need to turn over every stone until we find it."

Victor narrows his eyes, searching my face for clues, "Where are you headed?"

"I'm going to see Julian Warren," I announce as I reach for my keys.

His eyes flicker, widening a fraction. "That may not be a good idea," he warns with concern, lacing his words.

"The Blackharts may rule from high with our wealth and legacy," I start, my hand resting on the doorknob. "But Julian runs the streets. There isn't a whisper that he doesn't hear about down there."

For a moment longer, Victor holds my gaze, the unspoken risks hanging between us. Then, resigned, he nods. His chair creaks as he leans forward, burying himself once again in the maze of papers. I turn the handle and step out of the office with the door clicking behind me like the cocking of a gun. Whatever the cost, I'll find the answers we're looking for, even if I have to confront the devil himself.

The city lights blur as I navigate through the darkened

streets. My thoughts swirl as fiercely as the gears shift beneath the hood of my car. Julian Warren looms in my mind. He's a mystery wrapped in the intrigue of the streets he commands. His Hawthorn blood may course through his veins, but he's cut from a different cloth, a fabric twisted and hardened by life in the shadows, not the silken threads of privilege. He's the product of loveless passion, an affair William Hawthorn had with a stripper. Never acknowledged, Julian clawed his way to the top with the streets as his cradle, his schooling, and his kingdom.

As I drive, I can't help but acknowledge Julian's grit. He's transformed his neglect, his outsider status, into a dominion over the asphalt jungle. These streets answer to him now, and he's ensured his rule is absolute. Our paths have rarely crossed, primarily because he wants nothing to do with the elitist drama of his bloodline and because he's kept clear of my operations. The only thing he cares about is his little sister Seraphina. She doesn't know he exists, but that doesn't stop him from watching over her. He would never let harm come to her if it's within his power.

I respect that. There's an unspoken understanding between us. Two apex predators, each masters of their own domain, living by an unbreakable rule. The law of mutual respect. Divergent in our methods but similar in our iron wills to command our territories unchallenged. It's not a friendship. It's a recognition of power.

We coexist because we choose to adhere to boundaries set by unspoken consent, each to his own, because in our world, crossing those lines doesn't just mean stepping into another's territory. It means war. Neither of us is looking for a battle, not when there's so much at stake already. Tonight, that truce will be tested as I seek out Julian, not as an adversary, but as the closest thing to an ally I might find in these treacherous times.

The gates inch open, a silent admission granted by Julian's guards. Their scrutinizing eyes follow every move as my car purrs onto the vast estate. Surrounding me is an expanse of manicured lawns dotted with sculptures that would seem more at home in a museum than the front yard of his stronghold.

His house rises from the ground, a modern fortress clad in dark stone and glass, a stark contrast to the warmth of the grounds. Lights seep through the expansive windows, casting a golden glow that beckons with false promises of refuge. I don't let the grandeur fool me for a second. Julian's home is as much a lion's den as any back alley in his domain. The lavishness is just a prettier cage for the beast that dwells within.

I'm under no illusion about the man who commands this place. Julian may offer a smile with one hand while the other holds a dagger. As I step out of the vehicle, I'm acutely aware of the fact that he could be watching, assessing whether to greet me with a handshake or a bullet. His unpredictability is the only constant in a life governed by his peculiar code. He could decide my fate on a whim, that is, if I were any ordinary man trespassing in his domain.

However, fear has no grip on me here. Caution, yes, but not fear. My name alone carries a legacy that bends the rules of engagement. I don't give a damn about Julian's fickle nature. I'm a Blackhart, born to rule, not to bow. In this chess game of power, I'm the king who moves across the board unfettered. Julian knows this. I know this. I don't get ruled. I rule.

Before me, the butler approaches. His back is as straight as his years would allow. The silvery vestiges of his hair catch the luminescence from the porch light as he leans in with the whisper of strength left in his voice.

"Mr. Blackhart, it is a pleasure to see you. Mr. Warren is

waiting for you in his office," he intones with a reverberation that seems to imitate the prestige of the house behind him.

I mask my urge to chuckle with a simple nod. The pleasantry is unnecessary for two acquaintances whose circles rarely intersect by choice.

"Lead the way, Thomas," I say, the name rolling off my tongue with ease born from the few interactions we've had over the years. Thomas half-bows, a movement limited by old age, and turns to guide me through the maze corridors of Julian's mansion.

My lips almost curve with amusement. Formalities for the sake of appearances are a game for the public eye, not ours. We're far from friends, Julian and I, but the courteous veneer is just another play in the theatre of power. My footsteps resonate on the floor, a staccato rhythm marching me toward whatever pretense of civility Julian has prepared for this meeting.

The door to Julian's office swings open, and I catch the first glimpse of him, poised behind his desk as if he's the master of all he surveys. A nudge from Thomas breaks my brief fixation, and with that discreet prompt, the old butler takes his leave. I step into the room, and the air feels charged, heavy with unspoken omens. I gaze at the butler disappearing through the doorway and can't help the sardonic lilt in my voice.

"I see you're capable of being civilized," I remark, gesturing to Thomas's retreating back. "Not so animalistic after all."

Julian's lips twist into his signature sinister smile with a mixture of amusement and hidden barbs. "Only when the need calls for it," he replies smoothly. With a tilt of his head, he regards me with sharp, assessing eyes. "What brings you here, Damien?"

I stride across the room and sink into the chair opposite

him. My hands come to rest before me, fingertips tented, and I waste no more time with pleasantries. "Cut the shit, Julian," I say. "You know damn well why I'm here."

Julian picks up a file and tosses it to me. The file lands with a soft thud on the polished wood between us, and I can't stop my hands from reacting as I spread it open. Inside, there's a collection of documents, and a photograph sits on top. A recent one, of Isabella, taken without her awareness.

My fingers tighten involuntarily, and the edges of the photo crinkle ever so slightly in the grip of my sudden tension. It's a visceral reaction, one that I hasten to quell by easing my hold on the image before Julian can register the effect it has on me. With deliberate slowness, I adjust the photograph, setting it gently back into the file with my face betraying nothing of the storm that rages inside at the sight of her.

I look up at Julian with irritation creeping into my furrowed brow. "What does this have to do with anything?" I demand evenly, but my hands betray the urgency I feel.

Julian leans back in his chair, steepling his fingers as if he were about to unveil a plot twist in a melodrama.

"Isabella's father," he starts with a slow, measured tone. "He's a man whose vice for gambling left her with nothing but debts and regrets. He often found himself in hot water. A predicament from which only Isabella could get him out of."

I clench my jaw as my patience wears thin. "What does this have to do with Jackson?" I probe sharply.

Julian's eyes glint with a knowledge that suggests he knows more than he should.

"You must wonder why a man like him marries a woman like Isabella. It wasn't just a simple affair of the heart, Damien. Her father's connections, albeit to some rather unsavory characters, might have been... valuable to Jackson."

"Word on the street," Julian continues, and the smirk on

his lips grows wider. "Is that your brother tried to off you. But, as fate would have it, someone got to him first."

I curse under my breath, clamping down on the swell of irritation. "Who else knows about this?" My voice is edged with the menace that comes from being cornered.

Julian narrows his eyes like a predator enjoying the moment right before the kill.

"No one," he states coldly. "I made sure to cut out his tongue myself. I can't have rumors going around about the Blackharts. We may not be friends, but our power balances each other's rule. If some were to think there's a rival amongst you, they'd be gunning for your power. Then they'd come for me. I like where I am, and I want to keep it that way with as little bloodshed as possible. Not that I mind killing."

"So you think Isabella knows something?" I ask before narrowing my eyes to read Julian's expression.

He shakes his head, a motion dismissive and confident in its finality. "No, I don't think she knows anything, but someone does. Jackson was supposed to get a lot of money from somewhere, and his marriage to Isabella is no coincidence."

The revelation hits me like a physical blow, and in an instantaneous reaction fueled by a blend of fury and fear, I hop out of the chair. The sound of it skidding across the floor is a distant echo to the thunderous beat of my racing heart.

"Someone will try to kill her?" I shout, my composure shattering audibly like fragile glass on concrete.

Julian's laugh is mirthless and taunting like scythes through the tension.

"Last I heard, you tortured her. Now you're worried for her. Why is that?" He leans forward with his forearms resting on the desk.

Julian hands me a box with tattered documents inside. "I

had this gathered from Isabella's Father's office in her old house. This is her father's doing. Find him, and you'll get your answers."

"Don't you already know?" I snap as I grab the box.

Julian's eyes darken. "No. The fucking bastard disappeared. I can trace him to Jackson's wedding. After that, he vanished. Don't worry. if he turns up somewhere, I'll let you know."

"Thank you," I say.

"No problem," Julian says with a wolfish grin. "I'll let you know when I need you to return the favor."

I can't help but chuckle, a dry sound that echoes around the room. "Should have known there would be strings attached," I reply with bitter amusement.

Julian only shrugs as his eyes lock onto mine with a stony intensity. "Nothing is given freely in our world, Damien," he says, a cruel sort of truth hanging in the air between us.

I nod my acknowledgment before standing up to leave. Thomas, ever the perfect butler, escorts me out with a professionalism that belies the tension brewing beneath the surface.

As I head home, I dial Victor on my phone. "Switch your focus," I instruct, the words crisp and businesslike. "Look into Isabella's father."

Without waiting for a response, I hang up with my mind whirring with the new information Julian revealed. It's a tangle of half-truths and hidden motives, and I feel a strange sort of thrill as I unravel the threads. As I drive, my thoughts keep circling back to Isabella. The woman I can't seem to get out of my mind. Once home, I head straight to my office, intent on doing a little more digging on Isabella.

# CHAPTER 17

## Isabella

"Good morning, Destiny. You're looking as beautiful as ever," Jacob says from the counter, his voice pulling interrupting my thoughts.

I stand behind the counter pouring a cup of coffee for Mrs. Harmon, the early bird regular, when I hear him. I can't help but roll my eyes as I turn around.

"Hello, Jacob," I reply before setting the coffee pot down with a soft clank. "When are you going to stop flirting with me?" I can't keep a straight face, even as I pretend to chide him.

Jacob just laughs, the sound rich and easy. "I'm not flirting with you, Isabella. I'm just offering a friendly compliment." His smile is infectious, and despite my resolve, I laugh.

I've been back in my tiny town for three months now. Jacob popped up about a week after I returned and has been a fixture at the diner ever since. Eating breakfast, lunch, and dinner like it's his personal kitchen. At first, I suspected he was one of Damien's men, but he doesn't have that scary-suited-guy vibe.

Then I assumed he was hitting on me, but when I set

boundaries, he simply chuckled in that deep, rich laugh of his and assured me he wasn't interested romantically. He just found me 'interesting' and enjoyed our chats. Said I seemed nice and was just being friendly to a newcomer like himself. Since that clarification, things have been amicable between us, an easygoing rapport settling in.

I lean against the counter, a fleeting shiver traveling down my spine as I think back to Damien. Our last interaction plays in my mind like a dark, seductive memory so vivid I can almost feel it. His hands, both rough and gentle, had explored the contours of my body and awakened a raw hunger I hadn't known lay dormant within me. I remember how he made me feel. Alive with every nerve ending, singing with a desire so intense that it bordered on pain.

As I pick up the coffee cup, my hand trembles slightly, betraying the composed image I maintain. I can't shake the unnerving certainty that no man will ever touch me the way Damien did. Won't ignite a fire that seems impossible to extinguish. With each passing day, the longing only deepens, etching itself into my very core, leaving me restless and unsatisfied.

I shake those intruding thoughts away and carry Mrs. Harmon's coffee over to her with the steam curling up from the mug as I meander through the diner's early morning bustle. "Here you are," I say, setting down her cup. The rich aroma of coffee and breakfast foods fills the air as I weave back behind the counter.

"I take it you want your usual?" I ask Jacob, who's perched on one of the stools with a newspaper spread before him. He doesn't look up as he nods. "You got it," he responds, folding his paper with well-practiced creases.

"Bacon, eggs, and a side of hash browns, with black coffee coming right up," I chime, turning on my heel towards the kitchen.

In an instant, my steps halt. There's a shadow by the window, a silhouette that sends a shiver of unease through me. The stranger's gaze is fixed inward, and I can't look away. My abrupt stop causes Maggie, who emerges from the kitchen with a full plate, to bump into me.

"Destiny?" Jacob says in a tone filled with concern.

I twist back to Jacob, offering him a distracted glance before my eyes dart back to the window. Nothing. The figure has vanished just as quickly as it appeared.

"I'm so sorry, Maggie," I blurt out, the encounter with the stranger unsettling me more than I care to admit. My voice is a whisper of confusion mixed with uneasy apologies.

"That's okay," Maggie reassures me with her ever-present smile as she balances the plate like it's second nature. "At least I didn't drop the food." She brushes off the near mishap and carries on as if the pulse of the diner never skipped a beat, while I'm left with an unsettled feeling that lingers after the figure's disappearance.

The feeling of eyes on me is almost familiar now, like an unwelcome companion that lingers in the corner of my vision. Initially, I wrote it off as paranoia, a side effect of the chaos that had upended my life. But the strange occurrences have piled up. Little things are easily overlooked, yet they accumulate.

A cracked window in the morning when I'm certain I fell asleep without the nighttime air brushing against my skin. The front door, unlocked, when my mind argues I'd turned the key before bed. Maybe it's nothing. Maybe it's the quiet, trusting nature of this small town unraveling my usual vigilance.

The sensation of being followed and watched gnaws at me, sharp and persistent. I've started to double-check each window and every lock before I go to sleep. I keep a knife hidden beneath my pillow while a bat stands ready by the door. Damien's assurances that he'd leave me alone are as substantial as shadows, present but insubstantial.

Trust is as foreign to me now as the sense of safety once was. I sleep, I wake, and I move throughout my day with a vigilance that has woven itself into my muscle memory. My instincts scream that something isn't right, and I've learned it's better to listen and to prepare. Because if there's one thing that's certain, it's that trust is a luxury I can no longer afford.

”Destiny?” Jacob's voice penetrates my thoughts. He looks back towards the window before looking at me again. “Are you alright?”

"I'm fine," I manage to say with a practiced smile, though my pulse is still racing. "I thought I saw someone by the window, that's all." I'm not sure he's convinced, but there's no point in alarming him with my paranoia. "Let me get your food now."

"No rush," Jacob says, but there's a hint of something unreadable in his eyes. He slides off the stool, a fluid motion that seems too deliberate. "I'm going to run to the bath-room." His footsteps retreat quickly, leaving a knot of concern in my stomach.

I watch him go with a frown etching my brow deeper the further he gets. His hastiness doesn't sit right with me, but there are orders to fill and no time to ponder over Jacob's odd behavior. Turning on my heel, I push through the swinging kitchen door, and the warmth and clatter of pots greet me as I slip back into the rhythm of the diner. Maggie bursts into the kitchen, her apron dusted with flour and a grin plastered on her face.

"Girl, did you see the way he was looking at you? He's a hottie," she shrieks in a voice hitting a pitch that's pure excitement.

I roll my eyes. "He's not looking at me, Maggie. And don't

call him that," I say, trying to keep my focus on arranging the bacon on the plate in front of me.

However, Maggie is relentless. "Oh, come on. Anyone with eyes can see that Jacob is into you. I mean, why aren't you dating him?" she asks, nudging me in the ribs with her elbow.

I shake my head, feeling a smile tug at the corners of my mouth despite my exasperation. "Because he's not interested, Mag. We're just friends," I assert, but it's like talking to the wall. Maggie's grin grows even wider if that's possible.

"In that case," she says with a mischievous twinkle in her eye. "Since you're not going to claim him, I'm gonna put on my best moves. Watch him be in my bed by the end of the night!"

Her declaration is so outrageous that I can't help but burst into laughter. My laughter doubles when I see her check her reflection in the shiny side of the toaster, adjust her hair, reapply some lipstick, and give her cleavage an enthusiastic hoist before winking at me and strutting out of the kitchen.

"Yeah, good luck with that, Maggie," I call after her, still chuckling, and turn back to my work. I shake my head in amusement, and the weight of my earlier unease is momentarily forgotten.

I'm scooping the last of the eggs onto the plate when George walks into the kitchen. His hands are tucked in his apron pockets, and he has that concerned look he gets sometimes.

"How are you doing, kiddo?" he asks.

I glance up while balancing the plate in one hand. "Hey, George. I'm fine," I reply, but it's more of a reflex than an honest answer.

George arches an eyebrow, his voice laced with humor. "Are you sure? You're not going to disappear on me again, are you?"

His question reminds me of how I left things when I returned from that messy trip home. I had brushed it off with a vague explanation and a promise to keep my head down and work hard. I hated lying to him. "No disappearing act here," I chuckle, but the sound is hollow even to my own ears.

"You know I know something happened. You came back pretty banged up, kiddo." George's face softens, and I know an interrogation is coming. He raises his hand to stop me mid-breath. "You don't have to tell me what happened. Just tell me if you need help, and I'll help."

I look into George's kind eyes, and a surge of gratitude washes over me. It's a lifeline, knowing I have someone in my corner. The concern etched on his face feels like the embrace of family I've been missing. It's not often that someone cares, truly cares, without wanting something in return. In this moment, in the kindness of this man who's been like a father, I feel a flicker of hope that maybe, just maybe, I'm not as alone as I thought.

I summon a reassuring smile. One that's become second nature these days. "You don't have to worry. Everything is fine now," I tell him while hoisting the plate a little higher to signal the end of the conversation.

Escaping to the front, I push the kitchen door with a little more force than necessary. I can't help but let out a laugh when I spot Maggie, all but throwing herself at Jacob, who seems to find a spot on the wall fascinating.

"Here's your food," I say as I slide the plate onto the counter in front of him.

"Thank you," Jacob murmurs, quickly pulling away from Maggie's orbit.

My eyes flick to Maggie, and I can't resist. "Maggie, table 12 needs your attention."

Jacob shoots me a grateful look as she flounces away. "Thank you."

"Well, as funny as that was, you are a paying customer. Can't have you leaving and never coming back," I say with a light laugh.

Jacob leaves for work after his meal, and I find myself wondering, not for the first time, what he does. This is a small town, the kind where everyone knows everyone else's business, but somehow, Jacob's work remains a mystery. He doesn't clock in at any of the local stores; that much is clear. The rest of the day passes in a blur, each moment bleeding into the next. True to his pattern, he comes back like clockwork for lunch and dinner, his routine as punctual as the town clock.

Soon enough, the diner empties with its last patron departing with a satisfied smile and a wave goodbye. We clean the place from top to bottom, leaving it spotless and ready for another day of hustle and bustle. Walking home alone is no longer an option for me. Not after the last time.

There's a comfort in knowing that the car Seraphina gave me sits waiting at the curb. It's an older model, but it starts up without complaint. I haven't talked to Seraphina since I got back, and I feel guilty. However, I just need time to process and make sure things are truly fine before entering that life again.

The drive is short and uneventful, with the town streets quickly giving way to the familiar sight of my apartment building. The comfort it offers is immediate and enveloping, a welcome respite from the day's vigilance and forced smiles. I park the car and make my way inside, each step taking me closer to the sanctuary of my own space.

The spray of the shower drums against the tile in a rhythmic cascade that washes away the grime and tension from the day's work. Refreshed, with my skin tingling from the heat, I slip into comfortable clothes, feeling the soft fabric brush against my skin like a protective cocoon. I'm nestled under the covers with a book in hand.

In the quiet of the room, my mind races with conflicting emotions. I can't stop my mind from thinking about Damien. How each encounter left me more unsettled, a confusing blend of fear and an unbidden, growing warmth that I can't shake off. Especially after our last steamy encounter.

Suddenly, an unfamiliar creak pierces the calm. My heart stutters, then accelerates. In an instant, I'm no longer a casual reader but a survivor poised for confrontation. The knife, always nestled under my pillow, feels cold and heavy in my grasp as I slide out of bed, my movements silent, deliberate.

Peeking through the narrow slit of my partially open bedroom door, I see the front door inches open. I stumble back and press my spine against the cool wall, seeking the invisibility that shadows grant. My mind races with possibilities as the chill of fear wraps around me as tightly as a blanket. I'm prey in the eyes of an uninvited predator lurking at my doorstep.

I hold my breath as the blood in my veins pounds like a drumbeat too loud in my ears. The figure moves with muffled urgency. Drawers are being pulled open and shut with reckless abandon. They're looking for something, but I don't know what. My mind flits to the scant possessions that I call my own, none of which seem valuable enough to warrant such a desperate search. This a quiet, small town. Everyone is nice, so I can't imagine it's one of the townsfolk breaking in.

Suddenly, the intruder barges into my bedroom, and the bang of the door against the wall sends another spike of terror through me. Their shadow slices the room in disjointed angles as they toss my clothes and personal items aside.

As the figure turns, their eyes lock onto mine, the surprise barely registering before it's replaced by a grim determination. I can't hesitate. The knife in my hand becomes an extension of my will to survive. With my heart thundering, I lunge forward from behind the door.

Our bodies collide, and my momentum sends us both stumbling. The intruder is bigger and stronger, but panic heightens my resolve. The knife slashes towards them like a silver arc in the dim light, meeting resistance that yields too quickly. There's a grunt of pain and a curse, but they're not deterred. Their hands snatch at my wrists, seeking control, but my fear is a wild thing, clawing and thrashing for freedom.

We're a tangle of limbs and desperation. I kick, I bite, I fight with every shred of the terror that has lived inside me since the night I swore would never happen again. My breath comes in ragged gasps, but I can't stop. I won't stop.

"Where is it? The money!" the intruder hisses, his breath foul as it hits my face.

"I-I don't know what you're talking about!" I scream.

"He said you had it. That you'd give us the money," he insists, his eyes narrowing into slits of malice.

"I don't have any money!" The words tumble out in a mix of anger and fear, and my voice is barely recognizable to my own ears.

He doesn't listen. With a swift, practiced move, he wrestles the knife away from me. He raises the knife, the threat clear and imminent, but just as it seems, all is lost; he's lifted off of me as if he weighs nothing. He's thrown to the side with a force that speaks of raw power, and he hits the wall with a thud. Hovering over him is Jacob, and his face is a mask of fury and protection.

Jacob doesn't hesitate. He pulls out a gun and fires twice. The sharp bursts shock the air, and the intruder lies still.

Jacob takes out his phone. "Boss, someone attacked Isabella." Jacob gives a small nod. "Understood." Then he hangs up his phone.

He turns to me, his voice soft. "Are you alright?"

I realize that Jacob knows my name. My real name. Before any words can even take shape on my tongue, before I can voice the fear and relief battling within me, everything goes dark.

# CHAPTER 18

## Damien

I sit in my office with my fingers steepled tightly together, trying to contain the storm brewing within me. Jacob is here, in front of me, and I can see the concern etched on his face, but it does nothing to cool the heat of my anger. It's not that it's directed at him. Jacob did what he had to do to save Isabella. It's the fact that she was attacked under our watch that lights a fire in my gut I can't extinguish. My eyes lock onto his for a moment in a silent conveyance of the turmoil that I'm feeling.

"What happened, Jacob?" I ask, my voice revealing none of the anger churning inside me.

"I was watching Isabella as you instructed," Jacob starts, his eyes locked with mine, steady and sure. "Everything was normal until she froze at the window. It looked like she saw someone staring in. I made an excuse and said I had to use the bathroom so I could check it out."

I nod, urging him to continue, a silent command hanging between us.

"Nobody was out there when I got to the window," he continues, his brow furrowing. "I spent the day canvassing the town for any unregistered faces, any newcomers but came up with nothing. Went back to the diner for lunch and dinner, same as always, then stationed myself to watch for Isabella's shift to end."

"Then what happened?" I press, the pieces of a threatening puzzle starting to swarm in my head.

"She drove home. Everything was quiet, but then I saw one of her neighbors enter the building with a man. Seemed like a casual thing, so I didn't think much of it at first..." Jacob trails off for a second, his gaze hardening. "But something felt off. So I went in, found that woman on the ground, unconscious, and heard Isabella's screams."

I can feel the controlled fury in his voice, a mirror reflection of my own rage.

"That's when I bolted to her place," he says. "Busted through the door just in time to see her and the intruder fighting. I threw the bastard against the wall and shot him. Then everything went silent. Isabella passed out. I called you immediately after and brought her here."

I nod at Jacob, a silent dismissal hanging in the air between us. "You can go," I murmur, the words heavy with unspoken weight.

When the door clicks closed behind him, I lean back in my high-backed leather chair with a silent snarl curling the edge of my lips. I let the anger and the rage take over, and dark emotions roll through me like a storm.

Isabella... Sweet, loving, caring Isabella. Not at all like those women she's so often compared to. The socialites with their duplicity painted in rouge and perfumes. No, she is real and genuine, raw in her fear and strong in her vulnerability. Jackson had painted her the villain and tried to bend my perception. I growl under my breath, the sound of a primal rumble of warning to ghosts and shadows. I realize now how wrong I was. How wrong we all were about my brother. He wore a mask so perfect, so seamless, that no one saw the cracks until it was too late.

Sitting here, surrounded by security and luxury I once thought infallible, I've never felt anger like this. It burns in me and lights a fire in my veins. For every whispered lie, for every false lead, for every danger that touched Isabella due to this family's blind missteps... I will correct these errors, no matter the cost. Jackson's transgressions will not be the end of this. They will be the beginning of retribution.

The ring of the phone slices through my thoughts. It's an unwelcome intrusion. I glance at the caller ID to see my mother's name, and my stomach clenches with a mix of obligation and irritation churning within. I press the phone to my ear.

"Damien," her voice comes, sharp as a shard of glass. "Tell me you've found that whore who poisoned Jackson."

My grip tightens around the phone. The room feels colder suddenly. I settle the mask of calm over my features, a skill perfected over years of practice.

"Mother, I'm keeping tabs on Isabella," I respond, my voice even concealing the storm inside.

There's a dismissive scoff from her end, a sound that grates against my nerves. "Just kill the bitch and get it over with."

A heavy sigh escapes me before I can stop it. "Let me handle it, Mother. Mind your fucking business."

The line goes deathly quiet. "I'm sorry, Damien," she says, softer now. "The grief... it's making me act out."

I close my eyes, the sting of her silence sharper than her words. "It's okay, Mother," I find myself saying, the lie smooth and practiced. "Go, spend a day at the spa."

I don't wait for a reply before ending the call with a click that sounds far too final. The phone slips from my hand to the desk as I lean back with the chill of the room seeping into my bones.

The atmosphere in my office is oppressive, every dark, intricate panel of wood seeming to absorb my frustration. It's usually a place of control and power, where decisions are made with a cold, calculated mind. But today, the air is charged with tension, the lingering scent of leather and aged books doing nothing to ease the smoldering cauldron of emotions within me. Victor walks in and takes the seat on the couch as usual.

"I can tell by the look on your face that I'm not going to like what you have to say," I tell Victor as I note the dark clouds in his eyes.

"I dug up some information about Edward Storm," he starts, and I immediately lean forward with every muscle tensing as I listen to him.

Apparently, Edward Storm was seen as a pillar in the community. A businessman with a reputation that was unimpeachable. He was the diligent son-in-law at his late wife's family company, revered and successful. When cancer took hold of his wife, though, something in him shattered. Gambling became his solace, dragging him deeper down with drinks and adulterous nights.

After she passed, leaving a fortune that should've guaranteed comfort, he spiraled. Bad bets broke him, financial ruin clawed at his heels, and desperation inked his future with illegal dealings. He courted danger, brushing shoulders with our rivals and swapping his integrity for precarious prosperity.

The shocking divergence from the man he showed the world to the one lurking in shadows is almost a cliche, if not for the sting of reality. The gnawing question is *why*. Why marry Isabella off to Jackson, of all people? What dark prize could that union possibly present?

Victor's gaze is heavy, expectant. "We need to understand what Jack had over him and what made Edward throw Isabella into the lion's den. It's a piece we're missing, Damien."

I nod as the cogs turn fiercely in my mind. This isn't just about vengeance anymore. It's about unearthing a truth that changed the course of Isabella's life and redirecting my own in the process.

I point to the dusty, old box I'd gotten from Julian. "Get a few men on this," I instruct Victor. "Everything inside needs to be pieced together, every scrap of paper."

Victor narrows his eyes, curiosity piqued. "What's in the box?"

"It's information Julian collected from Isabella's childhood home," I respond tersely, feeling the edges of a puzzle pressing on my consciousness.

Victor's eyes widen momentarily. "He actually helped you?" he questions with a mixture of surprise and skepticism.

A gruff grunt escapes my lips as I lean back in my chair.

"Apparently, Julian has no desire to see our delicate balance upended. With the Hawthorns gaining more money and power, Julian would be staring down a barrel of problems. His assistance wasn't selfless. It was purely self-serving. He wants a favor in return."

A rueful laugh escapes Victor as he shakes his head.

"Should've known Julian would want something out of it," he says, though the humor doesn't quite reach his eyes. He hefts the box with a grunt. "I'm on it."

As Victor's form disappears through the doorway of my office, a silent acknowledgment hangs in the air. This is the dance of power we know all too well, a waltz of favors and debts in the shadows of our reality.

The quiet of the hallway feels stifling as I make my way from my office to where Isabella is sleeping. I reach the door with my hand pausing on the cool metal of the knob before pushing it open. The room is dimly lit, with the only light seeping in through the curtains. Shades of twilight caress the room in gentle blues and grays.

There, she lies. Isabella, her still form on the bed, is a portrait of vulnerability. She hasn't moved since Jacob, with his reckless concern, broke every speed limit to bring her here this morning. Now, her chest rises and falls with a rhythm that speaks of deep slumber, unaware of the chaos her presence has stoked in my world.

I reach out, my hand lightly tracing the contour of her cheek, and her eyelids flutter as if my touch is a whisper calling her back to consciousness. The barest smile begins to bloom across her face, a sweet, instinctual response that seems to draw on the warmth of dreams. Then, reality crashes in like a wave, washing away the remnants of sleep as she takes in my presence and the room that is not her own. The smile vanishes, and her body tenses.

With a sudden shift, she rolls away from me and onto her feet with the sheets discarded in a fluid, almost defensive motion. She stands there with a hard gaze, and her posture is coiled with anger. In an instant, Isabella has morphed from a slumbering innocence to a force of raw, unfiltered fury, staring me down as if my very existence has become an affront to her.

"Where am I," she asks.

"You're in my home," I reply, meeting her gaze with an even one of my own. "I had a guard bring you here for your safety."

"Jacob," she breathes out with her eyes widening in shock at making the connection. I only nod, confirming her realization that Jacob, the man she trusted, works for me.

"I've been keeping an eye on you," I confess, watching as her expression turns to one of anger and betrayal.

"Because you didn't believe me," she snarls. "You thought I was hiding something. That I knew something about this mess."

I don't deny it, as I keep my face as stoic as the walls around us. "At first, yes, that was the reason. But then... then I just wanted to keep you safe. Something is not right about this situation."

She screams, a raw sound of frustration and fear. "I have nothing to do with any of this!"

"The fact that you were attacked means you do," I counter firmly, unwilling to sugarcoat the gravity of her predicament.

Isabella's shoulders slump as defeat momentarily dims the fire in her eyes. "The intruder... he kept asking about money," she murmurs, more to herself than to me. "Whoever *they* are, said I would give it to them. I have no idea what they're talking about," she says, her voice a mixture of desperation and resignation. "I don't have any money..."

"They think you have money, Isabella. That's why they're after you," I say, keeping my voice level despite the frustration building within me. Her safety hangs by a thread, and it's hard not to let the urgency of the situation bleed through.

Isabella's eyes flash, and she stops pacing to face me. "My father... that asshole gambled away everything we had." Her voice crackles with a cocktail of rage and vulnerability. The painful admission has all the sharp edges of shattered glass.

I study her for a moment, choosing my words carefully as the room is heavy with the weight of unspoken fears.

"Someone out there has been led to believe differently. They're convinced you're sitting on a fortune." I pause, watching as realization takes shape in her gaze. "Since your father is missing, they're turning to you."

She starts pacing again like a caged animal, looking for an escape from an invisible trap. "I'm so sick of cleaning up his messes," she mumbles, the words fraught with weariness. "Why does this always happen to me? Why does he always drag me into his shit..." Her voice trails off into a hollow whisper.

I watch her determination take shape with each step she takes towards the door. Her voice is steady, with a newfound resolve that perforates the charged air between us.

"I'm getting out of here," she says with her hand reaching for the doorknob. "I'll just go somewhere else. I want to be as far away from you all as possible."

Her declaration echoes in the room, a clear testament to her will to escape the twisted play of events she's been forced into as a pawn on a chessboard she never agreed to play on. As she grasps the handle and turns it with a decisive click, I find myself at an impasse, torn between the need to protect her and letting her go.

She may have started off as the enemy, but she isn't any longer. I still burn with the need to find my brother's killer regardless of his betrayal. The people he tangled himself with are now after Isabella. I can never leave her now. Especially not after the night of passion we shared. I used to hate Isabella and what I thought she represented. When I thought she killed my brother, I wanted her to pay. Now that I know the kind of woman she is, I can't help the need to protect her. Her innocence calls to me.

Isabella Blackhart is mine.

Mine to protect.

Mine to keep.

It's time she realizes it.

# CHAPTER 19

## Isabella

The weight of Damien's footsteps is evidence of the urgency that surrounds us. To him, I must seem like a wild flame, untamed and fiercely unyielding. As I reach for my escape, attempting to turn the doorknob and flee from the gilded prison that his grand home has become, he is swift to react.

Before the cool metal can fully rotate under my fingers, Damien is there, keeping the door shut with a decisive thud that seals my fate. His hands encircle my arms and turn me around with an unspoken insistence. An insistence that isn't harsh but leaves no room for protest or escape.

"Let go of me, Damien," I snap in a voice so sharp it could cut through the tension that fills the room.

My anger hits him like a physical force, but it's laced with fear. A fear that he puts there. This has never been a game, but it's turning into a battle, one for my life and my trust.

"I can't do that, Isabella," he tells me, his grip firm yet careful not to hurt me. "You're not safe out there."

His voice is steady, a counterpoint to the chaotic emotions that flicker in my eyes like a storm.

"I have to get away from here," I plead with him.

Damien's grip tightens on my arms, and there's a flash of something dark and unyielding in his gaze. "You think you can walk away from me? I'm not just a chapter in your life, Isabella. I am the goddamn book. Every word that writes your future has my name on it."

"I have to leave," I tell him again.

"You can't just walk away from everything. It doesn't work that way," he snaps.

I try to shrug him off. "Watch me," I challenge as defiance rises within me like a tidal wave. The conflict ignites a strange, dangerous thrill in my veins. A mix of fear, anger, and something far more volatile.

"You're not understanding me," he bites out as his eyes drilled into mine like a storm brewing in those dark depths. "The empire I've built, his... our enemies. They won't care about your feelings or about what you want. You're in danger, whether you like it or not."

His words are like ice, stripping the heat from our argument, yet the heat between us is palpable. A fiery undercurrent to our standoff. I hate that a part of me wants to lean into his warmth to yield to that unspoken tension.

His thumbs stroke my skin absently, an odd tenderness clashing with the harsh words. I hate how it sends a shiver down my spine.

"Let go of me, Damien," I whisper, my voice betraying the storm inside me.

He releases me slowly as if each inch between us is reluctance made physical. "You can hate me and him all you want, but you can't be reckless with your life."

I step back to create distance from his maddening presence. "Don't pretend to care about my well-being now," I scoff as my anger flares again. "Where was this concern when Jackson's hands were around my throat?"

Damien's face tightens, his jaw setting in a hard line. "I

didn't know. I didn't like seeing you with him. Seeing you with him lit a fire in me that no ocean could douse. Be careful, Isabella, because playing with fire can be dangerous, especially when it's burning in the eyes of a man who considers you his."

"Yet you still treated me like shit," I snap.

"I said I was wrong," he growls lowly, his eyes never leaving mine. "I'm trying to protect you, damn it."

"I don't need your protection," I hiss, filled with false bravado.

Deep down, the uncertainty knots in my stomach, tightly coiled and ready to strike. Damien is a storm of a man, dangerous and unpredictable, and yet... I can't help but feel drawn to him. Every bitter argument is laced with an undercurrent that whispers of more than hatred, more than anger. But I refuse to acknowledge it. Not now. Not to him.

Damien steps closer, and his presence fills the space between us with an intensity that's suffocating.

"You do need my protection," he says, and I can't help but retreat until my back meets the wall.

"Why the sudden need to protect me?" I challenge as desperation seeps through my resolute façade.

His hands find the wall on either side of my head, caging me in, and I'm acutely aware of the heat radiating from his body. The atmosphere shifts, becoming charged with an electricity that speaks of carnal desire.

"I've walked through hell and back, but the thought of losing you terrifies me more than any demon I've faced. You've become my weakness, Isabella, and my ultimate strength," he whispers.

"I don't understand," I whisper. "You can have anyone you want. Why me?"

"You're not just anyone, Isabella," he murmurs, and his voice is a velvet caress that sets my nerves ablaze. "You're like fire. Scorching, illuminating, and impossible to ignore. I've felt the burn, and now I can't stay away." He leans in, and his breath ghosts over my skin. "I need to protect you because you challenge me, you captivate me, and damn it... I can't stay away from you." His gaze locks onto mine, fierce with a yearning that mirrors my own reluctant hunger.

"Don't," I plead when he leans in to kiss me.

I don't want to give into this pull again, even if my body wants it. The allure, the caresses, the kisses. If I give in, I'll fall for him, and if I fall for him, he'll have the power to hurt me. His brother has already done enough of that. Damien Blackhart is a threat to my heart and sanity.

"Everything will be alright, Bella," he whispers against my lips, giving me a nickname. "Trust me. I'll protect you."

I want to tell him that it won't be alright. That I can never trust him. Instead, I grab his crisp shirt like it's my lifeline. He closes the tiny distance between our mouths and kisses me. His tongue delves deep, and I arch my back, moaning from how right this feels. His hand moves up, clutching my hair and angling my head to kiss me deeper.

Goosebumps break out along my skin, and my center clenches in anticipation of what's to come because I know it's coming. Nothing has the power to stop me from giving in to Damien right now. My body remembers his. The way his hands touched my body. The way it felt to have him moving in and out of me. Everything. I've already slept with him once, so what's one more time.

My arms move to circle his neck as I press myself closer to him. He cups my ass before picking me up. I wrap my legs around him, locking my ankles as I rub my core against his hard length.

He spins around, walking in quick strides until he reaches the bed. I give a slight protest when he lays me down, wanting to keep his body as close to mine as possible. The protest is cut short when I see the look in his eyes. His hungry blue eyes speak to me, and I understand because they mirror my own. The desire I feel for him right now is visceral. It's all around me. It burns in my lungs with every breath I take. It pulses in my heart with each beat.

It rolls around in my gut, where electric shocks pulse, shooting waves of lust to my groin. I feel dirty and wrong. Close to insanity. Wanting Damien's touch doesn't make sense, and my mind knows this, but my head is no longer in control. My body wants him, if only for a kiss. Damn the consequences.

He pulls off my shirt before cupping my breast, and I hiss as a whimper escapes. My skin is burning from his touch. He pulls my nipple between his fingers, and my body hums in pleasure. Next, he removes my bra and sucks a nipple in his mouth, sucking on it like a man dying of thirst. I hold his head to my chest, moaning at how good this feels.

His hands make quick work of my pants, and as soon as they are off, his hand dives into my underwear. His fingers rub between my slick folds, and I can't stop the loud moan tearing from my throat. Just as quickly as he was there, he was gone, and I narrowed my eyes at his unnecessary teasing.

"One second, Bella," he says with a chuckle before stepping away.

I watch him undress. His crisp dress shirt falls to the ground, giving me a close look at his sculpted body. He's all hard, rigid muscles that would make any woman drool and forget their name. I watch his hand move to the zipper of his pants, and my core clenches, remembering how his dick made me feel. How he drove into me over and over again until I had the best orgasm of my life.

His pants fall, and I watch as he slowly pulls down his boxers. I bite my lip as I watch him stroke himself and wonder what it would be like to taste him on my tongue. I crawl across the bed, smirking as his eyes darken. I grab his dick and marvel at the velvet smoothness of it. Precum leaks from the tiny slit, and I move forward to lick it away. Damien hisses and grabs my hair in a hold that's firm and unyielding.

"What do you think you're doing," he growls in a tone full of possessiveness. "You want to taste me? Drive me wild with that sinful mouth of yours?"

"Yes," I tell him.

"Then have at it," he says as he loosens his grip. "This body is all yours, Bella."

He drags the tip over my lips, and I open my mouth to suck him deep. He growls at my needy whimper that escapes at the taste of him. His taste is salty and musky against my tongue. I suck him in again, enjoying the way his pulses on my tongue. I suck harder, bobbing back and forth as his breathing picks up. His hold tightens again when I take him deeper, using my hand to squeeze his base hard.

"Your mouth feels so good, baby," he whispers with desire. "Nothing has ever felt better."

My hand travels down to my dripping core, rubbing my clit to relieve some of the need. I moan around his dick, and using his grip, he pushes my head, pushing himself deeper and causing me to choke. My eyes water as I drag my mouth back to his tip. I push my fingers inside me, sending waves of pleasure through my core, and I feel Damien jerk in my mouth before he pulls out.

"Next time, I'll come down your throat," he says before pushing me back on the bed.

Damien attacks like a man possessed. He kisses me deep, and I lace my fingers in the silky strands of his hair as I rub my body against his. All too soon, he breaks off the kiss before trailing tiny kisses down my body. He reaches my hot center and swipes his tongue from my clit to my bottom, driving me crazy as he flicks up and down. He sticks his fingers inside me, and my whimper fills the quiet room. My toes curl, and my fingers tighten in his hair as I try to grind against his face. He pulls back, and I groan in frustration.

"I know you don't want to admit it," he whispers against me. "You and I have something. You can't deny what's between us. You feel it. I feel it. I'm going to show you that being with me is not a mistake, Bella."

He climbs back up my body and kisses me again. He rubs the head of his dick through my slickness, and I moan into his mouth.

"Damien," I whisper.

"I know," he says before thrusting into me.

I cry out as my body instantly clenches around him. My body is on fire, and I moan into his neck.

"See how we make each other feel?" he whispers against my ear as he moves slowly inside me.

I remain silent, wrapping my legs around him and moaning as he continues to move slowly. He growls in my ear before thrusting into me harder.

"That's okay, baby. You don't have to answer," he growls. "I'll fuck you so hard, and so often, you'll never think of us as a mistake."

He grips my ass hard and holds me in place. He slams into me so hard that I cry out at the mix of pleasure and pain. He slides out and pushes back in, setting a pounding rhythm, thrusting into me deeper and deeper. My nails sink into his back, raking down, and I'm sure he'll have marks when we finish. His thrust batters my walls repeatedly, causing a million tiny sensations to assault me all at once, propelling me higher toward orgasmic bliss that only he can give me.

As his cock fills me, each thrust more insistent than the last, heat floods through me. It's almost territorial, even as we both recognize the fleeting nature of this embrace. My hands journey up to cradle his face, desperately searching for the anchor of his eyes. When our gazes lock, a muffled murmur escapes my lips before sealing our mouths in a fervent kiss that eclipses thought. His pace intensifies, relentlessly propelling me towards a crest that looms dangerously close.

Then, as if a switch has been flipped, an overwhelming sensation seizes me. I freeze for a fraction of a heartbeat before arching back, and a strangled cry rips from my throat. My body clamps down on him, convulsing in ripples of pleasure that refuse to relent as if trying desperately to hold onto him forever.

"That's right, baby. Let go," he says, ramping up the pace of his thrusts as he chases his peak.

After a few more strokes, Damien roars above me. I feel his cock stiffening before he spills inside me. Our breaths intertwine as the silence envelops us, his form a weighted shield atop mine, melding into one another as though we're sculpted from the same fervent clay.

In this suspended slice of time, I surrender to the serenity that follows our storm, soaking in the warmth of the afterglow. I wince when Damien pulls out and rolls to the side. We lay next to each other, staring off into the distance, with neither of us knowing what to say next.

"Stay," he says, his voice barely above a whisper.

"Why should I stay, Damien?" My voice is quiet, almost lost in the stillness of the room. "Why should I trust you with my safety, with my life?"

He turns to me, his eyes searching mine with an intensity I don't want to acknowledge. "Because I can protect you, Isabella. I *will* protect you," he says with a certainty that both scares and comforts me.

"And once it's over?" I press, needing to know there's an end to this. That I won't be forever trapped in his gravity.

He takes my hand and entwines our fingers. "Once it's over, if you decide to leave, I won't stop you. You'll be free to go without any tether to me or the Blackhart name." His voice is a low promise threaded with an ache that I know reflects my own.

I consider his words, and the weight of my decision is heavier than the shadows around us. Would I ever be able to walk away from him, from us, regardless of his vow? The night stretches out before me, potent with the promise of more whispered secrets and stolen touches. I feel torn, ravaged by a war within. A storm against the calm. There's a gravity in his words, a pull as undeniable as the tide, and for a fleeting moment, I'm lost in the depth of his gaze, seeking an anchor in the storm of my emotions.

A part of me screams to flee, to unravel myself from the web of his influence and run toward the life I had planned. One of freedom, untethered from the likes of Damien Black-hart. Another part yearns to stay, to trust in the peace he offers and the safety promised in the fortress of his arms.

It's a gamble, a high-stakes game where my heart is on the line, and I'm terrifyingly close to placing my bet on him. If this is the wrong choice, if Damien is a siren leading me only to ruin, then I will bolt. I will leave, taking the shattered remnants of my haphazard dreams, and I'll never look back.

Yet here I lay with my resolve wavering on a decision that could undo me. I choose to stay, not out of weakness, but with a clandestine hope that somehow this tangled path may lead to redemption for both of us. With a reluctant nod, I concede with a heavy heart.

"Okay, Damien. I'll stay. For now." Deep within, I silently pray that choosing to stay in his arms doesn't mean sacrificing my heart.

# CHAPTER 20

## Isabella

It's been four weeks since I made the decision to stay with Damien. Four weeks of surprising tenderness and moments so sweet, they scare me. Damien treats me like a queen, with a gentleness I didn't know he possessed. We share breakfast each morning and dinner each night, with easy conversation and frequent laughter. The nights hold steamy encounters mixed with whispered intimacies and have only intensified the connection between us. My cheeks flush with the memory, a mix of pleasure and bashfulness swirling within me.

Yet, the need for my own space remains non-negotiable. I insisted on keeping my own room. Damien's jaw had tensed at that, a shadow of disapproval flickering in his eyes, but he didn't fight me on it. He agreed, albeit reluctantly. It's my sanctuary, a slice of independence that I cling to amongst the rapidly blurring lines of our unconventional relationship. It's proof that inside the fortress that is Damien Blackhart, I am still Isabella. Free, if not entirely unbound.

The presence of Jacob is a constant now, and his vigilant eyes trace my every move. He's a silent sentinel promised to guard my life. Despite the initial betrayal, the sting of his lies faded in the aftermath of his apology. I forgave him. How could I not when his actions were bound by duty? More convincingly, he had saved me when danger gnarled at my very door. His presence isn't suffocating, though. It's strangely comforting. Jacob shadows me with a respectful distance, and his presence unnoticed until he wants to be.

As I move through the days, he's there, blending into the environment with practiced ease but always there, watching and ensuring my safety. It's an odd partnership, one that treads the line between professional and personal because now he is part of my story, intertwined with the choice I made to stay in Damien's world. Everywhere I go, I feel his protective circle around me like an unspoken promise that I'm not in danger.

I take a deep breath of the aroma of the café's fresh coffee blending with the scent of old books. It's a quirky little place that Seraphina loves, half bookstore, half café. The walls are lined with shelves that climb toward the high ceiling, each one packed with tales and knowledge of every conceivable genre. A collector's paradise.

Plush armchairs and antique wooden tables are scattered throughout the space, offering cozy nooks for readers to lose themselves in a book or enjoy a warm drink. It's an eclectic mix of old-world charm and homey comfort. Soft jazz music plays subtly in the background, and the gentle hum of hushed conversations adds to the bookstore's tranquil ambiance.

It feels like a secret hideaway, a place where time slows and the world outside dims to a quiet whisper. My hands wrap tighter around the warm ceramic mug as I finally meet Seraphina's gaze. She's waiting, eyebrows raised in silent question.

My heart pounds as I sit across from her. The distance between us is measured in moments rather than meters. With the steam rising from my cup, a cloud of apprehension envelops me, thicker than the scent of coffee and old books that cling to the air. I haven't seen her since the night of my escape. Her gaze holds a mixture of concern and curiosity, and I struggle to hold it, afraid that she'll read the conflict that swirls within me like a brewing storm. Meeting Seraphina feels like stepping back into a past that's both haunting and heroic. She is my savior but also a reminder of all that I fled.

"Sera, it's been a wild ride," I begin, my voice barely above a whisper as if the words could somehow spill and shatter. "After the escape, I was in this tiny town, living a quiet life, waitressing at a local diner. Simple and serene. But it didn't last."

Seraphina's eyes are wide with concern. "What happened, Isa?"

I glance at Jacob a few tables away. "Damien found me. There was... kidnapping, torture. It's like I can never truly escape his gravity." I pause to sip my coffee. Its bitterness is a stark contrast to the sweetness of the pastries on our table.

"He let you go again?" her voice is a mix of hope and skepticism.

I nod. "I left and tried to restart, but someone attacked me in my new apartment. Then Jacob," I gesture subtly towards him. "He saved me. Damien sent him. Can you believe after everything, Damien's become...I don't even know, part of me?"

Seraphina reaches across the table and squeezes my hand. "Are you saying you're with him? After all he's put you through?"

"It's not that simple. There's tenderness I never expected, moments that feel normal, like we're a real couple," I say, feeling my cheeks warm with the confession.

"Do you trust him?" her question is sharp.

"I..." I trail off with my heart a knot of contradictions. "I want to, Sera. But trust is a luxury, isn't it? In our world, it's as dangerous as it is rare."

She gives me a look that's part understanding, part worry. "That is true. You're stronger than his chaos. Just remember that."

I smile wistfully. "I'm trying, Sera. Really, I am."

We sit there in silence, the soft murmur of the café around us blending into a lull of white noise. The minutes stretch out, filled with unspoken thoughts and the clinking of cutlery. Then Seraphina's voice cuts through the silence, gentle yet edged with the concern of a friend who has seen too much.

"Isa, are you really okay? You've been through an awful lot," she asks as her eyes search mine for the truth that my poker face might hide.

I offer her a small, reassuring smile before nodding. "Yes, Sera, I am. It's complicated, but I'm okay."

Her lips curve into a wry smile, and her tone lightens. "You haven't got a case of Stockholm syndrome, have you? Falling for your tormentor and all? You guys *are* in a relationship."

I laugh, a genuine burst of amusement that lightens the weight of our conversation. "Stockholm syndrome? No, and I wouldn't call it a relationship. It's... a mutually beneficial release of tension that we both enjoy," I say, figuring the euphemism wraps our arrangement in enough mystery to satisfy curiosity without revealing too much.

I lean back in the chair, feeling the old, carved wood press against my spine, grounding me to the moment. My mind whirls with memories, each one a sharp fragment of the picture that Damien and I have become. He's a storm of a man, relentless and fierce. He's put me through trials that would break most, and there was a time I would've given anything to escape his pull. My gaze flits to the window. Outside, the world moves on in blissful ignorance of the chaos that brews within me.

The attraction between us, undeniable and electric, has always been a force of nature. Our chemistry crackles with the intensity of a lightning strike in the air around us. I can't deny it, not even to myself, especially not when his touch still lingers on my skin.

And yet, as I sit here, I'm torn. Can a few tender moments and shared laughter erase the shadows of the past? The thought dances around the edges of my heart like a dangerous melody that tempts me towards forgiveness, towards trust. But forgiveness doesn't come easy, and trust... trust is a fragile thing that, once shattered, its shards are sharp and treacherous. Do I dare pick up the pieces?

I take a fortifying sip of my coffee, letting the heat seep into my bones. Can I fully give in? To lean into the fall and hope that the arms that have both harmed and held me will catch me this time? The battle between my heart's desires and my mind's warnings is a silent war that I wage within the confines of my ribcage.

I let out a soft sigh. Forgive and move on. The phrase is a siren's song, luring me to potentially treacherous shores. With Damien, I'm learning that some questions might not have ready answers, and maybe, just maybe, that's okay. For now.

The atmosphere shifts as I pivot the attention away from my chaotic world to hers. "How about you, Sera? What's been going on in your life?" I ask, eager for an update that's rooted in normalcy.

She shrugs a nonchalant gesture that's a little too casual. "Oh, things have been fine," she says, but the flicker in her eyes suggests the simplified answer is just the tip of an iceberg.

"What about Ethan?" I prod gently, recalling the countless times she had mentioned his name with that sparkle of interest in her eyes.

Her expression hardens, and her dismissive laugh is a tell-tale sign. "Ethan? He's out of the picture," she declares, then scoffs with a bitterness that's new to me.

I lean in, my curiosity piqued. "What happened?"

She looks away briefly as her fingers tap an impatient rhythm on the tabletop. "Let's just say he was a master of deception. The good guy act was just that, an act." She takes a deep breath, her voice steadying. "I caught him red-handed, or should I say, in the middle of the act, with some bimbo no less, when I showed up at his place. The truth couldn't have been clearer."

I feel a twinge of anger on her behalf, mixed with relief that she learned about his true colors now rather than later. "I'm sorry, Sera. You don't deserve that," I say earnestly.

She meets my gaze again with a resilient fire, replacing the earlier hurt. "It's fine. I'm better off without the lying, cheating scumbag."

Suddenly, the sound of gunfire erupts, shattering the calm like glass under a hammer. Bullets whiz through the air, tearing into bookshelves and scattering paper and debris. Time narrows to a pinpoint, and my pulse is a furious staccato in my ears. I barely register movement before Jacob is in motion, a blur of trained efficiency. He vaults over the tables with a protector's urgency, and with firm hands, he yanks both Seraphina and me down to the floor. We're pressed close to the ground, and the cool tile against my cheek offers a stark contrast to the chaos unfolding around us. Jacob covers us with his body like a human shield against the storm of lead, his eyes scanning for threats.

"Stay down!" he yells.

His command is needless. I'm frozen, and my breath

comes in shallow bursts as the reality of danger crashes over me with unforgiving clarity.

Ears ringing, the world recedes to the space between breaths and bullets. Jacob's return fire is a metronome of survival among the deafening roar.

He's calm, eerie in precision, even as he multitasks by shouting into his phone. "We're being attacked."

The line goes dead with urgency, his voice now a directive just for me. "Stay here and stay down."

As he moves away, phantom-like among the screams and shattering glass, the gunfire persists like a relentless storm. My heart feels like it's trying to escape. It's a wild thing inside my chest, pounding against the bone cage imprisoning it. It's hard to breathe, each inhale sharp and ragged as I try to remain as silent as death. The irony is not lost on me. Fear clutches at my throat, a tangible thing that makes swallowing impossible. The harsh staccato of gunfire is the only measure of time now, each shot echoing the rapid thrum of my pulse.

Terror grips me, a visceral and primal force, urging me to run, hide, escape. But I'm paralyzed, my body unresponsive under the weight of fear. Jacob's presence is both a comfort and a reminder of how dire the situation is. My mind frantically races. Snapshots of Damien, of laughing with Seraphina, of anything and everything dear flash before my eyes while the awful thought that I might never get to see them again claws through the fog of my terror.

Amid the terror, a wail pierces my focus. A kid, small, too young for such horror, is curled under a table corner, eyes big with fear.

"Just stay there," I shout in a voice strained with a more protective instinct than I've ever known.

Then, agony slices across my arm. My hand comes away painted in red, and the room spins slightly. Looking up, the specter of death is there with a gun pointing at my head. It's Jacob who cuts the final string of the gunman's intent. He collapses, and I'm yanked back harshly to the cold tiles. My heart thrashes against my ribs, every spark of pain from my bleeding arm a stark reminder of life, of the thin thread we're hanging by.

Jacob's fingers work furiously, ejecting the spent magazine and slamming a fresh one into the grip with practiced ease. He raises the gun, sights down the barrel, and fires with a methodical rhythm that belies the chaos. Bullets find their marks in a grim ballet, adding to the chaos that seems to stretch the seconds into lifetimes.

He moves slightly to shield my body with his own, a living barrier between me and the hail of lead. His arm muscles tense with each recoil, the signs of strain the only evidence that he's as human as I am among this insanity.

The barrage intensifies around us. Like more people joined the fray. It sounds like it's raining bullets, relentless and thunderous. I feel the vibration as each one hits. Among the terror, Jacob exhales in relief as the tension in his jaw eases.

"Help's here," he grunts, more to himself than to me.

I dare to raise my head and peer through the chaos. Damien is here, and he's the embodiment of retribution, with a gun in each hand. He moves with a lethal grace, his determination carved into the lines of his face. As he advances, each motion is fluid and deliberate, his presence a storm of vengeance against those who dare threaten us.

I watch, oddly detached, as the man I know so intimately transforms into a warrior, a beast in human form. His eyes, usually deep with complexity, are single-minded now. They contain no fear, only the clear intent to annihilate any threat that stands in his way. He's a striking image, like something from a visceral dream. Terrifying in power and hypnotizing in focus. Every takedown is swift, rooted in a primal instinct to protect and serve justice.

Then, as quickly as the chaos erupted, silence fell, heavy and absolute. Damien stands among the stillness, his chest heaving, guns lowered, as a guardian cloaked in the dust of turmoil. I see him clearly. He is not just a protector or a beast. He is the devil.

"Bella!" his voice cuts through the aftermath, urgent and laced with fear. "Where are you, baby?"

I try to respond, but the words get lost in a throat dry with dust and terror.

Jacob rises slightly, and his voice is a beacon of our location. "We're over here, boss."

I stand shaky on my feet as Damien materializes from the settling debris with his eyes scanning me and searching for harm.

His hands are on me, strong and reassuring. "Are you hurt anywhere?"

I stand here like a rag doll in the aftermath as Damien's hands roam over me with frenetic energy. His fingers are meticulous in their search, skimming over every inch to ensure no harm has come to me beyond the terror etched into my eyes.

The intensity in his gaze holds me captive, and I realize that the man before me, the one who has just wrenched us from the jaws of death, is fueled by a fear of losing something. Me. His touch is both frantic and gentle, a contrast that sums up the chaos we've been through. His hands eventually steady, grounding us both in the reality that I am, for the most part, unharmed.

"I'm okay. I—" I want to say I'm fine, but as he touches my arm, the world tilts at an odd angle. His fingers come away stained with a startling crimson, and my heart drops.

The searing pain shoots through my arm, unrelenting and

sharp, breaking through the numbness that had cloaked it. I can feel the heat of my blood as it trickles down my cold sweat-soaked skin. My head feels light, and those menacing black dots begin to swim across my vision, threatening to pull me into darkness. I grip Damien's arm, seeking an anchor to tether me to consciousness, trying to stay grounded in the midst of my fear and the pain that claws at my senses.

"It's a graze, Bella. You've been shot," his voice is calm, but his eyes betray the fierce protectiveness that always simmers below the surface.

"Damien, I think I'm going to..." The words trail off as my grip on reality loosens as I fight to stay awake.

Adrenaline wanes, leaving behind a bone-deep ache and a lightheadedness that has my knees buckling. The last thing I see before everything goes dark is the worry etched on Damien's face as he reaches to catch me. "Stay with me, Bella."

# CHAPTER 21

## Damien

My boots tap an impatient rhythm on the sterile linoleum as I pace back and forth like a caged animal. Anger courses through me. Hot, unyielding, and demanding action. In the silence of the waiting room, my voice comes out as a low growl, barely audible.

"Those fucking mother fuckers," I snarl.

The waiting room is a stark expanse of cold white. Each chair, tile, and wall bleached to a sterile purity that feels at odds with the chaos we've just escaped. The air is heavy with antiseptic scents, coating the inside of my nostrils with the odor of cleanliness that attempts to mask the underlying fear and pain this place knows all too well. Fluorescent lights hum above, casting an unforgiving glare on every surface, leaving no room for shadows or comfort.

It's a place of waiting, of not knowing, where time stretches and compresses with each tick of the clock. I'm trapped in an oasis of calm that's anything but tranquil.

"I'm going to kill whoever hurt her," I mutter to myself as my fists clench and unclench with restless energy. "They better count their fucking days."

I can't sit. The waiting is a silent killer more threatening than any bullet. I murmur into the void, vowing revenge and promising justice. My mind is swirling with the faces of their assailants, and their features burned into my memory. A hit list that won't be ignored.

"Not a single one will see daylight if she doesn't walk out of here," I snarl under my breath, each word a venomous promise. My heart refuses to settle, and each beat is a drum of war for those who dared to aim at her.

Memories of the phone call flash in my mind. The one where Jacob's voice, usually so steady, cracked with urgency, telling me they were under attack. I grabbed Victor, and we hauled ass over to the bookstore, where Isabella met Seraphina. Where she was supposed to be safe. The fear that clawed at my chest on the drive over, the thought of losing her, fuels the rage, brewing a storm inside me that I can barely contain.

I was a man possessed. A force of nature fueled by one singular motive. To reach Isabella. The air was thick with gunpowder, and the bodies of those who made the fateful decision to stand in my way were strewn across the floor as nothing but lifeless obstacles in my path. I left destruction in my wake, unapologetic and unyielding.

They say hell hath no fury like a man scorned, but they've never seen a man like me fight to save the woman who's slowly becoming everything to him. The men who dared attack don't get a chance to regret their choices. They don't get to wish they'd chosen differently. I made sure of that. With each pull of the trigger, I made sure they never lived another day to attack an innocent.

My fingers tremble slightly as I yank my phone from my pocket. I dial Victor with an urgency that's become second nature now.

The line clicks, and his gravelly voice is on the other end. "Yeah, boss?"

"Did you find anything?" I ask, struggling to keep the edge out of my voice.

After we arrived here, I could think of nothing else but to set Victor and Jacob on the trail of whoever dared to attack. Their resources are extensive, and their loyalty unquestioning, but this is personal.

"Yeah, we have Daniel, and it seems like he knows something," Victor says. "Since we were interrupted the last time we had him, I took him to the other location. No one will find us here. We'll get your answers."

"No!" I bark into the phone. "Strip him and hang him up. Wait until I get there. He's mine." My words carry the weight of a promise, a vow of retribution that will be kept. The lines between justice and vengeance blur in my vision, colored by the blood of the one I vow to protect.

My blood is seething with a need for vengeance so pure it's nearly sacred. I can almost taste the retribution in the air, a thick, copper tang of justice demanded by the violated sanctity of Bella's safety. They've awoken the beast, and there will be no reprieve, no mercy. Only the relentless force of my wrath.

The doctor strides into the waiting room, her expression one of firm professionalism, and I feel the phone slip slightly against my sweaty palm. The threat I leveled at this hospital hangs heavy in the air, an unspoken promise that they're painfully aware of. I keep my eyes locked with the doctor.

"How is she?" My voice is rough, all gravel and raw edges, every word a demand for the one thing I seek.

Isabella's safety. The implicit understanding is clear. They must give her the best care or face the full brunt of my power. They know it. I've made sure of that. I don't just want their best. I demand it.

The doctor's eyes hold a guarded relief, an emotion that seems almost out of place in the sterile chaos.

"She's stable, Mr. Blackhart," she begins, and every syllable amplifies the tension in my chest. "Isabella and the baby are fine."

The weight of the world lifts off my shoulders as the doctor confirms that it was just a graze. No stitches are needed.

I blink as the words 'and the baby' ricochet in my mind like a stray bullet. I'm stunned, speechless. She adds, almost as an afterthought, that Isabella can take over-the-counter painkillers if she needs them. Nothing stronger, though, because of the baby. My hands, which have been clenched into fists, slowly relax at my sides. This nightmare could've ended much differently. A surge of fierce protectiveness washes over me. Never again will they be at risk.

"Can I see her?" I manage to ask while keeping my voice steady, though my pulse races with the force of a raging river.

"Yes," she nods, signaling towards the hallway. "Come with me."

I follow as the knot in my chest loosens with each step. A baby. We're having a baby. I pocket away that jolt of joy, hiding it behind the iron façade that has become second nature. There will be time for softness later, away from prying eyes, when I can hold her in my embrace.

The hospital room is a stark white sanctuary that I step into. Isabella is sitting in the bed like a vision of resilience filling the hospital room. She looks much better than when I first brought her in. The flush of color has returned to her cheeks. Even now, in the aftermath of terror, her beauty is undiminished and perhaps even amplified by the strength she's unknowingly displaying. I stride quickly to her bedside as my eyes hungrily take in her form and seek evidence that she's truly unharmed.

"Are you okay?" I ask.

"I'm fine," she manages a soft smile, and her energy is a mere whisper of her usual fire. "It's just a flesh wound, Damien. Really."

Her words, meant to be comforting, stir a storm in me, but one look at her grit and grace and a reluctant laugh escapes me, half in disbelief, half from relief that she's speaking to me. She's alive.

"Every scar, every wound you carry, I carry twice over in my soul. You're cloaked in my shadows, Isabella, protected by my very being. Don't ever doubt that. Are you sure you're fine?" I ask again.

She gives me another small smile. "Yes, I'm sure."

I turn to the doctor with a low and commanding tone. "We need a moment."

My eyes hold a hard edge that brooks no argument. The doctor nods in understanding. Perhaps it's professionalism or the palpable intensity I exude that sways her, but she doesn't hesitate to leave. As the door clicks shut, I'm left alone with Isabella, and the silence enveloping us clashes with the chaos of my raging thoughts. Isabella's gaze catches mine with concern etched in her features despite her own ordeal.

"How's Seraphina?" she asks, her voice barely above a whisper.

"She's fine," I reassure her, feeling my body tense with the memory of the chaos. "After the shootout, I had Victor escort her home. She's safe, Bella," I tell her.

We sit here in silence, and I feel the chasm of my thoughts besieged with a madness of emotions. The news of her pregnancy lingers in the air between us, an invisible, seismic force that both terrifies and exhilarates me. I've never considered fatherhood. My life is filled with danger, and trust has always been a currency too expensive for me to deal out freely, especially to the women I've known.

But Isabella is irrevocably different. I'm falling for her, deeper each day, entangled in her strength and her spirit, envisioning a future I never dared to contemplate. Kids. With her, it doesn't just feel possible. It feels right. There's no room for doubt, not even a whisper, that she would be anything less than an incredible mother.

"So, I take it you know," her voice interrupts my thoughts, her tone soft but pointed. "If your silence is anything to go by." I can't help the way my eyes flit away momentarily, caught off-guard by her perceptiveness.

"Yes, the doctor told me," I admit, my voice betraying a fraction of the awe that's swelling in my chest. The room feels charged now, electric with the revelation that we're going to be parents. Despite the world's weight on my shoulders and the danger that lurks in the shadows, this single truth shines like a beacon. Our unexpected yet fiercely welcome light in the darkness.

"I didn't mean for this to happen. I didn't think about birth control because I was celibate with Jackson. Then you happened, and celibacy went out the window," she says tearfully, her voice a soft echo in the sterile room. "You must feel trapped now."

Picking up her hand, I bring it to my lips, kissing the back of it gently, trying to imbed strength through my touch.

"I feel anything but trapped, Bella," I tell her earnestly, locking my eyes with hers so she sees the truth in them.

"Now, what am I going to do," she murmurs, more to herself than to me. She's gazing at the ceiling, eyes glazed with the turmoil of our situation.

I know the question isn't meant for me, but I answer anyway.

"We'll get married," I say matter-of-factly as if it's the most obvious next step. "I'll have a priest waiting when we get home. My mother and sisters will be there too," I continue, already mapping out the future, making her a promise I intend to keep.

Her eyes widen as though I've just suggested we fly to the moon for lunch. She stares at me, and incredulity etches into every feature of her beautiful face. "Damien, have you lost your damn mind? We don't need to get married."

"But we do," I insist, my voice firm. "I won't have my child born a bastard. It's not just a label. It's about respect. Protection."

She scoffs while brushing a stray lock of hair from her face with a shaky hand. "It's not the 1950s. A marriage certificate is just a piece of paper. Our child will be loved and cared for. Married or not."

My jaw sets. I lean closer before lowering my voice. "As my wife, as a Blackhart, no one would dare to raise a hand against you. Everyone would know you're mine."

"Damien, I *was* a Blackhart, and we've seen how much that mattered," she snaps, her eyes flashing with the remembered pain of today's events.

"That was before you belonged to *me*. Before I made it clear how much you matter to me." My conviction pours into each word. We're two sides of the same coin, fierce in our stances, but I need her to see reason.

We go back and forth, our argument a fiery dance of stubborn wills. It's not just stubbornness that drives me. It's a raging need to keep her safe, to make her understand that this is the best way to protect her, our child, and our future. Eventually, her resistance begins to wane as she realizes the depth of my concern.

"Okay, Damien," she finally murmurs, her voice barely audible, a surrender that feels more like a victory for both of us. "We'll do it your way."

She doesn't say it with defeat but with a quiet strength

that only she possesses, and I know we'll be okay. We're going to face this, united as one.

I don't wait for another second. As soon as her agreement hangs in the air, I step out of the room. Pulling out my phone, I dial quickly, my fingers steady despite the adrenaline that pumps through my veins.

"Get a priest to my house. Within two hours," I bark the order into the phone to one of my men who knows better than to ask questions.

Next, I call my mother and sister. "Be at my house in an hour," I tell them, my voice leaving no room for debate. "It's important."

I don't wait for their response, their confusion, or their questions. I just end the call. I can explain later once all the pieces are in place. Right now, I need to act. To make sure nothing can stand in the way of securing my family's future.

I punch Victor's number into my phone. "Leave Daniel with just two guards," I command as soon as he answers. "Only give him water, nothing else."

Victor's response is a grunt, his understanding implicit without the need for further explanation. I continue with urgency threading my words together. "I need you back at my house later. Isabella and I are getting married. This is not up for debate."

A brief pause, and then his voice, tinged with sarcasm, cuts through. "Gonna make an honest woman out of her in the middle of a war zone, boss? Should I bring rice or a bulletproof vest as wedding decor?"

I can't help but let out a tense chuckle despite the seriousness of the moment.

"You're an ass," I reply, my lips curling into a reluctant smile. "Stop by the jewelers and grab rings, too," I tell him, and before he can say anything else, I end the call. Time is a luxury I can't afford to waste. Not now.

I push the hospital doors open and step into the privacy of the cool evening air, allowing myself a moment to just breathe. This may not be the most conventional way to get married, but with Daniel securely in our clutches, I can afford to give Isabella, my soon to be wife, my undivided attention for a few days. The word 'wife' evokes a smile that surprises even me. It sounds so right, so perfectly fitting for what she's about to become in my life. Maybe this won't be so bad after all. Maybe, in all of the chaos we're entrenched in, we've stumbled upon an unexpected kind of perfection.

I lean against the cold brick wall of the hospital, gazing up at the bright sky, making an unspoken vow to the sun. When all this is over, once the imminent threat that targets Isabella is quashed, I will give her the wedding she wholeheartedly deserves. An event marked by celebration, not desperation, filled with family and friends instead of guards and guns.

As fate would have it, life is a cruel and unpredictable dance, and if, by some foolish slip, I make an ass of myself, alienating the heart I yearn to protect, I know I'd go to the ends of the earth to win her back, to convince her to stay.

I stride back inside the hospital. The sterile tang of antiseptic collides with the resolve that's settled deep in my bones. I seek out the doctor with a single-minded focus with my footsteps echoing in the almost empty hallway. She's just where I expect her to be, and I don't hesitate.

"When can Isabella go home?" My question is pointed, unyielding as my gaze locks with hers.

The doctor meets my intensity with a nod, understanding the urgency without needing the gritty details of why.

"I'll get her discharge papers ready. She'll be free to go in about fifteen minutes," she says, already turning to make good on her word.

True to her promise, Isabella's paperwork is completed

with swift efficiency. Before long, I have her by my side, guiding her gently but firmly through the maze of hallways. She's quiet and steadier on her feet than I expected. In no time at all, she's in the passenger seat of my car as we drive toward the uncertain future that awaits us.

# CHAPTER 22

## Isabella

The drive to Damien's house is like a blur. This morning, I was in the comfort of a bookstore. Now, here I am in the passenger seat next to Damien, the afternoon sun casting long shadows on a day that has pivoted into the unexpected. I'm getting married today. Again, but this time, it's to Damien, a man whose resolution is as unyielding as the set of his jaw. He glances at me, his eyes reflecting a cocktail of determination and something softer.

A promise of not only safety but a partnership forged in the steel of necessity. I should feel overwhelmed, perhaps even frightened, but there's a certainty in the chaos, and it's rooted in the fierce protectiveness he exudes. As the scenery whisks by, a singular thought crystalizes with each passing mile. My life is changing irrevocably, and there's no one else I'd rather have by my side.

We pull up to the large, imposing house that somehow feels more like a fortress today than a home. I know the stakes are high. They loom over us like the dark clouds on the horizon threatening a storm. With an assuredness that belies the tension of the day, Damien helps me out of the car, his touch both grounding and comforting. The murmurs of voices from inside spill out as we make our way to the door. It's an odd mix of anticipation and fear that tugs at my gut. A reminder of the unexpected turn my life has taken in just a few hours.

"Damien," a voice calls out, unquestionably belonging to his mother. "We're in the sitting room. Come. Tell us what's going on."

There's an undeniable authority in her tone that sets my heart racing. Damien gives me a reassuring smile with the corners of his eyes crinkling in a way that suggests more than just amusement.

"This is going to be fun," he says, though the depth in his eyes tells me it's more battle than jest. "Come on. Let's get this battle over with."

With a faint nod, I follow him, clutching the fabric of my dress as if it could somehow shield me from the impending confrontation. We reach the door of the sitting room, and Damien pauses, giving my hand a firm, purposeful squeeze.

"No matter what they say, we are getting married. They will have to come to terms with you being in my life," he asserts with a conviction that sends warmth flooding through me.

His words are a fortress in their own right, strong and unyielding, an oath to face whatever comes our way. Together.

As the sitting room door swings open, a hush falls over the vast space. Damien's mother and his sister Aurora fix their gazes on me. A look of utter shock paints their faces. The air is thick with disapproval, and it's almost suffocating in its intensity.

Damien steps forward, his voice steady and commanding. "Mother, Aurora, thanks for coming."

The silence that follows is shattered when his mother's voice, cold as steel, slices through the tension. "So, you've found the whore who killed my son," she spits out, the words venomous, eyes narrowing dangerously. "Why is she here and not strung up somewhere waiting to be executed?"

Aurora stands abruptly with fire igniting in her eyes. "I'll kick her ass for daring to cross our family," she threatens as she takes a menacing step towards me.

Damien is quick to step in front of me like a shield. "Watch your tongues when speaking about Isabella," he snaps with an uncharacteristic edge to his voice, causing both women to recoil in surprise.

"What's gotten into you, Damien?" his mother demands with disbelief etched into every word. "Did she spread her legs for you too? Has she gotten in your head like Jackson?" she taunts, her words dripping with scorn.

"Sit down and shut up," Damien orders, his tone leaving no room for argument. They comply if only out of sheer astonishment, taking their seats across from us. Damien grasps my hand, and we sit opposite them.

"Isabella and I are getting married. The priest will be here within the hour," he states firmly, looking directly into his mother's outraged eyes.

The news hits them like a seismic wave, and their expressions morph quickly from anger to disbelief.

"You cannot be serious!" his mother's voice thunders.

"This is madness!" Aurora adds with a seething rage.

The room devolves into chaos as they explode with fury. The news of the impending wedding kindled a wildfire of indignation. The maelstrom of voices ramps up, each word a serrated dagger meant to rattle me. I feel Damien's hand, warm and steady, reassuring me. A silent vow that we're in this together. The air thick with hostility is choking.

Leaning towards Damien, my voice is barely above a whisper. "Maybe this isn't the right thing to do. They hate me, and

I—I don't want to be the reason for more conflict in your family."

Damien cups my cheek with a tender look. "Let the world challenge us. Let them come with their swords and judgments. They'll find us standing, unbreakable. You are the queen of my dark kingdom, Isabella, and I, your relentless king."

I'm speechless by his words. Meanwhile, his mom and sister are shouting in the background.

Damien's response slices through the clamor like a commandment. "Enough!"

The word echoes, absolute, and the room snaps to a heavy silence. Everyone's eyes fixate on him as the aftershock of his bellow fades. "Listen to me," he says with clarity that thrums with authority. "Isabella is not responsible for Jackson's death. She is going to be my wife. She is going to be the mother of my child."

The revelation hammers into the silence, and his mother's gasp is the crack in a dam about to burst. "She's pregnant?" The incredulity in her voice is mirrored on Aurora's face.

"Yes, she is," Damien affirms, each word a brick in the fortress he's building around me. "And you will accept her and treat her with respect."

The commandment lingers in the air, unquestionable and binding. His gaze doesn't falter as he addresses his family. "Wait here. We need to prepare." With those final words, he turns to me, and guides me out, leaving the turbulent sitting room and its stunned occupants behind.

As he leads me away from the chaos, we find sanctuary in a spare bedroom. The walls are bathed in soft pastel hues, and the ambiance calms my frayed nerves.

"This is where you'll get ready," he says with a tender but serious gaze. He runs a hand through his hair. A charming smile plays on his lips, and I can't help but smile back despite the turmoil within. "You know, tradition says a groom shouldn't see his bride before the ceremony," he teases, and with a playful wink, he's gone, leaving me wrapped in silence as the echo of his footsteps fades away.

Moments later, the door opens quietly and a maid steps in. Between her hands is a beautiful dress, more stunning than any I have ever imagined wearing. It's the kind of gown that tells a story. A perfect blend of elegance and boldness, much like my feelings at this moment. However, I thought I'd wear what I have on, but I thank Damien for making it so nice on such short notice. She lays the dress out carefully, and her hands are skilled and gentle as she helps me prepare.

The fabric of the dress cascades onto my skin like a whispered promise. Each layer of lace and silk a stark contrast to the unrest outside these walls. I watch my reflection as the maid works silently, securing each button with careful fingers that I wish were my mother's. She's not here, though, and the absence is a hollow ache in my chest. No maternal eyes to well with tears. No whispered blessings to cling to.

I always pictured my wedding day as a joyous occasion. I envisioned being enveloped in love and laughter, with my father's arm interlocked with mine as we walked down the aisle. A rite of passage accompanied by his proud smile. That vision crumbles with each sweep of the maid's gentle hands through my hair. This is not a union born of love. It is one necessitated by circumstance and dubious honor.

I should feel elation, yet all I feel is a spreading numbness as if with every pearl fastened, a piece of my dreams is stripped away. I'm doing this twice now, and both times, it feels like I am putting on a grand performance. Not stepping into a chapter of cherished togetherness.

The maid steps back as her work is now finished, and her eyes meet mine in the mirror. "You look beautiful," she says softly, with warmth touching her words and sincerity in her tone.

I catch a glimpse of myself, and the transformation is undeniable. A small smile curves my lips in a silent acknowledgment of her kindness.

"Thank you," I murmur, allowing myself this fragment of normalcy, this sliver of tradition in an otherwise untraditional day.

The mirror before me holds a beautifully adorned bride, yet I can see the sorrow in my own eyes. There's a haunting solitude that drapes over me. A veiled reminder of the glaring absence of those who should have been my rocks today. My heart weighs heavy with the stark realization. I'm making a sacrifice on the altar of obligation and assumed debts of honor.

As I stand before the mirror, the dress enveloping me in its splendor, I find myself reflecting on its significance. The gown, undeniably magnificent, is a masterful creation of chiffon and tulle layered intricately with the finest lace. Its bodice, expertly fitted, accentuates the contours of my form with a gentle embrace, while the skirt flares out in a sea of soft folds, whispering against the floor with every subtle movement.

The sleeves, sheer and delicate, kiss my arms with a touch that rivals a lover's caress. Ornate beading adorns the dress like drops of morning dew, each catching the light and casting prisms around the quiet room. It's more than a mere wedding dress. It's a work of art. Damien really did plan everything.

With meticulous care, a veil of delicate lace is secured gently upon my head. The maid offers a small, warm smile, one that suggests a depth of understanding, before signaling it's time to return to the sitting room. My breath steadies and my heart is a drumbeat beneath the dress as I follow her lead downstairs to the sitting room.

Damien stands there, and his presence is a fortress in the center of the room as his eyes immediately find mine. As our gazes lock, I'm in awe of the intensity within them. It's as if he's silently vowing to protect us against the world. At this moment, he is unbelievably handsome. The lines of his suit are tailored to mold his form like a second skin, complementing a stance that's both commanding and reassuring. The hint of vulnerability I notice only makes him more endearing, humanizing the strength he radiates.

His mother sits, and her demeanor is serene compared to before, yet the weight of her scrutiny is still there. Aurora, however, lets her anger pour from her gaze unabated. It's clear she distrusts and disapproves, and her glower speaks volumes of distaste. Their reactions pale as Damien steps forward. The desire emanating from him dissolves my apprehensions and empowers me to face this union.

His fingers intertwine with mine, and he leads me closer to the makeshift altar. His hand is steady, squeezing mine reassuringly as if to say, 'We're in this together.' The priest clears his throat, signaling the beginning of the ceremony, and the soft murmur of our small assembly quiets.

"Dear friends," the priest begins, his voice resonating in the room. "We are gathered here today in the presence of these witnesses to join Damien and Isabella in matrimony, which is an honorable estate. If any person can show just cause why they may not be joined together, let them speak now or forever hold their peace."

I stand beside Damien with my hand in his as the priest invites an objection that will not come. I find myself comforted by the pressure of his hand and the concern in his eyes that meets mine. He gives me a slight, reassuring nod, and my heart flutters with a mixture of anxiety and something akin to hope.

"Repeat after me," the priest says. "I, Damien," he

prompts, and Damien repeats in a strong, clear voice that counters the fragility of the moment. "I, Damien, take you, Isabella, to be my lawfully wedded wife."

The priest turns to me, and my heart races as I echo. "I, Isabella, take you, Damien, to be my lawfully wedded husband."

Damien continues, his voice steady. "To have and to hold, from this day forward."

My voice wavers with emotion as I vow. "To have and to hold, from this day forward."

"For better, for worse, for richer, for poorer, in sickness and in health," the priest leads Damien through the promise that feels heavier with each word.

Following in turn, I commit. "For better, for worse, for richer, for poorer, in sickness and in health."

Damien's eyes lock with mine. "To love and to cherish, till death do us part."

My throat tightens as I reciprocate the solemn oath. "To love and to cherish, till death do us part."

"According to God's holy ordinance, and thereto, I pledge myself to you," the priest continues.

Together, we speak, strength found in unity. "According to God's holy ordinance, and thereto, I pledge myself to you."

The priest gestures towards Damien, and with a fluent motion, he turns to face Victor, who holds out a small velvet box. Damien opens it to reveal our rings. My ring, a diamond wedding band, glistens with an array of intricately cut gems. It's an elegant ensemble, where each diamond, pristine and ethereal, is meticulously set in a band of polished platinum, reflecting the light with every subtle motion of my hand. The edges are soft and delicately carved to accentuate the stones, promising a comfortable embrace around my finger.

Damien's band is no less striking, yet it speaks of his character, being notably plain, robust, and timeless, with a finish that evokes strength and a lifetime of durability. In its simplicity lies its beauty, and a part of me thrills at the thought of these rings symbolizing our union. They're beautiful. Evidence of a sentiment that might grow in the long term.

The priest continues. "Damien, do you take Isabella to be your lawfully wedded wife, to live together in the holy estate of matrimony? Will you love her, comfort her, honor and keep her, in sickness and in health, and forsaking all others, keep you only unto her, for as long as you both shall live?"

"I do," Damien says firmly, his voice carrying a solemn promise.

The priest then turns to me, repeating the question. "Isabella, do you take Damien to be your lawfully wedded husband, to live together in the holy estate of matrimony? Will you love him, comfort him, honor and keep him, in sickness and in health, and forsaking all others, keep you only unto him, for as long as you both shall live?"

I open my mouth to speak, but as I look into Damien's eyes, I find myself getting lost in them. They hold a depth of emotion and a silent conviction that we can make it through whatever lies ahead. My surroundings begin to dissolve, the voice of the priest a distant echo as I stand there, gazing into the eyes of the man who is all at once a stranger and yet my rock in this stormy moment. The priest clears his throat, bringing me out of my thoughts.

"I do," I whisper.

Damien takes the ring from the velvet box, and with a tenderness that contradicts his steady hands, he slides it onto my finger. It's a perfect fit, snug against my skin. I, in turn, take his ring and, with slight trembling from the rush of emotions, place it on his finger. It sits there, a declaration of our commitment, simple yet so profound.

The priest looks at us with a smile. "I now pronounce you man and wife. You may now kiss the bride."

Damien's eyes meet mine with a spark of mischief and challenge in them. He smiles, a captivating, heart-stopping smile before he leans down and captures my lips with his. The kiss, wild and unrestrained, ignites a fire within me. It's passionate and full of a heat that surely isn't suitable for the eyes of our audience. At this moment, Damien doesn't care, and neither do I. His lips assert his claim over me in front of everyone here, especially his mother and sister. As we break away, breathless and flushed, I understand. This is Damien making it known that I am his, now and forever.

This journey to the altar wasn't one paved with the dreams of a young girl filled with tales of romantic love. It was one of necessity, of strategy. Yet, standing here, holding Damien's hand, something shifts within me. Perhaps it's the way his thumb rubs small circles on the back of my hand or the way he looks at me, not as a duty but with a genuine warmth. I allow myself a small smile as we turn, stepping together into our new life. Hand in hand, we make our way out of the room, and an unfamiliar sense of happiness bubbles inside me. At this moment, I entertain the thought that maybe, just maybe, marriage to Damien won't be so bad after all.

# CHAPTER 23

## Damien

I park the car behind the abandoned building. I can still smell the faintest hint of jasmine from Isabella's hair lingering in the air, and it twists something in my chest. Letting out a deep sigh, I lean my head back, my heart wrestling with frustration for having to leave her so soon. My wife. My thumb finds the wedding band on my finger, and I can't help but twirl it, feeling its newness against my skin. A smile unfurls across my face, unbidden.

Despite the chaos we had to navigate to get here, it's there, an undeniable symbol of my commitment to her. A reminder of vows exchanged and the quiet, unshakable conviction that it was the right decision. The metal glints in the waning sunlight, a beacon of the new life I've just begun with Isabella. My Isabella. With this ring, I'm not just tied to her legally, but in some intangible way that feels more permanent, more real. It's a weight I'm more than willing to bear.

I find myself drifting, lost in the weight of my thoughts. I reflect on the rushed vows we exchanged and how, despite the unconventional romance, I couldn't help feeling a pull towards her. A gravity that compelled me to show her the potential of 'us.' So, with a growing need to escape prying eyes and a stifling aftermath, I whisked her away to an island paradise. A place where the only sound was that of waves meeting the shore and the distant cry of seagulls. I wanted to prove to her, perhaps more to myself, that beyond the obligation and strategy, this could be something real.

On the island, a promise hung in the air like a salty breeze. We would set aside our pasts and allow ourselves to be two people learning the steps of a newfound dance. Isabella's laugh, clear and unburdened, became my favorite melody as we indulged in simple activities. We walked along the beach, with her hand in mine, feeling the cool, soft sand under our feet. We picked shells, laid on a blanket watching the stars, and had picnic lunches filled with fresh fruits that didn't demand much from her but offered much-needed peace and moments of shared joy. Her pregnancy didn't dampen her spirit. If anything, it brightened the fire in her.

And oh, how she came alive in the sanctity of our temporary haven. Her cravings were not just for the peculiar combinations of food. They extended to an insatiable appetite that brought both pleasure and closeness to our silent nights. The books I had secretly read talked of heightened senses, of hormones that painted every touch in a more vivid hue, yet nothing prepared me for the fervor with which she desired and was desired in return. Nights were a fever dream of caresses and whispered yearnings, and I was lost in the reverence of her needs.

It was a different kind of happiness. One that I had not known, branded with laughter and soft sighs instead of strategies and guarded conversations. In those fleeting days, bathed in the afterglow of a sunset or entwined in the sanctuary of our sheets, I began to believe in the potential of 'we' and 'us.' In a shared future that might just be crafted from the same fabric as those naive dreams I had once discarded. It was only a couple of days because that was all I could spare, but I vowed to take her anywhere she wanted to go if she kept smiling like that.

The sudden sound of a door slamming echoes through the silence, jolting me back to the present. Back to the life that runs on a parallel track to the one I just walked with Isabella.

Victor walks over. "Are you going to sit there all night?" he mocks. I can feel his gaze on me, impatient and expectant. "Or are we going to beat the shit out of Daniel?" he proposes, with a tone that suggests excitement rather than concern.

It pulls me out from the soft cocoon of reminiscence into the harsh reality of now. I sigh as my memories fold away like a storybook closing. Daniel, whom I left at the mercy of time and guarded space, had a week to reflect on his circumstances. Seven days that I hope have loosened his tongue. I turn the wedding band on my finger once more before letting my hand drop to my side. It's time for the other side of me to take over. The side that deals in shadows and hard choices. I step out of the car, closing the door behind me with a sense of purpose.

"Let's see if Daniel is ready to talk," I say, my voice steady, as I prepare myself for the night's necessary cruelties.

We push open the door to the abandoned building, and its hinges groan from disuse. The dim interior is lit by the sickly yellow glow of a single dangling bulb, and there, in the pooling shadows, is Daniel. His once sharp features are now gaunt, with skin pulled taut over high cheekbones. His hair, once meticulously styled, is now a matted tangle that clings to his sweat-slicked forehead.

The smell hits me next. A pungent mix of unwashed body, stale water, and a faint metallic tang that speaks of rusted chains and old blood. His eyes, rimmed with the red of strain and sleeplessness, flicker to me with a defiance that's dulled but not extinguished. The paleness of his skin makes the dark bruises marring his body stand out all the more. My nostrils flare at the stench, and a part of me recoils, yet there's an acknowledgment that this, too, is a necessary part of the dance we're locked in.

"You're going to answer my questions, Daniel. Who attacked my wife?" My voice is steady and measured, betraying none of the storm that brews within me.

Still, Daniel's response is wrapped in confusion as his swollen, cracked lips part with effort. "Who?"

"Isabella," I clarify.

A laugh, scratchy and weak, emerges from his throat. His words drip with venom. "Oh, the whore's married again? To you, no less! Man, she really gets around."

Rage flares up like wildfire. An inferno that blazes in my chest and roars in my ears. With restraint abandoned, my fist collides with his stomach. A physical rebuke of his disrespect. He doubles over with a gasp, and before I can check the fury that rides me, another blow crashes against his jaw, silencing the laughter and staining my knuckles with proof of his insolence.

"I'll ask again," I growl. "Who attacked my wife."

I stare down at Daniel, and my patience frays with every beat of silence. His bloody lips twist into a sneer.

"I'm not telling you shit," he hisses through bloodied teeth. "When my father hears about this... about you kidnapping me, there'll be hell to pay."

I can't help it. I chuckle, relishing the irony. "You think I'm afraid of your father?" My voice is chilled, hollow with mirth. "Listen carefully because I'll only say this once. She's mine. Every breath, every tear, every smile. Cross me or make her shed a single tear, and I'll make you beg for death long before I allow you the mercy of it."

Just as tension coils tighter in the room, the door creaks

open. Victor and I spin around with our guns raised, ready to neutralize any threat, but it's not necessary.

"No need to shoot, gentlemen," a familiar voice drawls from the doorway. Julian. I can feel the slightest shift in the atmosphere.

A mingling of resentment and curiosity. I lower my weapon, resigning to the twist of fate. "What are you doing here, Julian? How did you know we were here?"

His smile doesn't reach his eyes. "I keep my ear close to the ground. I know everything that happens in these streets."

I scrutinize Julian, taking in the poise with which he leans against the door frame. My grip on my gun loosens, but my senses remain alert. Julian isn't someone to be underestimated.

We watch as Julian's gaze slides to Daniel, who's trying to gather what's left of his defiance. "Hello, brother. I'd say it's nice to see you, but I'm not here for pleasantries."

Daniel responds with a glob of spit in his direction. "We're not brothers, you bastard," he snarls, his voice shredding on the effort.

Julian nods as if conceding a point. "That's true. Which is why I won't feel an ounce of remorse for what comes next."

He turns to face me with demand in his eyes. "I want in on this little... interrogation."

Victor's confusion is almost palpable. "Why get involved?" he asks bluntly.

"Daniel's connected to the scum who attacked Seraphina," Julian reveals with a hint of steel underlying his tone. "No one messes with my baby sister."

The room echoes with the dull thud of flesh against flesh. My face is a cold mask, my every nerve ending screaming in silent rage as I demand over and over. "Who attacked Isabella? Why do they want her?"

Victor, just as consumed by the need for answers, takes his

turn, his blows measured and calculated. Daniel, that stubborn fucker, just grins through the blood like a gory Cheshire cat in this twisted wonderland and tells us nothing.

Julian watches with sharp eyes, then steps forward with a subtle nod that signals it's time for his turn. "Let me," he says, and there's something chilling about his calm. Daniel's eyes flicker with a hint of real fear creeping in.

"Gonna sing like a bird now, Danny boy?" Julian taunts as he pulls something from his pocket.

The next minutes are a blur of sound and motion, and the atmosphere is thick with a sadistic kind of tension that even I'm not comfortable with. Then, when Julian's methods start to bear fruit, the room drops to a hush.

"Alright! Alright," Daniel gasps, the veneer of defiance cracked and broken. "It's Edward Frost... He's working with the Nightingales."

The name is like a punch to the gut. The Nightingales are vipers in human clothing. I let loose a string of curses, each a venomous expulsion of contempt for that name. The Nightingales are notorious, infamous in the worst ways, for dealing in the darkest corners of the criminal trade. Human trafficking. Souls are bartered and sold like cattle. Julian and I run our operations clean of such filth. As long as they kept their hands out of our territories, we turned blind eyes to their cancerous existence. Now, they've reached into my life. Out for Isabella. At that moment, our tacit truce crumbles to dust.

I grab him by the collar with an iron grip. "How does Jackson fit into all this?"

I demand, trying to piece together this treacherous puzzle. Daniel grimaces with pain stamped on his features, but his words tumble out now in a rushed bid for relief.

"Edward got his hands on a will. Old legal papers. Isabella's due for a fortune on her twenty-fifth. A massive one. But see, Ed's been bleeding chips," Daniel reveals with a bitter chuckle. "Owed sharks like Jackson more than he could ever pay back."

I release him slightly as my mind races. "And the deal? Spell it out."

Daniel coughs, and spittle of blood and desperation mix together. "It was all a set-up. Jackson marries Isabella for access, right? Edward, that snake, he planned to double-cross everyone from the get-go. He figured if Isabella... if she were out of the picture, he'd get it all. No intention of splitting anything. Look, Damien, he's the one who had your brother done in. I'll bet my life on it. Edward wants the cash, and with Isabella gone, it falls right into his lap."

A cold dread washes over me. So this is the game. Money. The root of betrayal and corruption. If Isabella dies, everything unravels, and the vultures swoop in. "And if she lives, they get nothing. Is that it?"

He nods, almost frantic now. "Exactly. Ed never wanted to share. Still doesn't. It's all for him. It's always been. And your wife has no idea about any of it."

The revelation hits me like a tidal wave of corroding acid. Her own father is the architect of her misery. I can feel the sting of betrayal as if I've been bitten by a snake. The animal rage in my blood simmers with each passing second over the greediness of that man. The man who should have protected her above all has marred her life in the worst way imaginable, and for what? Filthy money.

Julian's observation hauls me back from my thoughts. "Go, Damien. I'll handle things here. Go home to your wife. I'll make sure Daniel gets back home."

His tone is stringent, a taut line of certainty against the disorder I'm trying to contain. I hesitate as my instincts scream to stay, to make sure Julian doesn't bring another war in the middle of the shit we have going on.

Julian looks at me and sighs, his voice as cold as the steel in his eyes. "He'll be alive *and* in one piece."

Victor and I exchange a glance. We turn, heading for the door with the weight of every step pulsating with unspent fury.

Julian's voice stops me just as we cross the threshold. "Congratulations on your marriage, Damien."

I simply nod as I walk out the door. Outside, I pull Victor aside. "Scour the streets. I want every man available looking for Isabella's father. Keep eyes on the Nightingales. Sharp eyes." My orders come out clipped like shards of glass wrapped in iron. Victor nods, already moving to execute the command.

As I settle into the car, the leather of the seat feels cold and alien. The window rolls down with a smooth hum, and I catch Victor's attention one last time.

"Not a word of this, Victor. Not to anyone." My eyes lock with his, an unbreakable seal on my command. "Isabella can't find out. Especially not now," the words come heavy, laden with fear I can't show. "She's pregnant, and I can't have her stressed, understand?"

Understanding flickers in his eyes, and I see the promise there before I roll up the window, sealing myself away from the world I'm about to turn upside down.

As the cityscape blurs past, I can't shake the image of Isabella from my mind. Her smile, the curves of her body, the life we're building. My hands grip the steering wheel until my knuckles whiten as every fiber of my being is taut with the importance of keeping her safe. I grind my teeth, and the taste of my own frustration is bitter on my tongue. It's been a while since I've felt this cornered, this wrathful. They dare to target my wife, my unborn child? My jaw clenches as the cold determination sets in. There'll be no more games.

They've awakened a beast they had forgotten lay dormant.

I'm Damien fucking Blackhart, and the streets whisper my name with a mix of fear and respect. It's high time these would-be criminals remember why that is. I feel the darkness stir within me. The lethal calm that precedes the storm. They've chosen their fate the moment they crossed into my world. As the night folds around me, I become the shadow they should fear. My time has come to remind them.

# CHAPTER 24

## Damien

The Nightingale's have overstepped and trespassed into my domain. They've dared to lay hands on my wife. To shadow her with their vile intentions. It's a declaration of war, a signal that they are either foolishly brave or ignorantly seeking their demise. My mind is clear, laser-focused on the retribution that awaits. I know there's a storm on the horizon. It's dark and inevitable. The city's underworld will tremble. The ground will soak with the consequences of their audacity. I'll be ready. I have to be.

When the war descends upon us, as it surely will, I will stand unshaken. I'll erase them from our streets and from our lives with the cold finality of death itself. They've mistaken my patience for weakness, my silence for apathy. Soon, they'll understand the depth of their error. There will be no hesitation, no mercy. The Nightingales will fall, and peace will be bought with their blood. It's just a matter of when.

The moment I step through the doors of our home, the weight on my shoulders eases ever so slightly. Here, with Isabella, I can breathe. The soft light envelopes her like a halo, and for a fleeting moment, all is right in the world. I watch her, admiring her strength and the quiet way she moves about, unaware of the darkness her name is wrapped in. Despite that tension-filled day when I left her side to confront Daniel, I've been her constant shadow, ensuring she's alright.

Now, we sit together in the dimming light of the evening with her head resting against my chest and my fingers entwined with hers. In this, at least, I find solace. In her warmth. I her proximity. I'll do whatever it takes to keep this peace, this normalcy for her. She murmurs something about dinner, her voice a soothing balm, but my thoughts are on the storm brewing beyond these walls, of the retribution that's coming. Yet, for her, for the life she carries within, I'll wear the mask of calm a little longer. I'll keep the fury at bay and let love be my anchor in the storm. Isabella lifts her head from my chest and searches my face.

"You look tired, Damien. You should get some rest," she says, her voice laced with concern. For a moment, I'm tempted by the thought of succumbing to slumber next to her.

"I'll get rest when you're safe," I reply, my voice low but firm.

The image of her being attacked a week ago by those thugs flashes in my mind. The rage at her vulnerability bubbles within me, but I suppress it.

She lets out a gentle sigh, an expression of exasperation and a challenge. "I'm fine. There's no need to watch me every second of the day," she insists tenderly. "Plus, when you're not here, you have like ten guards watching me. I'm safe."

I gaze at her, and my hand instinctively reaches up to rub down her cheek, feeling the warmth of her skin. "You are my wife. The mother of my unborn child," I murmur, allowing my deep-seated fears to color my words. "Your safety is my number one priority. I won't rest until I eliminate the threat."

Her green eyes hold a depth of understanding, yet she sighs before speaking again. "Tell me what you know. Maybe I can help."

I shake my head, the motion a sharp dismissal of her offer. "No. I don't want you in this, love. It's too dangerous, and I'd lose my mind if something happened to you," I say with a finality that I hope will deter her.

Isabella's eyes widen as she processes my words, searching my face for the truth of them. "You really mean that, don't you?" she asks with a whisper of vulnerability in her voice. "Love..."

Without a word, I pull her on top of me, our physical closeness an unspoken reassurance. Gently, I frame her face with my hands, forcing her to see the sincerity in my eyes.

"I think it's time you realize just how much you mean to me, Bella," I say earnestly. "For a man who's lived in darkness, you're the only light I've ever craved. You've turned my world upside down, Isabella. I'll burn down anything that tries to take you from me."

She sucks in a breath, clearly taken aback by the intensity of my statement. I watch the emotions play across her face, seeing the moment she understands that this isn't just another protective measure. It's the confession of a truth she's never fully seen.

I sit here, holding her, and I can't help but think of all the ways I've tried to show her how vital she is to me. How central she's become to my world. It seems like every action and every decision has been a silent shout of that truth. As the thoughts churn in my mind, I realize with a jolt of frustration that it hasn't been enough for her to truly understand. She's the reason I'm gentler, the reason I pause to think twice, the reason I've contained the darkness that used to dominate my actions.

My life, once a solitary struggle for power, has been irrevocably altered by her presence. I want to shake the world for her and turn it upside down, just so she grasps the depth of my feelings. Yet here we are, with her still questioning the extent of my devotion, and it's like a dagger to my chest. The realization stings. That my love hasn't been as transparent as I believed.

The tenderness in my touch, the protective shadow I've become, my relentless pursuit of her safety. It's all for her. Yet, she hasn't fully gotten the hint. Leaning forward, I give her the softest of kisses, lingering just a moment so she can feel the weight of my feelings.

"I love you," I whisper against her lips, my voice barely a whisper yet loaded with all the emotion I hold in the depths of my soul. As I pull back, I lock my gaze with hers. "You're the most important thing in my life," I say with conviction, wanting her to know the full extent of my commitment. "I didn't marry you simply because you're pregnant with our child. I fell in love with you."

"You see darkness in me, and yet, you're the light I've always reached for. Don't doubt my love, Isabella. It's as fierce and possessive as the man before you, and it's yours, completely and irrevocably," I tell her.

She remains speechless, her eyes wide, reflecting a storm of emotions. My heart clenches as I watch her emotions shift from shock to surprise and then to a hesitation that claws at my insides. She's unsure, and it's as though I can physically feel the wariness that she's trying to hide. The silence stretches between us, loaded with unspoken words and the weight of my revelation hanging heavy in the air.

I hold my breath, willing her to understand, to see the raw truth in my confession. My gaze never falters. I want her to read in my eyes the certainty that she's become the axis of my existence.

Seizing the silence, I continue as my hand still caresses

her face. "This isn't just about wanting you, Isabella. It's about owning every moment that takes your breath away. You're not just in my world; you are my world. And I protect what's mine at all costs."

"We may have started off on opposing sides, drawn together by fate or chance, but our attraction, it's undeniable, like magnets drawn together. It's you and me, baby, against whatever comes our way," I profess, certain of this truth above all else.

I wrap my hand in her hair and pull her to me, losing myself in a kiss that speaks of all the unsaid words between us. Both of us moan at the contact. In this moment, it's as if I'm affirming that she's real, that she's truly with me, grounding me against the chaos that lies in wait. The kiss deepens, fueled by fears of what's to come and the relentless drive to protect. We are the eye of a storm, clinging to each other as everything clsc threatens to buckle under the impending storm.

As Isabella's nightgown hits the floor, the air between us charges with an electric tension, both heavy and intensely private. The sight of her figure, freer and more entrancing without the fabric barrier, seizes my attention completely. I feel a primal reaction stirring within me, a response that is both fiercely protective and deeply yearning.

My hand extends, not with urgency, but with reverence, to rest upon her slightly rounded belly where our future grows. The intimacy of the touch, the connection to both my wife and my unborn child, anchors me to this moment. I stare at her, the moonlight casting ethereal shadows that dance across her skin, and find the words spilling from my lips with a fervor I can't contain.

"You are my everything. When I think of all the danger out there, it's your face I see, your smile that I'm fighting to protect. This love, our family. It's my vow to you, stronger than any fear and mightier than any foe we face." My voice is unwavering, my conviction as clear as the star-studded sky above us.

I lift up and pull my boxers down, desperate to get inside of her. Once I kick them off, Isabella wastes no time lifting and sliding down my length. The moans we release echo through the room. She's so slick and hot, and it's heaven being inside of her. I grip her with an almost bruising force and pull her down onto me. Every time she lifts and comes down, my body raises to meet hers, thrusting fervently inside her.

We move faster and harder, her moans gaining in pitch, and I can tell she is close. Her orgasm rips through her, and her body shakes from the force of her orgasm. Wetness gushes between us, making it slicker for my cock. She slumps over, drained from the intense orgasm she just had. I pull out and turn her over to her hands and knees.

I don't give her time to adjust before thrusting inside her once again. With a desperate grunt, I pull out before entering her again, harder and deeper than before. She grabs the sheets and screams into the bed.

"That's right, baby," I tell growl breathlessly. "Take all of me."

My hands move from her hips to her shoulders, to her wrap around her hair. My fist tightens in her hair, and I pull her head back, using it as leverage to strengthen my thrusts. I lean forward, kissing her racing pulse and sucking, leaving my mark on her skin. She's starting to moan louder now, and I know she's getting closer to another orgasm. Reaching my arm around, I circle her clit furiously until she screams out in ecstasy. Whimpers and sobs pour from her mouth, but I don't let up my harsh pace.

"So fucking tight and wet, love," I moan as my cock jerks inside her as I get closer to coming.

I pull out, flip her over again, and slam back into her. When I come inside my wife, I want to look into her eyes.

"I love you," I tell her as I continue to thrust.

"I love your heart."

Thrust.

"I love your smile."

Thrust.

"I love the way you moan when I'm inside you."

Thrust.

"I love everything about you."

I crash my mouth against hers, our tongues dueling with each other as I deepen the kiss. I grasp her neck, yanking her to me so that were chest to chest. My thrust turns slow, torturous, and she moans again. It doesn't escape my notice that she doesn't say it back. I'll give her time. She doesn't have to say it right now. I'll do everything in my power to get her to love me, even if I spend the rest of my life trying.

"Damien," she moans in frustration because my slow thrusts aren't enough.

Her breathy moans do me in, and I think about the attack on her. How, if those asshole had succeeded, I wouldn't be here inside my wife right now. I feel a savage desire to claim her. To fuck her so hard and so deep that every inch of her knows it's mine. I drink the ecstasy from her lips and relish the feel of her soft curves in my hand. I lean back, grab her ass, and increase my pace. She clamps hard around my dick as she orgasms again. Her lips part, and needy sobs break free, mixing with moans as pleasure takes over her body.

I've never been so ravenous for her, and no matter how hard, how deep I go, I can't get enough. I'm starting to think that no matter how many times I fuck my wife, it will never be enough. I'm addicted to her pussy. I feel tingles of pleasure flow down my spine. My balls tighten, and I swell inside her, preparing to give her the biggest load I've ever given her. If she weren't already pregnant, this would definitely do the trick.

That last thought causes me to erupt. I snarl and pound inside her as I empty my seed into her depths. My arms tighten around her, and I drop my head to her shoulder as I come so fucking hard, I swear I see stars. I inhale deeply as I drag my nose over her skin. She smells like sex. Like me. I pull out of her, and we fall onto the bed, side by side.

Isabella's breathing steadies into the rhythm of sleep and the room is calmed by her peaceful presence. The afterglow of our fervent union still lingers on my skin, but there's an ache in my chest that hasn't subsided. She hasn't said it back. The three words that would bind her to me as I am irrevocably hers.

As I listen to the gentle cadence of her slumber, I promise myself again. I will spend every day showing her the depth of my affection, proving that my love is not just a fleeting emotion but a steadfast commitment. I know Isabella holds a tenderness for me in her heart, possibly skirting the edges of love, and that is a flame I vow to nurture until it matches the inferno in me.

The shrill ringing of my phone breaks the silence of the night, and my eyes snap to it immediately. Careful not to jostle Isabella, I slide out from the sheets, stealing a glance at her peaceful face. I pick up the phone from the nightstand, the screen's glow the only light guiding me through the darkness.

"Speak," I grumble into the phone with a low voice to keep from waking her.

I hastily grab my clothes and slide into my pants with swift movements. The cool fabric against my heated skin feels abrupt and alien after the warmth of our closeness. I button my shirt, not bothering with the precision I usually take. I snatch up my shoes, deciding against lacing them, and slip into them as I make my way toward the secrecy the night holds, leaving the serenity of her sleeping form unbroken.

"Boss, it's Victor. About the shredded papers..." There's a pause hanging in the air before he continues. "We've got nothing. Someone made damn sure to mix up the important stuff with a load of bullshit."

I clench my jaw as a curse slips between my lips, "Are you kidding me? And the Nightingales?"

Victor exhales wearily. "They're like shadows, Damien. We've got credible intel they're in town, but they might as well be ghosts."

Another curse escapes me, terse and biting. "Keep your eyes peeled. We can't let our guard down, not now."

"Got it," he says.

We end the call, and I'm already moving toward my office. If it weren't for my brother's damn betrayal, war wouldn't be at my doorstep. Yet that same betrayal brought Isabella into my life. Now, she's more than a presence in my bed. She's my wife, the mother of my child, the woman who owns my heart. Can I stay angry at Jackson for that? It's a debt I'll never be able to repay.

I stride into my office with the remnants of anger and frustration still burning through my veins. With a swift turn, I pour myself a drink. Each drop seems to echo in the silence of the room. I tilt the glass, letting the amber liquid coat the ice before bringing it to my lips. The smooth burn is a temporary distraction from the chaos that threatens to spill from my thoughts.

I wander over to the balcony doors and push them open, inviting the night breeze to sweep into the stifling stillness of the office. It's a welcome caress against my skin, and I close my eyes for a moment, allowing the coolness to temper the heat of my anger. The sounds of the nightlife filter through the open space. It's a world apart from the one within these walls, and for a brief moment, I let it enthrall me, offering an escape from the imminent threats and the weight of my duties.

Settling in my chair, I decided to power through some work, letting the soft clicks of the keyboard fill the void of the night. With Isabella's love in my hands and our future unwritten, I'm struck by the paradox of it all. Out of chaos has come the greatest gift. Before long, I'll slip back into bed, feeling her warmth against me once again, and for a moment, all will be right in the world.

# CHAPTER 25

## Isabella

Today is my doctor's appointment. I feel Damien's hand entwined with mine as we exit the house, and the familiar weight of his touch grounds me. I glance at the line of vehicles, one SUV stationed in front and one trailing behind us. There are more bodyguards than usual flanking us with their sharp eyes, scanning for any potential threats.

I can't help but feel a swell of gratitude for the extra precautions Damien insists on. It's evidence of his unyielding resolve to protect our growing family. The ride to the hospital passes in a blur, with my mind preoccupied with the flutter of nerves and excitement at the thought of my first checkup.

We pull up to a secluded back entrance and quickly disembark. The guards are swift, ushering us inside with practiced efficiency. Inside the hospital, the halls are silent, eerily devoid of the usual hustle and bustle, and I can't hide my bewilderment.

"Where is everyone?" I ask, seeking Damien's eyes for answers.

"I had it closed to outsiders today. Everyone around may know not to mess with me, but I'm not taking any chances."

His words ripple through me, a mix of reassurance and a stark reminder of the world we inhabit, where caution is not a luxury but a necessity.

The waiting room is a sterile void. I fidget in the stiff chair with my hands clasping and unclasping in my lap. My heart taps a rapid rhythm against my chest like an unsettling drumbeat that echoes my anxiety. The life growing inside me feels both wondrous and terrifying. Damien's hand, warm and reassuring, finds mine, and I cling to it like a lifeline.

His thumb strokes the back of my hand, a simple gesture that helps to anchor me against the surge of my racing thoughts. He's been wonderful since we discovered a baby was on its way. His excitement is a kind of balm to my own whirlwind of emotions. With him by my side, I feel strong enough to brace the tidal waves of my impending motherhood.

Damien leans in closer, his voice a soft murmur meant only for me. "Relax, love. It's going to be alright," he assures me with serene confidence that he seems to wear effortlessly, like his tailored suits.

I can't seem to echo his calm, and my words spill out in an anxious rush. "I can't, Damien. I just... can't.." The corners of my eyes prickle with the threat of tears.

"You can," he says. "Don't get lost in that pretty little head of yours."

"Damien, what if something's wrong with the baby? What if—" I start.

"Isabella," his voice is a gentle interruption, a soothing melody against the clamor of my fears. "Relax, baby. Stressing isn't good for either of you."

"But how can I? What if our baby isn't healthy? I've read about so many genetic disorders and the probabilities and the risks. It's all so overwhelming," I tell him.

He gives me a look, one that's meant to still the ocean

storming inside of me. "Isabella, come on, you know you can't think like that. Our baby is going to be just fine."

"You can't promise that. There's cystic fibrosis, there's Down syndrome, what if—" I continue in a rush.

His lips meet mine in an effective seal against the torrent of my spiraling thoughts. When he pulls back, his eyes hold mine in a steady gaze. "We'll handle it together, whatever comes our way. But for now, everything is fine, my love."

A gentleman in the doctor's coat strides forward with an air of confidence trailing in his wake. "Mr. and Mrs. Black-hart," he greets with a bow of his head and kindness in his eyes. "It is nice to see you."

Damien's hand tightens over mine, and with a guiding nudge, he introduces the man before me. "Bella, this is Dr. Nigel, the family doctor," he says as if the title alone should offer some form of comfort.

I study Dr. Nigel's face, searching the lines that time has etched onto his features. It takes a mere moment for the recognition to set like concrete in my stomach. He is the same doctor who was there when Jackson died

My voice, when I find it, is barely a whisper. "Nice to meet you, Dr. Nigel."

The words feel brittle on my lips, tasting of a time when his presence shadowed loss, not the potential joy of life we're here to celebrate today. As I stand beside Damien, facing Dr. Nigel, memories cascade through my mind like a relentless current. It feels like another lifetime when I was tethered to Jackson, where days melted into a monochrome of fear and desolation. That marriage was a storm, unrelenting and cruel, leaving scars hidden beneath the surface, a stark contrast to the gentle touch of Damien's hand in mine now.

Jackson's shadow had loomed over me, a threatening specter that dictated my every move, every breath. I was a bird in a gilded cage, clipped wings wrapped in silk, with a silent scream lodged in my throat. My former life was a carefully constructed façade, a smile painted on to cover the bruises of my spirit and the dread that nestled in the pit of my stomach each night.

Damien, however, is the dawn after the darkest night. Where there was once control and fear, Damien offers freedom and security. He loves without stipulations or suffocating expectations. His love empowers me, bolsters me through my insecurities, and lends me strength in the face of my anxieties. Just his presence, solid and unwavering, erases the years of being diminished.

I know he has his own shadows, we all do, but together, it's as if we turn to face them as one. In Damien's embrace, I have found not only a partner but a co-author of a new chapter, one painted in hues of hope and shared dreams. A chapter where our baby will be born into a legacy of love, not fear.

"Please follow me," Dr. Nigel says, bringing me back to the present.

As Dr. Nigel leads the way, the clinic's corridors seem to fold in on me, a maze that ends with an examination room. The doctor's coat whispers against the silent halls as he guides us, and I match my steps with Damien's, drawing courage from the rhythm of our synchronized strides.

We arrive at the room, and Dr. Nigel gives me a brief, professional nod. "Please disrobe from the waist down and lay on the table with the sheet covering you."

My cheeks flush at the commonplace request. I slip behind the paper-thin privacy curtain, shedding my clothes with fabric pooling at my feet like the discarded shells of my former fears. Once on the table, the sterile sheet crinkles beneath me, a flimsy barrier between my exposed skin and the table.

I hear the click of the door as Dr. Nigel returns, his voice carrying a chewed-over comfort. "When was your last period? Any morning sickness? Any unusual levels of stress lately?"

The questions line up like soldiers, and I muster my responses, each measured and precise, yet I can't help feeling self-conscious as I speak. Dr. Nigel finishes with his questions. His brow furrowed in concentration as he made notes in my chart. Then, he glances up at me with a reassuring smile.

"We're going to try seeing the baby through your belly first," he says with optimism threading his voice. "If you're far enough along, we won't need to use the transvaginal wand." He readies the ultrasound machine, and a moment later, I feel the cold press of jelly on my skin. I can't suppress a shiver.

"It's cold," I blurt out almost reflexively.

"Sorry," Dr. Nigel apologizes with a quick, almost sheepish smile. "I forgot to mention that the gel would be cold."

Damien's protective instincts flash in his eyes, and his hand tightens around mine. "Well, don't forget anything else that makes her uncomfortable," he growls with a hint of warning in his tone. "Or I'll make you *painfully* uncomfortable."

"Damien!" I hiss, my whisper sharp as a whip-crack in the quiet room. "Stop it!"

His concern is endearing, but his overprotectiveness can be a touch too fierce. I squeeze his hand as a silent plea for calm. After all, we're here for reassurance, not confrontation. The cold gel spreads over my skin as Dr. Nigel starts moving the ultrasound device across my belly. The small discomfort fades to the background as my eyes fixate on the screen, where a blurry image flickers in and out of clarity.

Dr. Nigel's hand is steady, his movements precise as he searches for the life inside me. I hold my breath as a hopeful tension tightens in my chest with each pass. The room is silent except for the murmur of the machine and the quiet shuffle as Damien shifts closer. Then the doctor pauses, adjusts the device slightly, and there it is. That tiny yet profound flicker on the screen.

"There's your baby," Dr. Nigel announces with a smile in his voice that echoes the joy swelling in my heart.

A wave of awe washes over me, rendering me breathless as I stare at the screen. Our baby, a tiny beacon flickering in the safe harbor of my womb. Tears prick my eyes as joy and wonder converge within my chest. My hand tightens around Damien's, our interlocked fingers a symbol of unity as we witness the miracle together.

I break into a smile, unstoppable and bright, reflecting the happiness blooming inside me. With each beat of that minute heart on the screen, the fears and scars of my past dissolve further into insignificance, overshadowed by the overwhelming love and promise to embrace us at this moment.

"Hello, little one," I whisper, my voice a tender caress for the life we've created.

Damien leans forward with his face etched with fierce determination. "Dr. Nigel," he begins, his voice firm and insistent. "Can you run through the health indicators you're seeing? Is everything developing normally?"

The doctor meets his gaze, nodding. "Absolutely. Let's look here," he says, pointing to the ultrasound screen. "The baby's heart rate is strong, and the growth measurements align with the expected range for this stage. Everything appears to be progressing just as it should."

"What about Isabella's health?" Damien inquires, his eyes never leaving Dr. Nigel's. "Are there signs of pre-eclampsia, gestational diabetes, anything I need to be prepared to handle?"

Dr. Nigel adjusts the screen slightly and replies. "No, Mrs.

Blackhart's blood pressure is in the normal range. We'll continue to monitor, of course, but for now, you both should just focus on maintaining a healthy lifestyle."

Damien's expression softens, but the concern doesn't entirely vacate his eyes. "And the activity restrictions, can we go over those? I want to make sure we're not doing anything to risk any complications."

"Of course," agrees Dr. Nigel patiently. "Let's ensure you're clear on everything. Mrs. Blackhart should avoid heavy lifting, extreme sports, and anything overly strenuous. Light exercise, like walking and pregnancy-appropriate yoga, can actually be beneficial."

Satisfied for the moment, Damien gives my hand another reassuring squeeze, and the intensity in his eyes is replaced with a hint of gratitude. "Thank you, Dr. Nigel," he says. "It means everything to have your expertise guiding us through this."

Damien is finished with his questions, and his focus is now locked onto the flickering form on the screen. "That's our baby," he whispers, the softness of his voice carrying the weight of amazement and love. There's raw emotion in his eyes, a mirror of my own heart as it overflows with affection for that tiny, pulsing image.

Dr. Nigel's warm voice comes as a gentle interruption. "You're approximately five months along. Everything's looking exactly as we'd hope at this stage." He looks between us, the unspoken question hanging in the air. "Would you like to see if we can determine the sex of the baby? Are you interested in knowing?"

Our eyes meet, Damien's gaze reflecting the same desire and decision that stirs within me. We nod at each other, the decision made without words.

"No, Dr. Nigel," I say, my voice firm. "We want to be surprised."

He understands, giving a curt nod as he prints out the image of our child. "Take this, then," he says with a smile, handing us the picture. "A little keepsake of today's visit."

Dr. Nigel offers a last encouraging nod, and his professional demeanor mingles with genuine warmth. "I'll see you at your next appointment, Mrs. Blackhart. Keep taking care of yourself and the little one."

His voice trails off as he gestures to the ultrasound image still glowing from the screen. With a gentle smile, he backs away, giving Damien and me a moment alone. The door clicks shut behind him, and the reality of the room closes in. Just the two of us and the presence of a future we can barely begin to comprehend. I sit up slowly, the paper gown crinkling with my movements and the faint sound somehow grounding.

I swing my legs over the examination bed with unhurried movements. I need to get dressed and step back into the flow of everyday life, but for just a few heartbeats more, I let myself revel in the rush of emotions and the shared look with Damien that says everything about our journey ahead.

We drive away from the hospital in a comfortable silence that's filled with unspoken dreams and plans for our future. I notice Damien taking turns I don't recognize, and my forehead creases with confusion. Glancing at him, I'm about to ask where we're heading when he breaks the silence.

"Mom called this morning and asked us to come by after your appointment," he says casually as he navigates through the less familiar streets. Pulling into the driveway of his mother's house, my stomach knots with apprehension.

"Damien, you know your mother has never liked me," I whisper, my voice laced with worry.

He reaches over, takes my hand in his, and presses his lips to my knuckles. "Don't worry, love," he reassures me firmly. "I won't let any harm come to you. If she so much as disrespects you, I'll cut her down quickly." I nod, drawing strength from his protective vow, and with a deep breath, I ready myself to face whatever waits inside.

As Damien and I enter his mother's house, I take a moment to appreciate the understated elegance of the space. The house is nice, its charm distinct from the grandeur of our home but no less luxurious. We're barely through the door when the butler greets us, his postured frame arching into a small bow. Without a word, he gestures us forward, leading the way to the living room.

The moment we step into the room, Damien's mother rises from her seat, and her presence is commanding yet not overbearing. My heart hammers in my chest as she looks directly at me, but her eyes are softer than I have ever seen them.

"Isabella, Damien," she says, her voice surprisingly gentle. "Thank you for coming." Despite myself, I am touched by her acknowledgment. It's an unexpected warmth in a place I had steeled myself to feel cold and unwelcoming.

We all take our seats in the living room, and the atmosphere is thick with unease. Damien's mother's gaze never leaves mine, and I feel as if I'm under a microscope, her critical eye searching for something within me. Then, she takes a deep breath and begins to speak, her voice carrying a gravity that is both unfamiliar and disconcerting.

"Isabella, I... I want to apologize to you," she starts, her voice laced with sincerity. "I know I've been... less than hospitable in the past. It was even worse after... after Jackson's death." She pauses, seeming to gather the strength to continue. "I let my prejudice interfere with you feeling welcome into our family. Then, I let grief cloud my judgment. Jackson....he wasn't a saint. He was reckless, careless even. Often got himself tangled up with the wrong people, and... I regret that I wasn't there for him. That we, as a family, couldn't save him from himself."

Her eyes meet mine with a vulnerability I've never seen in her before. "My behavior towards you came from a place of guilt. For that, I'm truly sorry. I would like to be a part of my grandchild's life, and I'd like to start over with you. I never gave you a fair chance, and I see that now."

The room is heavy with her words, and for several moments, I'm utterly speechless. Fortunately, Damien steps in. "Mom, give Isabella some time to process this," he says firmly.

His mother nods, a small semblance of relief in her eyes. "That's all I can ask for," she replies.

With the awkwardness still permeating every corner of the room, we eat a small meal. Few words are exchanged, and the clinking of cutlery on fine china fills the silence. As we leave, I find myself reeling from the shock like a coat I can't seem to shed.

# CHAPTER 26

## Damien

The city glides by in a somber dance of shadows and streetlights as the familiar path to the warehouse unravels before us. I can feel the weight of the gun at my side, which is always a constant companion. Beside me, Victor drives in silence as his eyes scan the road and our surroundings with practiced paranoia. Our cargo tonight isn't ordinary. It's another batch of untraceable weapons meant to strengthen our ranks and tighten our grip on the city's underworld.

It's lucrative, it's necessary, and it's dangerous. The tension is as thick as the darkness that surrounds the industrial district we're heading into. Every shipment like this is a risk. Every deal is a potential double-cross. However, we're no strangers to the knife-edge balance of power and threat. It's the lifeblood of our operations. As the warehouse comes into view, I ready myself for another night's work in the family business.

Victor breaks the silence, casting a glance my way. "So, how's married life treating you, boss?" he asks, a sly grin tugging at his lips.

I chuckle as I maneuver one hand to fish out the sonogram from my pocket. "It's great," I say as I pass the glossy image to him.

Victor squints at the image, then breaks into his signature mischievous grin. "The kid looks weird. No surprise, given what his father looks like."

I can't help but laugh and shake my head. "Shut the fuck up, Victor."

His laugh echoes through the car. "Never thought I'd see the day. Damien Blackhart, ensnared by a woman and happy about having a baby."

With a nod of acknowledgment, I focus back on the road. "Neither did I," I admit, my voice more somber than intended. I'm married with a kid on the way. Never in a million years did I think I'd be here. With my dead brother's widow, no less. It's crazy, but I have no regrets. Isabella is mine.

Victor eyes me with sudden understanding. "Holy shit, you're in love," he says with incredulity tinged with respect.

I can't suppress the smile that forms on my face. "Yeah," I confess. "I told her, but she hasn't said it back yet."

"That fucking sucks. Don't worry," he says, clasping my shoulder in solid reassurance. "I've seen you two together. She loves you, even if she won't admit it yet. She's got to acknowledge it herself first. That she's fallen for a guy who was her captor. Who almost destroyed her. Once that clicks, she'll be all over you, man."

"Thanks for the pep talk, Dr. Love," I reply with amusement, layering over the gratitude in my voice.

We share another round of laughter that fills the car, overlaying the tension of the business that lies ahead. My mind momentarily drifts away from the underworld's shadows to thoughts of Isabella. Every day, I see it more clearly. The way she looks at me is softer, more tender. She's changing, growing round with our child, and there's this glow about her that outshines the darkness I deal with daily. I find myself yearning to leave all the chaos behind, to immerse myself in the tranquility that surrounds her.

Time spent with Isabella unfurls a part of me I hadn't believed existed. A gentleness buried beneath layers of necessary ruthlessness. I fantasize about a life where my days are filled with her laughter and our future child's babble, rather than the cold metal of a gun and the stench of blood. She's my unexpected salvation, a beacon guiding me to a shore I never thought I'd want to reach. As we pull up to the warehouse, a cold prick of unease stabs at me. The front is deserted, void of the usual guards who should be standing watch.

"Damn it," I curse under my breath. "My own men can't even follow a simple schedule." Disappointment grinds inside me like a drill, twisting with the certainty that I'll have to remind somcone of their duties. With a heavy hand.

Stepping inside with Victor close behind, the atmosphere is thick with wrongness. My gaze darts through the dim interior, noting the crates of incoming arms scattered haphazardly. A spark of rage ignites within me. What the hell happened here? Not a single crate has been shuffled into place for tonight's operation.

A few more strides and the answer slams into me with the subtlety of a sledgehammer. My men are splayed across the concrete. Their stillness is unnatural and profound. Someone killed them. I don't think it was Jose because he seemed content with our agreement. He wouldn't just attack, especially knowing that I would retaliate tenfold. He doesn't have the manpower or army that I have. It doesn't make the Valdezs any less of a threat. They are a force to be reckoned with, but he'll think twice before attacking me.

"What the fuck?" Victor murmurs, his voice catching on a whisper of disbelief. My hand unconsciously edges towards the steel security of the gun at my side. This isn't just an infraction. It's sabotage. A blaring, bloodied declaration that someone is out to get me.

The acute sound of shattering glass yanks my attention toward the ceiling as an explosion of movement erupts throughout the warehouse. Men in dark tactical gear cascade down from above, guns already blazing a relentless hail of lead. Instinctually, Victor and I draw our weapons.

"Down!" I bark to Victor, shoving him towards the safety of the shipping crates as bullets kiss the concrete where our bodies stood moments before. Rounds pierce the air with piercing howls in a chaotic symphony of destruction that threatens to swallow us whole.

"Motherfucker! This is an ambush!" Victor seethes, his eyes blazing with fury as he returns fire systematically, trying to make every shot count.

I can't help but agree, feeling the adrenaline surge through my veins like wildfire. "No shit, Sherlock! Cover me!" I shout, slipping out of our cover to fire back. My movements are sharp and calculated under the rush of danger. Each thunderous burst from my gun syncs with my racing heartbeat.

As I duck back into cover, metal shards and wood splinters rain around us, splintering off the crates that barely shield us from the onslaught.

"Who the hell tipped them off?" I growl, glancing at Victor. His face is a mask of concentrated aggression, but I can see the wheels turning behind his glare.

"I don't know, boss. But we're sitting ducks if we don't move!" he yells, ejecting a spent magazine and slamming in a fresh one with practiced ease.

I nod, mapping out a path to a back exit in my mind. "On three, we make a break for the door. Lay down some cover. Then bolt for it. Follow my lead." My resolve steels as I set my jaw, preparing for the sprint through the ballet of bullets.

"Got it. Three, two, one. Now!" Victor shouts, and we leap from cover, weapons blazing as we weave our way to survival, our fate penned by the pull of triggers and the speed of our stride.

Bullets whiz by, shredding the air with their lethal song. Victor and I manage just a few short, desperate dashes before we're forced to duck behind a new line of crates. My ears are ringing, but it's William Hawthorn's voice that cuts through the chaos.

"Damien Blackhart," Hawthorn bellows over the relentless gunfire. "You thought you could take my son and torture him without repercussions?"

"Fuck you!" I scream back, defiance raising the hairs on the back of my neck. I rise barely enough to glimpse my targets and fire off a few more rounds with my heart hammering against my chest.

I can almost hear the smirk in Hawthorn's voice as he replies. "I'll give my thanks to your informant. It seems they always have accurate information."

I'm seething as the anger pulses through me with every beat of my heart.

"I'm going to enjoy inflicting pain on you," he promises, but it's a promise I intend to turn back on him.

Suddenly, Victor taps my shoulder, pulling me back to the grim reality. "We don't have enough bullets to take them on. We're not prepared for this," he whispers with irritation in his eyes.

Exhaling a shaky breath, I survey the weapon-littered warehouse. "We have a whole fucking warehouse full of guns, Victor. Grab one and fucking kill them," I snarl, willing my mind to stay sharp despite the racing of my pulse. With a nod, we both focus on surviving. No planning, just instinct and the glint of metal in our hands.

Bullets zip past, leaving trails of deadly intentions in the air. My hand is steady, even as the rest of me is a coiled spring, ready to react. We're outnumbered but not outgunned. Not yet. I glance at Victor, exchanging a nod that speaks volumes. We've been through hell together, but this, this is a situation that will burn away everything but our raw resolve to survive.

I squeeze the trigger and my gun answers with a bark that's almost reassuring. I can't afford the luxury of fear, can't indulge in the bitter taste of doubt. Instead, I aim and fire, aim and fire, a relentless determination driving each movement. I count the shots, calculating the odds with each exchange. The air thickens with the scent of gunpowder.

I duck behind a crate just as it splinters under a spray of bullets. Bits of wood and metal embed themselves in the walls. Death lingers close. I can almost feel its breath on the nape of my neck. I push it back, as I always do, forcing it to wait for another who might be less vigilant, less desperate to live.

We move like shadows, from cover to cover is a deadly choreography set to the rhythm of gunfire. Each breath comes short and fast, matching the tempo of our desperate defense. With every glance, every flickering thought, I'm searching for an escape, a way out. All I see are closed doors. All I hear is the music of warfare, a dirge that I refuse to be the crescendo of.

I hurl my emptied gun to the ground with a vow for retribution echoing in my mind. My arms coil, striking out like vipers. A fist crashes into the first attacker's jaw, and the impact vibrates through my arm. I feel his bone give, but there's no time to contemplate; I pivot.

An elbow meets another's temple, a dull thud over the sound of gunfire. He stumbles, but I'm already moving, lashing out a leg that hooks an assailant's knees. He falls, and I'm on him, driving my knee into his ribs. Each hit is a statement, an exclamation of my refusal to die.

Twisting, I block a punch, wincing as the force vibrates up my forearm, and retaliate with a head butt. Blood, theirs or mine, it doesn't matter, spatters. I'm an avatar of violence, channeling years of honed aggression with every strike, every bone-crushing connection between flesh and bone. A brief lull in the gunfire tells me it's time.

Lunging to the nearest crate, I flip open the top, fingers skimming over cold steel until they wrap around the grip of a semi-automatic. The magazine slams home. Chamber, round's ready. It's heavier than my handgun, promising a different kind of dance. I peek over the crate and squeeze the trigger. Bullets spit out, my controlled bursts of retaliation.

William's orders slice through the mayhem, each word dropping like cannon fire. "Don't stop! Take down, Victor. I want Blackhart alive!"

I bark out a cold laugh with adrenaline surging through my veins. "Good luck with that, Hawthorn!" I shout back, defiance fueling my resolve. My voice is rough, serrated with wrath as I unleash my challenge. "I'll put every last one of your men in the ground, and then, I'm coming for you!"

Gunfire punctuates my vow. I can almost feel the sinister weight of Hawthorn's gaze, but it doesn't slow me down. It ignites a fire inside me. This is more than survival now. It's the crushing weight of inevitability, and I am its relentless harbinger.

A blur of motion catches my eye. It's a gunman rounding the crate at an angle I didn't anticipate. In a rush of combat instinct, my fingers tighten on my weapon, but it's too late. He lunges, a hand clamps over mine as he wrenches the gun from my grip. We dive to the ground with our bodies entwined in a desperate struggle for control. His face is close enough that I can see the determination and fear behind his eyes.

His finger finds the trigger, squeezing off a round in wild

panic. A hot streak of pain sears up my arm as the bullet grazes flesh, adding fuel to the fury that's been burning within me since this fight commenced. Gritting my teeth against the sharp sting, I snake my arm free and strike him in the throat. It barely fazes him, and we continue to grapple on the cold concrete with each of us battling to gain the upper hand in this lethal dance.

Suddenly, the gunman produces a blade, and he succeeds in stabbing at my side. It's a shallow wound, but searing pain spreads from it like wildfire. With an explosive effort, I seize the moment, twisting his head at an unnatural angle with one decisive motion. His body goes limp as the life is extinguished from his eyes before he even hits the ground. I'm gasping with the copper tang of blood on my tongue when Victor's hand clasps my shoulder.

"Come on," he pants, urgency clear in his voice as he helps me to my feet. He's right. We can't lose momentum. It's the only thing keeping us a heartbeat ahead of the grave.

I'm half running, half stumbling towards the back door, with Victor's hand as my saving grace clamped firmly on my shoulder. As we burst into the damp night air, sirens sing in the distance, a foreboding lullaby for the unclaimed dead we're leaving behind. The cold against my skin feels like a reprieve from the stifling prison of gun smoke and blood.

Without a word, we sprint to the car. My hand fumbles with the handle, slick with blood, as we throw ourselves inside. We're moving before the doors even slam shut, and the tires screech a desperate goodbye to the grave we narrowly avoided.

In the basked sanctuary of the car, Victor rummages through the glove compartment with hurried, shaking hands. He retrieves a first aid kit.

"Fuck!" The word cuts through the air when he applies

the gauze to my side, and a hiss of pain escapes my lips before I can reign it in.

"Sorry," he mumbles, his motions growing steadier as he binds the makeshift dressing to my flesh.

The city lights bleed together as we race away, leaving the battlefield behind. On impulse, my phone is in my hand, and I'm barking orders to the loyal few who didn't join tonight's operation.

"Clean up the warehouse," I spit out, voice edged with adrenaline and pain. "I want it sterile. No trace of us, not a single shell casing." I don't need to see them to know they'll jump into action. The dead can't answer for their crimes, and the living won't if they can help it.

As we meld into the churning current of the city, the weight of survival settles in. Those Hawthorn bastards will scour the earth to pin us down, but tonight we're ghosts. Unseen, unheard, untouchable. Tonight, we're the wraiths of vengeance, and nothing will lead back to us. Not a bullet and not a body.

My pulse hammers in my ears, matching the thrum of the engine as we weave through the city streets. Every shadow, every alleyway whispers of the retribution I'm owed. Retribution isn't a hope. It's an inevitability that I'll forge with fire and blood.

"They'll pay," I murmur the words carving themselves into the night. I look over at Victor, my fierce resolve reflected in his nod. "We'll hit them where it hurts," I vow, a dangerous promise that thrills with the certainty of a storm on the horizon. Tonight, we embrace the dark, but tomorrow, we become the blade that carves our justice into the heart of the Hawthorn empire.

# CHAPTER 27

## Isabella

I balance the tray of steaming food carefully as I push the door open with my shoulder, stepping into the dimly lit room where Damien has been resting. The clink of the porcelain bowls barely cuts through the heavy silence. For three days, I've cleaned his wounds and changed bandages. I remember vividly the chill that flowed through me when he burst through the door with Victor shadowing him, both of them looking like they'd clawed their way out of hell.

"It's just a scratch, love," Damien had offered when he saw my face, his voice a rough whisper of reassurances I wanted to believe. Through the fear constricting my throat, I demanded, with an authority that seemed to surprise us both, that he let me tend to him. He's been a model patient ever since.

He sits up straight in the bed as fingers dance across the keys of his laptop with a focus I've come to recognize as part distraction, part determination. The door creaks as I step in, losing a battle with the silence, and his piercing gaze lifts to meet mine.

"Isabella," he begins, and there's a softness in his tone that feels incongruent with the hard lines of his wounded body. "You don't have to do all this. I should be taking care of you."

I set the tray down on the dresser, and the bowls clink together.

My hands are steady as I respond. "I am your wife, Damien. We take care of each other."

The laptop snaps shut at an abrupt end to the gentle clatter of keys. He scoots to the edge of the bed, an invitation without words. As I move closer, the world seems to shrink to the charged space between us.

"Come here, wife," he murmurs, exhilaration threading his voice, and there's a hint of playfulness in the way he extends his arms. The distance closes, and I'm in his lap, enveloped by his heat. There's a scent of antiseptic masked by the familiar cologne that insists he's very much alive and here with me. His lips capture mine in a soul-searing kiss that speaks volumes of gratitude and love, of survival against the odds.

He pulls back just enough to breathe life into his words. "Thank you for taking care of me. I'm fine, really."

There's no 'fine' in the way he clings to me. No mediocrity in the emotions that charge the air. His fingers trace patterns of promised tomorrows on my back, and despite the chaos of our world, in his arms, I find a momentary peace.

I sit up and shimmy down his body. My hands move to pull down his boxers, and his dick springs free, hard, and ready. For a moment, I'm unsure if I should do this, but the heated look in his eyes gives me courage. I wrap my hand around his cock and stroke it up and down. He lets out the sexiest moan, so I move my hand faster, pumping hard. My head dips down, and I lick his tip before putting his length in my mouth.

"Fuck," he groans, lifting his hips, pushing deeper in my mouth.

His hands tangle in my hair, moving my head so that I'm bobbing up and down at his pace. My tongue swirls around his sensitive head, and another moan comes from his mouth.

That's it, baby," he growls. "Take all of me. Suck harder."

My gaze lifts to his face, and the look he's giving me spurs me to go faster. Suck harder. His hips are lifting off the bed, pushing deeper into my mouth.

"Fuck. Fuck. Fuck," he says harshly.

It only takes a few more minutes, and he's shooting his load down my throat. His grip is so tight on my hair that it brings tears to my eyes, but I don't care. I'm making him feel good. Making him lose control, and I swallow every last drop.

"Jesus, Bella," he moans when he finishes.

"I hope that relaxed you," I tell him when I sit up.

"Consider me relaxed, babe," he says. "You take good care of your husband."

The doorbell rings, and I can't help but release an involuntary sigh. "That would be your mother," I inform him with a weariness I don't bother to hide.

Ever since the incident, she's been a perpetual presence here, apparently to tend to her injured son. Yet all she really does is march around the place, issuing commands to the staff as though running a military operation. There's something so clinical about her approach as if the warmth of motherhood has eluded her altogether, and she can't quite grasp why I'd dirty my hands with bandages and ointments. Despite my efforts, she scrutinizes my every move, a silent indictment of my place in this household.

"Don't sound so happy," Damien teases with a wry smile, pulling me from my thoughts.

"I'm not happy," I reply, unable to keep the edge from my voice. "All she does is dictate. This isn't her house."

In response, he enwraps me in a tight hug. "I know she can be tiring, but she's doing what she knows. Don't let it get to you," he whispers softly.

With a collective breath, we prepare ourselves and descend the stairs to greet the matriarch. To our mutual surprise, there stands Aurora next to his mother, her presence like a cold draft. She's made no secret of her disdain for me. Since the day Damien slipped a ring on my finger, she's been nothing but distant. A frosty satellite in our orbit.

We settle into the living room with the tension humming beneath the surface of our practiced civility. Damien's mother is perched at the edge of her seat like a queen in court, her eyes sharp and assessing as they land on him.

"How are you feeling, dear?" she inquires, her voice striking a careful balance between concern and formality.

Damien gives me a sidelong glance, a private joke shared in the arch of his brow. "I'm fine, Mom. Really," he reassures, shifting slightly to ease his discomfort. "Isabella's been magnificent, as always, but both of you are making much fuss about nothing."

His mother nods once, brisk and businesslike, and lets the subject drop as though it's an insignificant footnote. "Very well," she says, her eyes now focusing on the papers she brought with her. "Let us discuss the gala tomorrow night. It's crucial we present a united front, especially after recent... events."

I eye Damien as he addresses his mother and sister. "Tina has been handling all of the gala preparations in my absence," he assures everyone with a confident nod. "I trust her implicitly. Everything will be according to our standards, and it will be fine."

As if on cue, Aurora leans back with a derisive snort. "Speaking of standards," she says, her eyes skating over me with poorly disguised disdain. "I'd be surprised if Isabella can still fit into a dress for the gala. Hasn't she put on a bit of...comfort weight, brother?"

The words hang heavy, and before I can muster my pride, Damien's voice cuts through the tension like a blade. "Enough, Aurora," he growls, his tone leaving no room for argument. "You know she's pregnant. If you disrespect my wife again, you will not appreciate the consequences."

I know I've picked up a little weight, but I'm barely showing. I have a small bump, but it just makes me look fat, like I'm out of shape, not pregnant. I'm surprised Damien didn't put up a fuss about me going. He's been very adamant about me staying home, but I guess this is one of those things that require his presence, and he'd rather take me than leave me home.

Aurora's face twists into a sneer. "You should be ashamed, Damien. Ashamed for marrying and having a baby with your brother's widow. Jackson was right about you."

The air shifts, suddenly electric with accusation. Damien's eyes bore into Aurora with confusion. "What was Jackson right about?" he demands.

Aurora falters, her features softening as she glances down. "He said... he said you were losing your place, putting everyone else before the family. I didn't want to believe it, but now I see it," she murmurs. "I'm sorry. I just don't want anything to happen to you. I was always worried about both you and Jackson, and now with him gone..." She trails off, shaking her head.

Damien's voice is firm. "You should be apologizing to Isabella."

Aurora's lips purse. "Over my dead body," she sneers.

Before the bitterness can claw any deeper, I interject. "Damien, it's alright." I force a smile, keen to move past Aurora's spite. "Let's focus on the gala."

Finally, the heavy front door clicks shut behind Damien's mother and sister, their departure a sweet, if not brief, reprieve from the tension. I exhale for the first time in hours. No sooner has the wave of relief washed over me than Damien's phone interrupts the fleeting calm with its insistent jangle. He shoots me an apologetic look before stepping out to take the call. Alone, I pad to the kitchen to pour myself a glass of juice.

Charles, the butler, enters the kitchen, finding me alone in the echo of the day's events. His approach is quiet and respectful.

"Mrs. Blackhart," he begins, his voice as poised as ever. "Might I have a moment to discuss the dinner menu for this evening? The chef requests confirmation of your preferences so he can begin the preparations."

I offer him a weary nod, pushing aside the encounters with Damien's mother and sister. "Certainly, Charles. I think something light would be fitting for today. Perhaps a grilled salmon with a side of steamed vegetables? And for Damien..."

Charles patiently waits as I contemplate Damien's preferences, given the day he's had.

"He usually enjoys a hearty meal, but with the gala tomorrow, let's keep it lighter for him as well. Maybe the same as mine, but include a small serving of roasted potatoes. He loves those." I finish with a small smile. The familiarity of catering to Damien's likes brings a semblance of normality.

"Of course, Mrs. Blackhart. It shall be as you wish," Charles assures me, his demeanor as unruffled as the starched collar he wears. "And may I say, it's a pleasure to see you taking such good care of Master Damien, especially now." His words are simple and sincere.

"Thank you, Charles. I appreciate that," I tell him.

With a final nod of acknowledgment, Charles departs,

leaving me with my thoughts as the scent of citrus from my juice mingles with the faint, yet robust fragrance of the impending dinner.

I head upstairs, juice in hand, seeking the sanctuary of our bedroom. When I enter, I'm met with the sight of Damien, wincing slightly as he dons his shirt, a clear sign he hasn't fully healed.

"Where are you going?" I ask, trying to mask the concern in my voice.

Damien doesn't meet my eyes. "It's Victor," he begins, fastening his cuffs with deft fingers. "We got a tip on where to find some people I've been looking for."

There's a cryptic edge to his words, a veil he draws to guard me from the darker corners of his world.

But I'm not easily fooled. "You're not telling me every-thing. I know you want to keep me safe," I probe, acutely aware of his evasion. "Damien, remember what keeping secrets does? Keeping me in the dark is dangerous."

Damien sighs deeply, his muscles tensing as he faces the inevitable confrontation. "I have to do this, Isabella," he implores, but I'm not swayed.

"No, you don't," I counter, narrowing my eyes. "You're still recovering. Just stay... one more day. For me."

His eyes soften, the battles he fights internally mani-festing in his gaze. Then, as if a decision has been made, he smiles mischievously and takes out his phone. He dials and puts it on speaker.

The ringing punctuates the silence before Victor's voice booms from the speaker. "What's up? Are we heading out?"

"Sorry, Vic," Damien's tone is light, with a hint of laugh-ter. "My wife won't let me out to play. She says I need to stay home."

Victor's laughter fills the room, and I can't help but roll my eyes at such boyish conversation.

"He needs to recover for at least one more day. We have the gala after that. Then you boys can have all the fun you want. Just don't come back bleeding everywhere again," I assert, raising my voice for Victor's benefit.

"Yes, ma'am," Victor chuckles on the other end, the sound thick with amusement. "Damien, when you're done being bossed around by your wife, you know where to find me."

Damien tosses his phone on the bed and begins to unbutton his shirt once more. I watch, rooted to the spot by the door, as he peels the garment from his torso, revealing the bare skin beneath that hasn't yet healed from his recent encounter. His eyes lift to meet mine, and the intensity I see there makes my breath catch in my throat. That look, it's more than a silent conversation. Heat pricks at the surface of my skin, and goosebumps trail like a shiver across my arms as anticipation builds within me.

"I should be out tearing the city apart right now," Damien says. "I'm filled with an energy that feeds my vengeance. But since I can't do that, I'll fill up my time doing something else."

Damien stalks toward me, and when he gets closer, he rips my clothes from my body. He spins me towards the window, and I place my hands on the glass. Before I have time to think, Damien enters me like a man possessed. His thrusts are unrestrained and savage, filling me over and over again. I moan against the glass as I claw for a grip. His breathing is ragged as his body moves with uncontrolled force, filling me completely.

"Damien," I moan because there's nothing else I can say.

His hand wraps around my throat, bringing me back against his chest. His brutal grip on me gives him leverage as he hammers into me until I'm screaming so loud that his staff has to think he's killing me. Damien buries himself deep inside me, breathing harshly into my neck. His cock jerks, and I know he's close.

I move back against him, helping the friction so he can reach his peak. His grip on my throat tightens, and he moans into my neck as his cock jerks violently within me. His body is shaking as he comes so hard. My body feels like noodles when he pulls out of me and drags me to the bed to continue releasing that energy.

Lying in bed, the wind from the open windows intertwines with our calm breathing. Damien's hand draws comforting circles on my back, a rhythm that lulls my racing thoughts. He sighs contentedly, a sound that vibrates through the quiet room.

"Damien," I begin, my voice barely above a whisper. "Will our lives always be like this? Wrapped in danger?"

He doesn't hesitate to respond. "This is the life I lead, Isabella," he says, his voice steady. "Danger is part of the territory. But don't be afraid. I will do everything in my power to keep us safe."

I pause, feeling the weight of my next words. "But what if... what if it becomes too dangerous? If one day it's the only way to protect our child, would you let me leave?"

His arms tighten around me, pulling me into his chest. "If it's to protect our child, yes," he admits with a heavy heart. "I would let you leave. But there will be no divorce. That's off the table. I'll take care of what needs to be handled and bring you both home back to me, just like it's supposed to be."

"Okay," I tell him.

"In this life or the next, you're irrevocably mine. My heart beats in that chest of yours, and every shadow that falls on you is cast by me. Remember that, Isabella, whenever you think of running," he says before leaning back.

I'm silent while I take in the gravity of his promise. I care for Damien deeply, more than I ever thought possible, yet the dangers that shadow his life are real and unpredictable. Can I embrace this life with all its uncertainties, or will the risks prove too great? This is the decision I must face.

## CHAPTER 28

### Isabella

Tonight is the night of the gala, and Damien has spared no expense to ensure I am pampered throughout the day, treating me like the royalty he believes I am. Early in the morning, a masseuse arrives, using her skilled hands to deftly knead away the tension that had built up over the chaotic past weeks. As relaxation seeps into my muscles, I can't help but feel a growing sense of anticipation for the evening ahead.

Around midday, a hair stylist crafts my hair into an elegant updo, with loose, cascading curls that frame my face with a softness that belies the firm resolve within me. Each strand is meticulously placed, the result being both lush and refined. As the sun dips lower, a makeup artist brushes my face into a flawless canvas. Smokey eyeshadow makes my eyes smolder, while a touch of rose on my cheeks provides a delicate contrast to the boldness of my gaze.

Finally, the pinnacle of the transformation comes as I slip into my gown. It's a breathtaking creation, red silk that clings and falls in all the right places, with a daring slit up the side that promises a glimpse of leg with every step I take. The fabric catches the light and seems to glow with its own inner fire, a reflection of the passion I carry within me. I secure the delicate straps of my high heels.

I stand before the mirror, taking in the woman who stares back at me. The reflection shows a queen, regal and ready to face whatever the night may bring. Damien walks into the room, and his confident steps falter for a moment as he takes in my appearance.

"Beautiful," he mutters under his breath, and there's a heat in his gaze that sends a ripple of excitement through me.

"None of that, Mr. Blackhart," I say with a playful warning in my tone, but the words only seem to draw him closer.

In a few strides, he's right behind me, with his hands finding their way to my hips to bring me flush against him, my back to his chest. His touch is tender yet possessive, and I feel his fingers trace down to rest on the slight bump of our growing child. Thanks to the artful scrunching of the dress, the baby is cleverly concealed. Yet to him, I know, it's the most beautiful part of all. Damien leans down and kisses the nape of my neck, sending a shiver down my spine.

"Tonight," he whispers against my ear. "You'll outshine every woman there." His breath is warm on my skin, and his words weave a thrilling anticipation through me. "Every man in the room will have their eyes on you."

His hands tighten possessively on my hips, pulling me harder against him. "But that ring on your finger makes a very clear statement. They can look all they want, but you're taken. You're *mine*." The heat of his proximity sends desire coursing through me. My breathing becomes deeper, more deliberate. I close my eyes for a moment to collect myself.

With an effort, I steady my voice, turning my head to

murmur back at him. "I'm not worried about other men, Damien. You shouldn't be, either." It's a declaration mingled with the fiery confidence his love has kindled in me. He pauses for a heartbeat, then his grip relaxes, and he steps back.

In a swift, fluid motion, Damien catches my hand, his fingers interlacing with mine, and leads me away from the room. Together, we move through the house and step out into the cool embrace of the evening. The waiting vehicles stand like silent sentinels, ready to bear us off into a night that's ours to conquer.

The vehicle purrs to a stop in front of the venue, a beautiful edifice rising like a dream against the evening sky. Damien steps out first, commanding and assured, and then circles the car to open the door for me. His hand is a promise as it enfolds mine, leading me out into the flood of cameras and flashing lights.

"Smile, love," he murmurs, and I summon my brightest smile, the one I save just for him, hoping it hides the panic fluttering in my chest.

I step out of the car, and it's like stepping onto a stage. The lights are blinding, and the chatter of the crowd is a deafening roar in my ears. The smile on my lips feels like a mask, pasted on to present a brave face to the gawking world, and I pray that I don't look as terrified as I feel. Like a deer caught in a frenzy of camera flashes.

We weave through the frenetic sea of photographers, and voices are tossed at us like darts, most of them business-related, probing Blackhart Enterprises. For a moment, the chaos makes me forget the reality of our lives. That the public sees Damien only as a successful businessman.

"Who is this lovely lady hanging on your arm, Mr. Blackhart? Is she going to be added to the other notches on your bedpost?" The question slices through the buzz, crude and sharp. My heart stutters and a flush of humiliation scorches my cheeks.

Damien halts and turns, his eyes finding the source with a deadly glare. "This is my wife," he growls. "Show some fucking respect." His command is swift. Someone from his team steps forward, and the offending journalist is swiftly removed from the crowd, and his protests are lost to the night.

"No one knew you were married," he shouts in defense as he's escorted away.

Damien just shrugs, nonchalant, his voice cold steel. "Whether you knew or not doesn't give you the right to speak about women that way."

A shocked silence falls over the crowd. Damien's words are a direct challenge to the social order, where women are often seen as mere adornments. Without another word, he pulls me close, and we make our way inside, leaving the bewildered whispers behind us.

Inside the gala, the atmosphere is electric, and every detail is curated to perfection. Beautiful chandeliers cast a warm, golden glow over the room, and the air buzzes with the melody of a hidden orchestra. My fingers lightly brush the silk of my gown as Damien leads me through the throng of distinguished guests. With each introduction, I offer a genuine smile, and my responses are laced with a newfound ease that never accompanied me during my previous marriage. Here, with Damien, I find I'm not the awkward accessory I was once reduced to. I am a partner, an equal.

As the sea of faces parts to make way for us, I marvel silently at the splendor. I'm introduced to titans of industry, their heavy accolades slipping into our conversation as smoothly as Damien's hand rests on my back. His guiding presence is a constant assurance, and I bask in the respect that's readily afforded to us, to *me*, his partner, not just in life but in vision.

As Damien and I weave through the crowd, I can't help but feel a swell of pride. The elaborate chandeliers cast a soft glow on all the guests, and their laughter mingled with the gentle hum of the orchestra. My hand rests lightly on his arm as I smile at the people greeting me. I'm in the middle of introducing myself to a potential donor for the foundation when suddenly, a chill runs up my spine. A man I don't recognize approaches and sets his hand on my elbow.

"You must be Mrs. Blackhart," he says, a bit too familiar for my taste.

Before I can react, Damien's presence looms beside me, his voice controlled but dripping with danger. "Take your damn hands off my wife, or risk losing them."

I flinch in surprise. "Damien," I say in both admonishment and confusion.

The man hastily withdraws his hand as if my skin burns him, but he masks his fear with bravado and extends his hand to me, a clear attempt to salvage his pride.

But Damien is unrelenting. "If you so much as think of touching her again, you'll wish you hadn't been born," his words like a sharpened blade.

The gentleman makes a hasty retreat, looking for all the world as though the fires of hell nip at his heels. With a tight smile still plastered on my face, I turn to my husband.

"That was uncalled for, and you know it," I whisper low enough for only him to hear among a sea of onlookers.

Damien's response comes low and fierce. "You belong to me, Isabella. Anyone who dares to challenge that will answer to me."

His possessive assertion wraps around me, an unyielding chain that both comforts and constrains. "The world should know you wear my ring, breathe my air, and exist because I allow it. If anyone crosses that line, they will learn why I'm the one they fear in whispers."

I don't bother answering and just get back into the swing of things. The grandeur of the gala is overwhelming, every corner dripping with opulence and the heavy scent of ambition. I spot Seraphina in a gown that hugs her like the second skin of a creature born of moonlight and secrets.

Victor stands too close to be a coincidence. Their eyes lock on each other, a silent storm brewing in the scant space between them. I watch, curious and a touch envious of the palpable connection they share. As their gazes linger, the world around them blurs into irrelevance.

Victor lifts a hand, his fingers delicately moving a stray lock of Seraphina's hair with a care that borders on reverence. For a second, the air crackles with electricity. Seraphina stiffens, and I can see her eyes darting, a silent signal of her war between longing and the constraining reality of prying eyes. With a whisper that doesn't reach me, she steps away from him. I'm left wondering about the mystery of their interaction, questioning whether there might be burgeoning flames between them.

As Seraphina strides gracefully to find her seat, Victor's eyes shadow her every move, an intense gaze that could either guard or devour. I stifle a laugh, recognizing the dance of denial and desire. It mirrors my own turbulent resistance to Damien, a battle that ultimately led to a surrender far sweeter than any old victory.

Soon enough, we approach the table designated for the evening's dignitaries. Damien's mother greets us with warmth in her eyes that matches her smile, silently communicating her approval. However, Aurora offers nothing more than a frosty glare. I roll my eyes discreetly, taking my seat while silently vowing not to let her disdain disrupt the evening.

Damien leans down, his lips grazing my temple, a touch that sends a wave of calm through me.

"I'll be right back, love," he whispers.

He gives a subtle nod toward the guards standing watchfully to the side, a silent directive to guard me in his brief absence. I watch him walk away with the lines of his suit hugging his frame and every inch the CEO of Blackhart Enterprises. He's about to address the eager room.

My gaze follows him as he strides confidently up to the podium on the stage. His presence commands attention, silencing the buzzing conversations as everyone turns to look at him. He clears his throat lightly, and then his deep voice rolls over the crowd like smooth whiskey.

"Ladies and gentlemen, distinguished guests," he starts, his voice strong and assured. "Welcome to tonight's event. It's an honor to stand before you as we unite for a cause close to our hearts. The ongoing fight against childhood poverty. Tonight, your generosity will pave the way for a brighter future, providing education, healthcare, and stability. Let us remember that our shared humanity binds us in responsibility to the younger generation. Thank you all for your support and having big hearts. Together, we can make a difference."

A wave of applause cascades through the room as he concludes, the echoes of his message resonating with sincerity. For a moment, Damien surveys the crowd, but then his eyes lock onto mine, intense, full of pride, and something fiercer. My heart beats faster, responding to the silent conversation between us. He makes his way back to our table, each step measured and sure.

The plates arrive one after another in a symphony of culinary delight. Before me is a dish that is art on porcelain. Pan-seared salmon resting on a bed of wild rice drizzled with a delicate, herbed sauce. A colorful medley of seasonal vegetables adds vibrant contrast, and the aroma is enticing, promising flavors as rich as the setting.

Now, with the formalities set aside, a natural hum of conversations begins to bloom across the tables. The atmosphere is charged with a blend of business, philanthropy, and subtle elegance.

Laughter tinkles at a table nearby while a group of executives engage in a robust discussion to my left. I find myself drawn into a conversation about the impact of local non-profits, finding my voice and matching the passion with which Damien spoke earlier.

Turning to the elegantly dressed woman beside me, I engage in the dialogue. "I've heard about the local non-profits. They're making quite an impact on our city, aren't they?"

She nods emphatically, her eyes alight with joy. "Absolutely, Mrs. Blackhart. Organizations like these are lifelines. They provide essentials for children who would otherwise go without."

I respond with a sense of honesty despite not being as knowledgeable as I perhaps should be. "I might not know much about these organizations, but it's clear to me that any group dedicated to helping children is doing vital work. Hopefully, tonight's fundraiser will contribute significantly to their efforts."

Her smile is warm, and her reply assures me their intentions are as genuine as the cause. "Yes, they need clothes, shoes, school supplies... all the basics to have a decent start in life. And I assure you, we will make certain that every dollar from tonight is put to good use."

I feel a surge of respect for her and, by extension, for those gathered here tonight who share her passion. Smiling, I think to myself how refreshing it is to find that some people in our high society care about more than just their extravagant lifestyles. They care about making a difference for those who need it most.

"I need to use the restroom," I murmur to Damien before sliding the napkin from my lap. He nods, and as his hand rises, likely to signal one of his guards to accompany me, Aurora's sharp voice cleaves through the intimate gesture.

"I'll go with her," she interjects, eyes fixed on Damien, challenging him.

I blink, taken aback by her sudden offer. Damien's brow arches in surprise, scrutinizing his sister's intent.

"I'm trying to be nice, to make friends with Isabella," Aurora announces with a disarming smile. "Isn't that what you want?"

Damien's guard lowers, and with a cautious nod, he agrees. Side by side, Aurora and I weave through the tables and the swell of guests. As the noise of the gala fades behind us, Aurora turns to me with her face devoid of the pretense she displayed at the table.

"I don't like you," she says bluntly, and I feel the sting of her words. "You're not good enough for Damien, and he's losing his touch. You're a distraction, taking him away from his duties."

I stop, not willing to listen to her hatred. "Listen, if you're just going to spout bullshit, you can go back to the table," I say with a clipped tone, dismissing her words and presence.

Her lips twist into a smirk. "Nope, I'm going to see this through."

I release a weary sigh and continue walking, making a point to silence her existence in my mind, treating her spite as nothing more than background noise to an already long evening. As we approach the ladies' room, Aurora gestures dismissively to the door.

"Just over there, to the left. I see my friend," she says, disinterest coloring her voice. "Find me when you come out."

Without waiting for my response, she struts off, leaving me to the brief solace of the restroom hallway.

I make my way to the bathroom, grateful for a few moments of solitude. Locking the stall behind me, I take a long, much-needed breath to shake off the tension that Aurora's words have brought on. It doesn't take long to finish, and as I wash my hands at the sink. I catch my reflection in the mirror. My eyes are a little duller, and my posture is slightly more defeated. I'm ready for this night to end. I take another heavy breath, steadying myself for the return to the fray.

I push the door open and move into the hallway, scanning for Aurora, but she's nowhere to be seen. Slightly relieved, I head back towards the ballroom. That's when a man appears from the shadows. At first, I assume he's just another guest, perhaps wandering out from the function. His pace doesn't slow, and I expect him to brush past, but without warning, he's upon me, a flash of metallic glint in his hand. A knife.

He lunges, and I dart back instinctively, but not fast enough. The blade slices across my arm, a hot sear of pain following the sharp, cold shock. I stumble with fear surging through me and an anguished cry escapes my lips. It could have been fatal, but the attack is mercifully brief before I'm even fully aware of what's happening. One of Damien's guards is there, grappling with my assailant. They wrestle, a brief dance of violence that ends with the guard disarming the man and sending him crashing to the floor.

I'm shaking with a hand over my wounded arm, but when the guard turns to me, concern etched into his brow, I manage to tell him I'm okay. My voice doesn't sound like my own. It's then that I look for the man, the source of all this chaos, and he's gone. Vanished as though he were a ghost.

Suddenly, Aurora is at my side, her voice a sharp note of surprise. "What happened?" she asks, her eyes wide.

I'm about to answer when Damien is there, and his worry

for me radiates off him in waves. I don't get the chance to respond, and I'm not sure I could even if I tried because his presence draws all my focus. In his eyes, I see a storm of emotions, a fierce protectiveness that wraps around me stronger than any guard's embrace ever could.

Damien's voice slices through the chaos, authoritative and commanding, as he starts giving out orders. His presence is like a storm, and his words are the thunder that shakes the foundations of hesitation among his guards. Despite the exquisite setting of the gala, it feels like a charade has shattered, and all I can focus on is the tension in his jaw and the barely restrained anger in his eyes.

"We're leaving," he says sharply, and I don't bother to see if anyone's looking our way. In truth, I don't care.

As we move briskly away from the event, I can feel Damien's rage vibrating through his frame. He's shaking. The fury in him is so tangible, so raw, like a force unto itself.

"I knew I shouldn't have brought you," he mutters to himself with a note of self-reproach in his voice that cuts deeper than I expect. I stop him for a moment, reaching for him, needing to ground both of us in a reality that isn't marred by shadows and threats.

"I'm glad I came, Damien," I tell him firmly. I mean every word. The walls at home were closing in on me, suffocating. Tonight, I got to escape them, got to dress up, and feel radiant in his presence. "I got to dress up and look pretty for you," I say, trying to draw a smile from him to remind him of the delight we shared before things went so terribly wrong.

He pauses and looks at me as if seeing me for the first time this evening. "You're always beautiful, baby," he replies softly, and the anger in his gaze melts for a fleeting moment. His compliment wraps around me like a warm embrace, soothing the sting of the night's events.

I can't help but smile, even as my arm throbs in protest. I

take his hand, lacing our fingers together, a promise that his fears haven't come to pass. I'm alright. Yet my gesture seems to do little to chase away the storm that lurks within him, his anger a dark cloud that refuses to dissipate. Still, we walk on, side by side, into the uncertainty of the night.

# CHAPTER 29

## Damien

I sit behind my desk at work with the familiar weight of responsibility settling on my shoulders as I survey the paperwork that's piled up in my absence. It's been too long since I've been in this chair, in this room that smells faintly of leather and steel. There's an uneasy feeling that I can't shake off. The constant concern for Isabella. Despite my reluctance to let her out of my sight, security needs dictate that I can't keep her glued to my side. I've doubled the guards around her and our unborn child. It's the most rational decision to ensure their safety.

Victor stands in front of me, and his presence is as solid and reliable as ever. He lays out the plans with precision, his voice a steady hum in the quiet of my office. We have a lead. A possible location for the Hawthorns. They've been hiding ever since they ambushed us, and I vowed retribution. I'll take them out and then find and take out the Nightingales. The thought of taking action, of squashing this threat, brings a fierce satisfaction.

I want it to be swift and brutal. A strike that will send a message echoing through the underworld. You don't mess with the Blackharts and walk away unscathed. I lean forward, elbows on the desk, fingers interlocked, as the predator inside me stirs, ready to protect my family.

"Let's do it," I command, my voice a low growl of approval for the impending strike. This is not just any retaliation. It's a statement. A declaration that the Blackharts will not tolerate threats to our own.

"How many men do we have ready?" I feel a map of the Hawthorn's location being pushed into my hands, and I spread it out on the desk, and my eyes quickly take in the layout, entry points, and potential risks.

"We have two teams of six, Damien. The best of the best," Victor replies. His confidence is reassuring, but I need details and intricacies that go beyond just numbers.

I point to the map and trace the perimeter. "I want eyes on every entrance. Sniper support on the rooftops here and here," my fingers tap against the paper, indicating the high vantage points. "We go in at night. Use the cover of darkness to our advantage."

"And the entry point for our teams?" Victor asks, leaning over to follow my plan.

I glance at the maze of hallways and rooms laid out before me. "Team One will breach from the back entrance. It's less guarded but has the quickest access to the Hawthorns' inner sanctum. Team Two will create a diversion at the front. I don't want them to even whisper the word 'retreat' until we have the Hawthorns' cornered."

Victor nods while jotting down notes. "Explosives for the diversion?"

"No, too risky. We need precision, not chaos. Smoke and flash bangs should suffice. Disorient, displace, control," I state decisively. "And I will lead Team One personally. I want to look them in the eyes when their empire crumbles."

"You should stay back—" Victor starts.

I cut him off with a hard stare. "This is non-negotiable, Victor. I need to be there. This ends tonight." My voice is a low rumble, a promise of the retribution to come. "Take the rest of the day to prepare. We move as soon as it's dark."

Victor nods sharply, the plan set in stone. "We will be ready, boss."

I nod, rolling up the map, the lines and angles of battle etched into my mind. The Hawthorns have crossed a line, and tonight, they'll pay with their empire.

Victor exits, and the office door closes with a soft click, signaling the start of our plan. I settle deeper into my executive chair, trying to immerse myself in the mundane tasks of signatures and approvals. The things my secretary couldn't do in my absence. Yet each stroke of the pen feels heavy, dragging through my indecision like a blade. Time crawls by and the ticking of the clock syncs with my escalating need to return to Isabella. The distraction of work is futile. My mind is a fortress, and she is the uncontested regent within its walls.

I glance at my watch, aware of each minute that draws me further from the calm before the storm. Then, suddenly, I can't stand it anymore. The waiting, the distance. I rise from my desk as a resolute tide rises to claim the shore.

"Tina," I call out as I stride past my secretary's desk. "I'll be out for the rest of the day. Keep things running." She nods, accustomed to the abrupt changes in my schedule, a silent affirmation of understanding.

As I leave the confines of my office, the anticipation of seeing Isabella again hastens my steps. Tonight, I wage war for the safety of my family. But for now, all I want is to lose myself in the solace of her presence, if only for a moment, before the night unleashes its fury.

I storm into the house like a storm, with my every stride fueled by a fiery mix of purpose and need. The door slams shut behind me, and I call out her name, my voice laced with the raw urgency of a man with everything to lose. The moment she appears, my restraint shatters. I need her in every way imaginable. I pull her close, my lips crashing onto hers, conveying a desperate hunger that borders on madness. I need to get inside my wife. To get in between her legs. It's as close to heaven as I'm going to get.

This could be our last time, and I'm driven by the primal urge to be ensnared within her, to savor the intoxicating warmth of her body as if it's my last breath of air. I carry her to our bedroom, laying her on the bed with a fervor that blurs everything else out of focus. If this night doesn't end in our favor, she might be trapped in mourning once again. A widow bearing the cruelty of fate. However, I've orchestrated plans upon plans, leaving no stone unturned because failure is a specter that has no place in my world.

I am Damien fucking Blackhart. I conquer, I claim, I endure. Tonight, I vow to banish the shadow of death that looms over us because nothing, not even fate itself, will deny me the future we've built. I look into her eyes, giving a silent promise that I will return to her and let the world fade away as we ascend to a crescendo of passion and promise.

Isabella gasps in surprise at my urgency, her eyes alight with a flicker of astonishment and knowing. She can sense the storm brewing within me, the turbulent waves that are crashing against the shores of my restraint.

"What's gotten into you?" she asks with a breathy laugh, and the sound mingles with the air of our entwined existence.

I pause with my hands roaming over her as if to memorize every curve, every line, in case fate demands a ransom I can't pay.

"I need you, baby," I say in a voice thick with emotion before my lips claim hers in a kiss that speaks of raw need, of unspoken fears, and unbreakable bonds.

Dragging her clothes off her body and throwing them on the floor, I climb between her legs, and she spreads them willingly. I position myself at her entrance and thrust in, sinking to the hilt inside my wife. She moans, and a satisfied groan rumbles in my chest. This is heaven. This is what I need. I kiss her, delving deep and taking her moans into me.

"Tell me, baby," I whisper against her lips as I start to move inside her. "I need to hear the words."

She moans, and I know she knows what I want. She wraps her legs around my back, and her fingers grip my hair. Our eyes lock, and I can see it. I can see the love reflecting back in her beautiful eyes. I pull out of her, only to thrust back inside, hard. I'm addicted to her. My body moves against her as her moans spur me on. My pace becomes frenzied as I kiss her like I'll never get the chance again. I fuck my wife with everything in me until her moans turn into screams of ecstasy. I pound inside her, and the sounds of our slapping bodies fill the air.

"Say it," I demand, thrusting harder inside her. "Your beautiful eyes tell me, but I need to hear the words. Tell me, baby."

She trails her hand over my jaw before cupping my face. "I love you, Damien."

"Thank fuck," I growl and proceed to fuck my wife into oblivion.

I slide away from her, and she's unconscious before I even fully exit the bed, her breath evening out in the muted light of the room. I lost count of how many times I made her come and how many times I came, filling her up each time. Satisfaction warms me. I really wore her out.

With quiet movements, I dress in the shadows of our sanctuary. Her peaceful face beckons for one last touch, and I can't resist bending down to press a soft kiss on her forehead.

For a lingering moment, I allow myself to simply gaze at her, at this picture of peace that I'm so desperate to preserve.

As I leave the room, the gravity of the night ahead settles in my bones. It's time to shift focus. Our home behind me feels like a different world as I step out into the chilled evening air. Victor's waiting figure comes into view at our agreed time.

"Let's get this done," I say, my voice low, leaving no room for the chaos of emotions from the past hours. Tonight, I'm not just a man or a husband. I'm the architect of retribution, and every step from here on out is a step towards a future where she never has to fear again.

The night wraps around us like a cloak as we approach the Hawthorn's' compound. A sprawl of darkness was pierced by the guarded floodlights.

"This is it," I breathe out, my voice barely above a whisper. Victor nods, our eyes locking in a silent understanding. We've covered this. Every entrance, every exit, every possible scenario. My heart beats a relentless rhythm, but my hands are steady. This isn't just another mission. It's personal.

I signal the team with a subtle gesture, and like shadows, we dissolve into our roles. I skirt around to the back. There's a vulnerability there that we're about to turn into our entrance. The cutters are quiet in my hands as I sever the wire fence, the gap just wide enough for one man at a time.

Squeezing through, I allow myself a moment to adjust to the adrenaline that turns every sense up to its highest frequency. Then, I move, leading my team with precision. We work to dismantle their defenses, a silent dance of swift, decisive action. The electricity in the air is thick, and the danger only spurs us further.

I see one of Hawthorn's men patrolling, unaware of the storm that's about to break. I press myself against the wall and motion for my team to hold. My hand moves to my gun, but I only nod when he passes, silent as a ghost. Our plan doesn't call for unnecessary bloodshed. We are here for justice, not a massacre.

Then I'm at the door, priming a breaching charge that whispers death to the lock. The explosion is a muted thump, a footnote in the echo of the night. We burst inside, and for a second, chaos is our ally. We move on with a single-minded force of retribution as I lead us deeper into the heart of darkness where the Hawthorns wait. Tonight, they will learn the true cost of crossing Damien Blackhart.

Chaos erupts as if the night itself has come to life. Men rush out from every corner, their shouts fragmenting the silence, a discordant prelude to the all-out war that envelops us. Bullets whistle through the air, tearing past like deadly hornets enraged from their nest. I duck and weave, with my mind laser-focused on one thing alone: William Hawthorn. That bastard has to be here, hiding within the bowels of this fortress, and I will drag him into the light.

I exchange gunfire, popping off rounds with a sniper's precision. Each step forward is hard-won, a battle of wills etched in gunpowder and blood. My team flanks me, their presence a constant in the chaos, a symphony of determined might versus sheer desperation. In this maelstrom, I am both the eye and the storm, commanding order where there is none, bending this frenzied clash of lives to my formidable will. William Hawthorn will not escape my reckoning. Tonight, the scales of justice will be balanced by my hand.

"Victor," I hiss, keeping my voice to a whisper as we navigate the narrow corridor. Our boots are silent against the ground, our presence nothing but a shared breath among the shadows.

Victor glances at me with a nod, confirming he's listening. "Yeah?"

I gesture to the door at the end. "Reinforcements could

be coming through there. We need to seal it off to buy us more time."

"On it," he replies, swift and sure, peeling away with a couple of others to secure the passage.

I press on, and the thrill of the hunt sharpens my senses. My brow furrows as I hear the faintest noise, shifting beyond the next turn.

"Victor, hold up," I shout, hand signaling a halt. The silence answers like a challenge. "Do you hear that?" I murmur, my tone taut with vigilance.

He strains his ears for a moment, then nods subtly. "Backup generator. If we kill it, we'll have a better shot moving unseen."

"Agreed." I pause, weighing our next move. "Take point on that. I've got your six."

As he edges forward, I keep my weapon raised like a silent protector, shadowing his every step. The hum of the generator grows louder, like a mechanical heartbeat we're about to silence.

With a swift look between us, Victor cuts the power, plunging us into deeper darkness. "Let there be dark," he quips under his breath, a flash of dark humor that keeps the grim reality at bay.

I can't help but smirk, even now. "Nice one, Vic. Now, let's find Hawthorn before this darkness becomes permanent."

The darkness feels like an ally as we continue threading through the compound, our footsteps nearly inaudible. Gunfire erupts intermittently, piercing the stillness with its deadly bite. I move with a hunter's grace, ducking into the shadows as bullets ricochet off the walls. I can feel the adrenaline coursing through my veins, heightening every sense.

My fingers tighten around the grip of my weapon, ready to respond to the merest hint of movement. I exhale slowly, my breath steady despite the chaos. A shout catches my attention, and I pivot, squeezing the trigger and watching as a figure collapses. Another obstacle eliminated. We're inching ever closer to our prey through this maze of danger and deception, with each fallen enemy a grim reminder of the stakes at hand.

The corridor unexpectedly twists, and as I lean out to scan for threats, an explosion rocks the foundation. Dust and confusion become my cover as I find myself cut off from my men. Heart pounding with the urgency of the hunt, I push through the haze alone. Each step is methodical, loaded with the promise of retribution. I'm a man possessed, riding the edge of vengeance and duty.

I arrive at a heavy wooden door. Without hesitation, I kick it open and step through with my weapon aimed in front of me. There he is, William Hawthorn, in the flesh. There's no surprise in his eyes. Only the calm acceptance of fate.

"Damien Blackhart, as I live and breathe," William drawls. "You know, I should've warned my boy to stay clear of your kind. Messing with the Blackharts was bound to bite him."

I keep my gun steady, the metal a cold extension of my will. "Why did you?" I demand.

He laughs, coughing slightly. "The offer. Jackson's offer was too damn good."

"What offer?" My grip tightens.

His smile is a twist of cynicism and regret. "He told me he had the means to take you out. After that, we Hawthorns would reign supreme. He didn't want your territory. He craved money, the high life. We were to fund that existence in return. But you won't be surprised we planned to double-cross him. Once you were dead, why pay for a lap dog when we own the house?"

My blood boils. I can barely contain the rage. "Watch

your mouth about my brother," I snarl the words a venomous warning.

William raises an eyebrow in a silent challenge. "Even now, knowing he would have killed you, you defend him?"

"No one talks shit about my brother," I shoot back, unyielding.

His laughter is gravelly, unfazed by the gun I have on him. "But dear Jackson sold out every one. Joined hands with that trash Edward Storm. Storm got mixed with those Nightingales, the vile bunch, but we all had a... mutual understanding."

"And what was that?" There's a dangerous edge to my inquiry.

His smile turns sardonic. "You'll never know."

His hand moves too quickly toward his jacket. It's instinct. My finger squeezes the trigger before his gesture completes. The gunshot echoes with a resounding finality.

"Fuck!" My curse fills the room, rebounding off the walls.

William's body hits the ground with a heavy thud, and his last expression is a frozen grimace. I wanted him dead, yes, but his words had opened a darker abyss, one I needed to explore. The answers he held are gone, swallowed by the silence of death.

Victor bursts in, his presence slicing through the gritty silence of the room. "Boss, everyone has been neutralized. Except for that bastard, Daniel. He's not here," he reports, his gaze locked onto mine. I nod once, sharply, as I pivot on my heel to leave the room.

"Have we lost any men?" I ask without looking back, feeling the weight of potential loss in every step I take.

Victor's affirmation is like a blow. "We've lost six men total," he says, his voice steady but heavy with unspoken sorrow.

As we move through the house, I begin to issue

commands, my voice low and resolute. "Collect the bodies. Remove any traces of our presence here. If any of the men had families, pay for the funerals and give them severance. Make sure to convey our condolences," I instruct, my mind already calculating the cost of the night's actions.

"Okay," Victor replies, his footsteps in cadence with mine.

Upon reaching the entrance, I halt and face Victor squarely. "Set the house on fire when you finish. This isn't over by a long shot. William may have posed a threat, but he wasn't the biggest threat. We have to find the Nightingales," I say, my resolve burning fierce and unyielding. "Meet me at my home office tomorrow morning."

The cold night air bites at my skin as I step out of the pillaged house. I've always thought ridding the world of William Hawthorn would be the endgame. But the Nightingales have now made it to my list. A wry smile plays on my lips. Survival has always been a game of chess, and tonight, I've avoided being a pawn. Isabella's face floats into my mind, and I can almost hear her sigh of relief mixed with disapproval. I know she's praying for an end to this bloodshed, craving a semblance of normalcy that our lives constantly undermine.

But the chessboard has changed. There's no turning back. The engine of my car hums as I begin the drive home. My jaw sets, a silent vow etching itself deep within. I'll dismantle the Nightingales piece by piece. They think they can hide, but shadows are my domain. I swear on everything I hold dear, they will be eradicated. For Isabella, for my men, for the semblance of peace, we all damn well deserve.

# CHAPTER 30

## Isabella

"You cannot be serious!" I yell at Damien, and my voice bouncing against the walls of our bedroom. The fury and fear interlace as tightly as the fingers I've clenched at my sides.

"I never joke about your safety, Isabella," he says, but the sincerity in his voice does little to quell the anger in me.

"I'm not going to stay who knows how long at your mother's house while you go off into the night on a rampage," I tell him, the edges of my words sharp enough to cut through the tension hanging in the air.

"You'll be better protected there. With my guards and my mother's, you'll be safer," Damien responds, but his solution only deepens the gap of worry that pits my stomach.

I fold my arms and huff in agitation, feeling the walls closing in. "Ever since you came home from whatever mission you went on, you've been insufferable. I thought you caught whoever the bad guys were. You told me everything was handled!"

Damien sighs in frustration, the sound weighted with unspoken burdens. "It *was* handled. Now, there's another threat to take care of."

"I knew it. It's always going to be like this, isn't it? There will always be a new threat. When will we be safe? When can things be normal?" I implore, the vulnerability in my voice making me feel naked and exposed.

"You didn't marry a normal man!" Damien yells back, the rawness of his emotion taking physical form in the space between us, causing me to take a step back.

He notices the gap, sees the apprehension in my eyes, and scrubs a hand down his face. "It won't always be like this, baby," he softens, his eyes locking with mine, pleading for understanding. "Our love blossomed during chaos. We don't have a normal yet. Promise me that you will do this. Do this for me. Allow me to take out this last threat, and we can create our normal. I'll show you what normal looks like."

I'm quiet for a moment, letting the silence say what words cannot before I nod with a shaky breath.

"I'm sorry, Damien. It's just..." I trail off, blaming the pregnancy hormones for my outburst, though we both know there's more haunting me than the erratic whims of an expectant mother.

Damien walks forward, placing his hand where our baby is just beginning to make its presence known, my stomach still not round enough to broadcast the life within.

"It's okay," he whispers, his touch a soothing balm over my fears.

I grab my duffel bag from the closet, stuffing it with essentials. Clothes, toiletries, and the framed photo of Damien and me from our quick wedding. My movements are hasty, robotic, and driven by adrenaline. Damien waits by the door with concern etched into every line of his feature. We leave together with the still of the night enveloping us as we slip into his car.

As the vehicle glides through the dark streets towards his

mother's house, my heart sinks like a stone in deep water. The constant danger of being married to Damien, the never-ending shadow of guards, our lives punctuated by whispered threats, it's suffocating. Our child, this flicker of new life unwittingly introduced to such peril, tightens the knot of worry inside me.

I believe Damien. Of course I do. When he says he'll take care of it, I know he will. All of this is for a slice of normalcy we're chasing like a horizon that keeps pushing further away. Anger simmers within me, too, like a persistent flame. It's the secrecy, the sense of being protected but not trusted with the full weight of truth, that leaves me fuming. He shares, yes, but it's always veiled, always measured out like a rationed commodity.

Along this eerily quiet journey, my thoughts echo in the silence. Will it be like this forever? Our lives, a series of concealed truths and armored cars? Respect is built on trust, and how can I feel respected when I'm kept at arm's length from the realities of my own life? As the car sweeps into his mother's driveway, the unknown faces of tomorrow loom over me. I'm left wondering if our vows are now just another set of promises lost to the shadows we can't seem to escape.

We pull up to the house, and the sight of Victor's parked car sends confusion through me. Damien cuts the engine, and we step out into the cold night. Victor emerges, too, his slow movements betraying impatience. His passenger door opens, and a voice cuts through the quiet, sharp and accusing.

"Let go of me, asshole!" My head snaps up to Damien, seeking an explanation.

Damien sighs deeply, the exasperation visible as he pinches the bridge of his nose.

"Idiot," he mutters.

"Isabella?" The familiar voice of Seraphina pulls my gaze

towards her. "What the hell is going on?" My mouth opens, but no sound escapes. I'm as clueless as she is.

"Why did this *asshole* storm into my house, throw me over his shoulder, carry me to his car, stuff me inside, and drive like a maniac all the way here?" Seraphina demands with her fury directed at Victor.

Damien shoots Victor a glare that could cut glass. "I told Victor to ask if you would like to accompany Isabella to my mother's house, given that things are still shaky between them. He was not supposed to technically kidnap you," he explains, his voice a mixture of anger and apology.

"I would have come had you simply asked," Seraphina snaps, her eyes blazing towards Victor.

"Where's the fun in that," Victor replies with a smug grin, unfazed. "I like the fight in you. It makes me all tingly," he adds, the comment hanging in the air, unappreciated by everyone but him.

"I'll show you tingly, you bastard," Seraphina seethes, advancing on Victor with a glare sharp enough to rival the chill in the air. He just laughs, that irritating, self-assured chuckle that makes her blood heat.

"I love it when you talk dirty," he replies, clearly finding himself amusing. Seraphina's hands clench into fists at her sides, her comeback poised on her lips, but her words are cut short as the door swings open. Damien's mother, framed by the doorway, observes the scene with a disapproving eye.

"Do come in," she says dryly, though her tone leaves no room for warmth. As her gaze settles on Seraphina, her expression sours further. "You never said she was coming," she remarks with a narrowed look. "Hawthorns aren't allowed in my home."

A venomous "Bitch," slips from Seraphina's lips just under her breath, but I catch it.

Damien wastes no time and quickly ushers us all into the house, with his hand lightly pressed against my lower back, guiding me forward. The warmth of the foyer does little to mollify the chill of the confrontation outside. That's when I noticed her, Aurora. She's lounging on the sofa with an air of indifference that seems too calculated.

"What is she doing here?" The question tumbles out of my mouth before I can stop it, my surprise evident.

Aurora doesn't even bother standing. "This is my mother's house, Isabella. I don't need a reason to be here," she responds snidely.

Before the tension can escalate, Damien jumps in, authoritative, laying down his rules. "Mother, you can continue to do whatever you normally do. Just act like Isabella isn't here. She's here for the extra protection, not to interrupt your routine."

He turns toward Seraphina with a pointed look. "And that's why I invited you here, to keep her company."

Seraphina emits an audible snort at his choice of word, "invited." Damien cuts his eyes toward her, a silent warning, and she meets his gaze unflinchingly. The air is thick with unsaid words and brewing storms, but for now, we all stand under a forced ceasefire.

"That reminds me," Victor suddenly blurts out, effectively cutting through the thickness of the tension in the room.

He doesn't wait for a response. His tall frame disappears through the front door, leaving us in a strange, silent interlude. The door swings open barely a minute later, with Victor making his return, hands occupied with a couple of bags.

"I've got all the girly food you can think of," he declares, raising the bag to display his triumph.

I roll my eyes at his choice of words, yet somewhere within, I can't help but acknowledge a flash of gratitude for his forethought. It's an unexpected gesture from Victor, especially when suffocating under the heavy blanket of our current predicament.

Damien guides Seraphina and me to the movie room on the opposite end of the house, far removed from his mother's iciness. The space feels like a refuge with the lush sofas and dim lighting as a soft cocoon against the rest of the world.

I sense Damien's intention in placing us here is a strategic distance that shields us from the cold scrutiny and thinly veiled contempt we just encountered. Just before he leaves, he pulls me aside with his hands firm on my shoulders.

"You'll be safe here, I promise," he assures me with the kind of determination that brooks no argument. "I'll be back first thing in the morning."

Behind us, the murmured snipes of Seraphina and Victor float in the air as if they're in their own volatile world, arguing amongst themselves. I grasp Damien's hands, searching his eyes.

"Be careful," I whisper, the vulnerability of our situation never clearer than this very moment. He responds not with words but with a tender kiss on my lips, a silent vow that lingers when he pulls away.

"I love you," he whispers against my mouth, a warm breath of certainty.

"I love you too," I breathe out, holding onto that sentiment and him until the door closes behind him and Victor, leaving Seraphina and me in whispered echoes and the promise of safety until dawn.

Seraphina and I make ourselves comfortable, sinking into the plush cushions as the room fills with explosive sound effects from the action movie blaring on the screen. The smell of popcorn mingled with a myriad of snacks that Victor proudly presented floats around us.

Almost instinctively, we reach for the chocolate-covered almonds, and our eyes are glued to the screen. Something weighs on me, a conversation long overdue. I turn toward Seraphina, pausing to gather my courage.

"Hey, Sera, I—I need to say I'm sorry," I start, my voice barely above the movie's soundtrack. "For that day of the shootout. I know that's why... well, why we haven't really hung out since then."

Surprise flashes in Seraphina's eyes, and her focus shifts from the on-screen chaos. "Isabella, that's not it at all," she says earnestly. "I stayed away because I was scared. The feud between my family and the Blackharts is putting you in more danger just by being around me."

Her words knock the air out of my lungs. Damien never mentioned a feud, and a flare of anger ignites in me, but I quickly suppress it.

"I had no idea," I admit, stunned. "And I'm sorry for all of this mess."

Seraphina shakes her head fiercely. "No, don't be. It's not your fault, and frankly, it has nothing to do with us personally." Then, in a typical Seraphina move, she redirects the conversation. "Forget that for now. How are you doing? Really?" She nudges me with a concerned look.

A small smile creeps onto my face; the next words I'm about to say are both exhilarating and terrifying. "I'm... I'm pregnant, Sera."

The movie becomes a distant murmur as Seraphina processes my news. Then, her shock morphs into joy, and she leaps up, her excitement tangible. "You're going to have a baby? That means I'm going to be an aunt!" She envelopes me in a hug that's almost crushing, but it's the kind of embrace that speaks volumes more than words ever could, filled with love and unwavering support.

Seraphina's questions flow freely, and her eyes are wide with curiosity and amazement. "How far along are you? Have you thought of any names? Oh, and do you know if it's going to be a boy or a girl?"

I laugh, my heart feeling lighter than it has in weeks despite the shadow of danger that clings to the walls of this safe house.

"I'm five months along. No names yet. I mean, we just found out." I pat my stomach, still in awe. "And for the gender, we want it to be a surprise."

Our conversation fades as we settle back into the movie, the loud explosions once again filling the room. Then, a different kind of explosion shakes the house, not from the speakers but from the world outside. Ominous and real. Plaster dust sifts down from the ceiling, and the movie is forgotten as Seraphina and I lock eyes in fear.

Jacob slams the door open, his face urgent as his eyes scan the room until they land on us. "We need to go. NOW."

His voice is a command, one that brooks no argument and speaks volumes of the peril just beyond our thin veneer of safety. Panic tightens my chest, but I stand, ready to face whatever comes next.

I clutch Seraphina's hand tightly as we follow Jacob out of the room. His urgency is infectious, and a thin bead of sweat forms on my forehead. The distant echo of men shouting spirals into an audible discord, and the reality of danger crashes down on me. Gunfire cracks through the air in a staccato rhythm that has my heart racing in sync. Fear spikes through me like electrical currents, shocking my system into acute awareness.

Jacob moves with a lethal grace with his gun raised. His body twists and turns with a dancer's precision, each movement purposeful and every shot he fires striking with intention. Seraphina and I huddle close behind him, our footsteps a desperate whisper against the floor. We weave through the corridors of the house with the stench of gunpowder burning in my nostrils as a grim reminder of the razor-thin line between life and death.

I can't take my eyes off Jacob. Each thunderous boom from his gun serves as a fierce proclamation of our determination to survive. His protective instinct manifests in the stern set of his jaw and the unwavering focus in his eyes. Shouts and bodies blur around us, but Jacob's presence is a constant, a steady force leading us to safety among the violence.

Jacob's shots echo in quick succession. "Keep up!" he barks over his shoulder, eyes alert and scanning for threats.

I grip Seraphina's hand tighter, our pace quickening to match Jacob's. With a swift, almost silent motion, Jacob reaches an assailant, and in one fluid motion, he snaps the man's neck. The finality of the action sends a shiver through me, but there's no time to dwell on it. We turn sharply down another hallway, then begin our descent on a narrow staircase, with our feet barely whispering against the steps.

We are halfway down when a new sound prickles my ears. Footsteps from above follow us. Jacob doesn't hesitate. He pivots to cover our rear, his gun up and ready.

"Keep going down! I'm right behind you," he insists, his voice laced with an urgency that propels us forward even as fear tightens around my chest like a vice.

Seraphina and I don't look back. We can't afford to. Every step we take is one closer to safety, or so I hope. We reach the bottom, and that's when it happens. A loud thud resounds through the stairwell as something or someone hits Seraphina with brutal force from behind. She crumples to the ground before I can react, unconscious, her body limp and vulnerable.

I freeze for a second, and the bitter taste of dread floods

my mouth. My breath hitches as cold metal presses against my head. Through the dim light, I lock eyes with the intruder, his face shrouded by a ski mask, a silent demand in his gaze.

"She only wants you. Don't make a sound, and don't put up a fight," he hisses.

Panic claws at my insides, a desperate question forming in my mind. Who is she? But my instinct screams that compliance means doom. Adrenaline surges, and with the resolve I didn't know I possessed, I lash out. My foot crashes into his groin. He doubles over with the gun wavering in his hand. Seizing the moment, I deliver a fierce kick to his face, and down he goes, a crumpled heap of consequences on the floor. Breathless, I whirl around.

"Wake up," I plead, shaking Seraphina, my voice breaking. "Please wake up." Her stillness terrifies me. Jacob still hasn't come down the stairs. Desperation coils within me, my mind racing for answers we don't have time to find.

Gunfire still pierces the air, relentless and terrifying. I don't know where Damien's mom and sister could be in this chaos, and my heart clenches with worry for them. I continue to shake Seraphina, my hands trembling, refusing to let terror paralyze me.

"Seraphina, please," I whisper urgently.

Around us, the mayhem rages on, a storm of violence and fear, but I can't, I won't leave my friend vulnerable and alone. She's family to me. We've faced the world side by side, and I am determined to see us through this nightmare together. My resolve hardens. I will protect her at all costs. Desperation gives way to fierce determination as I scoop her limp body into my arms, prepared to carry her if I must. Failure is not an option. I stagger under her weight. Suddenly, a familiar voice slices through the air.

"I knew you'd put up a fight," it sneers.

I try to whip my head around to face the new threat, steeling myself for another confrontation. Before I can spot the speaker, something heavy crashes against my skull. A burst of white-hot pain flashes through my consciousness, and then, much like the lights that flicker and die above us, everything goes black.

**31**

---

# CHAPTER 31

---

## Isabella

Consciousness creeps back to me, sluggish and reluctant. My head throbs in time with my pulse, and pain races through me like sharp needles. As my eyes fight to open, reality warps in and out of focus, the world around me slowly taking shape. Walls, unfamiliar and cold, surround me, painting a picture of confinement I wish I could disbelieve.

Fingers fumbling, I realize with a sinking heart that I'm shackled to a chair, with my wrists chafing against the harsh bite of rope. A futile struggle ensues as I attempt to wriggle free, but the bonds hold fast, unyielding.

There's a single window barred from the outside, casting a funnel of daylight that seems to grasp at the otherwise dim interior. The furnishings are minimal. A metal table bolted to the floor, flanked by two chairs of the same unyielding material. On the table lies a pitcher of water and a glass beside it.

The air is still, scented with the faintest trace of lemon, an attempt at comfort, perhaps, in this cold and utilitarian space. Despite the lack of adornment, the room doesn't feel cramped. It's spacious enough, yet the emptiness serves as a constant reminder of my isolation. This is an old house made to look more maintained than it has been.

"Sera...phina," I gasp out, my voice a mere whisper against the thick silence that fills the room.

To my left, a soft moan answers me. It's Seraphina. She stirs with her own battle with consciousness etched on her face. Her eyes flutter open, heavy with disorientation. She scans the room, her confusion palpable as her gaze lands on me.

Shock registers in those deep, familiar eyes as reality sets in. Realizing she's bound just as I am, her body jerks in a reflexive attempt at escape. But like me, she is tethered, imprisoned by more than just ropes, by fear, by desperation. We are trapped, mutual recognition igniting a silent alarm between us as we face the unknown perils that wait in the shadows.

The door creaks open, drawing a stark line of light across the darkened room that momentarily blinds me. My eyes widen in response to the silhouette that's now framed by the doorway. It's Aurora, the last person I expected or wanted to see. Three men follow her in, faces stern and unreadable. Aurora's voice breaks the oppressive silence, smooth and cold as ice.

"Ah, you're finally awake," she states, her eyes examining me as if I'm nothing more than a specimen under her microscope. "You have caused more problems than you know. I didn't want to get my hands dirty, but you left me no choice."

I frown, jerking against my restraints, with confusion and anger mingling in my gut. "I don't know what you're talking about," I reply, but my voice sounds far less certain than I intend it to.

Aurora laughs a hollow sound that bounces off the walls and wraps around me like a chilling embrace. "You really are clueless, aren't you?" she taunts.

She begins to circle me, and I follow her with guarded eyes, my body tensing instinctively. Each step she takes sends a wave of ominous foreboding through me, and goosebumps rise on my skin despite the stuffy air. A visceral reaction to the predator prowling before me. Aurora stops back in front of me, her gaze cold and calculated. She pauses for just a moment, evidently savoring the control she holds over this twisted situation.

"I'd like to introduce you to someone," she declares with a sly edge to her voice and gestures toward the door they came through. I'm on high alert, muscles tensed and mind racing, until he walks in. My father. My eyes go wide as my heart slams against my chest.

"What the fuck!" I blurt out before I can stop myself. "What have you gotten me into this time, Dad? I don't have any money to help you. Why these people think that, I have no idea."

As I glare at him, the puzzle pieces are tumbling into place. This isn't just about money. If Aurora is involved, there's something much larger at play. She's a Blackhart, for god's sake. They're loaded with money. Fear twists in my stomach. It's not just the money they're after.

My father strides forward, and before I can even flinch, his hand cracks across my face. The stinging slap sends my head careening to the side, and a pained moan escapes me. I taste blood as I've bitten my cheek.

"Bitch! Why did you have to be so difficult," he hisses, his voice dripping with contempt.

"Don't touch her, you sick son of a bitch!" Seraphina's voice, raw and furious, cuts through the stunned silence following his outburst. There's a brief moment of tension. Then another smack sounds, this one not against my skin. Seraphina moans in pain, and the sound wrenches at my heart.

I can't see her from where I'm tied, but anger and worry swell within me like a turbulent storm. "Seraphina!" I shout, straining against the ropes. "Why are you doing this?"

My father's eyes burn into mine, simmering with anger as he leans in closer. "Because you're about to come into a large sum of money, and I need that money," he spits out, the words laced with venom.

Confusion washes over me. I have no knowledge of any money. I may be married to Damien, but it's technically not *my* money; it's his. My father's greedy eyes don't leave me, and it's clear that he believes this, whether it's a delusion of his desperate mind or a cruel fact, I'm yet to uncover.

"What are you talking about," I ask. My breath hitches, and a chill races down my spine.

"You see, your conniving grandparents set up a trust for you," my father continues, the venom in his voice betraying the jealousy he's probably fostered for years. "I found the documents while going through your mother's things. The bitch never told me about it."

His eyes are alight with a sick satisfaction as he delivers the next piece of the puzzle, a piece that feels like the missing weight to anchor the nightmare I'm trapped in.

"When you turn twenty-five, you'll inherit one hundred million dollars."

An incredulous laugh escapes me, mirthless and strained. Is this some twisted joke? The heavy click of a gun being cocked slices through my disbelief. I don't have to look to know it's aiming at me. The intent is clear: comply, or else. "But you see, I can't have access to it," he sneers.

My father's face contorts into a grotesque smirk as he delivers each word like a dagger aimed directly at my heart. "I owed Jackson a lot of money. He owed the Hawthorns a lot of money." His eyes flicker with a dark triumph, finding pleasure in revealing the twisted web of debts and deceit. "I told him about the money you're set to get and offered him to marry you for access to it."

He pauses, studying my reaction as if expecting gratitude for his vile matchmaking. "He happily agreed." A shiver of disgust runs through me as he speaks of my life like it's just another one of his shady deals. "He told me you were being difficult. Why couldn't you just be a good little wife, look pretty, and spread your legs whenever he wanted?"

The force of the revelation hits me like a physical blow, knocking the breath from my lungs. I want to scream, to rage against the injustice and the sheer violation of it all. It's unbearable the way my own father commodifies me, reducing me to nothing more than a bargaining chip in his sordid transactions. Rage and disbelief war within me as I meet his gaze, my eyes blazing with fury, utterly repulsed by the monster before me.

Aurora's words come slicing through the thick, fraught atmosphere, as precise and chilling as the rest of her. "My brother also made enemies with the Nightingales. It seems that he promised the Hawthorns and the Nightingales money. They caught wind of your little inheritance, and when Jackson refused to play by their rules, they poisoned him. Thanks to me."

My father resumes, his voice barely above a whisper, but each word etches into my memory with the permanence of a scar.

"The Nightingales... they found me. They would have taken me out, no second thoughts if I hadn't dangled you like a carrot." He hesitates, his eyes nothing short of predatory. "You see, the Nightingales, they deal in human trade. A dirty business. And Luke, Luke Nightingale, he made an offer to marry you. That would give him legal access to the money."

I stare at him, my breath ragged, as the web of deceit tightens around me. "I agreed," he continues, and I can hear the tacit resignation in his voice. "Once we got hold of the money, they wouldn't have cared what happened to you. They'd sell you to whoever offered the most. And me? I wouldn't have batted an eye." His confession hangs heavy in the air, a toxic mist that chokes the very life out of the room.

Tears sting the corners of my eyes, yet they refuse to fall. There's a hollowness in my chest, a void where trust and love for my father once resided. To be betrayed by one's own blood, sold like property into a spider's web of crime and cruelty, is a soul-shattering reality that claws at the inside of my skull.

I should feel panic. Instead, a deep, abyssal sadness wraps itself around my heart, squeezing until each shallow breath becomes a battle. His words render me into nothing more than currency in his eyes. A daughter exchanged for debts settled. The iron taste of blood in my mouth is now entwined with the bitter flavor of betrayal.

Desperation claws at the edges of my thoughts, but I focus, hanging onto every bitter confession that spills from Aurora's lips. "Jackson wanted to take Damien out. I was fully on board with that plan," she says with chilling nonchalance as if discussing the weather rather than murderous schemes. I blink, feeling as though the room is spinning around me. "Damien was getting weak."

Then, I feel her eyes on me, piercing and cold. "Then you came along, and even while married to Jackson, you were a distraction to Damien. His eyes followed you whenever you were in the room." Her voice is edged with disdain as if I'm a bug she's eager to squash underfoot. She shakes her head minutely, an executor disillusioned by her subject's faults.

"Then you had to go and marry him and get knocked up in the process." Her words spear through me, setting my blood on fire. I want to scream, to rail against her, but the ropes binding me are as tight as the trap I'm in.

A cold smile plays on her lips. "No worries, though. The plan still stays. I've been working with the Hawthorns and the Nightingales." Her casual revelation sends a shiver down my spine like a treacherous ballet of fear and anger twisting through me. Aurora's betrayal is a new cut in a body already etched with scars.

"You see, Isabella," he says, and I can't help but wince at the sound of my name on his lips. A name that once implied affection is now weaponized. "I found a little loophole. Let's call it a grey area." The smirk on his face grows wider, more insidious if that's even possible. "If you die and there's no husband or kids, then the money goes to your next living kin." He pauses for effect, his smile a grotesque distortion of joy. "That would be me." His laughter cuts the tension in the room, a chilling, malevolent sound that underscores the gravity of my situation.

A sickening knot forms in my stomach as he lays out his grotesque plan. To think that to him, my life and the life of my unborn child are nothing more than bargaining chips in his twisted game. I listen, my heart pounding in my ears as anger and fear collide within me. His words are calm, methodical even, as if he is explaining the rules of a board game.

"But you see," my father continues, the cruel glint in his eyes betraying his feigned concern. "That puts me in a predicament. If all the money goes to me, then the Nightingales would take it and kill me." He states this as a matter of fact, his selfishness and cowardice on full display.

"You're worth more to me alive than dead. You're Damien's wife, and you're pregnant with his spawn," he says, his voice dripping with venom. "That's leverage over him. The Nightingales will keep you. I'll demand money from Damien, and he'll pay. For some odd reason, he cares for your worthless ass." I feel the weight of each word like a physical assault.

"Your actions say otherwise. Clearly, she's not as worthless as you're claiming. Otherwise, why go through all this fucking trouble," Seraphina says, her words laced with a venom born of newfound courage. Someone hits her, and all I hear is her heavy breathing and the small, splattering sound of blood hitting the floor.

She glares defiantly at the man who struck her, her lips curling into a grotesque yet triumphant grin as she sports her bloodied smile. She spits, more blood than saliva, straight at him, the crimson stain on his shirt a mark of her unyielding spirit. "You hit like a bitch," she taunts, goading her assailant, daring him to reveal the cowardice we already see.

"Once I get my money, I'll disappear," my father continues, his plan unfolds with monstrous clarity. "When you turn twenty-five, the Nightingales will get their money. They'll lure Damien to rescue you and kill him. They can do what they want with you. Kill you and the brat for all I care." The ease with which he speaks of my life ending is a blow far greater than any physical pain. I'm left speechless, betrayed beyond words.

As Aurora speaks, fierce and resolute, her declaration hangs in the air. "And with Damien dead, I'll take over."

Seraphina's boisterous laugh, devoid of any mirth, slices through the heaviness in the room. "That's your plan?" she asks, surprise painting her face with a mocking smirk. "You really think in this man's world, they'll let a woman have power? That they'll listen to *you*?"

I watch closely as doubt shadows the edges of Aurora's hardened expression. Her response is quick and biting. "Yes, they will. I'm a fucking Blackhart!"

Her certainty doesn't waver, but there's a tremor in her voice, making her assurance seem almost childlike.

"You sound so stupid, and you look stupider," Seraphina responds.

With a rush of movement, Aurora strides over and delivers a stinging slap across Seraphina's face. "Shut up!" she snarls. The force behind her voice and hand is a clear signal of her desperation to cling to control.

The taste of iron and betrayal still lingers on my tongue, but beneath the terror and the fury, something cold and hard settles in my stomach. A realization. One that's sour and unwelcome yet undeniably true. I can't believe it. All of this. Every twisted, blood-stained moment is because of money and power.

The world I grew up in, the one I naïvely chose to marry into, worships at the altar of wealth and domination. Damien is the ruthless god who presides over it. I think of him now, his eyes that command with an iron fist, his charisma that enraptures and terrifies in equal measure.

In the privacy of our home, I've glimpsed his vulnerability, a whisper of tenderness that he dares show only to me. Aurora believes him weakened, but she doesn't truly know her brother. I know the other face of Damien, the one sculpted by shadows and stained with the blood of his enemies. He's not weak.

He's calculating, precise, a predator who waits patiently for the perfect moment to strike. Damien's capacity for blood and vengeance is unquenchable. His power is meticulously crafted and fiercely guarded. No, Damien isn't weak. He is the very embodiment of the cold, methodical force that rules our world.

A hysterical laugh bubbles up from my throat, sharp and uncontrollable. It cuts through the tension in the room like a knife, drawing wide-eyed stares at the absurdity of the sound. These guys are so stupid.

"You all think you're so clever," I gasp between erratic

breaths. "But you forgot one thing," I pause, my eyes methodically meeting each of them, making sure they feel the weight of my gaze. "My husband is Damien Blackhart."

The name tastes good on my tongue. "His heart is as black as his name, stained with the blood of his enemies. You've underestimated him, but I haven't. When he realizes I'm missing, he'll remind you exactly who he is."

My voice sharpens, cold as the steel of a blade. "He'll become a man on a war path, annihilating anything and everything that stands in his way because you are right about one thing. He does care for me. He cares for our unborn child. He will do anything to get to us. And I'll clue you in on a little secret."

I lean forward, as far as my bonds allow, a smirk playing on my lips before I deliver the final blow. "I'm the one that tames the beast. Without me around, no one will stop him. You've just sealed your fates."

**32**

# CHAPTER 32

## Damien

I grip the steering wheel until my knuckles turn white, each turn taking us closer to my mother's house, each turn a silent scream of fury. Victor breaks the silence, his own anger a palpable force.

"This is bullshit, Damien. They played us like amateurs," he spits out, his eyes scanning the road as if expecting our enemies to appear out of thin air.

"I know," I growl, the words coming out like shards of glass. "Someone fed us bad intel on purpose, to make us look like fools, to waste our time while my wife sits at home worried..." I can't finish the sentence, the rage boiling within me threatens to erupt at any moment.

"We'll find them, brother," Victor assures me, not a hint of doubt in his voice. "We'll bring hell down on every single one of those Nightingale bastards. We will end them."

A harsh laugh escapes me, hollow and devoid of humor. "They think they can hide? They think they can make me look like a fool?" My grip on the wheel tightens further if that's even possible. "They have no idea who they're dealing with. I will tear down every hiding hole, every stronghold, until I get my hands on them."

Victor nods a cold determination settling on his features. "We'll make them regret ever crossing the Blackharts," he says, his voice steady now. "We'll find them, Damien. And when we do, the Nightingales will pay with blood."

My blood boils in my veins, each heartbeat a drum of war in my chest. They've tried to make a fool of me, and that doesn't just stir my fury. It ignites it like a wildfire that cannot be contained. The streets fly by in a blur, and with each passing second, the image of the betrayer's face takes form in the back of my mind. When this is over, when the pieces are back in their rightful order, I'm going to find that low life. The one who dared to feed us bad intel.

I can almost feel the satisfying crunch of bone beneath my fists already. The thought fuels me, a promised calm to the raging storm within. There will be no mercy, no hesitation. Just the swift, brutal justice that's been a long time coming. They've made it personal, and I'll make sure the price they pay is steeped in their own blood and regret.

As we pull up to my mother's house, a knot tightens in my gut. "Something isn't right," I mutter as my senses heighten.

The front door is ajar, and there's a gaping hole in the side of the house like an open wound. My heart races and fear interlaces with the fury. I slam on the brakes, leaving the car running, and swing the door open.

"Isabella!" Her name tears from my throat, raw and laced with dread as I sprint towards the house.

Each step pumps more adrenaline through my veins. She's been my anchor during these dark times. Without her, the beast threatens to break loose. I can't let that happen. Not now. Not when she needs me most.

The house stands before me like a grim picture of chaos and violence. Walls that once echoed with laughter now bear the scars of brutality. The plaster is punctured by bullets, and the artwork is shredded by shrapnel. I tread over the shattered glass and look around.

As I move further in, overturned furniture and the remnants of my mother's treasured collectibles lay strewn about. Bullet holes pepper the walls as if a madman had danced while spraying lead. There were no cries of pain or whispers of movement, just bodies lying around, unnaturally still.

"Isabella!" Her name rips from me again, desperation coloring it with a sharp edge. "Isabella! Where are you, baby? Come on. Answer me."

Behind me, Victor's voice rises and falls, calling for my mother, Aurora, Seraphina, and Jacob. The syllables bounce off the walls with a hollow echo. His voice, once laden with fury, now carries an undercurrent of worry. No reply comes, and the silence that swallows his words is far more terrifying than the sound of any gunshot. It's the silence of a void, a vacuum where life should be, and it grips my heart with icy fingers.

A shuffling noise cuts through the suffocating stillness, snatching our attention. Victor and I whip around, weapons raised in an instinctual, deadly dance we've performed countless times. The silhouette of a figure teeters on the edge of clarity. It's Jacob stumbling in with his face glistening with a sheen of blood and his clothing torn to ribbons.

We lower our guns as Victor steps closer to him, his voice tainted with controlled anger. "Jacob, what the hell happened?"

Jacob's words come out in ragged, pained bursts. "It was an ambush. The Nightingales, they knew we'd be scattered. They waited for the right moment to strike. They took Isabella and Seraphina."

A fury, colder and more dangerous than before, blossoms

within me as I listen to his labored breathing. His struggle to stand illustrating the brutality of his ordeal. Victor's fists clench and unclench with each shuddering breath Jacob takes, his own rage a mirror of mine.

Victor's voice comes out raw, laced with unexpected ferocity. "Was Seraphina hurt?" I glance at him, my eyes narrowing instinctively at the growl, the unfiltered rage in his tone I had never heard before.

Jacob nods weakly. "I saw her lying at the bottom of the stairs when I was shot. I couldn't get to them. They carried her and Isabella out of here."

"Fucking bastards!" Victor roars, his fists clenching as if ready to tear apart the enemies with his bare hands.

Leaving Victor stewing in his fury, I press on through the house, opening doors, urgently searching. Distress and anger twist inside of me like barbed wire as the reality sets in. I still haven't laid eyes on my mother or Aurora. Every empty room is a silent scream, confirming my worst fears that the carnage has claimed more than just the physical structures. It's personal. A trail of terror left in their wake.

My breath hitches in my throat as I push open another door, and the scene before me punches the air from my lungs. There, among the carnage, is my mother sprawled on the floor. Her eyes, once so full of defiance and fiery spirit, are now glassy, emotionless, eternally fixed on some invisible horizon. A wave of numbness crashes over me, and the room spins as the truth anchors itself deep within my core. The beast inside me, lurking beneath the surface, howls in despair and fury.

Victor's heavy footsteps approach from behind, quick and chaotic. He swears vehemently, his voice sharp enough to slice through the thick tension that fills the room. With rough hands, he seizes my shoulder and spins me around, his finger jabbing towards the wall. Written in her blood is a macabre message.

*"Time to pay. We have something you want. Now, give us what we want. We'll contact you soon"*
*– Nightingale*

The bloodied words are more than a threat. They're a declaration of war. My eyes harden with resolve, steely and unforgiving. They've taken from me, and for that, the Nightingales will face a reckoning they can't even begin to imagine.

My mind races, haunted by the terror that must have gripped Isabella in those harrowing moments. The thought of her fear is a razor-sharp blade twisting in my gut. She's out there, pregnant and vulnerable, a plaything at the mercy of the Nightingales. It's more than I can bear. My wife is caught in the clutches of such cruelty. How her heart must have pounded, each beat a drum sounding the alarm of her capture.

I can almost hear her pleas, the silent screams for help that I couldn't answer. Now, as she waits, surely her spirit is fighting to stay alive, to stay hopeful for me to find her. The beast within me paces, ravenous for the reckoning that's due. For every second of fear they've instilled in her, there will be an ocean of retribution. I swear it.

Something clicks inside of me. I'm more beast than man now, the change coming over me as natural as a full moon's call to a hidden werewolf. I turn to Victor, my words more growl than speech. "Track Isabella. Assemble the men. I'll meet you at the warehouse. Stock up on weapons because we're going hunting."

Victor's eyes are hard with the same anger, but he's cautious. "Where are you going?" he demands.

I don't hesitate. "I'm going to recruit someone more ruthless than me." And with that, I leave the house without looking back.

I stalk toward my car with determined strides, jump in, and take off toward my destination. I thank my lucky stars that I secretly had Victor put a tracker in Isabella's ring. She never knew, never felt the light touch of me sliding it off her finger during the night, and it was back before she woke up the next morning.

My foot presses harder on the gas pedal. Normally, I wouldn't dare approach Julian for help, but this is a special case. The Nightingales didn't only take Isabella. They have Seraphina, too. That alone will cause Julian to thirst for blood. No one messes with his baby sister.

I speed through the gates at Julian's estate, every part of my being screaming the urgency of the situation. Decorum and subtlety have no place here. I can't afford the niceties of a well-mannered visit. As my car skids to a halt in front of the house, Julian is already outside with his gang flanking him and their weapons at the ready. A small army bristling with hostility.

"What the fuck, Blackhart," Julian growls at my sudden appearance, his posture radiating danger. "Do you have a fucking death wish?"

I get out of the car, lifting my hands in the universal gesture of peace, showing I'm unarmed and not here to fight. "I need your help," I say, my voice even, eyes locked onto his. "You'll want in on this. The Nightingales took my wife."

Julian quirks an eyebrow, the suspicion plain on his face. "What makes you think I'll help you?"

There's a moment of calculation in my response, a second where I choose my words with the care of a man walking on a knife's edge.

"They didn't just take Isabella," I say slowly, deliberately lowering my hands and meeting his fierce gaze with an intensity that matches my own desperation. "They took Seraphina too. She wasn't among the bodies at my mother's house."

His body goes rigid, the muscles in his jaw clenching so tight it looks like they might snap. Julian's formidable composure gives way to a storm of fury that seems to emanate from him in waves. "Those body-stealing, shit-kicking, low life's kidnapped my baby sister?"

Julian's heavy boots pound the ground as he stomps down the stairs, eyes ablaze with a fury that seems to ignite the very air around us.

"What the fuck was my sister doing at your mother's house, Blackhart?" he bellows, each word like a bullet shot from a gun.

I roll my eyes, already tired from the night's grim discoveries. "Your sister is my wife's best friend, asshole," I reply, my voice flat and weary. "Isabella was staying there for her safety while I went to hunt the Nightingales, but we got bad intel. They ambushed my mother's house while we were away."

For a moment, Julian just stares, his eyes drilling into me as if trying to find the lie in my words. Then, like a trap snapping shut, his arm whips forward, and his fist connects with my face.

"What the fuck!" I shout, staggering back from the force of the blow.

"That's for not protecting my sister," Julian seethes, his chest heaving with ragged breaths.

I taste blood and feel it trickle from my nose, wiping it away on my shirt before locking eyes with Julian again.

"I'll help you. I'm not doing this because you asked. The Nightingales brought me into this the moment they attacked my sister. What's the plan?" he demands, his anger now edged with a keen sharpness of purpose.

I take a breath, steadying myself. "Victor is tracing her location now," I say, regaining my equilibrium. "Meet me at my warehouse on Main in twenty minutes."

I stride into the dimly lit warehouse, every muscle coiled tight, eyes scanning for Victor. "Did you get her location?" I bark the moment I spot him.

Victor turns, his face a hard mask under the flickering fluorescents. "Yeah, they're about two hours away, in the middle of nowhere. We don't have eyes or ears over there. We'll be going in blind."

Nodding, I feel the icy resolve harden in my chest. "That's why we're taking all the firepower we can."

"And of course, you'll have me and my hooligans," Julian's voice echoes as he saunters through the doors, gang trailing like shadows.

"Tell me the plan," he demands, the tension in his voice as sharp as the knives we carry.

I look between the men, my eyes steel. "We split into two teams. Victor, you lead the first team around the back and create a diversion. They'll be expecting a frontal assault. Meanwhile, Julian and I will take the second team and move in under the cover of the chaos. We stay in constant contact. If you find the women, you radio in. No heroics. We extract and regroup. We do this clean and by the numbers."

Victor nods and heads to an arsenal laid out on a nearby table. We're systematic as we arm ourselves, handguns sliding into side holsters and back holsters, the cold metal familiar and oddly comforting. Ankles get a lighter piece, something quick to draw. I tuck a knife into my boot and another at my back, hidden but easily reached.

Julian smirks as his own weapons are a mirror of deadly intent. "After all this time, you still know how to gear up for a war."

"This isn't war," I correct him, checking the clip on a gun. "It's a massacre."

I make my rounds, my gaze hawk-like as I double-check the weapons and gear of my men. Each firearm is cleared, and each magazine is fully loaded, and not a single pin is out of place. It's more than thoroughness. It's a silent vow to myself. No fuckups, not this time.

These weapons are the key to retrieving Isabella and my child, to bring them home safely where they belong. As I move towards Julian's crew, intent on inspecting their equipment as well, Julian steps in front of me, blocking my path.

"My guys are good," he says sharply, eyes leaving no room for questioning his authority.

I glare at him, the muscles in my jaw tensing with the effort to hold back a retort. Time is slipping away like grains of sand in an hourglass. I can't waste it feuding with the help. So, I turn away, biting back any comments, because every minute we stand here is another minute Isabella and our child are in the hands of the Nightingales.

The air in the warehouse is electric, crackling with the collective tension of predators poised for the hunt. Everyone's demeanor is taut, coiled energy, and focused rage, barely restrained by discipline and the need for quiet calculation. They understand what's at stake. This isn't just another skirmish in the underbelly of the city's criminal wars. It's personal. The beast inside me, an insidious shadow that quivers with the promise of violence, is ravenous now, its thirst for blood a burning echo in my veins.

It thrashes against the barriers of my control, demanding release, hungry for the taste of retribution. My hands itch for the weight of my gun, the cold caress of the trigger under my finger, even as my mind plots the downfall of those who dared to target my family. They've awakened a fury they cannot comprehend, let alone contain. The Nightingales will know what it means to go up against Damien Blackhart. Their mistake will be their last.

We finish gearing up in silence, each lost in our own thoughts of vengeance and rescue. The air is thick with the promise of violence, but it's nothing compared to the shared understanding hanging between us. We get our people back, or we don't come back at all.

# CHAPTER 33

## Damien

The roar of the engine fills my ears like a snarling beast that matches the adrenaline coursing through my veins. I grip the steering wheel, knuckles white and aching, as the convoy of vehicles behind me eats up the miles of road. Each second is an eternity. I'm desperate to get to Isabella. To tear her away from the Hell she must be enduring.

Images of her in distress, in danger, fuel my rage and feed the frenzied pace of my heart. I make a silent vow to myself, a promise that cracks with the intensity of my resolve. When Isabella is back and safe in my arms, I'm going to spend the rest of my life ensuring she never feels an ounce of fear again.

Nothing, and no one, will be allowed to shadow our lives like this, not when I'm done. The Nightingales will regret their mistake. That's the only guarantee they'll have. After the carnage I leave behind, it will be a long, cold day in Hell before anyone dares to cross me again. I won't stop until every last one of them is made an example of. They will learn the price of their audacity. They will understand fear.

We hit the dirt road with gravel crunching under our tires in record time as the last of the sun's rays bleed out over the horizon. We pull over, two miles shy of the target location Victor gave us. The air outside is cool and heavy with the scent of dust and untamed wilderness. We kill the engines and slide out of the vehicles.

I lead my group silently, our boots muffled against the natural underbrush. Underneath the faint glow of moonlight, the large house finally comes into view. The large, forsaken structure looks like it hasn't seen life in decades. The windows are broken, and its siding is weathered and peeling. The sight of it sends a shiver through my spine, not from fear but from the thought of Isabella being held in such a place.

It's a blight in the desolation. We press forward, each of us a silent shadow moving with lethal purpose through the night, closing in on the house that seems as dead as the silence that envelopes it.

"Positions," I whisper, the word barely a breath. Our eyes meet, and I see the fire of a shared mission reflected back at me.

Victor nods, his voice just as muted. "Northwest corner is covered. Snipers in place."

Julian's hand lands on my shoulder, squeezing once, a tacit signal of solidarity. "My guys will take the east wing. We're not letting anyone slip out with Isabella."

"Keep it tight," I command, my gaze hardening. "No one goes in solo. We do this as one unit, or not at all."

Victor's affirmation is a short, sharp nod. "Understood, boss."

Julian's grin is cold and lethal. "It's time to hunt," he says, and the words hold all the promise of the vengeance we're about to deliver.

I check the grip on my weapon, feeling the familiar weight settle into my hands. "Let's move," I say, and as one, we step deeper into the shadows, ready to reclaim what is ours.

The door shatters under the force of my boot, and splinters dance through the air like a sinister ballet. Chaos erupts instantly as we burst through. The sound of gunfire is a deafening roar, intertwining with the chorus of shouts and curses. Bullets are whizzing past, stitching patterns of deadly intent in the walls and furniture. I duck, feeling a hot rush of air as a round narrowly misses my head. My heart is hammering in my chest, pounding out a rhythm of survival and rage.

"Move, move, move!" My voice is a raw surge above the chaos that drives my men forward.

The night is shattered by the staccato of assault rifles. The air is heavy with the pungent tang of gunpowder. Each burst of noise is a potential end, a life possibly snuffed out. I return fire, and the recoil is a solid punch against my shoulder as my focus narrows to the spaces where the enemy hides.

Adrenaline surges through my veins like liquid fire, sharpening my senses and guiding me through the battleground this house has become. Men are falling; some of them are mine, and it's a hollow ache, a promise of grief to be settled later. For now, there's only the fight, the unyielding drive to find Isabella.

Every fallen foe is a step closer to her, every cleared room a potential haven of reunion. I can't afford to think, only to act. The need to protect and reclaim what's mine fuels every movement. This chaos is my realm, and I will reign over it with an iron resolve until she is back in my arms.

I press my back against the cold wall. A bullet whizzes by, grazing the space where my head was a heartbeat ago. I can't hesitate. Not even for a second. Thrusting the barrel of my gun around the corner, I squeeze the trigger, the sound of return fire ripping through the air.

The gunman is relentless as his footsteps draw nearer like the shadow of death looming with every step he takes. Then, a resounding crack. A sniper's shot pierces through the window, shattering glass and expectations. The gunman's stride falters, and he stumbles and collapses onto the hardwood in a grotesque dance of finality.

Breathing hard, I cast a glance toward the window, acknowledging the sniper's precision with a swift nod. No words, no thanks can be exchanged in this hell. Only the silent language of survival. I take a quick breath, check the corridor, and then, with the determination that fuels my every move, I dive back into the fray with my weapon leading the way.

"We're almost clear downstairs," I say as the pulse of the battle thrums through my veins. The din of gunfire is a constant now, a drumbeat pushing us towards the endgame.

"Head upstairs. We'll cover you," Victor responds, his face a mask of cool determination as he reloads his weapon with practiced ease.

In the background, Julian is almost a blur, his movements punctuated by the staccato rhythm of his gun firing and the wild, unsettling laughter that follows each of his shots.

"Both of you head upstairs. I'm having too much fun with these guys," Julian yells over the noise, reloading with a manic gleam in his eyes. "I'll catch up when our playtime is over!"

Victor and I exchange a glance, his nod signaling the plan. Upstairs is where they're likely keeping Isabella. Every moment counts, and yet Julian's frenzy buys us the precious time we need. We each grip our weapons tighter and plunge into the heart of the house, ascending the staircase two steps at a time, leaving Julian to his chaotic waltz with danger.

The staircase creaks under our hurried steps as we reach the landing. The door at the end of the hallway bursts open, and a hail of gunfire forces us to scatter. My instincts kick in, and I lunge to the left, crashing into a room and fumbling for cover. Bullets chew through the doorway, splintering the wood mere inches from where my hand grips my gun.

Heart racing, I pivot with my weapon raised, scanning the room. It's empty, save for the dust motes stirred into a frenzy by the chaos. Outside, I hear Victor and the men return fire through the deafening barrage, the sound of their struggle resonating through the floorboards.

I press my body against the wall, and the plaster digs into my back as I sidestep toward the window, seeking a different angle. There's no visual on the shooters, but I can hear them, their shouts merging with the relentless sound of gunfire. I lean around the corner, squeezing off a few rounds. They're met with an immediate response of bullets whizzing past my face as I jerk back into safety.

"We can't hold this position!" one of the men yells to Victor. I steal a glance down the hallway. They're pinned down by too much firepower bearing down on them. I know we can't stay like this, and each second costs us. With a deep breath, I prepare for the gamble of a rapid move, ready to do what must be done to tilt the odds back in our favor.

I reach into my pocket, and my fingers wrap around the familiar cold metal of the grenades. In one swift motion, I pull the pins, the tiny clinks drowned by the sound of gunfire. With precision honed by countless battles, I hurl the grenades toward the enemy's position. They arc through the air like harbingers of destruction.

Get down!" I bark, my voice a commanding force as I lean out of the doorway. I duck back into the room and press my body to the floor just as the hallway explodes in a deafening blast with the shockwave rumbling beneath me.

"Woo hoo!" Julian's voice ricochets through the air, cutting through the lingering echo of the blast. "Who knew you had it in you, Blackhart."

My body hums from the adrenaline, and I push myself up off the floor, my hands patting down my clothes, sending plumes of dust back into the air. The gunfire has ceased, granting us a moment's reprieve in the otherwise relentless battle. I quickly inspect my gun, pulling back the slide to check for any jams before slamming a fresh magazine into place.

"Shut up, Julian," I grunt with a mix of irritation and relief.

My eyes scan the area for Victor. "Victor? Are you alright?" I call out, hoping to hear his familiar voice.

A short pause feels like an eternity before his voice grumbles back through the dust-filled air.

"Yeah, boss. Next time, give us more notice before you start blowing up shit. I'm not going to be able to hear right for a year." His figure emerges from the settling debris, coated in a film of grey but unmistakably alive.

We push off the walls, readying ourselves once more. The grenade has left a gaping hole in the middle of the hallway floor, with jagged edges and splintered wood now adding to the chaos. Cautiously avoiding the hole, we advance with a keen awareness. Our formation is tight and precise, a silent understanding among us that there can be no room for error.

I signal to Victor with a subtle gesture, my hand brushing against my weapon as we both edge around the deceivingly peaceful abyss the grenades carved out. The dance of death resumes, our movements deliberate and efficient as we sweep through the house once again, the weight of our intent clear and palpable in the air.

I barely register the sudden resurgence of gunfire before it's upon us. Bullets zip past with lethal intent. Victor and I return fire, our movements synchronized by necessity and survival instincts rather than communication. In the fraction of a second when my attention shifts to reload, the world tilts violently. An unseen force slams into my side. An assailant tackles me, unbalancing my practiced stance, and we're sent careening through the wall.

The structure gives way as if it's made of paper rather than plaster and wood. Splinters and dust erupt around us. There's no time to process the shock, only to react as gravity claims us both. We crash down to the first floor, landing with a thunderous impact. The floor beneath us relinquishes its integrity, and we plunge through, enveloped in a cloud of debris and disorientation. My ears ring, and for a moment, the battle above is muffled, the chaos paused by our unexpected descent. But survival is a relentless drive, and I scramble to orient myself, ready to confront the attacker despite the fall.

I stand up, drawing my weapon, ready to shoot the fucker that tackled me. Suddenly, the gun is knocked out of my hand. Pain explodes across my chest as I'm struck by a brutal kick, sending me staggering back into yet another wall. Dust and grit bite into my eyes as I struggle to straighten up, squinting through the haze.

As my vision clears, I'm met with the sinister silhouette of Luke Nightingale, the progeny of Dorian Nightingale, a man as notorious as his father. A twisted smile creeps across his face as his eyes glint with the thrill of the hunt. I face him, my resolve hardening like steel. There's no backing down. Not now. Not against him.

The distant clamor of gunfire and venomous shouting filters down through the broken floorboards, but it fades behind the curtain of my focus. I am fixed, resolutely, on the man in front of me. Luke's every breath is a taunt, his confidence sickening, but I harbor no doubt. Julian's men, Victor, and my men; they're skilled and relentless. They'll mop up Nightingale's lackeys without me. This, Luke and I, this is personal, and it's exactly where I need to be. Muscles tense, I circle, eyes locked on Luke as we both understand the unspoken truth. Only one of us is walking away from this.

"I'm going to kill you, Blackhart," Luke snarls. "Your pretty little wife is now mine."

My blood boils as Luke's words slither through the air, each one laced with venom. "You think you can intimidate me, Nightingale? Lay a finger on my wife, and I swear—"

"Swear what, Damien? Your empty threats mean nothing here," he sneers, his voice dripping with malice. "I'll take your sweet wife and sell her off. Can you imagine how much she'll fetch? Especially now, with the child. I hear pregnant women have an increased appetite. She'll be quite the prize."

Clenching my fists, I fight to keep my rage in check, knowing that losing control could be fatal. "You're sick, Luke. You touch either of them and—"

His maniacal laughter cuts me off. "Oh, and if it's a girl, your precious daughter? I've got a client with a particular taste for innocence," he says with a grotesque smile.

"Your interest in her isn't just unfortunate; it's lethal. I don't do warnings twice, and I don't share what's mine. Back off now, and you might live to see tomorrow," I spit out, feeling a surge of hatred like never before. "Keep going, and you won't."

"Oh, but I will, Blackhart." Luke's eyes gleam with dark triumph as he circles me like a predator. "I always get what I want."

Not if I have anything to do with it. "We'll see about that," I growl, my resolve as sharp as a knife's edge. "This ends now."

Without warning, I lunge at Luke, fists aimed at his smirking face. He meets my attack with equal ferocity, blocking my strike and countering with a brutal jab to my ribs. Our dance is dangerous, a rhythmic exchange of punches and kicks, our heavy breaths punctuating each vicious connection. As our fists fly, the hunters become the hunted, each of us vying to be the last one standing.

In the narrow space cluttered with debris, a glint of steel catches my eye. Almost as if mirroring my thoughts, Luke brandishes a knife, its blade reflecting the scant light. Without hesitation, I draw my own. Our weapons flash between us as an extension of our feral intent. Metal clashes against metal as we swipe and stab, each attack with a deadly promise to end the other's life.

He is relentless, and so am I. We are two sides of the same coin, tarnished by violence and vengeance. Luke comes at me with a furious overhead strike, but I parry it aside, the force of his attack sending vibrations up my arm. I retaliate, aiming for his side, only to have my knife knocked away by the savage twist of his wrist.

Pain flares where his blade slices my shoulder, the bright sting of blood joining the mix of sweat and grit. I grab my other knife, and with narrowed eyes, I see an opening and surge forward. My blade finds purchase, cutting through fabric and skin. We are locked in a deadly embrace, and the boundary between hunter and prey is blurred as we bring our fight to its grim conclusion.

"You won't win, Blackhart," Luke says with a laugh.

"I won't win?" I scoff, blood dripping from the fresh wound on my shoulder. "You've already lost, Luke. You just haven't felt it yet."

Luke's laughter echoes through the decrepit room. The sound is sinister, maddening. "Oh, Damien. Your delusions are almost endearing. I'll enjoy breaking you. Watching as you realize all the sordid things I'll do to your beloved wife... And your child. It's quite a future I have planned for them."

I lunge forward, but it's a feint. I want him close, want him to feel the certainty of my words. "You aren't doing a damn thing, Luke. Not to them. Not to anyone. You're over. You've forgotten who you're fucking with."

He tightens his grip on the knife, ready for another

round. But this isn't a fight. This is a reckoning. "You think you're a wolf among sheep? I'm the goddamn reaper, Luke, and I'm here for you."

"My dear Damien, you truly believe you're death incarnate?" A twisted smile contorts Luke's face as he prepares to strike. Unfortunately, his confidence is misplaced. Every moment has led to this.

"Yes," I reply, my voice is thunder to his lightning. "And I've come to collect your soul."

I narrow my gaze, focusing all my energy on the fight. Luke is strong, no doubt about it, but my will is ironclad, fueled by the need to reach Isabella to protect our child. Every muscle in my body is taut, ready to respond. I feint to the left, a move Luke anticipates, his grin spreading as he prepares to counter. But it's a ruse. In a flash, my true attack is underway as I spin right, exploiting a gap in his guard like a swift and silent promise.

Luke's eyes reflect a split-second of realization, a flicker of surprise that his experience and cruelty could not anticipate. My hand, clasping the knife with unerring precision, drives the blade forward. The sharp point pierces through clothing, skin, and, finally, the heart. His body goes rigid against mine. His sneer turns into a grimace. His eyes, once alight with the thrill of power and sadism, start to dim as the life within them leaves.

"I'm sorry, Isabella," I whisper, not for the life I take but for the violence she despises, the darkness that I promised to shield her from. As Luke Nightingale's strength fades away, my resolve only hardens. I will get to her. Whatever it takes.

# CHAPTER 34

## Isabella

I let out a loud, defiant laugh, even as the ropes bite into my wrists. "Do you hear that? I told you," I say, my voice echoing through the still room. "My husband will tear this house down to get to me."

Aurora, my father, and the men gathered in the room stare at me in stunned silence. But beneath their stoic façades, I see it. The unmistakable glimmer of fear flickering in their eyes. Aurora takes a hesitant step back, and I can't help but chuckle, the sound harsh and mocking.

"What's wrong? Afraid? You should be. Because when he gets here, and he will get here, your last breaths will be in agony for ever thinking you could take us from him."

Suddenly, the sound of gunfire erupts, punctuated by shouts that are muffled yet frantic, resonant through the walls of this cursed place. The house shakes with the violence of it all as if the very foundation is rebelling against the horrors it's been forced to witness.

The men jump to their feet, their previous arrogance replaced with the chaotic scramble of the terrified. It's chaos, and for the first time since I was taken, I smile. Not because

I enjoy the terror but because I know that Damien is coming. He is the storm itself, and he will stop at nothing to find me. Aurora's command slices through the tension in the room like a blade.

"Guard the door!" she barks, and the men hastily comply, their weapons now pointed at the door.

Their eyes are wide, and their movements are jittery. I'm watching, calculating, as the gunfire and shouts from beyond these walls continue, unwavering for a few more agonizing minutes. And then, as if the world has suddenly lost its voice, quiet descends with suffocating absoluteness.

It's in the silence that it happens, a loud pop, jarringly out of place. The two men at the door don't even have a chance to turn before they collapse, their bodies hitting the floor with thuds that resonate through my bones.

"It came from the window!" my father's voice screeches with panic, undercutting the authority it once held. "Everybody get down."

My heart is racing, but not from fear. It's anticipation, a twisted sense of victory even while I'm tied to a chair. Damien is here, and hell follows with him. The door bursts open and in walks Damien, Victor, another guy I've never seen before, and a group of men.

"Isabella," Damien breathes with a sigh of relief. Then he gazes around the room, his eyes widening in shock. "Aurora? Are you alright?" He asks. "Did they hurt you?" Aurora stands there like a deer caught in headlights. "Why aren't you tied up?" Damien asks.

"Because she's in on this whole ordeal," Seraphina says.

"Seraphina, are you alright?" Victor asks her. The gaze he's sending her causes me to scrunch my eyebrows.

"I'm peachy," she says with a bloody smile.

"Who hurt her," Victor says when he sees the blood on her mouth. "Who hit her."

Seraphina tilts her head. "That asshole over there."

Victor raises his gun and fires two shots faster than you can blink. The guy that hit Seraphina hits the floor with a thud.

"And people call me a hot head," the mysterious man said.

"Shut up, Julian," Victor snaps.

"I'm just saying," Julian replies. "I never knew you guys were as bloodthirsty as me. We'll have to do this again sometime."

The tension in the room clings to my skin, thicker and more visceral than the dust I in the air. Aurora stands petrified, her façade of control shattered, revealing the naked trepidation beneath and the fear of consequences she never anticipated. My father's posture, once composed and imposing, is now hunched, quivering like a leaf in the grip of an impending storm. Their fear rolls off in thick waves, clashing with the seething, almost tangible rage emanating from Damien, Victor, and Julian.

Damien's eyes burn with a ferocity that matches the inferno I envision surrounding us. The righteous anger of a man whose world has been threatened. Fury glows in Victor's gaze like a protective inferno searing for justice. Julian is covered in an aura of untamed violence, exuding a hunger for carnage as if reveling in it were his natural state. The air crackles, charged with the impending wrath of retribution and the sweet scent of vindication.

Damien's voice cuts through the tense air, every word laced with incredulity. "Aurora, what the hell is happening? How are you involved in this?"

"Fuck!" my father bellows, and the veins in his neck bulge visibly as he paces like a caged animal. "Do you have any idea what you've cost me, Isabella?" He turns to face the room, eyes wild with disarray. "I orchestrated a masterpiece, a scheme that would've secured my money!" His hands are clenched into fists, trembling at his sides.

"But no," he spits, whirling to point an accusing finger at Damien. "You, with your righteous crusade, had to come storming in here, killing everyone to rescue her worthless ass!"

I can't help but interject, my voice icy as it cuts through his tirade. "Your *masterpiece* involved selling out your own daughter. How did you expect it to end?"

He ignores me, continuing to rave, turning towards Aurora. "And you! You were supposed to make sure the Nightingales took Isabella. My plan was perfect!"

I watch as Aurora pivots, and her eyes shoot daggers at my father. "Shut the fuck up!" Her voice shatters the chaos, sharp and commanding, leaving silence in its wake.

The tension mounts, but it's Damien's voice that booms in the room. "What was your plan, Aurora? Were you scheming with Jackson?" Damien's eyes widen as realization dawns. "You're the informant."

A sardonic laugh escapes Aurora as she stares at Damien with defiance. "Yes, once you were dead, I would have all the power," she sneers. "I was tired of living in our mother's image. Of being in your shadow. Of being treated like a commodity instead of a person!" Her words are laden with years of pent-up frustration, ringing through the suddenly still air.

"Our mother is dead because of you!" Damien yells.

"Good riddance to her," Aurora replies as she walks over and starts untying me.

Julian's laughter grates on my nerves. "Man, and I thought my family was fucked up," he says, oblivious to the tense atmosphere. "Your family drama is like a soap opera."

I barely register the cold metal against my temple as my father points his gun at me. His expression is a maelstrom of hatred and desperation. Damien's voice slices through the room, sharp and deadly.

"Don't touch her," he warns, the threat carried in the timbre of his voice.

My father, perhaps driven to madness by his rapidly unraveling plans, ignores the command. The gunshot from Damien's weapon is a cracking whip in the air. My father crumples, his eyes wide with an incredulity that mirrors surprise. It betrays a final moment's realization that mirrors shock rather than acceptance.

The last of Aurora's men edges closer to Seraphina, and with a fluidity that belies his earlier levity, Julian points his gun, no trace of humor left in his glare.

"Touch my sister and die," he snarls a command that echoes with a chilling finality. I'm bewildered at how swiftly he shifts from carefree to callous.

The man lifts his hands calmly, signaling peace. "I'm just going to untie her," he claims, and that simple gesture momentarily lowers the weapons trained on him.

"Sister?" Seraphina questions, her voice threading through the heavy silence that's fallen after the gunshot's echo.

Confusion laces her tone. It's as if she's grappling with a puzzle that doesn't fit. Julian's caring look softens the otherwise hardened lines of his face, reflecting a tenderness that seems almost out of place in the charged air.

"You're my little sister," he explains, a note of protectiveness threading his words. "You don't know me because I don't associate with the Hawthorns, but I've been watching over you since you were born." There's a gravity to his confession, a weight to the words that suggest years of secrets tucked away in the shadows of our family's legacy. "You're the only thing good that's come from that family."

Seraphina's eyes widen. She's visibly trying to connect the dots, to make sense of the revelation that's unraveling the fabric of what she thought was true. "Who are you?" The question hangs in the air, poised between skepticism and the need to know.

"I'm Julian Warren," he says. His name carries a reputation even I've heard whispers of. A man who commands the streets, a ghost in the underworld, and a mystery until now. There's pride in his nod, a silent acknowledgment of the power he wields. "And Ethan won't be sticking his dick in another woman ever again. No one cheats on my sister and gets away with it."

The bluntness of his words cuts through the tension, leaving a raw edge in its wake. Seraphina just stares, lost in the enormity of the moment, trying to absorb the magnitude of Julian's existence in a world she thought she understood.

As the man loosens the binds around Seraphina's wrists, I feel the tension bleed out of my shoulders; the relief is short-lived, though. No sooner does Seraphina stand than a sharp pain scorch my scalp. Aurora grabs a fistful of my hair and yanks me back, using me as a shield between her and the anger of the room. My scalp burns, and my eyes water from the sudden assault.

Victor reacts with the swiftness of a striking snake, with his arms wrapping around Seraphina and pulling her out of harm's way, close to his chest.

"Take your fucking hands off my sister if you want to walk out of here alive," Julian spits out towards Victor, the threat in his voice leaving no room for negotiation.

I catch the brief moment of hesitation in Victor's eyes before he concedes, releasing Seraphina but staying within an arm's reach as if an invisible lifeline connects them.

"Release Isabella," Damien's voice booms in the room.

Instead of complying, Aurora's grip on my hair tightens, with a twisted sneer distorting her features. Pain laces through my head as she uses me to defy Damien's command.

I suppress a cry, not giving her the satisfaction, even as the primal fear begins to coil in my stomach.

"No," she hisses.

Aurora backs up, dragging me clumsily with her as a living barricade. There's the cold press of metal against my palm, and I realize she's pushed a gun into my hand while still maintaining control over me with her gun. There's a dangerous dance of power-play. Her words slither into my ears.

"Thank you for doing all of the heavy lifting, brother," She sizes Damien up with eyes full of venom and the twisted satisfaction of betrayal. "Now, I'll get the money and the power." I can feel the hard insistence of the gun she's pressing into my side.

"Shoot Damien," she orders me in a voice of steely calm and underlying madness.

I'm shocked by her demand. "What?" is all I can muster, my voice breaking. "I'm not killing my husband." The words feel surreal, even as I hear them.

Unsatisfied with my response, Aurora pulls my hair tighter, tilts my head back, and jams the gun against me with more force. Pain radiates through my scalp, and the chilling metal feels like it's seeping into my bones. Desperation begins to singe my thoughts, and I'm acutely aware of the magnitude of the moment. Choices, consequences, life, and death are all poised on the edge of a knife.

Aurora's words are cold and calculating, the kind that chills blood even in the frenzy of chaos. "Either you kill him, or I will. If you die, no one gets the money. If Damien dies, I get an empire. It's a win-win for me. You're my leverage out of here."

Her lips curl into a malicious smile, eyes gleaming with the thrill of her ultimatum. "You want to save your baby, right? You have to choose. Your baby or Damien."

Desperation grips at my heart. My hand trembles, the gun

in my grasp a monstrous weight. Tears sting the edges of my eyes, but my gaze fixes on Damien. My husband. My love. The man I can't imagine a life without. Somewhere deep inside, the fierce maternal instinct to protect my unborn child claws its way to the surface, demanding attention. I'm torn between an unthinkable act and an unspeakable loss.

"I don't understand," I choke out, my breath hitching with every jarring tug of my hair. "You wanted me alive for the money. Now you want to kill me?" Aurora's cold shrug seems to move in slow motion, exhibiting a callous calculation that makes my blood run colder.

"I win whether you live or die," she states matter-of-factly. Her gaze pierces into me, devoid of empathy. "I only need you alive to walk out of here. But if you kill my brother, I promise I will leave you and that bastard child alone."

"There's a problem with your thinking," Julian's voice cuts through the chaos, sharp and clear. I peer in his direction through my blurred vision. "You fucked with my sister. There's nowhere you can go that I won't hunt you down and tear you to pieces. All the Blackhart money in the world won't save you."

In that instant, Aurora's façade of control flickers, her eyes betraying a glimmer of doubt. Then, suddenly, chaos erupts. The man who had been leaning silently in the corner makes his move, a blur of motion towards Aurora. No hesitation marks her response. Her gun fires with a crack that splits the tension like thunder, and he drops, lifeless.

"No one fucking move!" Aurora's scream slices through the thick air, her command a heinous declaration above the fallen man's silent form. The weight of my choices feels as heavy as the gun pressed into my hand.

Damien's eyes are steel as they meet Aurora's, and the words he utters are steady, filled with a terrifying calm.

"Release Isabella," he says, his voice carrying the weight of command and a trace of a plea. "And I won't retaliate. This can end without more bloodshed."

Aurora's laugh, sharp and mocking, cut the air. "You think I'm a fool?" she scoffs, pressing the barrel of the gun harder into my side. A whimper escapes my lips despite my resolve not to show fear. "Raise the gun and kill Damien, or I will kill your baby." Her threat chills me to the bone; her cruelty knows no bounds.

Then she twists the gun deeper with her next venom-dripped words. "I won't even kill you. I'll shoot you in the stomach, so you suffer the loss..." Her eyes narrow with malicious delight. "...and hope the gunshot does enough damage to where you can't get pregnant again."

My heart pounds against my ribcage like a trapped bird desperate for escape. The gun in my hand feels like it weighs a thousand pounds. I stare at Damien, my vision blurred with tears, and I see my world hanging in the balance: my future, my love, my child.

I raise the gun, its weight now an anchor pulling me into an abyss I can never return from. My hands shake uncontrollably, a physical manifestation of the unbearable turmoil churning inside me. I catch Damien's gaze. His eyes, wide with a cocktail of fear and resignation. In that brief eye contact, an unspoken conversation born of love and shared secrets passes between us.

I love Damien more than I have ever loved anything or anyone. He is my heart, my sanctuary, my steadfast ship in the most violent of storms. Equally, the love for our unborn child is a fierce, primal force. It is visceral and raw. It is my body's every instinct to protect this unseen life that has made a home within me. This cruel deadlock that Aurora has forced us into is shattering. Each second frays more of the thin fibers holding my sanity together.

A silent scream builds in my throat as I'm torn between

the two loves of my life. The gun trembles in my hands like a living thing, mirroring the violent quake of my soul as every breath becomes a battle, every heartbeat a war drum signaling the approach of an unthinkable moment of decision.

"Okay. I'll do it," I whisper, feeling the words like stones in my mouth. They're heavy with a false resignation that must be convincing enough to fool Aurora for a moment.

"I know you will," she says, smirking with the assurance of someone who holds all the cards.

"First, I have to say something," I wheeze, and the tears in my eyes are real, but they're not for what she thinks.

I have to buy myself some time. My arm is shaking from the burden of the gun I'm holding. It's heavy, and my strength is waning. I need to make my move soon before my chance slips away.

Aurora's impatience is palpable. "What?" she snaps, her voice laced with threat and irritation.

I take a staggered breath and let the tale come out. "When I was young, I learned to do a flip. I've even done it with other people," I say, stalling, my words weaving a confusing web.

"What the fuck are you talking about," Aurora snaps again, her composure breaking like thin ice under the weight of her dwindling patience.

"This," I grit out, desperation lending me a momentary burst of strength.

In one fluid motion driven by adrenaline, I lean forward. The element of surprise is on my side as I use Aurora's body-weight against her, flipping her over my head with one move. Her body hits the ground with a thud, and the air is knocked from her lungs. My foot finds its way to her chest, holding her down, my weight an advantage for the first time.

"You threatened my husband and child," I snarl. "Sister-in-law or not, you're dead to me." The gun, now more an instrument of justice than a monstrous weight, is steady in my hand as I aim it at Aurora's head.

Her eyes widen, a wordless plea for mercy she doesn't deserve, as her own fingers fumble for the gun she's lost. She lifts her arm in defiance, or perhaps one last act of desperation, but it's too late. My resolve solidifies into action.

I squeeze the trigger, and a single shot rings out. It hits true, right in the middle of her forehead. Aurora's hand goes limp, and the gun slides out of reach. Silence stretches over the chaos of the room, and for a moment, it feels like the whole world goes silent with it.

My hands are trembling. The aftershocks of adrenaline and horror make my fingers loosen before I release the gun. It hits the ground with a thud, a metallic punctuation to the nightmare we've just lived through. A sob, raw and wrenching, erupts from somewhere deep inside me, and suddenly, Damien's arms envelop me, pulling me into a refuge built of apologies and promises.

"Isabella, I'm so, so sorry... This should never have happened to you," he murmurs against my hair. His voice is thick with regret, shaking with an intensity that resonates through his embrace.

"I'm going to make this up to you," he continues. "Even if I have to spend the rest of my life doing so."

Tears break free, streaming down my cheeks and nestling into the warmth of his embrace. I'm taken over by an overwhelming torrent of emotions, a maelstrom of fear, relief, and love.

Minutes bleed into one another as I cry. When the storm subsides into a drizzle, humor flickers, fragile but defiant. "Do you have any more crazy family members I should know about? Because I'm not sure our baby can handle inheriting psychotic tendencies."

A soft chuckle vibrates against me before Damien's lips

find mine. The laughter gives way to a kiss, deep and all-consuming.

The moment shatters with the grotesque soundtrack of gagging. "My eyes can't take it anymore. Can you swap spit outside?" Julian groans. I glance over to see Victor holding Seraphina protectively. Her face is hidden in his chest and leaves me with questions that buzz like flies.

The ominous click of a gun cocking slices through the air. "I'm going to shoot you if you don't take your hands off her," Julian asserts, steel wrapped in venom.

Seraphina whirls around, fury blazing in her eyes. "I'm seeking comfort. He's giving me comfort. Stop threatening him," she snaps back, her voice a wild thing unleashed. "You say you're my brother, but you're treating me like property."

Shock washes over Julian's face. "I'm sorry, that was not my intent." I watch as Damien and Victor exchange glances, wide eyed with shock at Julian's rare concession.

"Seems like someone doesn't want to make their little sister mad," Damien teases, a wry smile touching his lips.

Julian's glare could curdle milk, but there's an undercurrent of relief there, too. A relief that maybe, just maybe, we've all come through this closer than before.

Everything is over. Damien calls in more of his men to clean up and demolish the house, erasing any hint of the nightmare that just unfolded. As we move through the debris and crumpled bodies, each step takes us further from the chaos. He and I walk the distance to the vehicles parked on the edge of this emotional battleground, our footsteps heavy with exhaustion and hearts burdened with what-ifs.

Sliding into the passenger seat, I glance at the rearview mirror one last time, watching as the house disappears from view as we drive away. The engine hums to life under Damien's skilled hands, and a profound sense of gratitude washes over me. Gratitude that we're leaving together hearts still beating, lives still entwined.

In this moment, everything else can wait. 'Our normal,' I muse; whatever shape it takes, it is ours to rebuild. With a contented sigh, I lean back in my seat, feeling Damien's warm hand encasing mine, his thumb caressing my skin in gentle, soothing strokes.

"I love you, Isabella," he says, his voice tinged with an emotion that echoes the depth of the day's events. I intertwine my fingers with his, anchoring myself in the reality of his presence.

"I love you too, Damien," I reply, letting the weight of those words carry us toward a future we'll forge together, scars and all.

# CHAPTER 35

## Isabella

The sun is setting, and as I stand in the warmth of its fading rays, I can't help but reflect on the turbulent turn our lives have taken. Since the kidnapping, wild rumors have circled like vultures over roadkill, painting a tale of tragedy for the Blackharts, Hawthorns, and Nightingales. A boat party gone awry, ending in an unforgiving sea. That's the official story, at least.

Whispers in the underworld tell a different narrative. One where Damien became the grim reaper of souls and Julian the embodiment of vengeance. It's a story that's bred a new kind of silence, one lined with fear and unspoken respect.

We held funerals for Damien's mom and sister about a week after my kidnapping. I stood next to Damien with my hand in his, offering what little strength I could. As usual, he stood there in his unflappable manner. People came in droves, offering hushed condolences that slipped through the air like sighs. Each phrase uttered was the same 'I'm sorry for your loss'.

They shuffled past, acknowledging me with nods and the briefest of smiles, but none dared to utter a word of the past, of the union I had with Jackson. I'm certain it's the fear of what lies within Damien's heart that silenced their tongues. Damien's reputation made it clear that he wouldn't tolerate any slander about his wife.

After the funerals, we found our normal. Damien had gone back to Blackhart Enterprises, giving his assistant Tina some much-needed vacation. He may still have his fingers in the darker dealings of the family business, but every evening, without fail, he walks through the front door in time for dinner. It turns out, I did have an inheritance, but I decided to put it away from our child, or children, if we decide to have more. The months flew by, and my body swelled with the life inside me. Damien attended every doctor's appointment, making sure things with me and the baby were fine.

I couldn't help but complain about the extra pounds and the way my feet disappeared beneath the gentle, rounded bump of my belly. It felt as though I waddled more than walked. Damien would just look at me with a sparkle of something deep and loving in his eyes. He assured me I was beautiful, and his words wrapped around me like a warm, comforting shawl. Each time his gaze lingered over my protruding belly, it darkened with a promise, a silent pledge that set my heart beating.

"Can't wait to do it all over again," he would murmur, and it sent shivers down my spine.

Me? I can barely think about going through another pregnancy when the end of this one seems like a distant dream. The readiness to meet our baby buzzes through me like a frenetic energy I've no outlet for. Each moment, I'm acutely aware that our child could announce its arrival at any given second.

"Hi, baby," Damien's voice interrupts my thoughts.

It's a gentle tether pulling me back to the now. I've been sitting on the couch with the TV playing softly in the background, delivering a movie I haven't really been watching. I turn towards him with a smile, feeling a warm flutter in my chest.

"Hey, you're home early," I say.

He strides in with that familiar confidence, shrugging off his suit jacket and handing it to the butler, who disappears with practiced discretion. Damien closes the gap between us and leans down, his lips meeting mine in a deep kiss. His presence and his touch are something I've grown to crave more with each day that passes.

"I missed my wife," he murmurs against my lips, the words mingling with warmth and the faint scent of his cologne.

He pulls back just enough to look at me as his hands find their way to my belly. "How's our little one today?"

I let out a sigh of frustration. "Our little one seems to be claiming more real estate by the minute. I can barely manage to get up and down from this couch without a crane," I reply. "Plus, these cravings have to stop. I ate peanut butter with peppermint today. Eww."

Damien's chuckle is warm, and the sound echoes in the quiet room. His eyes shine with a mix of love and mischief. A shriek escapes me as he scoops me up from the couch effortlessly as if my expanded form weighs next to nothing.

"What are you doing?" I ask as a giggle bubbles from my throat.

He plants a tender kiss on my nose, and there's a glint in his eyes, a mix of playfulness and desire.

"I'm taking my wife upstairs," he whispers with a mischievous warmth. "I've got a feeling that you had another craving that hasn't been satisfied yet."

His words send a liquid thrill through my veins. My skin tingles from the heat of his gaze. His hands, strong and assured, remind me of the passion we've managed to keep going. Despite the belly that has redrawn the contours of my body, the intimacy between us has only grown more profound, with Damien discovering ways to keep the physical connection as fervent as before. The anticipation of his touch, the thought of him moving inside me, lights a fire in my belly.

My eyes lock with his. "Lead the way."

I curl up against Damien on our bed with my head resting in the nook of his arm. His fingers trace idle patterns on my back as we're both satisfied with our recent lovemaking.

"I love you, Isabella," he says softly.

"I love you too, Damien," I whisper back.

Our past, with its scars and ghosts, may never be entirely behind us, but ahead lies a future. A canvas ripe for our creation. At this moment, that's all we need. Damien's steady heartbeat is a rhythmic promise against my ear, lulling me into a sense of peace. The soft rise and fall of his chest are a reminder of life's simple continuities.

The gentle ebb and flow that whispers of normalcy and warmth. A glaring contrast to the wild tides we've weathered together. As I drift into sleep, cradled in the love that's become my sanctuary, I can't help but smile. Despite all the odds, I am genuinely happy with how my life has turned out. Sharp pains shoot through me, unexpected and brutal, dragging me from the depths of sleep.

"Damien," I gasp as I nudge him frantically.

He just mumbles, lost in whatever dream has him in its grip.

"Damien!" I finally yell, punching his shoulder with more force than I intended to.

He bolts upright, suddenly wide awake with his weapon drawn in seconds. "What's wrong?" he asks, his sleep-addled brain struggling to catch up.

"Put that away. It's time," I manage to breathe out, the words a cue that sets him into motion like nothing else could.

Damien puts his weapon away and leaps from the bed. He scrambles around, snatching the baby bag with one hand and my hospital bag with the other, and somehow, his own bag is slung across his shoulder. Each motion is frenzied and a little chaotic. Meanwhile, pain grips me again, and I follow behind him as best I can, pacing my breaths with each step calculated against the waves of contractions.

He's a blur, a frantic shadow stumbling down the stairs as he rushes to the car. He's a ball of nerves punctuated by the jangle of keys and the slam of our front door. I hear the engine rev to life, and as the car roars away, I'm still on the steps of the staircase.

"Oh, Damien, you silly man," I sigh, half in exasperation, half in affection.

Moments later, tires screech and Damien bursts through the door again, remorse painting his handsome features.

"Baby, I'm so sorry I left without you," he breathes out, a mix of apology and relief.

I can't help but smile. His love and fervor in these moments erase any irritation of being momentarily forgotten. Taking his extended hand, we walk to the car together. To the world, Damien might be a figure to fear, a demon cloaked in darkness, but to me, he's an unrivaled source of strength and tenderness. An unfailing soft teddy bear when it matters most.

The world outside blurs as Damien speeds towards the hospital and each surge of pain knits my brows tighter.

"Damien, slow down," I pant, but he's riding the gas pedal like our baby has a timer.

"Okay, baby," is all he says, his eyes steady on the road while his hand finds mine, squeezing gently.

Slumped in the passenger seat, my back arches with

another contraction. "God, I'm never doing this again, Damien. You and your lethal sperm are staying away from me!"

The words are half-growl, half-grunt, and I'm only half-joking.

He doesn't argue. "Okay, baby," is all he says in a gentle whisper.

Upon arrival, we're ushered into the delivery room, and hospital staff work around me, strapping on monitors that beep and buzz. I grind my teeth with every beep that seems to echo the skyrocketing scale of my pain.

"I mean it, Damien! You're not coming near me after this!" I yell at him.

His face is the picture of agreement, almost angelic with concern. "Okay, baby," he murmurs every time, but his eyes twinkle with a hint of amusement that says he knows I don't mean it.

Labor stretches on, each hour a tiny eternity marked by the relentless waves of contractions. They rise and fall, robbing me of breath, of composure, like the tide working to erode my resolve. Damien is beside me, his hand an anchor amidst the storm, lending me the strength I'm starting to doubt I possess.

"Push, Mrs. Blackhart," Dr. Nigel coaches, his voice a distant lighthouse guiding me through the fog of pain.

I push and push, each effort an enormous task, until finally, a sharp cry pierces the room. Relief floods through me, and the tension breaks like a snapped string.

"Congratulations! You have a baby girl!" Dr. Nigel announces.

The nurses move swiftly as they check and clean the fragile new life before me. Then, she's on my chest, her warmth seeping into my own cold weariness.

"She's beautiful," I breathe out with tears of joy falling down my cheeks.

"Just like her mother," Damien says before his lips brush my forehead in a kiss that speaks of pride and love.

He looks at me with a question in his eyes. "What shall we name our daughter, love?"

"Elizabeth," I say, my voice a whisper as I say the name of my dear late mother.

Damien's voice is soft, almost reverent. "Donna for middle."

My heart swells with love, and I nod in agreement. "Elizabeth Donna Blackhart. I love it."

It feels right. The name is a perfect blend that resonates with the legacy we carry and the future we forge.

My eyes grow heavy now that the adrenaline is receding. Exhaustion leaves me in a gentle lull of contentment. Damien takes Elizabeth gently into his arms, and I drink in the sight of them. My family.

"Get some rest," he tells me with a smile in his voice. "Everything is just right."

I close my eyes, and sleep overtakes me with the image of Damien and Elizabeth etched into my soul. Damien is correct. Everything is just right.

Something feathery light brushes my cheek, and I groan, swiping at the irritation. A soft, mischievous giggle echoes through the tranquility of the room. The faint pitter-patter of tiny feet signals motion, and the bed shifts behind me, signaling the presence of another person. Another giggle, full of innocence and mirth, dances in the air.

"There's a tiny creature sneaking around our room, love. Shall I apprehend it?" Damien's voice, thick drowsiness, adds a playful note to the morning. I can't help but let out a small laugh with my heart swelling with warmth.

Suddenly, a tiny, joyful scream pierces the room, and I feel a miniature, energetic body launch onto the bed.

"I think a little tickling would be a fitful torture for waking the beast," Damien declares in a mock monster growl.

He commences what we've lovingly dubbed 'the tickle torture,' and the room instantly fills with bubbly giggles, the sound a musical proof of the joy and love living within these walls.

"Stop, Daddy!" Elizabeth's young voice cuts through the laughter, her command both stern and giggling. "No tickle torture today." As the peals of laughter fade and the tickling ceases, Damien obeys her tiny decree.

Then, small hands gently cup my face as Elizabeth leans in, putting her small face just an inch from mine. Her disregard for personal space is comical and endearing.

"Still sleep, Mama?" she asks, innocence and curiosity mingling in her bright eyes, and I can't help but smile at my beautiful, impish alarm clock.

"Not anymore," I tell her before placing a small kiss on the tip of her nose.

Elizabeth falls back onto the bed with another infectious giggle, her bright eyes sparkling with untamed joy.

"Today is my special day!" she shrieks, her voice bubbling over with excitement.

I prop myself on one elbow, feigning ignorance. "Really?" I ask, my lips curving into a smile. "And why is today so special?"

"It's my birthday, mama!" Elizabeth exclaims, her small hands clapping together in delight.

The simple statement fills me with a rush of love and a hint of nostalgia. Another year has passed, marking the growth of our little miracle. The moment is interrupted by a knock on the door, and in comes Mrs. Collins with her usual efficiency cloaked in concern.

"Apologies, Mr. and Mrs. Blackhart," Mrs. Collins says, stepping into the room. Her gaze shifts to Elizabeth, her expression firm but not unkind. "Young madam, we do not wake your parents," she chides gently.

Elizabeth's shoulders slump slightly, her exuberance dimming a little. "I'm sorry," she says as her little toes draw circles on the comforter.

"It's alright," I hurry to reassure both Elizabeth and Mrs. Collins, my voice soothing the ruffled feathers of the morning. "We were getting up anyway."

Mrs. Collins surveys the scene, the lines of her face softening just a tad. Giving a curt nod, she then turns her attention back to Elizabeth. "It is time for breakfast," she informs her, her hand extended towards our daughter.

With one last excited glance at us, Elizabeth hops off the bed, takes Mrs. Collins' hand, and together, they make their way to the door, which closes behind them with a soft, definitive click. Left in the quiet wake of their departure, Damien and I exchange a look.

The look Damien gives me is one I've come to know intimately. It's full of heat, desire, and undying love. In moments like these, he seamlessly transforms from the playful, doting father into the man whose hunger for me is as clear as day. How he manages this swift transition, I can't say, but the shift in his gaze is more than enough to ignite a fire within me.

His eyes, dark and piercing, send a clear message that resonates deep in my core. My breath hitches slightly, recognizing the silent promise of what's to come. The unspoken conversation between our eyes has always been our secret language.

Damien lunges at me like a man on a mission. A laugh escapes me as I fall back on the bed. His mouth covers mine in a searing kiss before he moves to my neck, sucking on it and leaving his mark. I can feel his hard length rubbing up and down my center before his hand pulls my underwear down.

My underwear gets caught on my legs, and I kick them off before widening my legs as he positions himself. In one smooth thrust, he's buried deep inside me, and I moan from the pleasure of it. His mouth moves to mine again, his tongue dueling with mine as he thrusts slowly.

"Mmm," he moans from my slickness.

It's always like this with him. One look and I'm instantly wet, hot, and ready for him to devour me whole. Damien pulls out and slowly thrusts back in again, stretching me in a way only he can. I moan into the kiss, moving my hips to give him better access. To get deeper. Goosebumps cover my body as a fire lights inside me, boiling my blood as I lose myself in the pleasure he gives me with each agonizingly slow thrust.

"Damien," I moan into his mouth because I need more.

He breaks the kiss before sitting up, grabbing my hips, and thrusting harder. His pace increases, and his thrust becomes deeper. The sound of slapping bodies fills the air, mixed with our heavy breathing. My moans become louder, and I'm getting close. Close the cliff that will send me off to the land of orgasmic pleasure. I finally erupt in his arms, pulling him closer to hide my wails in his neck. I'm consumed by this man. He owns me, body and soul.

I lay back and let him use my body to reach his peak. His breathing becomes erratic, and he leans down, kissing me like he'll never kiss me again. He gives a few more thrusts and moans into my mouth as he finds his release. He pulls from my body, and semen drips onto the sheets, leaving a mess that I'm sure will make the maid blush when washing them.

"Good morning, wife," Damien's voice is husky, his words a tender stroke as his hand trails along my cheek. I can't help but smile up at him, feeling the warmth of our shared love enveloping me like a familiar blanket.

"Good morning, husband," I reply, still basking in the afterglow of our passionate connection. "It seems like someone woke up with quite the appetite this morning."

There's a playful hint in my voice, acknowledging the fervor with which he greeted the day and me. Damien's reply comes not just in words but in action as he leans in to kiss me deeply once more.

"I can't help it," he murmurs against my lips, the vibrations sending tingles down my spine. "I can never get enough of you. Your body is perfection. It's heaven being between your legs."

"Well, I guess it's good to get a taste of heaven now because our day is about to be hell," I say with a laugh that's more nervous than humor.

Today isn't just any day. It's the day our home turns into a proverbial zoo, buzzing with squealing children hopped up on cake and excitement. Elizabeth is turning five, and the thought of managing about ten little ones of the same age is admittedly daunting.

At first, Damien was set against throwing a party, but all it took was one glimpse of Elizabeth's glistening eyes. The thought of no party was too much for her to bear. I've never seen him buckle under pressure, but he gave in quickly to his little princess. She truly has him wrapped around her little finger.

"Think of today as practice," Damien says as he gets out of bed.

"Practice?" I question, amusement lacing my tone as I watch his bare back, muscles shifting as he moves towards the closet.

"Yes, practice. Elizabeth is turning five, love. It's time to give her that sibling I've been trying to give her," he states decisively, rummaging through his clothes.

I can't help but laugh, the sound bouncing warmly off the walls. Yes, Damien has been quite vocal about adding to our family.

"You wanted a football team, Damien," I admonish playfully, propping myself up on my elbows. "I'm not pushing that many kids out of my vagina. I'm no baby factory." Despite my words, I send him a sweet smile. "But you are correct. It's time for Elizabeth to have a sibling."

Damien walks out of the closet with a gleam in his eye and charges at me. I can't contain the scream that slips out, followed by a peal of laughter as I scoot upwards on the bed, holding my hands out in defense.

"None of that, Mr. Blackhart. We can practice the baby making some more after the party," I tell him.

He growls, a playful, frustrated sound, and walks back to the closet, clearly conceding, leaving an echo of unfulfilled desire hanging in the room.

The water from the shower washes away the remnants of passion, clearing our minds and preparing us for the day ahead. We dress quickly, exchanging knowing glances and soft kisses in between tying shoes and buttoning shirts. Then we're off to prepare. I wanted us to do everything. The living room becomes a whirlwind of color as Damien inflates balloons and I drape streamers across the walls. Our kitchen overflows with scents of baked treats and finger foods as we swiftly move through the motions. Everything is coming together nicely.

I place the last dollop of frosting on the cake, the pink hues and glimmering sprinkle of five candles completing the scene. The doorbell rings just as I set the cake on the designated dessert table.

"I'll get it," I call out before I make my way to the door.

Flipping the latch and pulling the door open, I see Seraphina, who's practically overflowing with bags of all shapes and colors.

"Aunt Sera has finally arrived!" she announces. "Where's my little monster?" she asks eagerly as her eyes glint with the playful title we've bestowed upon Elizabeth.

"She's out back," I tell her, laughter spilling from my lips as she darts like a fairy on a mission, slipping through the rooms and heading straight for the garden where our daughter is playing.

Just as I move to close the door, a black leather boot wedges itself firmly into the doorway. I glance up to see

Victor. His face is almost hidden behind a fortress of meticulously wrapped presents.

"A little help would be nice," he grumbles.

I roll my eyes and take a few gifts, enough for him to actually see where he's going. I step aside, granting him entry. Together, we maneuver through the sea of balloons and streamers to reach the present table that's quickly becoming overflowing with just his and Seraphina's gifts alone.

"Seraphina's here," Victor says, a note of surprise and timidity lacing his voice, so uncharacteristic of the man I know to be as unfazed as Damien in nearly every situation. His reaction to seeing Seraphina sends a furrow of confusion across my brow. His usual poise is absent, replaced by a hesitancy that piques my curiosity.

"I'll be right back," he mutters before making his way toward Sera with brisk steps.

I can't help but watch their interaction, as subtle as they believe it to be. They speak in hushed tones, their bodies rigid with a tension that's palpable even from a distance. My eyes widen in astonishment when Victor gently cups Seraphina's cheek, his gaze softening as he looks at her with uncharacteristic tenderness.

It's a fleeting moment, for Seraphina allows it only for an instant before pulling away with her eyes darting around to check if they have become the subject of any unwanted attention.

She says something to Victor, I can't make out the words, but his reaction is evident. His eyes widen with a mixture of surprise and something else. Fear? Concern? It's hard to tell. Seraphina steps away, leaving Victor momentarily still before he gathers himself and returns to the festivities.

I'll have to ask Seraphina what the was about. I make a mental note to ask about it later. Today is not the day for family mysteries. Today is Elizabeth's day, and I'll let nothing distract me from making it as perfect as possible for my baby girl.

The party is in full swing. Smiles and laughter light up the room, echoing off the walls like a melody of pure joy. Colors swirl as the children dash around with giggles bursting from their lips while Damien, my Damien, chases them, growling and pretending to be a monstrous beast from their wildest imaginations. The kids shriek with delight, weaving around furniture and slipping under his outstretched arms. On the veranda, mothers lounge comfortably, sipping lemonades and sinking deep into conversations, their laughter mingling with the kids'.

It's a perfect scene from an outsider's view. A normal family doing normal things. No one would suspect the silent guards concealed in the shadows, their eyes vigilant for the hint of any threat that might dare to intrude upon us. Damien may still be the CEO of Blackhart Enterprises, but he is the king of the elite underworld. His name may whisper fear in his enemies, but they are his enemies, nonetheless. The joyful chaos makes it easy to ignore the doorbell's distant chime as it reaches my ears. I'm too caught up in the moment, giggling as I watch my husband fall into his role as the cherished monster.

"Hey, kiddo!" a cheery voice pulls me from the playful scene.

"George!" I say as my face breaks into a wide smile. "I'm so glad you came."

George has been my rock, the unwavering support I stumbled upon when my life was a whirlwind of chaos and uncertainty. From the moment I darted into his quaint little town, seeking refuge, to this moment of love and happiness. When the turmoil calmed at home, I returned to his diner in that sleepy town. Not just to tie up the loose ends of my retreat but to offer him the truth he deserved. He knew there was more beneath my restless gaze, and when I finally bared my soul, his reaction was nothing short of fatherly.

Much to my surprise, he insisted on meeting Damien, the man entangled deeply in my life. Their first encounter was a battle of auras, Damien's perilous edge clashing with George's paternal shield. Neither man was willing to fold, but they uncovered a shared resolve to see me safe and content. Their initial tension softened into a cautious respect. He's been a presence in our lives ever since. Elizabeth even calls him Grandpa. My thoughts scatter as Maggie's voice slices through the warmth of the moment.

"What am I, chopped liver?" she says with a mock pout, and in an instant, we're all laughing.

The party buzzes with the carefree exuberance of children and the bubbling chatter of adults. I'm basking in the warmth of family and friends, celebrating Elizabeth's birthday. When I glance over, I see Seraphina flitting from group to group, like the master social butterfly she is. She laughs and shines brightly, illuminating everything with her presence, but pointedly avoids Victor, who watches her every move with hawk-like intensity. His eyes follow her, never straying long.

The joyous chorus of "Happy Birthday" fills the air, sweet and slightly off-key, as Elizabeth blows out her candles with a toothy grin. It's a whirlwind of wrapping paper and ribbons as she opens her presents, her gasps of delight punctuating every reveal. Then comes the moment for cake. The slices are generous, and the frosting is decadent. A sugary delight that I ensure reaches every plate. As I cut the last piece of cake, a voice penetrates the happy din, fresh and mocking.

"Sorry, I'm late. It seems my invitation got lost in the mail." Julian makes his presence known. Since he and Damien worked together to rescue Seraphina and me, Julian has enjoyed an unusual orbit within our circle, coming and going at random times.

"Julian," Damien acknowledges with a nod. "Come have some cake."

Unspoken conversations hang between them. Men of power in an uneasy truce. Julian nods before producing a present for Elizabeth. He walks over to sit on the table with the rest of the gifts she's opening. His strides falter for a heartbeat as he nears Maggie, stocked with a gift in hand, setting it among the others. His eyes rake over her, appraising, while Maggie's cheeks bloom with the sudden heat of his gaze.

"Hello, beautiful," Julian says, his voice carrying a hint of charm and mischief.

"Hi," Maggie replies, her voice a whisper threaded with shyness.

I watch from a distance, the exchange seeming innocent to an unsuspecting eye, but the intensity in Julian's gaze doesn't escape me. It's heated, piercing, almost predatory. Maggie is blissfully unaware of the depth of the waters she's dipping her toes into.

"What is your name?" he inquires, his voice smooth as velvet yet weighted with an allure that could ensnare the strongest will.

"Maggie," she answers with a hint of a tremor in her voice.

Julian's smile then broadens, and all at once, it's clear he's taken an interest that won't easily wane.

"I look forward to getting to know you, Maggie," he states with a promise that seems to seal some unspoken pact before he turns away, his footsteps deliberate as he moves to join the men on the other side of the room.

I file away the encounter for a later conversation with Maggie. Blissfully ignorant of our world's intricacies, she's like a rare bloom in a thicket of thorns. I can't let her unknowingly get caught up in it. Catching my breath from the festivities, I can't help but smile, my gaze sweeping over the lively scene. If you had asked me years ago, I never would have dreamed that life could unfold so beautifully. The laughter of friends, the warmth of family, and the strength of love surround me.

A perfect picture of my new life. Damien catches my eye from across the room, communicating without words, and I know we share the same sense of contentment. We have weathered storms to find peace in each other's arms, and as we look forward, I'm eager to see what the future holds for us, for this joyous life we've built together.

# ACKNOWLEDGMENTS

**Thank you for reading! If you enjoyed the book, please consider leaving a review!**

This journey of bringing my words to the world has been one of the most fulfilling adventures of my life, and it would not have been possible without the support and love from a circle of incredible people.

To my family, thank you for your unwavering belief in my dreams, for the quiet sacrifices you've made to give me the time and space to write, and for the endless encouragement on the days when the words wouldn't flow. Your faith in me has been the bedrock of my resolve.

My friends, you are my chosen family. Your enthusiasm for my project, your readiness to listen to my ideas (and frustrations), and your celebrations at each small victory have meant everything. Thank you for the laughter, the distraction, and the shoulders to lean on.

To the countless members of online writing and self-publishing communities, thank you for sharing your wisdom, experiences, and encouragement. Your guidance on everything from character development to the intricacies of self-publishing has been invaluable. This book is better because of your generous spirit.

A special thanks goes out to my beta readers and early reviewers. Your feedback was crucial, helping me see my work through fresh eyes and refine it further. Your constructive criticism and praise have both humbled and inspired me.

And to you, the reader, for giving this book a chance. Writing might be a solitary endeavor, but it is the connection with you, the reader, that truly brings a book to life. Your support is not just appreciated; it is the reason I write.

Last but not least, I want to acknowledge the countless cups of coffee, the late-night inspiration, and the quiet moments of reflection that fueled this book's creation. This journey has been mine alone in many ways, but it has been enriched by the presence and support of so many.

From the depths of my heart, thank you to everyone who has been a part of this incredible journey. Here's to many more stories to come.